also by
SCARLETT ST. CLAIR

When Stars Come Out

HADES X PERSEPHONE
A Touch of Darkness
A Touch of Ruin
A Touch of Malice

HADES SAGA
A Game of Fate

ADRIAN X ISOLDE
King of Battle and Blood

a TOUCH of DARKNESS

SCARLETT ST. CLAIR

Bloom books

Published by Bloom Books, an imprint of Sourcebooks
P.O. Box 4410, Naperville, Illinois 60567-4410
(630) 961-3900
sourcebooks.com

Originally published as *A Touch of Darkness* in 2019 by Scarlett St. Clair.

Library of Congress Cataloging-in-Publication Data is on file with the publisher.

Printed and bound in the United States of America.
LSC 42

Ashley Elizabeth Steele
&
Molly Kathleen McCool
Thank you for loving me.
Best friends forever.

CHAPTER I
The Narcissus

Persephone sat in the sunlight.

She'd chosen her usual spot at the Coffee House, an outdoor table in view of a crowded pedestrian street. The walkway was lined with shade trees and box gardens teeming with purple aster and pink and white sweet alyssum. A light breeze carried the scent of spring and the honeyed air was mild.

It was a perfect day, and though Persephone had come here to study, she was finding it hard to concentrate because her eyes were drawn to a bunch of narcissus flowers that sat in a slender vase on her table. The bouquet was sparse—only two or three slender stems—and their petals were crisp, brown, and curling like the fingers of a corpse.

The narcissus was the flower and symbol of Hades, the God of the Dead. They did not often decorate tables, but coffins. Their presence at the Coffee House probably meant the owner was in mourning, which was really the only time mortals worshipped the God of the Underworld.

Persephone always wondered how Hades felt about that or if he cared. He was more than just the King of the Underworld, after all. Being the wealthiest of all the gods, he'd earned the title of Rich One and had invested his money in some of the most popular clubs in New Greece—and these weren't just any clubs. These were elite gambling dens. It was said Hades liked a good bet and rarely accepted a wager other than the human soul.

Persephone had heard a lot about the clubs from other people while at the university, and her mother, who often expressed her dislike for Hades, had also spoken out against his businesses.

"*He has taken on the role of puppet master,*" Demeter had chided. "*Deciding fates as if he were one of the Moirai himself. He should be ashamed.*"

Persephone had never been to one of Hades's clubs, but she had to admit, she was curious—about the people who attended and the god who owned it. What possessed people to bargain their souls? Was it a desire for money or love or wealth?

And what did it say about Hades? That he had all the wealth in the world and only sought to add to his domain rather than help people?

But those were questions for another time.

Persephone had work to do.

She dropped her gaze from the narcissus and focused on her laptop. It was Thursday, and she had left school an hour ago. She'd ordered her usual vanilla latte and needed to finish her research paper so she could concentrate on her internship at *New Athens News*, the leading news source in New Athens. She started tomorrow, and if things went well, she'd have a job after she graduated in six months.

She was eager to prove herself.

Her internship was located on the sixtieth floor of the Acropolis, a landmark in New Athens as it was the tallest building in the city at 101 floors. One of the first things Persephone had done when she'd moved here was take an elevator to the top floor observatory where she could see the city in its entirety, and it had been everything she'd imagined—beautiful and vast and thrilling. Four years later, it was hard to believe she would be going there on an almost daily basis for work.

Persephone's phone buzzed on the table, drawing her attention. She found a message from her best friend, Lexa Sideris. Lexa was her first friend when she'd moved to New Athens. She'd turned around to face Persephone in class and asked her if she wanted to pair up for their lab. They'd been inseparable ever since. Persephone was drawn to Lexa's edginess—she had tattoos, hair as black as night, and a love of the Goddess of Witchcraft, Hecate.

Where are you?

Persephone responded, *The Coffee House.*

Why? We need to celebrate!

Persephone smiled. Ever since she'd told Lexa about landing her internship two weeks ago, she'd been hounding her to go out for drinks. Persephone had managed to postpone the outing, but she was quickly running out of excuses and Lexa knew it.

I am celebrating, Persephone texted. *With a vanilla latte.*

Not with coffee. Alcohol. Shots. You + Me. Tonight.

Before Persephone could respond, a waitress approached holding a tray and her steaming latte. Persephone came here often enough to know the girl was as new as the narcissus. Her hair was in two braids, and her eyes were dark and laced with heavy lashes.

The girl smiled and asked, "Vanilla latte?"

"Yes," Persephone said.

The waitress set Persephone's mug down and then tucked her tray under her arm.

"Need anything else?"

Persephone met the girl's gaze. "Do you think Lord Hades has a sense of humor?"

It wasn't a serious question, and Persephone thought it funnier than anything, but the girl's eyes widened, and she responded, "I don't know what you mean."

The waitress was clearly uncomfortable, probably at hearing Hades's name. Most tried to avoid saying it, or they called him *Aidoneus* to avoid drawing his attention, but Persephone wasn't afraid. Maybe it had something to do with the fact that she was a goddess.

"I think he must have a sense of humor," she explained. "The narcissus is a symbol of spring and rebirth." Her fingers hovered over the wilted petals. If anything, the flower should be her symbol. "Why else would he claim it as his?"

Persephone stared back at the girl, and her cheeks flushed. She stammered, "L-let me know if you need anything."

She bowed her head and went back to work.

Persephone snapped a picture of her latte and sent it to Lexa before taking a sip.

She put her earbuds in and consulted her planner.

Persephone liked organization, but more than that, she liked being busy. Her weeks were packed—school on Monday, Wednesday, and Thursday, and up to three hours each day at her internship. The more she did, the more excuses she had for not returning home to see her mother in Olympia.

Next week, she had a history test and a paper due for the same class. She wasn't worried, though. History was one of her favorite subjects. They were discussing the Great Descent, the name given to the day the gods came to Earth, and the Great War, the terrible and bloody battles that followed.

It wasn't long before Persephone became lost in her research and writing. She was reading a scholar who claimed Hades's decision to resurrect Zeus and Athena's heroes had been the deciding factor in the final battle when well-manicured hands slammed her laptop shut. She jumped and looked into a pair of striking blue eyes, set in an oval face framed with thick, black hair.

"Guess. What."

Persephone took out her headphones. "Lexa, what are you doing here?"

"I was walking home from class and thought I'd stop by and tell you the good news!"

She bounced back and forth on the balls of her feet, her blue-black hair bobbing with her.

"What news?" Persephone asked.

"I got us into Nevernight!" Lexa could barely keep a handle on her voice, and at the mention of the famous club, several people turned to stare.

"Shh!" Persephone commanded. "Do you want to get us killed?"

"Don't be ridiculous." Lexa rolled her eyes, but she lowered her voice. Nevernight was impossible to get into. There was a three-month waiting list, and Persephone knew why.

Nevernight was owned by Hades.

Most businesses owned by the gods were extremely popular. Dionysus's line of wines sold out in seconds and were rumored to contain ambrosia. It was also exceedingly common for mortals to find themselves in the Underworld after drinking too much of the nectar.

Aphrodite's couture gowns were so coveted, a girl killed for one just a few months ago. There was a trial and everything.

Nevernight was no different.

"How did you manage to get on the list?" Persephone asked.

"A guy at my internship can't make it. He's been on the waiting list for two years. Can you believe how lucky? You. Me. Nevernight. Tonight!"

"I can't go."

Lexa's shoulders fell. "Come on, Persephone. I got us into Nevernight! I don't want to go alone."

"Take Iris."

"I want to take *you*. We're supposed to be celebrating. Besides, this is part of your college experience!"

Persephone was pretty sure Demeter would disagree. She had promised her mother several things before coming to New Athens to attend university, among them that she would stay away from the gods.

Granted, she hadn't kept many of her promises. She'd changed her major halfway through her first semester from botany to journalism. She would never forget her mother's tight smile or the way she'd said, *"how nice"* between gritted teeth when she'd discovered the truth. Persephone had won the battle, but Demeter declared war. The day after, everywhere she went, one of Demeter's nymphs went too.

Still, majoring in botany was not as important as staying away from the gods, because the gods didn't know Persephone existed.

Well, they knew Demeter had a daughter, but she had never been introduced at court in Olympia. They definitely didn't know she was masquerading as a mortal. Persephone wasn't sure how the gods would react to discovering her, but she knew how the entire world would react, and it wouldn't be good. They would have a new god to learn and to scrutinize. She wouldn't be able to exist—she would lose the freedom she had just gained, and she wasn't interested in that.

Persephone didn't often agree with her mother, but even she knew it was best she led a normal, mortal life. She wasn't like other gods and goddesses.

"I really need to study and write a paper, Lexa. Plus, I start my internship tomorrow."

She was determined to make a good impression, and showing up hungover or sleep-deprived on her first day wasn't the way to go about it.

"You've studied!"

Lexa gestured to her laptop and stack of notes on the table. But what Persephone had really been doing was studying a flower and thinking about the God of the Dead.

"And we both know you've already written that paper. You're just a perfectionist."

Persephone's cheeks flushed. So what if it was true? School was the first and only thing she was good at.

"*Please,* Persephone! We'll leave early so you can get some rest."

"What am I going to do at Nevernight, Lex?"

"Dance! Drink! Kiss! Maybe gamble a little? I don't know, but isn't that the fun of it?"

Persephone blushed again and looked away. The narcissus seemed to glare back at her, reflecting all her failures. She had never kissed a boy. She had never been around men until she'd come to college, and even then she kept her distance, mostly out of fear her mother would materialize and smite them.

That was not an exaggeration. Demeter had always warned her against men.

"*You are two things to gods,*" she'd told Persephone when she was very young. "*A power play or a plaything.*"

"*Surely you are wrong, Mother. Gods love. There are several who are married.*"

Demeter had laughed. "*Gods marry for power, my flower.*"

And as Persephone had gotten older, she had come to realize that what her mother said was true. None of the gods who were married actually loved each other and instead spent most of their time cheating and then seeking revenge for the betrayal.

That meant Persephone was going to die a virgin, because Demeter had also made it clear that mortals weren't an option either.

"*They…age,*" she'd said in disgust.

Persephone had decided not to argue with her mother about how age didn't matter if it was true love, because she'd come to realize that her mother didn't believe in love.

Well, not romantic love at least.

"I…don't have anything to wear," Persephone tried weakly.

"You can borrow anything from my closet. I'll even do your hair and makeup. Please, Persephone."

She pursed her lips, considering.

She would have to sneak away from the nymphs her mother had planted at their apartment and strengthen her glamour, which would cause problems. Demeter would want to know why Persephone was suddenly in need of more magic. Then again, she could blame the extra coverage on her internship.

Without glamour, Persephone's anonymity would be ruined, as there was one obvious characteristic that identified all gods as Divine, and that was their horns. Persephone's were white and spiraled straight into the air like those of a greater kudu, and while her usual glamour had never failed around mortals, she wasn't so sure it worked for a god as powerful as Hades.

"I don't really want to meet Hades," she said at last.

Those words tasted bitter on her tongue, because they were really a lie. A truer statement would be she was curious about him and his world. She found it interesting that he was so elusive and the bets he made with mortals completely appalling. The God of the Dead represented everything she wasn't—something dark and tempting.

Tempting because he was a mystery and mysteries were adventures, and that was what Persephone really craved. Maybe it was the journalist in her, but she'd like to ask him some questions.

"Hades won't be there," Lexa said. "Gods never run their own businesses!"

That was true, and probably truer of Hades. It was well-known that he preferred the dark gloom of the Underworld.

Lexa stared at Persephone for a long moment and then leaned across the table again.

"Is this about your mom?" she asked in a low voice.

Persephone stared at her friend for a moment, surprised. She didn't talk about her mom. She figured the quieter she was about her, the fewer questions she'd have to answer and the fewer lies she'd have to tell.

"How did you know?" It was the only thing Persephone could think to say.

Lexa shrugged. "Well, you never talk about her, and she came by the apartment a couple weeks ago while you were in class."

"What?" Persephone's mouth dropped open. This was the first time she had heard of this visit. "What did she say? Why didn't you tell me?"

Lexa put up her hands. "Okay, first, your mom is scary. I mean, she's gorgeous just like you, but"—Lexa paused to shiver—"cold. Second, she told me not to tell you."

"And you listened to her?"

"Well, yeah. I sorta thought she would tell you. She said she hoped to surprise you, but since you weren't home, she'd just call."

Persephone rolled her eyes. Demeter had never called her. That was likely because she'd been there looking for something.

"Did she come into our apartment?"

"She asked to see your room."

"Dammit." Persephone was going to have to check

10

the mirrors. It was possible her mother had left an enchantment so she could check up on the goddess.

"Anyway, I got the sense that she's...overprotective."

That was the understatement of the year. Demeter was overprotective to the point that Persephone had virtually no contact with the outside world for eighteen years of her life.

"Yeah, she's a bitch."

Lexa raised her brows, looking amused. "Your words, not mine." She paused and then hedged. "Wanna talk about it?"

"No," Persephone said. Talking about it wouldn't make her feel any better—but a trip to Nevernight might. She smiled. "But I'll go with you tonight."

She'd probably regret the decision tomorrow, especially if her mom found out, but right now she was feeling rebellious, and what better way to rebel than going to the club of her mother's least favorite god?

"Really?" Lexa clapped her hands. "Oh my gods, we'll have so much fun, Persephone!" Lexa jumped to her feet. "We have to start getting ready!"

"It's only three."

"Uh, yeah." Lexa pulled at her long, dark hair. "This hair is gross. Plus, it takes forever to style and now I have to do your hair and makeup too. We need to start now!"

Persephone didn't make any move to leave. "I'll catch up with you in a moment," she said. "Promise."

Lexa smiled. "Thank you, Persephone. This will be great. You'll see."

Lexa hugged her before practically dancing down the street.

Persephone smiled, watching Lexa go. At that

11

moment, the waitress from earlier returned and reached to take Persephone's mug away. The goddess's hand shot out, holding the girl's wrist tight.

"If you report to my mother anything but what I tell you, I will kill you."

It was the same girl from earlier with her cute braids and dark eyes, but beneath the young college girl glamour, a nymph's features rang true—small nose, vibrant eyes, and angled features. Persephone had noticed earlier when the girl had delivered her drink but hadn't felt the need to call her out. She was just doing what Demeter told her to do—spying. But after the conversation with Lexa, Persephone wasn't taking any chances.

The girl cleared her throat and didn't meet Persephone's gaze. "If your mother discovers I lied, she'll kill me."

"Who do you fear most?" Persephone had learned long ago that words were her most powerful weapon.

She tightened her hold on the girl's wrist before releasing her. The nymph cleaned up quickly and ran away. Persephone had to admit, she felt bad for the threat, but she hated being followed and she hated being watched. The nymphs were like Demeter's claws, and they were lodged in Persephone's skin.

Her eyes fell to the dying narcissus and she caressed the wilted petals with the tips of her fingers. At Demeter's touch, it would have swelled with life, but at her touch, it curled and crumbled.

Persephone might be the daughter of Demeter and the Goddess of Spring, but she couldn't grow a damn thing.

CHAPTER II
Nevernight

Nevernight was a slender obsidian pyramid with no windows, taller than the bright buildings around it, and from a distance, it looked like a disruption in the fabric of the city. The tower could be seen from anywhere in New Athens. Demeter had said the only reason Hades built the tower so tall was to remind mortals of their finite lives.

Persephone was beginning to grow anxious the longer she stood in the shadow of Hades's club. Lexa had gone to talk to a couple of girls she recognized from school up the line, leaving Persephone to hold their place alone. She was out of her element, surrounded by strangers, preparing to enter another god's territory, and wearing a revealing dress. She found herself folding and unfolding her arms, unable to decide if she wanted to hide the low cut of the outfit or embrace it. She'd borrowed the pink sparkly number from Lexa, who was far less shapely. Persephone's hair fell in loose curls around her face, and Lexa had applied minimal makeup to show off her natural beauty.

If her mother saw her now, she'd send her right back to the greenhouse, or, as Persephone had come to refer to it, the glass prison.

That thought sent her stomach into a spiral. She looked around, wondering if Demeter's spies were about. Had her threat to the waitress at the Coffee House been enough to keep the girl silent about her plans with Lexa? Since she'd told her best friend she'd come tonight, her imagination had run wild with all the ways Demeter might punish her if she was caught. Despite her mother's nurturing ways, she was a vengeful punisher. In fact, Demeter had a whole plot in the greenhouse dedicated to punishment—every flower that grew there had been a nymph, a king, a creature that incurred her wrath.

It was that wrath that made Persephone paranoid and had her checking every mirror in her house when she'd returned to the apartment earlier.

"Oh my gods!" Lexa was a vision in red, and eyes tracked her all the way back to Persephone's side. "Isn't it gorgeous?"

Persephone almost laughed. She wasn't as impressed with the grandeur of the gods; if they could flaunt their wealth, immortality, and power, the least they could do was help humanity. Instead, the gods spent their time pitting mortal against mortal, destroying and reforming the world for fun.

Persephone looked up at the tower again and frowned. "Black's not really my color."

"You'll sing a different tune when you lay eyes on Hades," Lexa said.

Persephone glared at her roommate. "You told me he wasn't here!"

Lexa placed her hands on Persephone's shoulders and looked her in the eyes. "Persephone. Don't get me wrong, you're hot and all, but...what are the actual odds you'll catch Hades's attention? This place is packed."

Lexa had a point—and yet, what if her glamour failed? Her horns would catch Hades's attention. There was no way he'd pass up the chance to confront another god on his premises, especially one he'd never met.

Persephone's stomach knotted, and she fidgeted with her hair and smoothed her dress. She wasn't aware that Lexa was watching her until she said, "You know, you can just be honest and admit you'd like to meet him."

Persephone's laughter was shaky "I don't want to meet Hades."

She wasn't sure why it was so hard to say she was interested, but she couldn't bring herself to admit that she might actually want to meet the god.

Lexa gave her a knowing look, but before her best friend could say anything, shouts came from the front of the line. Persephone peeked around to get a look at what was going on.

A man tried to take a swing at a large ogre guarding the entrance to the club—one of the notoriously ruthless and brutal creatures Hades employed to guard his fortress. Of course, it was a terrible idea; the ogre didn't even blink as his hand closed down on the man's wrist. Out of the shadows, two more ogres emerged, large and dressed in black.

"No! Wait! Please! I just want—I just need her

15

back!" the man wailed as the creatures grabbed him and dragged him away.

It was a long while before Persephone could no longer hear his voice.

Beside her, Lexa sighed. "There's always one."

Persephone shot her an incredulous glance.

Lexa shrugged. "What? There's always a story in the *Delphi Divine* about some mortal trying to break into the Underworld to rescue their loved ones."

The *Delphi Divine* was Lexa's favorite gossip magazine. There were few things that rivaled her obsession with the gods—except maybe fashion.

"But that's impossible," Persephone argued.

Everyone knew Hades was notorious for enforcing the borders of his realm—no soul in and no soul out without his knowledge.

Persephone had a feeling it was the same for his club.

And that thought sent shivers down her spine.

"Doesn't keep people from trying," Lexa said.

When she and Lexa stepped into the ogre's line of sight, Persephone felt exposed. One glance at the creature's beady eyes, and she almost called it quits. Instead, she crossed her arms over her chest and tried to avoid looking at the monster's misshapen face for too long. It was covered in boils and its underbite exposed razor-sharp teeth. Even though the creature couldn't see through her glamour—her mother's magic surpassed that of the ogres—she knew her mother had many spies across New Athens. She couldn't be too careful.

Lexa gave her name, and the ogre paused as he spoke into a mic pinned to the lapel of his jacket. After a

16

moment, he reached forward and pulled open the door to Nevernight.

Persephone was surprised to find that the small space they entered was dim and silent, and the two ogres from earlier had returned and now occupied the space.

The creatures raked their gazes over Lexa and Persephone and asked, "Purses?"

They opened their clutches so the two could check for prohibited materials, including phones and cameras. The one rule at Nevernight was that photos were forbidden. In fact, Hades had this rule for any event he attended.

"How would Hades even know if some curious mortal snapped a photo?" Persephone had asked Lexa earlier when she explained the rule.

"I have no idea how he knows," Lexa admitted. *"I just know that he does, and the consequences aren't worth it."*

"What are the consequences?"

"A broken phone, blackballed from Nevernight, and a write-up in a gossip magazine."

Persephone cringed. Hades was serious, and she guessed that made sense; the god was notoriously private. He hadn't even been linked to a lover. Persephone doubted Hades had taken a vow of chastity like Artemis and Athena, and yet he managed to stay out of the public eye.

She sort of admired that about him.

Once they were cleared, the ogres opened another set of doors. Lexa grabbed Persephone's hand and pulled her through. A blast of cool air hit her, carrying the scent of spirits, sweat, and something akin to bitter oranges.

Narcissus. Persephone recognized the scent.

The Goddess of Spring found herself on a balcony overlooking the floor of the club. There were people everywhere—crowded around tables playing cards and drinking at the bar shoulder to shoulder, their silhouettes ignited by a red backlight. Several plush booths were arranged in cozy settings and packed with people, but it was the center of the club that drew Persephone's attention. A sunken dance floor held bodies like water in a basin. People moved against each other in a mesmerizing rhythm under a stream of red light. Overhead, the ceiling was lined with crystal and wrought-iron chandeliers.

"Come on!" Lexa pulled Persephone down a set of stairs to the ground floor. She held on tight to Lexa's hand, afraid she would lose her as they wove through the crowd.

It took her a moment to figure out which direction her friend was going, but they soon reached the bar, squeezing into a space only big enough for one person.

"Two manhattans," Lexa ordered. Just as she reached for her clutch, an arm snaked between them and threw down a few dollars.

A voice followed, "Drinks on me."

Lexa and Persephone turned to find a man standing behind them. He had a jawline as sharp as a diamond and a head of thick, curly hair as dark as his eyes, and his skin was a beautiful, burnished brown. He was one of the most handsome men Persephone had ever seen.

"Thanks," Lexa breathed.

"No problem," he said, flashing a set of pretty, white teeth—a welcome sight compared to the ogre's grisly fangs. "First time at Nevernight?"

Lexa answered quickly, "Yes. You?"

"Oh… I'm a regular here," he said.

Persephone glanced at Lexa, who blurted exactly what Persephone was thinking. "How?"

The man offered a warm laugh. "Just lucky, I guess." He extended his hand. "Adonis."

He shook Lexa's hand and then Persephone's as they gave him their names. "Would you like to join my table?"

"Sure," they said in unison, giggling.

With their drinks in hand, Persephone and Lexa followed Adonis to one of the booths they had seen from the balcony. Each area had two crescent-shaped, velvet couches with a table between them. There were already several people there—six guys and five girls—but they shifted so Lexa and Persephone could have a seat.

"All, this is Lexa and Persephone." Adonis pointed to his group of friends, saying their names, but Persephone only caught those who were closest to her—Aro and Xerxes were twins, sporting the same ginger hair, spray of freckles, pretty blue eyes and willow-thin bodies. Sybil was blond and beautiful, her long legs peeking out beneath her simple white dress; she sat between the twins and leaned over Aro to speak to Persephone and Lexa.

"Where are you all from?" she asked.

"Ionia," Lexa said.

"Olympia," Persephone said.

The girl's eyes widened. "You lived in Olympia? I bet it was beautiful!"

Persephone had lived far, far away from the city proper in her mother's glass greenhouse and hadn't seen much of Olympia. It was one of the most popular tourist destinations in New Greece, where the gods held Council and kept sprawling estates. When the Divine were away, many of the mansions and surrounding gardens were open to tour.

"It was beautiful," Persephone agreed. "But New Athens is beautiful too. I…didn't really have much freedom in Olympia."

Sybil offered a sympathetic smile. "Parents?"

Persephone nodded.

"We're all from New Delphi, came here for college four years ago," Aro said, gesturing to Sybil and his brother.

"We like the freedom here too," Xerxes joked.

"What are you studying?" Persephone asked.

"Architecture," the boys said in unison. "College of Hestia."

"I'm in the College of the Divine." Sybil said.

"Sybil is an oracle." Aro pointed to her with his thumb.

The girl blushed and averted her eyes.

"That means you'll serve a god!" Lexa's jaw dropped.

Oracles were coveted positions among mortals, and to become one, they had to be born with certain prophetic gifts. Oracles acted as messengers for the gods. In ancient times, that meant serving in temples; now it meant serving as their press manager. Oracles gave statements and organized press circuits, especially when a god had something prophetic to communicate.

"Apollo's already got his eye on her," said Xerxes.

Sybil rolled her eyes. "It's not as wonderful as it sounds. My family was not happy."

Sybil didn't need to say it for Persephone to understand. Her parents were what the Faithful and the god-fearing called Impious.

The Impious were a group of mortals who rejected the gods when they came to Earth. Having already felt abandoned by them, they were not eager to obey. There had been a revolt, and two sides were born. Even the gods who supported the Impious used mortals like puppets, dragging them across battlefields, and for a year, destruction, chaos, and fighting had reigned. After the battle ended, the gods had promised a new life, something better than Elysium (apparently, Hades didn't like that too well), but the gods delivered—they threaded together continents and dubbed the landmass New Greece, splicing it into territories with great, gleaming cities.

"Well, my parents would have been ecstatic," Lexa said.

Persephone met Sybil's gaze. "I'm sorry they weren't excited for you."

She shrugged. "It's better now that I'm here."

Persephone got the feeling she and Sybil had a lot in common when it came to their parents.

Several shots later, the conversation lapsed into hilarious stories of the trio's friendship, and Persephone became distracted by her surroundings. She noticed small details like strands of tiny lights overhead that looked like stars in the dark above, single-stemmed narcissus on the tables at each booth, and the wrought-iron rails of the second story balcony where a lone figure loomed.

That was where her gaze stayed, meeting a pair of shadowy eyes.

Had she thought earlier that Adonis was the most handsome man she'd ever seen?

She'd been wrong.

That man was now staring at her.

She couldn't tell the color of his eyes, but they ignited a fire under her skin, and it was like he knew; his full lips curved into a harsh smile, drawing attention to his strong jaw covered in dark stubble. He was big, well over six and a half feet tall, and dressed in darkness from his inky hair to his black suit.

Her throat went dry and she was suddenly uncomfortable. She fidgeted and crossed her legs, instantly regretting the move, because the man's gaze fell there and held for a moment before sliding back up her frame, snagging on her curves. The fire pooled low in her stomach, reminding her of how empty she felt, how desperately she needed to be filled up.

Who was this man, and how could she possibly feel this way about a stranger? She needed to break this connection that had created such a suffocating energy between them.

All it took was seeing a pair of delicate hands slip around the man's waist from behind. She didn't wait to see the woman's face; she turned toward Lexa and cleared her throat.

The group had moved on to talking about the Pentathlon—an annual athleticism competition with five different sporting events, including a long jump, javelin throw, discus throw, a wrestling match, and a series of short races. It was hugely popular in the highly competitive cities of New Greece, and while Persephone wasn't really a sports fan, she did love the spirit of the Pentathlon and enjoyed cheering for New Athens in the tournament. She tried to follow the conversation, but her body was charged, and her mind was on other things—like how it would feel to be taken by the man on the balcony. He could fill this emptiness, feed this fire, end her suffering.

Except that he was obviously taken—and if not taken, otherwise engaged with another woman.

She resisted looking over her shoulder to see if he remained on the balcony until her curiosity won out, but when she looked, the balcony was empty. She frowned, disappointed, and craned her neck, searching the crowd.

"Looking for Hades?" Adonis joked, and Persephone's gaze snapped to his.

"Oh, no—"

"I heard he was here tonight," Lexa interrupted.

Adonis laughed. "Yeah, he's usually upstairs."

"What's upstairs?" Persephone asked.

"A lounge. It's quieter. More intimate. I guess he prefers the peace when he's negotiating his terms."

"Terms?" Persephone echoed.

"Yeah, you know, for his contracts. Mortals come here to play him for things—money or love or whatever. The fucked-up part is, if the mortal loses, he gets to pick the stakes. And he'll usually ask them to do something impossible."

"What do you mean?"

"Apparently he can see vices or whatever. So he'll ask the alcoholic to remain sober and the sex addict to be chaste. If they meet the terms, they get to live. If they fail, he gets their soul. It's like he wants them to lose."

Persephone felt a little sick. She hadn't known the extent of Hades's gambling; the most she'd heard was that he asked for the mortal's soul, but this sounded much, much worse. It was…manipulation.

How did Hades know these mortals' weaknesses? Did he consult the Fates or possess this power himself?

"Is anyone allowed up there?" Persephone asked.

"If you're given the password," Adonis said.

"How do you get the password?" Lexa asked.

Adonis shrugged. "Hell if I know. I don't come here to bargain with the God of the Dead."

Though she had no desire to enter into a bargain with Hades, Persephone did wonder how people came by the password. How did Hades accept a wager? Did mortals offer their case to the god who then deemed it worthy?

Lexa stood, grabbing Persephone's free hand. "Persephone, bathroom."

She dragged her across the crowded floor to the restroom. While they waited at the end of the long line, Lexa leaned toward Persephone, a huge smile plastered on her face.

"Have you seen a more attractive male?" she gushed.

Persephone's brows lowered. "Adonis?"

"Of course, Adonis! Who else?"

Persephone would have liked to inform Lexa that while she was ogling Adonis, she'd missed the man who truly deserved the term. Instead, she said, "You're smitten."

"I'm in love."

Persephone rolled her eyes. "You can't be in love. You just met him!"

"Okay, maybe not love. But if he asked me to carry his babies, I'd agree."

"You are ridiculous."

"Just honest." Lexa grinned. Then she looked at

Persephone seriously and said, "It's okay to be vulnerable, you know?"

"What do you mean?" Persephone's question was snappier than she intended.

Lexa shrugged. "Never mind."

Persephone wanted to ask her to elaborate, but before she could, a stall opened, and Lexa took it. Persephone waited, sorting through her thoughts, trying to figure out what Lexa might have been talking about, when another one opened.

After Persephone emerged from the restroom, she looked for Lexa, expecting her to be waiting, but didn't see her among the crowd. She looked toward the balcony where Hades supposedly made his deals; had her friend wandered up?

Then her gaze met a pair of sea-green eyes: a woman was leaning against the column at the end of the stairs. Persephone thought she looked familiar but couldn't place her. Her hair was like gold silk and as radiant as Helios's sun, her skin the color of cream, and she wore a modern version of a peplos that matched her eyes.

"Looking for someone?" she asked.

"My friend," Persephone said. "She was wearing red."

"She went up." The woman tilted her chin toward the steps, and Persephone followed her gaze. "Have you been there?"

"Oh, no, I haven't," Persephone said.

"I can give you the password."

"How did you get the password?"

The woman shrugged. "Here and there." She paused. "So?"

25

Persephone couldn't deny she was curious. This was the thrill she'd been seeking—the adventure she craved. "Tell me."

The woman chuckled, her eyes glittering in a way that made Persephone wary. "Pathos."

Tragedy. Persephone found that horribly ominous.

"Th-thanks," she said and headed up the spiral steps to the second floor. As she topped the stairs, she found nothing but a set of dark doors embellished with gold and a gorgon standing guard.

The creature's face was badly scarred—evident even with the white blindfold covering her eyes. Like others of her kind, she once had snakes in place of hair. Now, a white hooded cloak covered her head and hid her body.

As Persephone approached, she noticed the walls were reflective, and she caught herself in the surface, observing the blush of her cheeks and the brightness of her eyes. Her glamour had weakened since she'd been here. She hoped if anyone noticed, she could blame it on the excitement and alcohol. Persephone wasn't sure why she felt so nervous; maybe it was because she didn't know what to expect beyond those doors.

The gorgon lifted her head but did not speak. For a moment, there was silence, and then the creature inhaled, and she froze.

"Divine," the gorgon purred.

"Excuse me?" Persephone asked.

"Goddess."

"You are mistaken."

The gorgon laughed. "I may have no eyes, but I know a god when I smell one. What hope have you of entering?"

"You are bold for a creature who knows they speak with a goddess," Persephone said.

The gorgon smiled. "Only a goddess when it serves you?"

"Pathos!" Persephone snapped.

The gorgon's smile remained, but she opened the door and asked no more questions. "Enjoy, my lady."

Persephone glared at the monster as she entered a smaller, smoky room. Unlike the main floor of the club, this space was intimate and quiet. Overhead, there was a single, large chandelier that provided enough light to illuminate tables and faces but not much else. There were several clusters of people gathered, playing cards, and none of them seemed to notice her.

When the door clicked shut behind her, she started to explore, looking for Lexa, but found herself distracted by the people and the games. She watched as graceful hands dispensed cards and listened as players at the tables bantered back and forth. Then she came to an oval table where the occupants were leaving. She wasn't sure what drew her to it, but she decided to sit.

The dealer nodded. "Madam."

"Do you play?" a voice asked from behind her. It was a deep rumble she felt in her chest.

She turned and met a pair of endless eyes. The man from the balcony stood in her shadow. Her blood heated to an unbearable level, making her flush. She squeezed her crossed legs together and clenched her hands into fists to keep from fidgeting under his gaze.

Up close, she was able to fill in a few gaps in her assessment of his appearance. He was beautiful in a dark way—in a way that promised heartbreak. His eyes were

27

the color of obsidian and framed by thick lashes, his hair pulled into a bun at the back of his head. She had been right that he was tall; she had to tip her head back just to meet his gaze.

When Persephone's chest started to ache, she realized she had been holding her breath since the man approached. Slowly, she drew in air and, with it, the smell of him—smoke and spice and winter air. It filled every empty place inside her.

As she stared, he took a sip from his glass, licking his lips clean. He was sin incarnate. She could feel it in the way her body responded to his—and she didn't want him to know. So she smiled and said, "I'm willing to play if you're willing to teach."

His lips quirked, and he raised a dark brow. He took another drink, then approached the table, taking a seat beside her. "It's brave to sit down at a table without knowing the game."

She met the man's gaze. "How else would I learn?"

"Hmm." He considered, and Persephone decided she loved his voice. "Clever."

The man stared like he was trying to place her, and she shivered.

"I have never seen you before."

"Well, I've never been here before," she said and paused. "You must come here often."

His lips quirked. "I do."

"Why?" she asked. Persephone was surprised she said that aloud—and so was the man. His brows rose. She tried to recover. "I mean—you don't have to answer that."

"I will answer it. If you will answer a question for me."

She stared at him for a moment, then nodded. "Fine."

"I come because it is...*fun*," he said, but it didn't sound like he knew what that was. "Now you—why are you here tonight?"

"My friend Lexa was on the list," she said.

"No. That is the answer to a different question. Why are you here tonight?"

She considered his question, then said, "It seemed rebellious at the time."

"And now you aren't so sure?"

"Oh, I am sure it's rebellious." Persephone dragged her finger along the surface of the table. "I'm just not sure how I'll feel about it tomorrow."

"Who are you rebelling against?"

She looked at him and smiled. "You said one question."

His smile matched hers and it made her heart beat harder in her chest. "So I did."

Staring back at those endless eyes, she felt he could see her—not the glamour or even her skin and bones but the core of her, and it made her shiver.

"Are you cold?" he asked.

"What?"

"You've been shivering since you sat down."

She felt her face redden. "Who was that woman with you earlier?"

Confusion clouded his face and then cleared. "Oh, Minthe. She's always putting her hands where they don't belong."

Persephone paled. Minthe sounded like a mistress, and if that was the case, she wasn't interested. "I...think I should go."

He stopped her with a hand on hers. His touch was electric and warmed her from the inside out. She pulled away quickly.

"No," he said, almost commanding, and Persephone glared at him.

"Excuse me?"

"What I mean to say is, I haven't taught you how to play yet." His voice lowered to a mesmerizing rumble. "Allow me."

It was a mistake to hold his gaze, because it was impossible to say no when she did. She swallowed and managed to relax. "Then teach me."

His eyes burned into her before falling to the cards. He shuffled them, explaining, "This is poker."

She noted that he had graceful hands and long fingers. Did he play piano?

"We will play five-card draw and we'll start with a bet."

Persephone looked down at herself—she hadn't brought her clutch, but the man was quick to say, "A question answered, then. If I win, you will answer any question I pose, and if you win, I will answer yours."

Persephone grimaced. She knew what he was going to ask, but answering questions was far better than losing all her money and her soul, so she said, "Deal."

Those sensual lips curled into a smile, which deepened lines on his face that only made him look more attractive. Who was this man? She guessed she could ask his name, but she wasn't interested in making friends at Nevernight.

While dealing each of them five cards, the man explained that, in poker, there were ten different rankings, the lowest being the high card and the highest being the royal flush. The goal was to draw a higher rank than the other player. He explained other things, like checking, folding, and bluffing.

"Bluffing?" Persephone echoed.

"Sometimes, poker is just a game of deception… especially when you're losing."

Persephone looked at her hand and tried to remember what he'd said about the different ranks. She laid her cards down, face up, and the man did the same.

"You have a pair of queens," he said. "And I have a full house."

"So…you win," she said.

"Yes," he replied and claimed his prize immediately. "Who are you rebelling against?"

She smiled wryly "My mother."

He raised a brow. "Why?"

"You'll have to win another hand if I'm going to answer."

He dealt another and won again. This time, he didn't ask the question, just looked at her expectantly.

She sighed. "Because…she made me mad."

He stared at her, waiting.

She smiled. "You never said the answer had to be detailed."

His grin matched hers. "Noted for the future, I assure you."

"The future?"

"Well, I hope this isn't the last time we'll play poker."

Butterflies erupted in her stomach. She should tell him this was the first and final time she would come to Nevernight.

Except she couldn't make herself say the words.

He dealt again and won. Persephone was getting tired of losing and answering this man's questions. Why was he so interested in her anyway? Where was that woman he'd been with earlier?

"Why are you angry with your mother?"

She considered this question for a moment. "She wants me to be something I can't." Persephone dropped her gaze to the cards. "I don't understand why people do this."

He tilted his head. "You are not enjoying our game?"

"I am. But...I don't understand why people play *Hades*. Why do they want to sell their soul to him?"

"They don't agree to a game because they want to sell their soul," he said. "They do it because they think they can win."

"Do they? Win?"

"Sometimes."

"Does that anger him, you think?" The question was meant to remain a thought in her head, and yet the words slipped out between her lips.

He smirked, and she could feel it deep in her gut. "Darling, I win either way."

Her eyes went wide, and her heart stuttered. She stood quickly, and his name fell from her mouth like a curse.

"Hades."

His name on her tongue seemed to have an effect on him, but she couldn't tell if it was good or bad. His eyes darkened, and his smile lines melted into a hard, unreadable mask.

"I have to go."

She spun and left the small room.

This time, she didn't let him stop her; she hurried down the winding steps and plunged into the mass of bodies on the main floor. All the while, she was highly aware of the spot on her wrist where Hades's fingers had touched her skin. Was it an exaggeration to say it burned?

It took her a while to find the exit, and when she did, she pushed through the doors. Outside, she took a few deep breaths before hailing a taxi. Climbing inside, she sent a quick text to Lexa, letting her know she was leaving, and while she felt bad, it didn't seem fair to make Lexa leave early just because she couldn't stay in that tower another minute.

The force of what she'd done hit her.

She'd allowed Hades, the God of the Underworld, to instruct her, touch her, play her, and question her.

And he had won.

But that wasn't the worst part.

No, the worst part was that there was a side of her—a side she'd never known existed until tonight that wanted to run back inside, find him, and demand a lesson in the anatomy of his body.

CHAPTER III
New Athens News

Morning came fast.

Persephone checked the mirror to ensure her glamour was in place. It was weak magic because it was borrowed, but it was enough to hide her horns and turn her bottle-green eyes mossy.

She reached up to apply a touch more glamour to her eyes. They were the hardest to get right, and it took the most magic to dull their bright, abnormal light. As she did, she halted, noticing something on her wrist.

Something dark.

She took a closer look. A series of black dots marked her skin, some smaller, others larger. It looked like a simple, elegant tattoo had been inked on her arm.

And it was wrong.

Persephone turned the faucet on and scrubbed her skin until it was red and raw, but the ink didn't move or smear. In fact, it seemed to darken.

Then she remembered yesterday at Nevernight when

Hades's hand had covered hers to keep her from leaving. The warmth of his skin transferred to hers, but when she fled the club later, that warmth turned to a burn, which only intensified when she went to bed last night.

She'd turned on the light several times to inspect her wrist but found nothing.

Until this morning.

Persephone lifted her gaze to the mirror and her glamour rippled from her anger. Why had she obeyed his request to stay? Why had she been blind to the fact that she had invited the God of the Dead to teach her cards?

She knew why. She'd been distracted by his beauty. Why hadn't anyone warned her that Hades was a charming bastard? That his smile stole breath and his gaze stopped hearts?

What was this thing on her wrist, and what did it mean?

She knew one thing for certain: Hades was going to tell her.

Today.

Before she could return to the obsidian tower, however, she had to go to her internship. Her eyes fell to a pretty embellished box her mother had given her. It sat on the corner of her vanity and held jewelry, but when her mother gave her the box at twelve, it had contained five gold seeds. Demeter had crafted them from her magic and said they would bloom into roses the color of liquid gold for her, the Goddess of Spring.

Persephone planted them and did her best to nurture the flowers, but instead of growing into the blossoms she expected, they grew withered and black.

She would never forget the look on her mother's face when she found her staring at the wilted roses—shocked, disappointed, and in disbelief that her daughter's flowers grew from the ground like something straight out of the Underworld.

Demeter had reached forward, touched the flowers, and they flared with life.

Persephone never went near them again and avoided that part of the greenhouse.

She looked at the box and the mark on her skin burned as hot as her shame. She couldn't let her mother find out.

She searched through the box until she found a bracelet wide enough to cover the mark. It would have to do until Hades removed it.

Persephone returned to her room but didn't make it far when her mother materialized in front of her. Persephone jumped, and her heart felt like it wanted to jump out of her chest.

"By the gods, Mother! Can you at least use the door like a normal parent? And *knock?*"

On a normal day, she wouldn't have snapped, but she was feeling on edge. Demeter couldn't find out about Nevernight. Persephone did a quick inventory of everything she'd worn last night—the dress was in Lexa's room, the shoes in her closet, and she'd shoved the jewelry in her purse, which hung on her doorknob.

The Goddess of Harvest was beautiful and didn't bother to glamour up to hide her elegant, seven-point antlers. Her hair was blond like Persephone's, but straight and long. She had glowing skin and her high cheekbones were naturally rosy like her lips. Demeter lifted her pointed chin, assessing Persephone with critical eyes—eyes that changed from brown to green to gold.

"Nonsense," she said, taking Persephone's chin between her thumb and forefinger, applying more magic. Persephone knew what she was doing without looking in the mirror—covering her freckles, brightening the color in her cheeks, and straightening her wavy hair. Demeter liked when Persephone resembled her, and Persephone preferred to look as little like her mother as possible. "You might be playing mortal, but you can still look Divine."

Persephone rolled her eyes. Her appearance was just another way she disappointed her mother.

"There!" Demeter finally exclaimed, releasing her chin. "Beautiful."

Persephone looked in the mirror. She had been right—Demeter had covered up everything Persephone liked about herself. Still, she managed a forced, "Thank you, Mother."

"It was nothing, my flower." Demeter patted her cheek. "So tell me about this *job.*"

The word sounded like a curse coming from Demeter's lips. Persephone ground her teeth together. She was surprised by how fast and furious the anger tore through her. "It's an internship, Mother. If I do well, I might have a job when I graduate."

Demeter frowned. "Dear, you know you do not have to work."

"So you say," Persephone muttered under her breath.

"What was that?"

Persephone turned to her mother and said louder, "I want to do this. I'm good at it."

"You are good at so many things, Kore."

"Don't call me that!" Persephone snapped, and her mother's eyes flashed. She'd seen that look right before Demeter thrashed one of her nymphs for letting her wander out of sight.

Persephone shouldn't have gotten angry, but she couldn't help it. She hated that name. It was her child-hood nickname, and it meant exactly that—*maiden*. The word was like a prison, but worse than that, it reminded her that if she stepped too far out of line, the bars of her prison would solidify. She was the magic-less daughter of an Olympian. Not only that, she borrowed her mother's magic, and that tether made obeying her even more important. Without Demeter's glamour, Persephone couldn't live in the mortal world anonymously.

"Sorry, Mother," she managed, but she didn't look at the goddess when she spoke. Not because she was embarrassed but because she really didn't mean the apology.

"Oh, my flower. I don't blame you." Demeter placed her hands on her daughter's shoulders. "It's this mortal world. It's creating a divide between us."

"Mother, you're being ridiculous." Persephone sighed, placing her hands on either side of Demeter's face, and when she spoke again, she meant every word. "You are all I have."

Demeter smiled, holding her daughter's wrists. Hades's mark burned. She leaned in a little, as if to kiss Persephone's cheek. Instead, she said, "Remember that."

Then she was gone.

Persephone released her breath, and her body withered. Even when she had nothing to hide, dealing with her mother was exhausting. She was constantly on edge, preparing for what she would find unacceptable next. Over time, Persephone thought she had hardened herself against her mother's unwanted words, but sometimes they pierced her.

She distracted herself by focusing on choosing her outfit for the day, a pretty, light pink dress with ruffled sleeves, a pair of white wedge shoes, and a white handbag. On the way out, she stopped to check her reflection in the mirror, pulling glamour from her hair and face, returning her curls and freckles. She smiled, recognizing herself once again.

She left the apartment, feeling happier as she stepped into the morning sun. Persephone didn't have a car and she didn't have the ability to teleport like other gods, so she either walked or took the bus when she needed to get around New Athens. Today, since it was warm, she decided to walk.

Persephone loved the city because it was so unlike what she'd grown up with. Here, there were mirrored skyscrapers that sparkled under Helios's warm rays. There were museums filled with histories Persephone had only learned when she moved here, buildings that looked like art, and sculptures and fountains on almost every block. Even with all the stone and glass and metal, there were acres of parks with lush gardens and trees where Persephone had spent many evenings walking. The fresh air reminded her she was free.

She inhaled now, trying to ease her anxiety. Instead, it traveled to her stomach where it knotted, made worse by the inked bracelet around her wrist. She had to get rid of it before Demeter saw it and her few years of freedom turned into a lifetime in a glass box.

It was usually that fear that kept Persephone cautious.

Except for last night. Last night, she'd felt rebellious, and despite this strange mark on her skin, she'd found Nevernight and its king to be everything she had ever desired.

She wished that weren't so. She wished she'd found Hades repulsive. She wished she hadn't spent last night recalling how his dark eyes had trailed her body, how she'd had to tip her head back just to meet his gaze, how his graceful hands had shuffled the cards.

How would those long fingers feel against her skin? How would it feel to be swept into his strong arms and carried away?

After last night, she wanted things she had never wanted before. Soon, her anxiety was replaced with a fire so unfamiliar and intense, she thought she might turn to ash.

Gods. Why was she thinking like this?

It was one thing to find the God of the Dead attractive and another thing to…*desire* him. There was absolutely no way anything could happen between them. Her mother hated Hades, and she knew without asking that a relationship between them was forbidden. She also knew that she needed her mother's magic more than she needed to quench this fire roaring inside her.

She neared the Acropolis, its dazzling, mirror surface almost blinding her, and made her way up the short flight of steps to the gold and glass doors. The lower level of the floor had a row of turnstiles and security guards—necessary for the businesses located in the high rise, with Zeus's advertising company, Oak & Eagle Creative, among them. Zeus's admirers were known to wait in crowds outside the Acropolis just for a glimpse of the God of Thunder. Once, a mob had tried to storm the building to reach him, which was sort of ironic considering Zeus was rarely at the Acropolis and spent most of his time in Olympia.

Zeus's business wasn't the only one in need of security, though. *New Athens News* broke some difficult stories—stories that infuriated gods and mortals alike. Persephone wasn't aware of any retaliation, but as she moved through security, she knew these mortal guards wouldn't be able to stop an angry god from storming the sixtieth floor for revenge.

After security, she found a bank of elevators that took her up to her floor. The doors opened into a large reception area with the words *New Athens News* overhead. A curved glass desk sat beneath it, and a beautiful woman with long dark curls greeted her with a smile. Her name was Valerie; Persephone remembered her from her interview.

"Persephone," she said, coming around the desk. "It's good to see you again. Let me take you back. Demetri is expecting you."

Valerie directed Persephone to the newsroom beyond the glass partition. There, several metal and glass desks were arranged in perfect lines across the floor. There was a flurry of activity—phones ringing, paper shuffling, keys tapping as writers and editors pounded out their next articles. The smell of coffee was strong, like the whole place ran on caffeine and ink. Persephone's heart thudded in her chest with the thrill of it all.

"I saw you were from New Athens University," Valerie said. "When do you graduate?"

"In six months."

Persephone dreamed of the moment she'd walk across that grand stage to receive her degree. It would be the pinnacle of her time among mortals.

"You must be so excited."

"I am." Persephone glanced at Valerie. "What about you? When do you graduate?"

"In a couple years," Valerie said.

"And how long have you been here?"

"About a year," she said with a smile.

"Do you plan to stay when you graduate?"

"In the building, yes, just a few floors up at Oak & Eagle Creative," she grinned.

Ah, Zeus's marketing company had sourced her.

Valerie knocked on the open door of an office at the very back of the room. "Demetri, Persephone's here."

"Thanks, Valerie," Demetri said.

The girl turned to Persephone, smiled, and left, allowing room for her to enter the office and catch her first glimpse of her new boss, Demetri Aetos. He was older, but it was clear he had been a heartbreaker in his prime. His hair was short on the sides, longer on top, and flecked with gray. He wore black-framed glasses, which gave him a scholarly air. He had what Persephone would consider delicate features—thin lips and a smaller nose. He was tall but thin beneath his blue button-up, khaki slacks, and polka-dot bow tie.

"Persephone," he said, coming around his desk and stretching out his hand. "It's good to see you again. We are happy to have you."

"I'm happy to be here, Mr. Aetos," she said as she took his hand.

"Call me Demetri."

"Okay...Demetri." She couldn't help smiling.

"Please, sit!" He indicated a chair, and she took a seat. Demetri leaned against his desk, hands in his pockets. "Tell me about yourself."

When Persephone had first moved to New Athens, she hated this question, because there was a point when all she could talk about was her fears—closed spaces, feeling trapped, escalators. Over time, though, she'd had enough experiences, and it had become easier to define herself by what she liked. "Well, I'm a student at New Athens University. I'm majoring in journalism and I'll graduate in May..." she started, and Demetri waved his hand.

"Not what's on your resume."

He met her gaze, and she noticed that he had blue eyes.

He smiled. "What about you—your hobbies, interests...?"

"Oh." She blushed and thought for a moment. "I like baking. It helps me relax."

"Oh? Tell me more. What do you like to bake?"

"Anything, really. I've been challenging myself at sugar cookie art."

His brows rose and his smile stayed. "Sugar cookie art, huh? That's a thing?"

"Yes, I'll show you."

She pulled out her phone and found a few photos. Of course, she had only taken pictures of her best cookies.

Demetri took the phone and swiped through the photos. "Oh, nice. These are great, Persephone."

He met her gaze as he returned her phone.

"Thank you." Persephone hated the cheesy smile those words brought to her face, but no one but Lexa had ever told her that.

"So you like to bake. What else?"

"I like to write," she said. "Stories."

"Stories? Like fiction?"

"Yes."

"Romance?" he guessed.

It was what most people assumed, and the blush on Persephone's cheeks wasn't helping her case. "No, actually. I like mysteries."

Demetri's brows rose again, almost meeting his hairline. "Unexpected," he said. "I like it. What do you hope to gain from this internship?"

"Adventure." She couldn't help it. The word slipped out, but Demetri seemed pleased.

"Adventure." He pushed away from his desk. "If adventure is what you desire, *New Athens News* can give it to you, Persephone. This position can look like anything you wish—it's yours to craft and manage. If you want to report, you can report. If you want to edit, you can edit. If you want to get coffee, you get coffee."

Persephone only had an interest in getting coffee for herself, but she didn't bother telling him that. She didn't think she could be any more excited, but as Demetri spoke, she had the overwhelming feeling that this internship would change her life.

"I'm sure you know that we find ourselves in the media a lot," he smiled wryly. "Ironic, considering we are a news source."

New Athens News was well-known for the number of lawsuits filed against them. There were always complaints of defamation, slander, and invasion of privacy. Believe it or not, those weren't the worst accusations leveled against the company.

"I couldn't believe when Apollo accused you of being members of Triad," Persephone said.

Triad was a group of Impious mortals who actively organized against the gods, supporting fairness, free will, and freedom. Zeus had declared them a terrorist organization and threatened death to any caught with their propaganda.

"Oh yeah." Demetri raised his brows and rubbed the back of his neck. "Completely ludicrous, of course, but that didn't keep people from believing it."

Probably the worst thing to come from it was that, as a result of Zeus's condemnation, the Faithful organized into cults and started a manhunt of their own, killing several who were openly Impious, uncaring if they were associated with Triad or not. It was a horrific time, and it had taken Zeus longer than necessary to come out against the cults. *New Athens News* said so themselves.

"We seek truth, Persephone," Demetri said. "There's power in truth. Do you want power?"

He didn't even know what he was asking.

"Yes," she said. "I want power."

This time when Demetri smiled, he showed his teeth. "Then you will do well here."

Demetri showed Persephone to her desk, which sat just outside his office. She settled in, checking drawers, noting what supplies she would need to ask for or buy, and stored her purse. A new laptop sat on top of the glass desk. It was cool to the touch, and when she opened it, the dark screen reflected the face of a man behind her. She turned in her chair and met a set of wide, surprised eyes.

"Adonis," she said.

"Persephone." He looked just as handsome as he had last night, only more professional with his lavender button-up and coffee cup clutched in one hand. "I had no idea you were our new intern."

"I had no idea you worked here," she said.

"I'm a senior reporter, mostly focused on entertainment," he said rather smugly. "We missed you when you left last night."

"Oh, yes, sorry. I wanted to prepare for my first day."

"Not going to fault you for that. Well, welcome."

"Adonis," Demetri called as he stepped back into the doorframe of his office. "Mind giving Persephone here a tour of our floor?"

"Not at all." Adonis smiled at her. "Ready?"

Persephone followed him, eager to witness the fast-paced environment of her new office. She was happy to see a familiar face, even if she had just met him last night. It made her feel more comfortable here.

"We call this the workroom. It's where everyone follows leads and investigates," he said.

People looked up from their desks and waved or smiled at her as they passed. Adonis indicated a wall of glassed-in rooms.

"Interview and conference rooms. Break room. Lounge." He pointed to a huge room with various casual sitting areas and warm, low light. It was cozy, and there were already several people nesting. "You'll probably prefer to write in here when you get the chance."

Adonis showed her to the supplies closet, and she raided it for pens, sticky notes, and notebooks. While he helped her carry her supplies back to her desk, he asked, "So what kind of journalism are you interested in?"

"I'm leaning toward investigative reporting," she said.

"Oh, a detective, huh?"

"I like research."

"Any subject in particular?" he asked.

Hades.

The god's name popped into her head without warning, and she knew it was because of the mark on her wrist. She was anxious to get to Nevernight and figure out what it was.

"No, I just…like to solve mysteries," she answered.

"Well then, maybe you can help us figure out who's been stealing lunches from the fridge in the break room."

Persephone laughed.

She got the feeling she was going to like it here.

CHAPTER IV
The Contract

Less than an hour after leaving the Acropolis, Persephone stood outside Nevernight, pounding on the pristine, black door. She'd taken the bus here and it had nearly driven her insane. She couldn't sit still. Her mind had stirred up all sorts of fears and anxieties over what the mark might mean. Was this bracelet some sort of... *claim?* Was it something that would bind her soul to the Underworld? Or was it one of his horrible contracts?

She was about to find out, if someone would just answer this damned door!

"Hello!" she called. "Anyone there?"

She continued to pound on the door until her arms hurt. Just when she thought about giving up, the door flew open, and the ogre who had been staffing it last night glared at her. In the daylight, he was even more gruesome looking. His thick skin sagged around his neck, and he stared at her with small, squinted eyes.

"What do you want?" His words were a snarl, and it

wasn't lost on her that he could crush her skull with his hand alone.

"I must speak with Hades," she said.

The ogre stared at her and then slammed the door closed.

That really pissed her off.

She banged on the door again. "Bastard! Let me in!"

She'd always known ogres existed and had learned some of their weaknesses by reading a few books from Artemis's Library at school. One of them? They hated being called names.

The ogre tore the door open again and snarled at her, blowing his stinking rot breath in her face. He probably thought it would scare her away, and it had doubtless worked on others in the past, but not on Persephone. The mark on her wrist drove her. Her freedom was at stake.

"I demand you let me in!" She curled her fingers into her palms. She considered how much space remained in the doorway. Could she get past the huge creature? If she moved quickly enough, his girth would probably throw him off-balance.

"Who are you, mortal, to demand an audience with the God of the Dead?" the creature asked.

"Your lord has placed a mark on me, and I will have words with him."

The creature laughed, beady eyes shining with amusement.

"*You* would have words with him?"

"Yes, me. Let me in!"

She was growing angrier by the second.

"We are not open," the creature responded. "You will have to come back."

"I will not come back. You will let me in now, you big, ugly ogre!"

Persephone realized her mistake as soon as the words were out of her mouth. The creature's face changed. He grabbed her by the neck and lifted her off the ground.

"What are you?" he demanded. "A tricky little nymph?"

She clawed at the ogre's steel skin, but he only pressed his meaty fingers deeper into hers. She couldn't breathe, her eyes watered, and the only thing she could do was drop her glamour.

When her horns became visible, the creature released her as if she burned. Persephone staggered and inhaled deeply. She pressed a hand to her tender throat but managed to stay on her feet and glare at the ogre in her true form. He lowered his gaze, unable to look upon her or meet her bright, eerie eyes.

"I am Persephone, Goddess of Spring, and if you would like to keep your fleeting life, then you will obey me."

Her voice shook. She was still rattled from being handled by the ogre. The words she had spoken were her mother's, used at a time when she'd made threats against a siren who refused to help her search for Persephone when she wandered away. Persephone had only been a few feet away, hiding behind a shrub, and she'd overheard her mother's crude words and filed them away, knowing that without powers, words would be her only weapon.

The door opened behind the ogre, and he stepped aside, lowering to his knees as Hades strode into view.

Persephone couldn't breathe. She'd spent all day remembering what he looked like, recalling his elegant but dark features, and yet her memory was nothing compared to the real thing. She was pretty sure he was wearing the suit from last night, but the tie around his neck was loose, and the buttons of his shirt fell open at the neck, exposing his chest. It was like he'd been interrupted in the middle of undressing.

Then she remembered the woman who had wrapped her arms around his waist—*Minthe*. Perhaps she had interrupted them. She took great satisfaction from that thought, even though she knew she shouldn't care.

"Lady Persephone." His voice was heavy and seductive, and she shivered.

She forced her eyes level with his. They were equals, after all, and she wanted him to know it because she was about to make demands. She found him studying her, his head tilted to the side. Being under his gaze in her true form felt strangely intimate, and she wanted to call up her glamour again. She had made a mistake—been so angry and so desperate, she'd exposed herself.

"Lord Hades," she managed with a curt nod. She was proud her voice did not shake, though her insides did.

"My lord." The ogre hung his head. "I did not know she was a goddess. I accept punishment for my actions."

"Punishment?" Persephone echoed, feeling increasingly exposed in the daylight outside the club. It took Hades a moment to peel his gaze from Persephone and look upon the ogre.

"I laid my hands upon a goddess," the monster said.

"And a woman at that," Hades added unhappily. "I will deal with you later. Now, Lady Persephone." He stepped aside and let her enter Nevernight.

She stood in the dark as the door closed behind her.

The air was heavy, charged with an intensity she felt deep in her belly, and thick with his scent. She wanted to inhale and fill her lungs with it. Instead, she held her breath.

Then he spoke against her ear, his lips brushing feather-light over her skin. "You are full of surprises, darling."

She inhaled sharply and twisted to face him, but when she did, Hades was no longer near her. He had opened the door and was waiting for her to enter the club.

"After you, Goddess," he said. The word wasn't used mockingly, but it was full of curiosity.

She passed the god and stepped onto the balcony overlooking the empty floor. The place was immaculate, the floors were polished, the tables glossy. It was impossible to tell that this place had been packed wall to wall last night.

She turned and saw Hades waiting. When she met his gaze, he descended the stairs and she followed.

He crossed the floor, heading for the winding stairs and the second floor. She hesitated.

"Where are we going?" she asked.

He paused and turned toward her. "My office. I imagine that whatever you have to say to me demands privacy?"

She opened and closed her mouth, looking around the empty club. "This seems pretty private."

"It isn't," he said and headed up the stairs without another word. She followed.

When they came to the top of the steps, he took a right—away from the room she'd been in the night before—toward a black wall elaborately embellished with gold. She couldn't believe she hadn't noticed it. Two large doors bore images of vines and flowers curling around Hades's bident, raised in gold relief. The rest of the wall was patterned with gilt floral designs.

She probably shouldn't be so surprised that the God of the Dead chose to decorate with flowers—the narcissus was his symbol, after all.

Her eyes were drawn to Hades as he opened one of the gilded doors. She was not eager to be in an enclosed space with him. She didn't trust her thoughts or her body.

This time, he called her out. "Will you hesitate at every turn, Lady Persephone?"

She glared. "I was just admiring your decor, Lord Hades. I didn't notice this last night."

"The doors to my quarters are often veiled during business hours," he replied and then indicated the open door. "Shall we?"

Once again, she gathered her courage and approached. He didn't leave much room for her to pass, and she brushed against him as she stepped into the room.

She found herself in Hades's office. The first thing she noticed were the windows that overlooked the club floor. There were none to the outside, but the space was warmly lit and oddly cozy, even with its black marble floor. Maybe it had something to do with the fireplace against the wall. A couch and two chairs made a lovely sitting area, and a fur rug only added to the comforting aesthetic. At the far end of the room, elevated like a throne, was a large obsidian slab that acted as Hades's desk. From what she could tell, there was nothing on it—no paperwork or pictures. She wondered if he used it at all or if it was just for show.

Immediately in front of her was a table upon which a vase of bloodred flowers rested. She rolled her eyes at the floral arrangement.

Hades closed the door, and she stiffened. This was dangerous. She should have confronted him downstairs where there was more space, where she was better able to think and breathe without inhaling him. His boots tapped against the floor as he neared, and her body grew taut.

Hades stopped in front of her. His eyes scoured her face, lingering on her lips for a split second before lowering to her neck. When he reached out to touch her, Persephone's hand clamped down on his arm. It wasn't that she feared him as much as she feared her reaction to his touch.

Their eyes met.

"Are you hurt?" he asked.

"No," she said, and he nodded, carefully pulling his arm free of her grasp. He crossed the room, Persephone assumed to put distance between them.

Then she remembered she was in her true form and started to raise her glamour.

"Oh, it's a little too late to be modest, don't you think?" Hades said, piercing her with those beautiful dark eyes.

He tugged his tie free, and she watched it slip from his neck before lifting her eyes to his. He wasn't smirking like she expected. He looked...primal. Like a starved animal that had finally cornered his prey.

She swallowed. "Did I interrupt something?"

She wasn't sure she wanted an answer.

The corner of his mouth lifted. "I was just about to go to bed when I heard you demanding entrance to my club."

Bed? It was well past noon.

"Imagine my surprise when I find the goddess from last night on my doorstep."

"Did the gorgon tell you?"

She stepped further into the room, glaring. Hades's lips quirked, amused.

"No. Euryale did not. I recognized your magic as Demeter's, but you are not Demeter." Then he tilted his head again. "When you left, I consulted a few texts. I had forgotten Demeter had a daughter. I assumed you were Persephone. Question is, why aren't you using your own magic?"

"Is that why you did this?" she demanded, removing the bracelet she'd used to cover the mark on her skin and holding up her arm.

Hades smirked.

Actually smirked.

Persephone wanted to attack him. She clenched her hands at her sides to keep from vaulting across the room.

"No," he said. "That is the result of losing against me."

"You were *teaching* me to play," she argued.

"Semantics," he shrugged. "The rules of Nevernight are very clear, Goddess."

"They are anything but clear, and you are an asshole!"

Hades's eyes darkened. Apparently, he didn't like being called names any more than the ogre did. He pushed away from the desk, striding toward her, and Persephone took a step back.

"Don't call me names, Persephone," he said and then reached for her wrist. He traced the bracelet all around, making her shiver. "When you invited me to your table, you entered into an agreement. If you had won, you could have left Nevernight with no demands on your time. But you didn't, and now we have a contract."

She swallowed, considering every horrible thing she'd heard about Hades's contracts and his impossible terms. What darkness would he pull from deep inside her?

"And what does that mean?" Her voice was still biting.

"It means I must choose terms."

"I don't want to be in a contract with you," she said between her teeth. "Take it off!"

"I can't."

"You put it there. You can remove it."

His lips twitched.

"You think this is funny?"

"Oh, darling, you have no idea."

The word *darling* slid across her skin and she shivered again. He seemed to notice, because he smiled a little bit more.

"I am a goddess," she tried again. "We are equals."

"You think our blood changes the fact that you willingly entered into a contract with me? These things are law, Persephone." She glared at him. "The mark will dissolve when the contract has been fulfilled." He said it like that should make it all better.

"And what are your terms?" Just because she was asking didn't mean she was going to agree.

Hades's jaw was tight. He seemed to be restraining himself—maybe he wasn't used to being ordered around.

When he lifted his head and stared down at her, she knew she was in trouble.

"Create life in the Underworld," he said at last.

"What?" She hadn't been prepared for that, though she probably should have been. Wasn't her greatest weakness her lack of power? An irony considering her divinity.

"Create life in the Underworld," he said again. "You have six months—and if you fail or refuse, then you will become a permanent resident of my realm."

"You want me to grow a garden in your realm?" she demanded.

He shrugged again. "I suppose that is one way to create life."

She glared at him. "If you steal me away to the Underworld, you will face my mother's wrath."

"Oh, I am sure," he mused. "Much like you will feel her wrath when she discovers what you've so recklessly done."

Persephone's cheeks flushed. He was right. The difference between them was that Hades didn't seem at all fazed by the threat. Why should he be? He was one of the Three—the most powerful gods in existence. A threat from Demeter was a pebble thrown.

She straightened, raising her chin and meeting his gaze head-on. "Fine." She felt the pressure of Hades's hand on her wrist like a shackle and tore her hand free. "When do I start?"

Hades's eyes glittered. "Come tomorrow. I'll show you the way to the Underworld."

"It will have to be after class," she said.

"Class?"

"I'm a student at New Athens University."

Hades looked at her curiously and nodded his head. "After...*class*, then."

They stared at each other for a long moment. As much as she hated him right now, it was hard not to enjoy the sight of him. "What about your bouncer?"

"What about him?"

"I'd prefer he not remember me in this form." She lifted her hand to her horns, then called up her glamour. It relaxed her a little to be in her mortal form.

Hades watched the transformation as if he were studying the form of an ancient sculpture. "I'll erase his memory...after he is punished for his treatment of you."

Persephone shivered. "He didn't know I was a goddess."

"But he knew you were a woman and he let his anger get the best of him. So he will be punished." Hades said it as matter-of-fact, and she knew there was no arguing.

"What will it cost me?" she asked, because she knew who she was dealing with, and she had just requested a favor from the God of the Dead.

His lips twitched. "Clever, darling. You know how this works. The punishment? Nothing. His memory? A favor."

"Don't call me darling," she snapped. "What kind of favor?"

"Whatever I want," he said. "To be used at a future time."

She considered this for a moment. What would Hades want from her? What could she possibly have to offer him? Maybe it was that thought that made her agree, or the fear that her mother would discover she'd showed her true form. Either way, she said, "Deal."

Hades smiled. "I will have my driver take you home."

"That's not necessary."

"It is."

She pressed her lips together. "Fine," she gritted out. She didn't really feel like taking the bus again, but the idea that Hades would know where she lived was unsettling.

Then the god clasped her shoulders, leaned forward, and pressed his lips to her forehead. The move was so sudden she lost her balance. Her fingers tangled into his shirt to steady herself, nails grazing the skin of his chest. His body was hard and warm, and his lips were soft on her skin. When he pulled away, she couldn't gather herself enough to be angry.

"What was that for?" she asked, her voice a whisper.

Hades maintained that infuriating smirk, like he knew she couldn't think straight, and brushed a finger across her heated cheek.

"For your benefit. Next time, the door will open for you. I'd rather you not piss Duncan off. If he hurts you again, I will have to kill him, and it's hard to find a good ogre."

Persephone could just imagine.

"Lord Hades, Thanatos is looking for you—oh—"

A woman entered the office from a hidden door behind his desk. She was beautiful, her hair parted in the center, as red as flame. Her eyes were sharp and brows arched, lips full and lush and crimson. All her features were pointed and angled. She was a nymph, and when she looked at Persephone, there was hatred in her eyes.

It was then Persephone realized she was still standing close to Hades, her hands tangled in his shirt. When she tried to pull away, his hands tightened on her.

"I did not know you had company," Minthe added tightly.

Hades didn't look at the woman. Instead, his eyes remained on Persephone. "A minute, Minthe."

Persephone's first thought was: *So this is Minthe.* She was beautiful in a way Persephone wasn't—a way that promised seduction and sin—and she loathed the jealousy she felt.

Her second thought was: Why did he need a minute? What more could he have to say?

Persephone didn't see Minthe leave because she couldn't force her gaze away from Hades.

"You haven't answered my question," Hades said. "Why are you using your mother's magic?"

It was her turn to smile. "Lord Hades," she said, drawing a finger down his chest. She wasn't sure what made her do it, but she was feeling brave. "The only way you are getting answers from me is if I decide to enter into another gamble with you, and at the moment, it's not likely."

Then she took the lapels of his jacket and straightened them, her eyes falling to the red polyanthus flower in the pocket of his suit jacket. She looked up at him and whispered. "I think you will regret this, Hades."

She touched the flower, and Hades's eyes followed the movement. When her fingers brushed the petals, the flower wilted.

CHAPTER V
Intrusion

Hades's driver was a cyclops.

She tried not to look so surprised when she saw the creature standing in front of a black Lexus outside Nevernight. He was not like the cyclopes depicted in history. They had been beastly creatures—large like a mountain, layered with rock-hard muscle, and fanged. This man was taller than Hades and all legs, with broad shoulders and a thin build. His eye was hooded but kind, and he smiled when he saw Persephone.

Hades had insisted on escorting Persephone outside. She was not eager to be seen in public with the god, though she wasn't so sure that thought had crossed Hades's mind. He was probably more concerned about getting her off his premises as soon as possible so he could get some rest…or whatever he'd been about to do before she interrupted.

"Lady Persephone, this is Antoni," Hades said. "He will ensure you make it home safe."

Persephone raised a brow at the God of the Underworld. "Am I in danger, my lord?"

"Just a precaution. I wouldn't want your mother banging down my door before she has a reason to."

She has a reason to now, she thought angrily, and the mark on her wrist pulsed, sending a wave of sensation through her. She met his stare, intending to glare and communicate her anger, but she found it difficult to think at all. The God of the Dead had eyes like the universe—vibrant, alive, vast. She was lost in them and all they promised.

She was thankful when Antoni distracted her from those dangerous thoughts. Nothing good would come out of finding Hades interesting. Hadn't she learned that already?

"My lady," Antoni said, opening the rear car door.

"My lord." She nodded to Hades as she twisted from him and slid into the black leather interior.

Antoni shut her door carefully and then folded himself into the driver's seat. They were on the road quickly, and it took everything in her power not to look back. She wondered how long Hades stood there before returning to his tower—if he was laughing at her boldness and her failure.

She stared down at the flashy bracelet that covered the black mark. In this light, the gold looked brassy and cheap. She pulled it off and examined the markings on her skin. The only thing she could think to be thankful for at this moment was that the mark was small enough and placed where it could be easily hidden.

Create life in the Underworld.

Was there even life in the Underworld? Persephone

knew nothing about Hades's realm, and in all her studies, she had never found descriptions of the land of the dead—just details of its geography, and even those seemed to conflict. She supposed she would find out tomorrow, though the idea of returning to Nevernight to make the descent into the Underworld filled her with anxiety.

She groaned. Just when everything seemed to be working out for her too.

"Will you be returning to visit Lord Hades?" Antoni asked, glancing in the rearview mirror. The cyclops had a pleasant voice, warm and spiced.

"I'm afraid I will," Persephone said absently.

"I hope you'll find him pleasing. Our lord is often alone."

Persephone found those words strange, especially in light of the jealous Minthe. "He doesn't seem so alone to me."

"Such is the case with the Divine, but I am afraid he trusts very few. If you ask me, he needs a wife."

Persephone blushed. "I am certain Lord Hades isn't interested in settling down."

"You'd be surprised by what the God of the Dead is interested in," Antoni replied.

Persephone didn't want to know Hades's interests. She already felt like she knew too many, and none of them were good.

Persephone watched the cyclops from her seat in the back.

"How long have you been in service to Hades?"

"The Three freed my kind from Tartarus after we were placed there by Cronos," he replied. "And so we have repaid the favor by serving Zeus, Poseidon, and Hades from time to time."

"As a driver?" She didn't mean to sound so repulsed, but it seemed a menial task.

Antoni laughed. "Yes, but our kind are great builders and blacksmiths too. We have crafted gifts for the Three and shall continue."

"But that was so long ago. Surely you've repaid their favor?" Persephone asked.

"When the God of the Dead gives you life, it is a favor that will never be repaid."

Persephone frowned. "I don't understand."

"You have never been to Tartarus, so I don't expect that you will." He paused, then added, "Do not misunderstand. My service to Hades is my choice, and of all the gods, I am glad to serve him. He is not like the other Divine."

Persephone really wanted to know what that meant, because from what she knew about Hades, he was the worst of the Divine.

Antoni arrived outside her apartment and squeezed out of the driver's seat to open her door.

"Oh, you don't have to—I can open my own door," she said.

He smiled. "It is my pleasure, Lady Persephone."

She started to ask him not to call her that but then realized he was using her title, as if he knew she was a goddess, yet she wore her glamour. "How did you—"

"Lord Hades called you Lady Persephone," he explained. "So I will too."

"Please…it's not necessary."

His smile widened. "I think you should get used to

it, Lady Persephone, especially if you visit us often, as I hope you will."

He shut the door and bowed his head. Persephone wandered to her apartment in a daze, turning to watch as Antoni drove away. This day had been long and bizarre thanks to the God of the Dead.

There was no reprieve from it either, because Lexa stood in the kitchen when Persephone came inside—and pounced.

"Uh, whose Lexus dropped you off in front of our lame apartment?" she asked.

Persephone wanted to lie and claim that someone from her internship had dropped her off, but she knew Lexa wouldn't believe that. She was supposed to be home two hours ago, and her best friend had just watched as she'd literally been chauffeured to their home.

"Well...you're never going to believe this but... Hades."

While she could admit to that, she wasn't ready to tell Lexa about the contract or the mark on her wrist.

Lexa dropped the mug she was holding. Persephone flinched as it hit the floor and shattered. "Are you kidding?" Persephone shook her head and moved to grab a broom; Lexa followed. "Like...*the* Hades? God of the Dead Hades? Owner of Nevernight Hades?"

"Yes, Lexa. Who else?"

"How?" she sputtered. "Why?"

Persephone started sweeping up the ceramic pieces. "It was for my job." It wasn't technically a lie. She could call it research.

"And you met Hades? You saw him in the flesh?"

Persephone shivered at the word, recalling Hades's

haphazard appearance. "Yeah." She turned away from Lexa and grabbed the dustpan, trying to hide the furious blush staining her cheeks.

"What does he look like? Details. Spill!"

Persephone handed Lexa the dustpan, and she held it as Persephone swept up the shattered mug. "I...don't know where to begin."

Lexa smiled. "Start with his eyes."

Persephone sighed. It felt intimate to describe Hades, and part of her wanted to keep him all to herself, though she was well aware she was only describing a toned-down version of the god. She had yet to see him in his true form.

There was a strange anticipation that followed that thought, and she realized she was eager to know the god in his divinity. Would his horns be as black as his eyes and hair? Would they curl on either side of his head like a ram's or reach into the air, making him even taller?

"He's handsome," she said, though even that word didn't do him justice. It wasn't just his looks; it was his presence. "He's...power."

"Someone has a crush." The smug smirk on Lexa's face reminded Persephone that she was too focused on what the god looked like and not enough on what he did.

"What? No. No. Look, Hades is handsome. I'm not blind, but I can't condone what he does."

"What do you mean?"

"The bargains, Lex!" Persephone reminded Lexa of what they'd learned from Adonis at Nevernight. "He preys upon desperate mortals."

Lexa shrugged. "Well, you could ask Hades about it."

"We're not friends, Lexa." They would never be friends.

Then Lexa bounced on her feet. "Oh! What if you wrote about him? You could investigate his bargains with mortals! How scandalous!"

It *was* scandalous—not only because of the content but because it would mean writing an article about a god, something very few did for fear of retaliation.

But Persephone wasn't afraid of retaliation; she didn't care that Hades was a god.

"Looks like you have another reason to visit Hades," Lexa said, and Persephone broke into a smile.

Hades had offered her easy access. When he'd pressed his lips to her forehead, he'd said it was for her benefit. She wouldn't have to knock to enter Nevernight again.

The God of the Underworld would definitely regret meeting the Goddess of Spring—and she looked forward to that day. She was Divine too. Though she had no power of her own, she could write, and maybe that made her the perfect person to expose him. After all, if anything happened to her, Hades would feel Demeter's wrath.

On her way to class at New Athens University, Persephone stopped to purchase an assortment of bangles. Since she would have to wear Hades's mark until she fulfilled their contract, she wanted to accessorize her outfits accordingly. Today she wore a stack of pearls, a classic touch to compliment her bright pink skirt and white button-up.

Her heels clicked against the concrete sidewalk as she rounded the corner and the university came into view.

Each step meant time was passing, which meant an hour, a minute, a second closer to her return to Nevernight.

Today Hades would take her to the Underworld. She'd stayed up into the night considering how she was to fulfill their contract. She'd asked if he wanted her to plant a garden, and he'd shrugged—*shrugged*—"*That is one way*," he'd said.

What was that supposed to mean, and what other ways could she possibly create life? Wasn't that why he'd chosen this challenge—because she had no power to fulfill the task?

She doubted it was because the Lord Hades wanted beautiful gardens in his desolate realm. He was interested in punishment, after all, and from what she'd heard and witnessed from the god, he did not intend the Underworld to be a place for peace and pretty flowers.

Despite how angry she was with herself and Hades, her emotions were at odds. She was both intrigued and nervous to descend into the god's realm.

Mostly, though, she was afraid.

What if she failed?

No. She closed her eyes against the thought. She couldn't fail. She wouldn't. She would see the Underworld tonight and make a plan. Just because she couldn't coax a bloom from the ground with magic did not mean she couldn't use other methods. Mortal methods. She would just have to be careful. She would need gloves—it was that or kill every plant she touched—and while the garden ruminated, she would look for other ways to fulfill the contract.

Or break it.

She did not know much about Hades except what

her mother and mortals believed about him. He was private, he did not like intrusions, and he did not like the media.

He was really going to dislike what she had planned for today, and suddenly she had the thought—could she make Hades mad enough that he would release her from this contract?

Persephone passed through the entrance of New Athens University, a set of six columns crowned with a piece of pointed stone, and entered the courtyard. The Library of Artemis rose in front of her, a pantheon-style building that she had taken pleasure in exploring her freshman year. The campus was easy to navigate, laid out like a seven-point star—the library being one of the seven points.

Persephone always cut through the center of the star, which was the Garden of the Gods, an acre of land full of the favored flowers of the Olympians and marble statues. Though Persephone had walked this path many times to class, today felt different. The garden was like an oppressor, and the flowers were enemies, their smells mixing in the air—the thick scent of honeysuckle mingled with the sweet smell of the rose accosting her senses.

Did Hades expect her to grow something this grand? Would he really sentence her to life in the Underworld if she failed to deliver his request in six months?

She knew the answer. Hades was a strict god; he believed in rules and boundaries, and he'd set them yesterday, not even fearing the threat of her mother's wrath.

Persephone passed Poseidon's pool and its towering statue of a very naked Ares with his helm atop his head and shield in hand. It wasn't the only statue of a naked god in the garden, and normally she gave it little thought, but today her gaze was drawn to the large horns atop Ares's head. Her own felt heavy under the glamour she wore. She'd heard a rumor when she moved to New Athens that horns were the source of the Divine's power.

Persephone wished that were true. It wasn't even about having power now. It was about freedom.

"It's just that the Fates have chosen a different path for you, my flower," Demeter had said when Persephone's magic never manifested.

"What path?" Persephone asked. *"There is no path, only the walls of your glass prison! Do you keep me hidden away because you're ashamed?"*

"I keep you safe because you have no power, my flower. There is a difference."

Persephone still wasn't sure what sort of path the Fates had decided for her, but she knew she could be safe without being imprisoned, and she guessed at some point Demeter had agreed, because she'd let Persephone go—albeit on a long leash.

She tensed when she smelled her mother's magic— bitter and floral. Demeter was near.

"Mother," Persephone said when Demeter appeared beside her.

She wore a human glamour—not something she often did. It wasn't that Demeter disliked mortals— she was incredibly protective of her followers—more that she merely knew her status as a goddess. Demeter's mortal mask was not so different from her Divine appearance. She kept the same smooth hair, the same

70

bright green eyes, the same luminous skin, but her antlers were veiled. She chose a fitted emerald dress and gold heels. To onlookers, she had all the appearances of a sharp businesswoman.

"What are you doing here?" Persephone asked.

"Where were you yesterday?" Demeter's voice was curt.

"It sounds like you already think you know the answer, so why don't you tell me?"

"Do not treat this with sarcasm, my dear. This is very serious—why were you at Nevernight?"

Persephone tried to keep her heart from racing. Had a nymph seen her? "How do you know I was at Nevernight?"

"Never mind how I knew. I asked you a question."

"I went for work, Mother. I must return today too."

"Absolutely not," Demeter said. "Need I remind you a condition of your time here was that you stay away from the gods? *Especially* Hades."

She said his name like a curse, and Persephone flinched. "Mother, I have to do this. It's my job."

"Then you will quit."

"No."

Demeter's eyes widened, and her mouth hung open. Persephone was sure that in all her twenty-four years, she'd never told her mother no. "What did you say?"

"I like my life, Mother. I've worked hard to get where I am."

"Persephone, you do not need to live this mortal life. It is...changing you."

"Good. That's what I want. I want to be me, whatever that is, and you're going to have to accept that."

Demeter's face was stone cold, and Persephone knew what she was thinking—*I do not have to accept anything but what I want.*

"I have heeded your warnings about the gods, especially Hades," Persephone added. "What are you afraid of? That I'll allow him to seduce me? Have more faith in me."

Demeter paled and hissed, "This is serious, Persephone."

"I am being serious, Mother." She checked her watch. "I have to go. I'll be late for class."

Persephone sidestepped her mother and left the garden. She could feel Demeter's gaze burning her back as she went.

She would regret standing up for herself, she was sure of it. Question was, what punishment would the Goddess of Harvest choose?

———

Class went by in a blur of furious notes and droning lectures. Normally Persephone was attentive, but she had a lot on her mind. Her conversation with her mother was gnawing away at her insides.

Though Persephone was proud she stood up for herself, she knew Demeter could whisk her away with a snap of her fingers back to the glass greenhouse. She was also thinking about her conversation with Lexa and how she could start research for her article. She knew an interview would be essential, but she wasn't eager to be in an enclosed space with Hades again.

She was still feeling off at lunch, and Lexa noticed.

"What's wrong?"

Persephone considered how to tell her friend her mother was spying on her. Finally, she said, "I found out my mom's been tracking me. She...sorta found out about Nevernight."

Lexa rolled her eyes. "Doesn't she realize you're an adult?"

"I don't think my mother has ever seen me as an adult." And she didn't think she ever would, evident by her use of the nickname Kore.

"Don't let her make you feel bad for having fun, Persephone. Definitely don't let her keep you from doing what you want."

But it was harder than that. Obeying meant she could stay in the mortal world, and that was what Persephone wanted, even if it wasn't as fun.

After lunch, Lexa came with Persephone to the Acropolis. She claimed it was to see where she worked, but Persephone suspected she wanted a glimpse of Adonis—and she got one, because he intercepted them as they passed the front desk.

"Hey," he said and smiled. "Lexa, right? It's good to see you again."

Gods. She couldn't blame Lexa one bit for falling under Adonis's spell. This man was charming, and it helped that he was remarkably handsome.

Lexa grinned. "I couldn't believe it when Persephone told me she worked with you. What a coincidence."

He looked at Persephone. "It was definitely a pleasant surprise. You know what they say, small world, huh?"

"Adonis, a moment?" Demetri called from his doorway, and they all looked in his direction.

"Coming!" Adonis glanced back at Lexa. "Good to see you. Let's all go out sometime."

"Careful, we'll hold you to that," she warned.

"I hope you do."

Adonis hurried off to join Demetri, and Lexa looked at Persephone. "Tell me—is he as handsome as Hades?"

Persephone didn't mean to scoff, but there was no comparison. She also didn't mean to offer a resounding "No."

But she did.

Lexa raised a brow and smiled, then leaned forward and pecked Persephone on the cheek. "I'll see you tonight. Oh, and make sure you follow up with Adonis. He's right—we should go out together."

With Lexa gone, Persephone deposited her belongings at her desk and went to make coffee. Post lunch, she was feeling tired, and she needed all her energy for what she was about to do.

When she returned to her desk, Adonis stepped out of Demetri's office. "So about this weekend."

"This weekend?" she echoed.

"I thought we could go to the Trials," he said. "You know, with Lexa. I'll invite Aro, Xerxes, and Sybil."

The Trials were a series of competitions whose contestants hoped to represent their territory in the upcoming Pentathlon. Persephone had never been, but she'd seen and read coverage in the past. "Oh... Well, actually, before we discuss that, I was hoping you might help me with something."

Adonis brightened. "Sure. What's up?"

"Has anyone here ever written about the God of the Dead?"

Adonis laughed, then stopped himself. "Oh, you're serious?"

"Very."

"I mean, it's kind of hard."

"Why?"

"Because it's not like Hades forces these humans into gambling with him. They do so willingly and then face the consequences."

"That doesn't mean the consequences are right or even fair," Persephone argued.

"No, but no one wants to end up in Tartarus, Persephone."

That seemed to contradict what Demetri had to say on her first day—that *New Athens News* always sought truth. To say she was disappointed was an understatement, and Adonis must have noticed.

"Look…if you're serious about this, I can send you what I have on him."

"You'd do that?" she asked.

"Of course," he said and grinned. "On one condition—you let me read the article you write."

She had no problem sending Adonis her article and welcomed the feedback. "Deal."

Adonis delivered. Shortly after he returned to his desk, she received an email with notes and voice recordings detailing deals the god had made with several mortals. Not everyone who wrote or called were victims of Hades; some were families of victims whose lives had been cut short due to a lost bargain.

In total, she counted seventy-seven different cases. As she read and listened, a common thread emerged from the interviews: all the mortals who'd gone to

Hades for help were in desperate need of something—money or health or love. Hades would agree to grant whatever the mortal asked if they won against him at a game of his choice.

But if they lost, they were at his mercy. And Hades seemed to delight in offering an impossible challenge.

An hour in, Adonis dropped by to check on her. "Finding any of it useful?"

"I want to interview Hades," she said. "Today, if possible."

She felt impatient—the sooner she got this article out, the better.

Adonis paled. "You want to...*what?*"

"I'd like to give Hades a chance to offer his side of things," she explained. Everything Adonis had on him was from the perspective of the mortal, and she was curious how the god saw bargains and mortals and their vices. "You know, before I write my article."

Adonis blinked a couple times and finally found his words. "That's not how this works, Persephone. You can't just show up at a god's place of business and demand an audience. There's a... There are rules."

She raised a brow and crossed her arms over her chest. "Rules?"

"Yes, rules. We have to submit a request to his PR manager."

"A request that will be denied, I'm assuming?"

Adonis glanced away, shifting on his feet as if Persephone's questioning made him uncomfortable.

"Look, if we go there, at least we can say we tried to reach him for comment and he denied us. I can't write this article without trying, and I don't want to wait."

Not when I can enter Nevernight at will, she thought. Hades would regret kissing her when he saw how she planned to use his favor.

After a moment, Adonis sighed. "Okay. I'll let Demetri know we're heading out."

He started to turn, and Persephone stopped him. "You haven't...told Demetri about this, have you?"

"Not that you plan to write this article."

"Can we keep it a secret? For now?"

Adonis smiled. "Yeah, sure. Whatever you want, Persephone."

———

Adonis parked on the curb in front of Nevernight, his red Lexus glaring against the black backdrop of Hades's obsidian tower. Even though Persephone was determined to follow through with this interview, she had a moment of doubt. Was she being too bold in assuming she could even use Hades's favor in this way?

Adonis came up beside her. "Looks different in the daylight, huh?"

"Yeah," she said absently. The tower did look different—harsher. A jagged cut in a sparkling city.

Adonis tried the door, but it was locked, so he knocked and offered no time for someone to answer before retreating. "Looks like no one's home."

He definitely did not want to be here, and Persephone wondered why he hesitated to confront the god when he came to his club so often at night.

As Adonis turned away from the door, Persephone tried it—and it opened.

"Yes!" she hissed to herself.

Adonis looked back at her, puzzled. "How did you… It was locked!"

She shrugged. "Maybe you didn't pull hard enough. Come on."

As she disappeared into Nevernight, she heard Adonis say, "*I swear it was locked.*"

She descended the stairs, entering the now-familiar club. Her heels clicked against the glossy black floor and she looked up into the darkness of the tall ceiling, knowing that this floor could be seen from Hades's office.

"Hello? Anybody home?" Adonis called.

Persephone cringed and resisted the urge to tell Adonis to shut up. She'd had it in her head that she'd go upstairs to Hades's office and catch him off guard, though she wasn't so sure that was a great idea. She considered yesterday, when he'd answered the door disheveled.

At least if she surprised him, she might learn the truth about whatever was going on between him and Minthe.

As if summoned by her thoughts, the redheaded nymph emerged from the darkness of the room, dressed in a fitted black dress and heels. She was just as lovely as Persephone remembered. The Goddess of Spring had met and befriended many nymphs, but none of them looked quite as severe as Minthe; she wondered if that was the result of serving the God of the Underworld.

"Can I help you?" Minthe had an inviting and smoky voice, but it didn't hide the sharpness of her tone.

"Hi." Adonis brushed past Persephone, suddenly finding his confidence and extending his hand. Persephone was surprised and slightly frustrated when Minthe took his hand and offered a smile. "Adonis."

"Minthe."

"Do you work here?" he asked.

"I am Lord Hades's assistant," she replied.

Persephone looked away and rolled her eyes. *Assistant* seemed like a loaded word.

"Really?" Adonis sounded genuinely surprised. "But you're so beautiful."

It really wasn't Adonis's fault. Nymphs had that effect on people, but Persephone was on a mission and growing impatient.

Adonis held Minthe's hand longer than necessary until Persephone cleared her throat, and he dropped it.

"Uh...and this is Persephone." He gestured to her. Minthe said nothing; she didn't even nod. "We're from *New Athens News*."

"So you're a reporter?" Her eyes flashed, and Adonis probably took it as interest in his occupation, but Persephone knew otherwise.

"We're actually here to speak with Hades," she said. "Is he around?"

Minthe's eyes burned into her. "Do you have an appointment with *Lord* Hades?"

"No."

"Then I'm afraid you cannot speak to him."

"Oh, well, that's too bad," Adonis said. "We'll come back when we have an appointment. Persephone?"

She ignored Adonis, glaring at Minthe. "Inform your lord that Persephone is here and would like to speak with him." It was a command, but Minthe smiled, unfazed, looking at Adonis.

"Your counterpart must be new and therefore ignorant to how this works. See, Lord Hades does not give interviews."

"Of course." Adonis wrapped his fingers around Persephone's wrist. "Let's go, Persephone. I told you, there is a protocol we need to follow."

Persephone looked at Adonis's fingers wrapped around her wrist and then met his gaze. She wasn't sure what look she gave him, but her eyes burned, and anger rose hot in her blood. "*Let. Me. Go.*"

His eyes widened and he released her. She turned her attention back to Minthe.

"I am not ignorant of how this works," Persephone said. "But I demand to speak with Hades."

"*Demand?*" Minthe crossed her arms over her chest, brows rising to her hairline, and smiled wickedly. "Fine. I'll tell him you *demand* to see him, but only because I will take great satisfaction in hearing him turn you away."

She twisted on her heels and melted into the darkness. Persephone wondered for a moment if she really was going to tell Hades or send an ogre to kick them out.

"Why would Hades know your name?" Adonis asked.

She didn't look at him as she replied, "I met him the same night I met you."

She could feel his questions building in the air between them. She just hoped he wouldn't ask them.

Minthe returned looking pissed, and that filled Persephone with glee, especially since the nymph had been so sure Hades would turn them away.

She lifted her chin and said tightly, "Follow me."

Persephone thought about telling Minthe she didn't need a guide, but Adonis was here, and he was already curious. She didn't want him knowing she had been here yesterday or about her contract with the God of the Dead.

Persephone offered Adonis a glance before following

Minthe up the same set of twisting stairs she'd followed Hades up yesterday and to the ornate gold and black doors of his office. Adonis offered a low whistle.

Today Persephone focused on the gold rather than the flowers. She supposed it was fitting he would choose gold; he was the God of Precious Metals, after all.

Minthe didn't knock before she entered Hades's office and strode ahead, hips swaying. Perhaps she hoped to hold Hades's attention, but Persephone felt his gaze on her the moment she entered the room. He tracked her like prey from his place near the windows, and she wondered how long he had been watching them below.

Judging by how rigid he stood, she guessed he'd been there a while.

Unlike yesterday when she had demanded entrance into Nevernight, Hades's appearance was pristine. He was an elegant chasm of darkness, and she might have thought to be terrified if she wasn't so angry with him.

Minthe paused and nodded. "Persephone, my lord."

Her tone had taken on that sultry edge again. Persephone imagined she used it when she wanted to bend men to her will. Perhaps she forgot Hades was a god. She shifted, turning to face Persephone again, standing just behind the god. "And...her *friend*, Adonis."

It was at the mention of Adonis that Hades's eyes finally left Persephone, and she felt released from a spell. Hades's gaze slid to her counterpart and darkened before he nodded to Minthe. "You are dismissed, Minthe. Thank you."

Once she was gone, Hades moved to fill a glass with amber liquid from a crystal decanter. He did not ask them to sit or if they wanted any.

That wasn't a good sign. He intended this meeting to be very short.

"To what do I owe this…*intrusion?*" he asked.

Persephone's eyes narrowed at the word. She wanted to ask him the same—because that was what he'd done, intruded into her life.

"Lord Hades," she said and took her notebook out of her purse, where she'd written down the names of every victim who had called the paper with a complaint. "Adonis and I are from *New Athens News*. We have been investigating several complaints about you and wondered if you might comment."

He lifted the glass to his lips and sipped but said nothing. Beside her, Adonis offered a nervous laugh. "Persephone is investigating. I'm just…here for moral support."

She glared at him. *Coward.*

"Is that a list of my offenses?" Hades's eyes were dark and void of emotion. She wondered if this was how he welcomed souls into his world.

She ignored his question and read a few of the names on the list. After a moment, she looked up. "Do you remember these people?"

He took a languid sip of his liquor. "I remember every soul."

"And every bargain?"

His eyes narrowed and he studied her a moment. "The point, Persephone. Get to the point. You've had no trouble with it in the past. Why now?"

She felt Adonis look at her, and she glared at Hades, her face flush with anger. He made it sound like they'd known each other far longer than two days. "You agree to offer mortals whatever they desire if they gamble with you and win."

"Not all mortals and not all desires," he said.

"Oh, forgive me. You are selective in the lives you destroy."

His face hardened. "I do not destroy lives."

"You only make the terms of your contract known after you've won! That's deception."

"The terms are clear; the details are mine to determine. It is not deception, as you call it. It is a gamble."

"You challenge their vice. You lay their darkest secrets bare—"

"I challenge what is destroying their life. It is their choice to conquer or succumb."

She stared at him. He spoke in such a matter-of-fact tone, as if he'd had this conversation thousands of times. "And how do you know their vice?"

It was the answer she had been waiting for, and at the question, a wicked smile crossed Hades's face. It transformed him and hinted at the god beneath the glamour. "I see to the soul," he said. "What burdens it, what corrupts it, what destroys it—and challenge it."

But what do you see when you look at me?

She hated to think he knew her secrets and she knew nothing about him.

And then she snapped. "You are the worst sort of god!"

Hades flinched but quickly recovered, eyes flashing with anger.

"Persephone—" Adonis warned, but Hades's warm baritone quickly drowned him out.

"I am helping these mortals." He took a deliberate step toward her.

"How? By offering an impossible bargain? Abstain from addiction or lose your life? That's absolutely ridiculous, Hades."

"I have had success," he argued.

"Oh? And what is your success? I suppose it doesn't matter to you as you win either way, right? All souls come to you at some point."

His gaze turned stony and he moved to close the distance between them, but before he could, Adonis stepped between him and Persephone. Hades's eyes ignited, and with a flick of his wrist, Adonis went limp and collapsed to the floor.

"*What did you do?*" Persephone started to reach for him, but Hades grabbed her wrists, keeping her on her feet and drawing her into him. She held her breath, not wanting to be this close, where she could feel his warmth and smell his scent.

His breath caressed her lips as he spoke. "I'm assuming you don't want him to hear what I have to say to you. Don't worry. I won't request a favor when I erase his memory."

"Oh, how kind of you," she mocked, craning her neck to meet his gaze. He bent over her, his hold on her wrists the only thing keeping her from falling onto her back.

"What liberties you take with my favor, Lady Persephone." His voice was low—too low for this kind of conversation. It was the voice of a lover—warm and impassioned.

"You never specified how I had to use your favor."

His eyes narrowed a fraction. "I didn't, though I expected you to know better than to drag *this* mortal into my realm."

It was her turn to narrow her eyes. "Do you know him?"

Hades ignored the question. "You plan to write a story about me? Tell me, Lady Persephone, will you detail your experiences with me? How you recklessly invited me to your table, begged me to teach you cards—"

"I did not beg!"

"Will you speak of how you flush from your pretty head to your toes in my presence and how I make you lose your breath—"

"Shut up!"

As he spoke, he leaned closer. "Will you speak of the favor I have given you, or are you too ashamed?"

"*Stop!*"

She pulled away, and he released her, but he was not through. "You may blame me for the choices you made, but it changes nothing. You are *mine* for six months— and that means, if you write about me, I will ensure there are consequences."

She tried hard to keep from shivering at his possessive words. He was calm as he spoke, and it unnerved her because she had the distinct impression he was anything but calm on the inside.

"It is true what they say about you," she said, her chest rising and falling. "You heed no prayer. You offer no mercy."

Hades's face remained blank. "No one prays to the God of the Dead, my lady, and when they do, it is too late."

Hades waved his hand, and Adonis awoke, inhaling sharply. He sat up quickly and looked around. When his eyes landed on Hades, he scrambled to his feet. "S-sorry," he said. He looked at the floor and didn't meet Hades's gaze.

"I will answer no more of your questions," Hades said. "Minthe will show you out."

Hades turned away, and Minthe appeared instantly, hair and eyes aflame, dead set on Persephone. She had the fleeting thought that she and Hades would make quite the intimidating pair and she didn't like it.

"Persephone." Hades's voice commanded her attention as she and Adonis turned to leave. She paused at the door and looked back. "I shall add your name to my guest list this evening."

He still expected her tonight? Her heart fell into her stomach. What sort of punishment would he add to her sentence for her indiscretion? She had the contract, and she already owed him one favor.

She stared at him for a moment and all his darkness seemed to blur together, except for his eyes, which burned like a fire in the night.

She strode from the office, ignoring Adonis's shocked expression.

Once they were outside Nevernight, Adonis muttered. "Well, that was interesting."

Persephone was barely listening. She was too distracted by what had transpired in Hades's office, appalled by his misuse of power and his corrupt belief that he was *helping*.

"You said you only met Hades once before?" Adonis asked as they got into his car.

"Huh?"

"Hades, you've met him once before?"

She stared at him a moment. Hades had said he

would erase Adonis's memories, but at that question, she wondered if it had worked.

"Yes," she admitted hesitantly. "Why?"

He shrugged. "There just seemed to be a lot of tension between you two, like...you have a history."

How was it that a few hours of history between them felt like lifetimes? Why had she invited Hades to the table? She knew she'd regret that decision for the rest of her life. This kind of deal had claws, and there was no way she was getting out of this without scars. There was too much at stake, too much that was forbidden. Persephone's freedom was wrapped up in this—and the threat came from all sides.

"Persephone?" Adonis asked.

She took a breath. "No. We don't have history."

CHAPTER VI
The Styx

What do you wear on a tour of the Underworld?

It was a question Persephone had been asking herself since she left Hades's office earlier that day. She should have asked more questions. Would they be hiking? What was the weather like below? She was tempted to wear yoga pants just to get a reaction out of him, but then she remembered she was going to Nevernight first, and they had a dress code.

In the end, she picked a short silver dress with a low neckline and heels that sparkled. She stepped off the bus in front of Hades's club and approached the entrance, ignoring jealous stares from the impossibly long line. The waiting bouncer was not Duncan, but he was still an ogre. Persephone wondered how Hades had punished the monster for his treatment of her. She had to admit, she'd been surprised by the God of the Dead in that moment; he hadn't defended her because she was a goddess, he'd defended her because she was a woman.

And despite his many flaws, she had to respect that.

"My name is   " she started.

"You need not introduce yourself, my lady," the ogre said.

Persephone reddened and hoped that no one in the line closest to her could hear. The ogre reached and opened the door, bowing his head. How did this creature know her? Was it the favor Hades had bestowed upon her? Was it visible somehow?

She met the ogre's gaze. "What is your name?"

The creature looked surprised. "Mekonnen, my lady."

"Mekonnen," she smiled. "Call me Persephone, please."

His eyes widened. "My lady—I couldn't. Lord Hades, he would—"

"I will speak with Lord Hades." She placed her hand on the ogre's arm. "Call me Persephone."

Mekonnen offered a crooked smile and then swept his hand out in a dramatic fashion, bowing at the waist. "Persephone."

She laughed and shook her head. She'd talk to him later about the bowing, but for now, if he never called her "my lady" again, she'd see that as a victory.

She entered the club and made her way to the floor, but just as she came to the end of the steps, a satyr approached. He was handsome in his black button-up, with shaggy dark hair, a goatee, and dark horns that curled out of his head.

"Lady Persephone?" he asked.

"Just Persephone," she said. "Please."

"Apologies, Lady Persephone. I speak as Lord Hades commands."

Was she going to have this conversation with everyone? "Lord Hades has no say over how I am to be addressed." She smiled. "Persephone it is."

The corners of his lips curled. "I like you already. I am Ilias. Lord Hades wishes me to apologize on his behalf. He is otherwise engaged and has advised me to show you to his office. He promises he will not be long."

She wondered what was holding him up. Perhaps he was sealing another terrible contract with a mortal…or with Minthe. "I'll just wait at the bar."

"I'm afraid that will not do."

"Another command?" she asked.

Ilias offered an apologetic smile. "I'm afraid this one must be obeyed, Persephone."

That annoyed her, but it wasn't Ilias's fault. She smiled at the satyr. "Only for you, then. Lead the way."

She followed the satyr as he cut through the thickening crowd and along the familiar path to Hades's office. She was surprised when he followed her inside. He walked to the bar where Hades had served himself earlier in the day. "Can I get you anything? Wine, perhaps?"

"Yes, please. A cab, if you have it." If she was going to spend the evening with Hades and in the Underworld, she wanted a drink in her hand.

"Coming right up!"

The satyr was so cheerful, she found it hard to believe he worked for Hades. Then again, Antoni had seemed to revere the god. She wondered if Ilias felt the same.

She watched as he selected a bottle of wine and began to uncork it. After a moment, she asked, "Why do you serve Hades?"

"I do not serve Lord Hades. I work for him. There is a difference."

Fair enough. "Why do you work for him, then?"

"Lord Hades is very generous," the satyr explained. "Don't believe everything you hear about him. Most of it isn't true."

That piqued her interest. "Tell me something that isn't true."

The satyr chuckled as he poured her wine and slid the glass across the table.

"Thank you."

"My pleasure." He bowed his head a little, placing his hand against his chest. When he looked at her again, she was surprised by his seriousness. "They say Hades is protective of his realm, and while that is true, it isn't about power. He cares for his people, protects them, and he takes it personally if anyone is harmed. If you belong to him, he will tear the world apart to save you."

She shivered. "But I don't belong to him."

Ilias smiled. "Yes, you do, or I wouldn't be serving you wine in his office." He bowed. "If you require anything, you must simply speak my name."

With that, Ilias was gone, and Persephone was left in the silence. It was quiet in Hades's office; the fireplace didn't even pop. She wondered if this was a form of punishment in Tartarus. It would definitely have driven her insane.

After a moment, she walked to the wall of windows that overlooked the main floor of the club. She had the strange feeling that this was how the Olympians once felt when they lived in the clouds and looked down upon the Earth.

She studied the mortals below. At first glance, she saw clusters of friends and couples, their worries banished by the drinks in their hands. For them, this was a night of fun and euphoria—not too unlike the one she had on her first visit. For others, though, their visit to Nevernight meant hope.

She picked them out one by one. They gave themselves away by their longing glances at the spiral staircase that led to the second floor where Hades made his deals. She noted the slumped shoulders of the stressed, the glistening sweat on the brows of the anxious, the rigid posture of the desperate.

The sight made her sad, but they would be warned soon enough not to fall prey to Hades's games. She would make sure of it.

She turned from the window and approached Hades's desk; the huge piece of obsidian looked as if it had been cleaved from the earth and polished. Persephone wondered if it had come from the Underworld.

She trailed her fingers along its smooth surface. Unlike her desk, which was already covered in sticky notes and personalized with photos, his was free of clutter. She frowned. That was disappointing; she'd hoped to glean something useful from the contents, but this one didn't even have drawers.

She sighed and turned around, remembering that Minthe had appeared from a passage behind Hades's desk. Looking at the wall now, there was no indication a door existed. She stepped closer, leaning forward to inspect the wall—seamless.

The door probably responded to Hades's magic, which meant it should respond to her favor. She ran her hand over the smooth surface—until her hand sank into the wall. She gasped and recoiled quickly, heart beating hard in her chest. She inspected her hand front and back but found no wounds.

Curiosity overwhelmed her then, and she looked over her shoulder before she tried again, pushing farther into the wall. It gave way like liquid, and when she stepped through on the other side, she found herself in a hallway lined with crystal chandeliers. The light kept her feet in shadow, and when she took a step forward, she fell and landed hard on something sharp.

The impact took her breath away. Panicked, she inhaled in gasps until her breathing returned to normal. It was then she realized she'd fallen on a step. The light overhead barely touched the outline of a staircase.

Persephone struggled to her feet despite a sharp pain in her side. She took off her pumps and left them behind, making her way down the steps at a steep incline. She kept her hand pressed to her side and the other on the wall, afraid that if she fell again, she'd break her ribs.

By the time Persephone reached even ground, her legs and side ached. Ahead, a blinding but hazy light filtered into a cave-like opening. She stumbled toward it and walked right into a field of tall, green grass speckled with blooming white flowers. In the distance, an obsidian palace jutted against the sky, beautiful but ominous, like clouds full of lightning and thunder. When she looked behind her, she discovered she'd traveled down a great black mountain.

So this is the Underworld, she thought. It looked so normal, so beautiful. Like a whole other world beneath the world. The sky here was vast and alight, but she couldn't spot a sun, and the air was neither warm nor cold, though the breeze that moved the grass and her hair made her shiver. It also carried a mix of scents—sweet florals, spice, and ash. That was how Hades smelled too. She wanted to inhale it, but even shallow breaths hurt after her fall.

She wandered farther from the mouth of the mountain, keeping her arms crossed over her chest, hesitant to touch the delicate white flowers for fear they would wilt. The farther she walked, the angrier she became with Hades.

All around her was lush vegetation. Part of her had wanted the Underworld to be full of ash and smoke and fire, but here she found…life.

Why had Hades charged her with such a task if he already excelled at creating it?

She continued with no destination other than the palace. It was the only thing she could see beyond the huge field. She was surprised no one had come after her yet; she'd heard that Hades had a three-headed dog that guarded the entrance to the Underworld. She wondered if it was her favor that helped her pass into this place unknown.

Except that she sort of wished someone would come along, because the longer she walked and the heavier she breathed, the more her side hurt.

Soon she found her way barred by a river. It was an unsettling body of water, dark and churning, and so wide she could only see the vague coloring of foliage on the other side.

This must be the Styx, she thought. It marked the boundaries of the Underworld and was known to be guarded by Charon, a daimon, also called a guiding spirit. He took souls into the Underworld on his ferry, but Persephone saw no daimon and no ferry. There were only flowers—an abundance of narcissus spilled over the side of the river.

How was she supposed to cross this? She looked back at the mountain—she'd come too far to turn back now. She was a strong swimmer, except that the pain in her side might slow her down. Aside from the width, it looked rather unassuming—just dark, deep water.

Persephone stepped closer to the bank. It was wet, slippery, and steep. The flowers growing along the incline created a sea of white—a strange contrast against the water, which looked like oil. She tested it with her foot before slipping into the river completely. The water was cold, and her breathing became labored, which made the pain in her side worse.

Just as she set a decent pace, something clamped down on her ankle and pulled. Before she could scream, she was dragged under the water.

Persephone kicked and clawed, but the more she struggled, the tighter the grip and the faster the thing moved, deep into the river. She tried to twist to get a look at what had snatched her, but a spasm of pain made her cry out, and water spilled into her mouth and down her throat.

Then something clamped down on her wrist, jerking her roughly as the thing pulling her feet halted. When she looked at what held her wrist, she tried to scream but inhaled water instead.

It was a corpse. Two vacant eyes stared back at her, bits of skin still clinging to parts of its skeleton face.

She was caught between the two as they pulled her

up and down, stretching her body to the point of pain. They were soon joined by two more who took hold of her remaining limbs. Her lungs burned and her chest ached, and she felt pressure building behind her eyes.

I'm going to die in the Underworld.

But then one of the dead let go to attack the others, and the rest followed soon after. Persephone took her chance and swam as fast as she could. She was weak and tired, but she could see Hades's strange sky brightening the surface of the river above, and the freedom and air it promised motivated her.

She broke the surface just as one of the dead caught up with her. Something sharp bit into her shoulder and dragged her under again. This time, she was saved as someone from the riverbank managed to grab her wrist and drag her from the water, the dead thing wrenching free with a vengeance. A scream tore through her, and suddenly she couldn't take in air.

She felt solid ground beneath her, and a musical voice commanded her to breathe.

She couldn't—it was a combination of the pain and the exhaustion. Then she felt the press of a mouth against hers as air pushed into her lungs. She rolled over and heaved, water spilling onto the grass. When she was finished, she collapsed onto her back, exhausted.

A man's face loomed over hers. He reminded her of sunshine with his golden curls and bronzed skin, but it was his eyes she liked the most. They were gold and brimming with curiosity.

"You're a god," she said, surprised.

He smiled, showing a set of dimples on either side of his face. "I am."

"You're not Hades."

"No." He looked amused. "I am Hermes."

"Ah," she said and laid her head back down.

"Ah?"

"Yes, ah."

He grinned. "So you've heard of me?"

She rolled her eyes. "The God of Trickery and Thieves."

"I beg your pardon. You forgot trade, commerce, merchants, roads, sports, travelers, athletes, heraldry..."

"How could I have forgotten heraldry?" she asked absently and then shivered, staring up at the dim sky.

"You're cold?" he asked.

"Well, I was just pulled from a river."

He took off his cloak and covered her. The fabric suctioned to her skin, and it was then she remembered that she'd worn that short, silver dress to Nevernight.

She flushed. "Thank you."

"It is my pleasure," he said, still watching her. "Shall I guess who you are?"

"Oh yes. Entertain yourself," she said.

Hermes looked serious for a moment and tapped his full lips with his finger. "Hmm. I think you are the Goddess of Sexual Frustration."

Persephone barked laughter. "I think that's Aphrodite."

"Did I say sexual frustration? I meant Hades's sexual frustration."

Just as the words were out of his mouth, a blast of raw power threw him back. His body made the ground shake as he landed, tossing up dirt and rock.

Persephone sat up despite the pain and turned to

find Hades towering over her in his sharp black suit. His eyes were glimmered darkly and his nostrils flared.

"Why did you do that?" she demanded.

"You try my patience, Goddess, and my favor," he replied.

"So you are a goddess!" Hermes said triumphantly, rising from the rubble unscathed.

She glared at Hades.

"He will keep your secret, or he will find himself in Tartarus."

Hermes brushed dirt and rock from his arms and chest. "You know, Hades, not everything has to be a threat. You could try asking once in a while—just like you could have asked me to step away from your goddess here instead of throwing me halfway across the Underworld."

"I'm not his goddess! And you—" Persephone looked at Hades. Hermes's brows rose with amusement as she struggled to her feet, because up until now, she'd been glaring up at them both from the ground. "You could be nicer to him. He did save me from your river!"

Once she was on her feet, she regretted moving. She felt dizzy and nauseated.

"You wouldn't have had to be saved from my river if you had waited for me!"

"Right, because you were otherwise engaged." She rolled her eyes. "Wonder what that means."

"Shall I get you a dictionary?"

Hermes laughed, and Hades turned on him. "Why are you still here?"

Persephone swayed, and Hades lunged, catching her before she hit the ground. The impact jarred her side, and she moaned.

"What's wrong?" he demanded.

"I fell on the stairs. I think I…" She took a breath and winced. "I think I bruised my ribs."

When she met his gaze, she was surprised to see he looked worried. She recalled Ilias's words from earlier—*he takes it personally if anyone is harmed in his realm.*

"It's okay," she whispered. "I'm okay."

Then Hermes said, "She has a pretty nasty gash on her shoulder too."

And the worry she'd seen burned away with his anger. His jaw tightened, and he lifted Persephone into his arms, careful not to jar her.

"Where are we going?"

"To my palace," he said and teleported, leaving Hermes alone on the riverbank.

CHAPTER VII
A Touch of Favor

"Are you well?" Hades asked.

Persephone closed her eyes when they teleported because it usually made her dizzy. Now she looked up, meeting his gaze, and nodded.

Hades settled her on the edge of a bed covered in black silk sheets. She looked around, discovering he'd brought her to a bedroom. It reminded her of Nevernight with its shiny obsidian walls and floor, and despite all the black, the room was somehow comfortable. Perhaps it had to do with the roaring hearth opposite the bed, the fur rug at her feet, or maybe the wall of French doors that led to a balcony overlooking a forest of deep green trees.

Hades kneeled on the ground before her, and she felt a little panicked, hands trembling. "What are you doing?"

He said nothing as he pulled Hermes's cloak from her body. She hadn't been prepared or she would have fought for it; instead, she stilled, exposed under Hades's gaze. He sat back on his heels as his eyes traveled over her body, lingering longest on her torn shoulder, catching in all the places her silver dress clung. She drew an arm over her chest, trying to maintain some modesty as Hades came up onto his knees, bracing his arms on either side of her. From this angle, his face was level with hers. She felt his whiskey-laced breath on her lips when he spoke.

"Which side?" he asked.

She kept his gaze a moment before reaching for his hand and pressing it to her side. She was surprised by her boldness but rewarded with his warm, healing touch. She moaned and leaned into him. If anyone entered his room at this point, they might think he was listening to her heart with the way he was positioned—pressed between her legs, head turned away.

She took a few deep breaths until she no longer felt the ache of her bruised ribs. After a moment, he turned toward her but did not pull away.

"Better?" His voice was low, a husky whisper that trailed over her skin. She resisted the urge to shiver.

"Yes."

"Your shoulder is next," he said, standing.

She started to turn her head to get a glimpse at the wound, but Hades stopped her with a hand on her cheek.

"No," he said. "It's best if you don't look."

He turned from her then and stepped into an adjacent room, and she heard the sound of running water. While she waited for him to return, she rested on her side, eager to close her tired eyes.

"Wake, my darling." Hades's voice was like his touch—warm, luring. He kneeled before her again, blurry at first, and then coming into sharp focus.

"Sorry," she whispered.

"Do not apologize," he said and set to work cleaning the blood from her shoulder.

"I can do this," she said and started to rise, but Hades held her in place and met her gaze.

"Allow me this," he said. There was something raw and primal in his eyes she knew she couldn't argue with, so she nodded.

His touch was gentle, and she closed her eyes. So he would know she wasn't asleep, she asked questions. "Why are there dead people in your river?"

"They are the souls who were not buried with coins," he said.

She opened one eye. "You *still* do that?"

He smirked. She decided she liked when he smiled. "No. Those dead are ancient."

"And what do they do? Besides drown the living."

"That's all they do," he replied matter-of-factly, and Persephone paled. Then she realized that was their purpose. *No souls in, no souls out.* Anyone who found their way into the Underworld without Hades's knowledge would have to cross the Styx, and it was not likely they would survive.

She fell silent after that. Hades finished cleaning her wound, and once again, she felt his healing warmth radiate through her. Her shoulder took far longer than her ribs, and she wondered just how bad the injury had been.

Once he was done, he placed his fingers under her chin. "Change," he said.

"I...don't have anything to change into."

"I have something." He helped her to her feet,

directed her behind a screen, and handed her a short, black satin robe.

She looked at the piece of fabric and then at him. "I'm guessing this isn't yours?"

"The Underworld is prepared for all manner of guests."

"Thank you," she said curtly. "But I don't think I want to wear something one of your lovers has also worn."

She wished he would have told her there were no lovers, but instead he frowned and said, "It's either this or nothing at all, Persephone."

"You wouldn't."

"What? Undress you? Happily, and with far more enthusiasm than you realize, my lady."

She spent a moment glaring at him, and then her shoulders sagged. She was exhausted and frustrated and not interested in challenging the god. She took the robe from him. "Fine."

He gave her the privacy she needed to change. She stepped out from behind the partition in the robe and immediately fell under Hades's gaze. He stared at her for a long moment before clearing his throat, taking her wet dress, and hanging it over the screen.

"What now?" she asked.

"You rest," he said and lifted her into his arms. She wanted to protest—he had healed her, and despite her weariness, she could walk—but being in his arms made her feel flush and shy, so she remained quiet, unable to speak. Hades held her gaze even as he laid her down and drew the blankets over her body.

Her eyes were heavy with sleep.

"Thank you," she whispered and then noted the harsh set of his face. Frowning, she said, "You're angry."

She reached out to smooth his knitted brows, tracing her finger along the side of his face, over his cheek, and to the corner of his lips. He did not relax under her touch, and she withdrew quickly, closing her eyes, not wanting to witness his frustration.

"Persephone," she said.

"What?" he asked.

"I want to be called Persephone. Not 'lady.'"

"Rest," she heard him say. "I will be here when you wake."

She didn't fight the sleep that came.

———

Persephone's eyes felt like sandpaper when she opened them. For a moment, she thought she was home in her bed, but she quickly remembered she had almost drowned in a river in the Underworld. Hades had brought her to his palace, and she now lay in his bed.

She sat up quickly, closing her eyes against her dizziness. When it passed, she opened them again and found Hades sitting in a chair, watching her. In one hand, he held a glass of whiskey, apparently his drink of choice. He had shed his suit jacket and wore a black shirt with the sleeves rolled up and the buttons halfway undone. She couldn't place his expression, but she felt that he was upset.

Hades took a sip of the whiskey, and the fire behind him cracked in the silence that stretched between them. In that quiet, she was hyperaware of the way her body was reacting to him. He wasn't even doing anything, but in these close quarters, she could smell him, and it ignited a fire in the pit of her stomach.

She found herself wishing he would speak—*say something so I can be mad at you again*, she thought. When he didn't oblige, she prompted him.

"How long have I been here?" she asked.

"Hours," he replied.

Her eyes widened. "What time is it?"

He shrugged. "Late."

"I have to go," she said but didn't move.

"You have come all this way. Allow me to offer you a tour of my world."

When Hades stood, his presence seemed to fill the room. He downed the last of his whiskey, walked to where she sat on the bed, grasped the covers, and drew them away. As she slept, the robe he had given her loosened, exposing a sheath of white skin between her breasts. She held it closed, her cheeks flushed.

Hades pretended not to notice and held out his hand. She took it, expecting him to step away when she got to her feet, but he remained close and kept a hold of her fingers. When she finally looked up, he was watching her.

"Are you well?" His voice was deep and rumbled through her.

She nodded. "Better."

He drew his finger along her cheek, leaving a trail of heat. "Trust that I am devastated that you were hurt in my realm."

She swallowed and managed to say, "I'm okay."

His gentle eyes hardened. "It will never happen again. Come."

He led her onto the balcony outside his room, where the view was breathtaking. The colors of the Underworld were muted but still beautiful. The gray sky provided a backdrop for the black mountains, which melded with a forest of deep green trees. To the right, the trees thinned, and she could see the Styx's black water snaking through the tall grass.

"Do you like it?" he asked.

"It's beautiful," she answered, and she thought he looked pleased. "You created all of this?"

He nodded only once. "The Underworld evolves just as the world above."

Her fingers were still laced with his, and he tugged, leading her off the balcony, down a set of stairs that emptied into one of the most beautiful gardens she had ever seen. Lavender wisteria created a canopy over a dark stone path, and clusters of purple and red flowers grew wildly on either side of the trail.

The garden awed her and angered her. She turned on Hades, pulling her hand from his. "You bastard!"

"Names, Persephone," he warned.

"Don't you dare. This—this is beautiful!" It made her heart ache and was something she longed to create. She stared longer, finding new flowers—roses of inky blue, peonies in pink, willows and trees with dark purple leaves.

"It is," he agreed.

"Why would you ask me to create life here?" She tried to keep her voice from sounding so despondent, but she couldn't manage it, standing at the center of her dream manifested outside her head.

He stared at her for a moment, and then, with a

wave of his hand, the roses and peonies and willows were gone. In their place was nothing but desolate land. She gaped at Hades as she stood in the ruins of his realm.

"It is illusion," he said. "If it is a garden you wish to create, then it will truly be the only life here."

She stared half in awe, half in disgust at the land before her. So all this beauty was Hades's magic? And he maintained it effortlessly? He was truly a powerful god.

He called the illusion back, and they continued through the garden. As she followed Hades, the scents accosted her—sweet roses, musky boxwood, peppery geraniums, and more. The smell of dense foliage reminded Persephone of the time she spent in the green-house where her mother's flowers bloomed so easily and the promise she'd made never to return. Now she realized she would just trade one prison for another if she failed to fulfill the terms of their contract.

Finally, they came to a low stone wall where a plot of land remained barren, and the soil at their feet was the color of ash.

"You may work here," he said.

"I still don't understand," Persephone said, and Hades looked at her. "Illusion or not, you have all of this beauty. Why demand this of me?"

"If you do not wish to fulfill the terms of our contract, you have only to say so, Lady Persephone. I can have a suite prepared for you in less than an hour."

"We do not get along well enough to be housemates, Hades." His brows rose, and she lifted her chin. "How often am I allowed to come here and work?"

"As often as you want," he said. "I know you are eager to complete your task."

She looked away and bent to scoop up a handful of the sand. It was silky and fell through her fingers like water. She considered how she would plant the garden; her mother could create seeds and sprout them out of nothing, but Persephone couldn't touch a plant without it wilting. Perhaps she could convince Demeter to give her a few of her own seedlings. Divine magic would have a better chance in this dirt than anything a mortal might offer.

She thought through her plan, and when she rose to her feet, she found Hades watching her again. She was getting used to his gaze, but it still made her feel exposed. It didn't help that she only wore his black robe.

"And…how shall I enter the Underworld?" she asked. "I'm assuming you don't want me to return the way I came."

"Hmm." He tilted his head thoughtfully to the side. She had only known him for three days but had seen him do this before when he was particularly amused; it was a move he made when he already knew how he was going to act.

Even with that knowledge, she was surprised when he took her by the shoulders and pulled her flush against him. Her arms shot out, fitting against his chest, and when his lips met hers, she lost her grip on reality. Her legs gave out, and Hades's arms slipped around her, holding her tighter. His mouth was hot and consuming. He kissed her with everything—his lips and teeth and tongue—and she reciprocated with just as much passion. Though she knew she should not encourage him, her body had a mind of its own.

As her hands moved up his chest and around his neck,

Hades made a sound deep in his throat that both thrilled and frightened her. Then they were moving, and she felt the stone wall at her back. When he lifted her off the ground, she wrapped her legs around his waist. He was so much taller than her, and this position allowed him to trace her jaw with his lips, nip at her ear, and kiss down her neck. The sensation made her gasp, and she arched against him, driving her fingers through his hair, loosening the tie that held his dark strands in place, and when his hands moved under her robe, grazing soft, sensitive skin, she cried out, gripping his hair in her hands.

That was when Hades pulled away. His eyes lit with a need she felt deep in her core, and they struggled to catch their breath. For a long moment, they remained still. Hades's hands were still under her robe, gripping her thighs. She wouldn't stop him if he continued. His fingers were dangerously close to her core, and she knew he could feel her heat. Still, if she gave in to this need, she couldn't say how she might feel after, and for some reason, she didn't want to regret Hades.

Maybe he sensed that too, because he pried his fingers from her flesh and lowered her to the ground. His dark hair fell in waves well past his shoulders, creating a dark halo around his face. "Once you enter Nevernight, you have only to snap your fingers, and you will be brought here."

The color drained from her face, and she stopped breathing for a moment. *Of course*, she thought. *He was bestowing favor.* In the aftermath of the kiss, Persephone felt ashamed. Why had she allowed this? Why had she allowed things to get so intense? She knew not to trust the God of the Underworld—not even his passion.

She tried to push him away, but he didn't budge.

"Can't you offer favor another way?" she snapped.

He looked amused. "You didn't seem to mind."

She blushed and touched her tingling lips with shaking fingers. Hades's eyes flashed, and for a moment, she thought he might pick up where they'd left off.

And she couldn't let that happen.

"I should go," she said.

Hades nodded once, then wrapped his arm around her waist.

"What are you doing?" she demanded.

Hades snapped his fingers. The world shifted, and they were in her room. She gripped Hades's arms, light-headed. It was still dark outside, but the clock beside her bed read five in the morning. She had an hour before she had to be up and ready for work.

"Persephone." Hades's voice was a low rumble, and she met his gaze. "Never bring a mortal to my realm again, especially Adonis. Stay away from him."

She narrowed her eyes. "How do you know him?"

"That is not relevant."

She tried to draw away from him, but he kept her where she was, pressed against him.

"I work with him, Hades," she said. "Besides, you can't give me orders."

"I'm not giving you orders," he said. "I am asking."

"Asking implies there's a choice."

She wasn't sure it was possible, but Hades held her tighter. His face was inches from hers, and she found it hard to meet his eyes because her gaze kept falling to his mouth—the memory of the kiss they'd shared in the garden a phantom on her lips. She shut her eyes against it.

110

"You have a choice," he said. "But if you choose him, I will fetch you, and I might not let you leave the Underworld."

Her eyes flew open, and she glared at him. "You wouldn't," she said between her teeth.

Hades chuckled, leaning in so that when he spoke, his breath caressed her lips. "Oh, darling. You don't know what I'm capable of."

Then he was gone.

CHAPTER VIII
A Garden in the Underworld

Lexa sat across from Persephone outside the Yellow Daffodil. They'd walked to the bistro from their apartment to have breakfast before they went their separate ways—Persephone to the Library of Artemis and Lexa to Talaria Stadium to meet Adonis and his friends for a day of Trials.

Stay away from him. Hades's voice echoed in Persephone's head as if his mouth were against her ear, and she shivered. Despite his warning, she would have gone with Lexa, but she had a god to research, a garden to plant, and a bargain to win. Still, she wondered why Hades disapproved of Adonis. Did the King of the Underworld know his warning would only make her more curious?

"Your lips are bruised," Lexa observed.

Persephone covered her mouth with her fingers. She'd tried to cover the discoloration with foundation and lipstick.

"Who did you kiss?"

"Why do you think I kissed someone?" Persephone asked.

"I don't know that *you* kissed anyone. Maybe *someone* kissed you."

Persephone flushed. Someone had kissed her, but not for the reasons Lexa was thinking. *He was just bestowing favor*, Persephone reminded herself. *He would do just about anything to ensure you don't disturb him again.* That included offering her a shortcut to his realm.

She wouldn't let herself romanticize the God of the Dead.

Hades is the enemy. He is your enemy. He tricked you into a contract and challenged you to use powers you don't have. He will imprison you if you fail to create life in the Underworld.

"I'm just guessing since you left the apartment at ten last night and didn't come home until, like, five this morning."

"H...how did you know that?"

Lexa smiled, but Persephone could tell her friend was a little hurt by her sneakiness. "I guess we both have secrets. I was up talking to Adonis. I heard you come in."

What she'd heard was Persephone tiptoeing into the kitchen for water after Hades had teleported to her bedroom, but she didn't correct her. Instead, she focused on the part of Lexa's reply that was news to her.

"Oh. You and Adonis are talking?"

It was Lexa's turn to blush, and Persephone was glad she could redirect this conversation even if she wasn't sure how to feel about her best friend dating her coworker. Plus, she had yet to figure out why Hades disliked him. Was it simply that she had brought him to Nevernight or something more?

"It doesn't mean anything," Lexa said.

Persephone knew she was just trying to keep her expectations low. It had been a long time since she had been interested in someone. She'd fallen hard and fast for her first college boyfriend, a wrestler named Alec, a man who was incredibly handsome and charming…until he wasn't. What Lexa had at first thought was protectiveness soon became controlling. Things escalated until one night, he'd yelled at her for going out with Persephone and accused her of cheating on him. At that point, she'd decided things had to end.

It was only after things ended that Lexa learned Alec hadn't been faithful to her at all. The whole thing had broken her heart, and there was a time when Persephone wasn't sure Lexa would ever recover.

"We were making plans for today and just…kept talking," Lexa continued. "He's so interesting."

"He's interesting?" Persephone laughed. "You're interesting. Fashionista. Witch. Tattoos. What more could a guy want?"

Lexa rolled her eyes and promptly ignored her compliment.

"Did you know he was adopted? It's why he became a journalist. He wants to find his biological parents."

Persephone shook her head. She didn't know anything about Adonis except that he worked at *New Athens News* and had regular access to Nevernight, which was ironic considering Hades really didn't seem to like him.

"I can't imagine what that's like," Lexa said absently. "To exist in the world without really knowing who you are."

She couldn't know how painful her words were.

The bargain Hades had forced upon Persephone had reminded her just how much she didn't belong.

Once Lexa left for the Trials, Persephone took a coffee to go and headed to the Library of Artemis and the sanctuary of its beautiful reading rooms named after the nine Greek Muses. Persephone liked all of them, but she had always been drawn to the Melpomene Room, which she entered now. She wasn't sure why it was named after the Muse of Tragedy, except that a statue of the goddess stood at the center of the oval room. Light streamed through a glass ceiling, pouring over several long tables and study areas.

She'd come here in search of a book, and while she looked, she trailed her fingers over leather binding and gold lettering. Finally, she found what she was looking for: *The Divine: Powers and Symbols.*

She carried the volume to one of the tables and sat down to open it, turning the pages until she found his name in bold letters across the top of one.

Hades, God of the Underworld.

Just seeing his name made her heart race. The entry included a sketch of the god's profile, which Persephone traced with the tips of her fingers. No one would recognize him in person from this picture because it was too dark, but she could see familiar features—the arch of his nose, the set of his jaw, the strands of his long hair falling to his shoulders.

Her eyes dropped to the information written on the rest of the page, which detailed how Hades became the God of the Underworld. After the defeat of the Titans, he and his two younger brothers drew lots—Hades was given the Underworld, Poseidon the sea, and Zeus the skies, each with equal access over the Earth.

She often forgot that the three gods had equal power over the Earth, mostly because Hades and Poseidon didn't often venture outside their own realms. Zeus's descent to the mortal world had been a reminder, and Hades and Poseidon were not going to stand by while their brother took control of a realm they all had access to. Still, Persephone hadn't considered what that meant for Hades's powers. Did he share some of her mother's abilities to call forth storms and famine?

She continued reading until she came to the list of Hades's powers; her eyes widened as she read it, and she couldn't tell if she was more afraid or awed by him.

Hades has many powers, but his primary and most powerful abilities are necromancy, including reincarnation, resurrection, transmigration, death sense, and soul removal. Because of his ownership of the earthly realm, he can also manipulate earth and its elements and has the ability to draw precious metals and jewels from the ground.

Rich One indeed.

Additional powers include charm—the ability to sway mortals and lesser gods to his will—as well as invisibility.

Invisibility?
That made Persephone very nervous. She was going

to have to withdraw a promise from the god that he would never use that power with her.

She turned the page and found information on Hades's symbols and the Underworld.

The narcissus is sacred to the Lord of the Dead. The flower, often in colors of white, yellow, or orange, has a short, cup-shaped corona and grows in abundance in the Underworld. It is a symbol of rebirth. It is said Hades chose the flower to give the souls hope of what is to come when they are reincarnated.

Persephone sat back in her chair. This god did not seem like the one she'd met a few days ago. That god dangled hope before mortals in the form of riches. That god made a game out of pain. The one described in this passage sounded compassionate and kind. She wondered what had happened in the time since Hades had chosen his symbol.

"I have had success," he'd said. But what did that mean?

Persephone decided she had more questions for Hades.

When she was finished reading the passage on the Underworld, Persephone made a list of the flowers mentioned in the text—asphodel, aconite, polyanthus, narcissus—and then found a book on plant varieties that she used to take careful notes, making sure to include how to care for each flower and tree.

She grimaced when the instructions called for direct sunlight. Would Hades's muted sky be enough? If she were her mother, the light wouldn't matter. She could make a rose grow in a snowstorm.

Then again, if she were her mother, a garden would already be growing in the Underworld.

When Persephone finished, she took her list to a flower shop and asked for seeds. When the clerk—an older man with wild, wispy hair and a long, white beard—came to the narcissus, he looked up at her and said, "We do not carry *his* symbol here."

"Why not?" she asked, more curious than anything.

"My dear, few invoke the name of the King of the Dead, and when they do, they turn their heads."

"It sounds like you have no wish to exist happily in the Underworld," she said.

The shopkeeper paled, and Persephone left with a few extra flowers, a pair of gloves, a watering can, and a small shovel. She hoped the gloves would keep her touch from killing the seeds before she got them in the ground.

After she left the shop, she traveled straight to Nevernight for the third day in a row. It was early enough that no one was waiting outside to get into the club. As she approached, the doors opened, and once she was inside, she took a deep breath and snapped her fingers like Hades had showed her. The world shifted around her, and she found herself in the Underworld, in the same spot where Hades had kissed her.

Her head spun for a few moments. She had never teleported on her own, always using borrowed magic. This time, it was Hades's magic that clung to her skin, unfamiliar but not unpleasant, lingering on her tongue, smooth and rich like his kiss. She flushed at the memory and quickly turned her attention to the barren land at her feet.

She decided she would start near the wall and plant

the aconite first, the tallest flower, which would bloom purple. Then she moved on to the asphodel, which would bloom white. The polyanthus was next and would grow in clusters of red.

Once she had a plan, she lowered to her knees and started to dig. She settled the first seed into the ground and covered it with thin soil.

One down.

Several more to go.

Persephone worked until her arms and knees hurt. Perspiration beaded across her forehead, and she wiped it away with the back of her hand. When she finished, she sat back on her heels and surveyed her work. She couldn't quite describe how she felt, staring at the grayish plot, except that something dark and uneasy edged its way into her thoughts.

What if she couldn't do this? What if she failed to meet the terms of this contract? Would she really be stuck here in the Underworld forever? Would her mother, a powerful goddess in her own right, fight for her freedom when she discovered what Persephone had done?

She pushed those thoughts aside. *This is going to work.* She might not be able to grow a garden with magic, but nothing was preventing her from trying it the mortal way…except her deadly touch. She would have to wait a few weeks to find out if the gloves worked.

She picked up the watering can and looked around for a place to fill it.

Her gaze fell on the garden wall. It might give her enough height to locate a fountain or a river.

She stepped carefully so as not to disturb her freshly planted seeds and managed to scale the wall. Like everything else Hades owned, it was obsidian and almost resembled a vicious volcanic eruption. She navigated the rough edges carefully, only falling once, but caught herself, cutting her palm. She hissed at the stab of pain, closing her fingers on sticky blood, and finally made it to the top of the wall.

"Oh."

Persephone had glimpsed the Underworld yesterday, and yet it still managed to surprise her. Beyond the wall was a field of tall green grass stretching on for what seemed like miles before ending in a forest of cypress trees. Cutting through the lengthy grass was a wide and rushing river. From this distance, she couldn't quite make out the color of the water, but she knew it wasn't black like the river Styx. There were several rivers in the Underworld, but she was too unfamiliar with its geography to even guess which one might be in the field beyond.

Still, it didn't really matter—water was water.

Persephone climbed down from the wall and started across the field, watering can in hand. The tall grass scraped across her bare arms and legs. Mingled with the grass were strange orange flowers she had never seen before. Now and then, a breeze stirred the air. It smelled like fire, and while it wasn't unpleasant, it was a reminder that, though she was surrounded by beauty, she was still in the Underworld.

As she waded through the grass, she came upon a bright red ball.

Strange, Persephone thought. It was a larger than normal ball, almost the size of her head, and as she bent to pick it up, she heard a low growl. When she looked up, a pair of black eyes stared back from the tall grass.

She screamed and stumbled backward, ball in hand. One—no, three powerful-looking black Dobermans stood before her, sleek coats shining, cropped ears twitching. Then she noticed their gazes were focused on the red ball she held in her hand. Their growls turned into whines the longer she held it.

"Oh." She glanced down at the ball. "You want to play fetch?"

The three dogs sat tall, tongues lolling out of their mouths. Persephone threw the ball and all three bolted; she laughed as she watched them fall over each other, racing to claim it. It wasn't long before they returned, the ball in the jowls of the one in the center. The dog dropped it at her feet and then the three sat back obediently, waiting for her to throw it again. She wondered who had trained them.

She tossed the ball again and continued until she reached the river. Unlike the Styx, the water here was clear and ran over rocks that looked like moonstones. It was beautiful, but just as she moved to draw water, a hand clamped down on her shoulder and drew her back. "No!"

Persephone fell and looked up into the face of a goddess.

"Do not draw water from the Lethe," the goddess added. Despite the command, her voice was warm. She had long black hair, half of it pulled back, and the rest fell over her shoulders, past her waist. She dressed in ancient clothing—a crimson peplos and a black cloak. A set of short, black horns protruded from her temples, and she wore a gold crown. She had beautiful but stern features—arched brows accentuating almond-shaped eyes set in a square face.

Behind her, the three Dobermans sat, tails wagging.

"You're a goddess," Persephone said, getting to her feet, and the woman smiled.

"Hecate," she said and bowed her head.

Persephone knew a lot about Hecate because of Lexa. She was the Goddess of Witchcraft and Magic. She was also one of the few goddesses Demeter actually admired. Maybe that had something to do with the fact that she wasn't an Olympian. In any case, Hecate was known as a protector of women and the oppressed—a nurturer in her own way, even though she preferred solitude. "I'm—"

"Persephone," she said, smiling. "I have been waiting to meet you."

"You have?"

"Oh yes." Hecate's laugh seemed to make her glow. "Since you fell into the Styx and had Lord Hades in an uproar."

Persephone blushed.

"I'm sorry I scared you, but as I am sure you've learned, the rivers of the Underworld are dangerous, even to a goddess," Hecate explained. "The Lethe will steal your memories. Hades should have told you that. I will scold him later."

Persephone laughed at the thought of Hecate scolding Hades. "Can I watch?"

"Oh, I would only think to reprimand him in front of you, my dear."

They smiled at each other, and Persephone said, "Um, but do you happen to know where I might find some water? I just planted a garden."

"Come," Hecate said, and as she turned, she picked

122

up the red ball and threw it. The three dogs took off through the grass. "I see you have met Hades's dogs."

"They're really his?"

"Oh yes. He loves animals. He has the three dogs, Cerberus, Typhon, and Orthrus, and four horses, Orphnaeus, Aethon, Nycteus, and Alastor."

Hecate led Persephone to a fountain buried deep in Hades's gardens. As she filled the container, Persephone asked, "Do you live here?"

"I live in many places," Hecate replied. "But this is my favorite."

"Really?"

"Yes." Hecate smiled and looked out at the landscape. "I enjoy it here. The souls and the lost, they are my loves, and Hades is kind enough to have given me a cottage."

"It's far more beautiful than I expected," Persephone admitted.

"It is to all who come here." Hecate smiled. "Let's water your garden, shall we?"

Hecate and Persephone returned to the garden and watered the seeds. Hecate pointed to several of the markers Persephone had used to remember what and where she had planted.

"Tell me, what are these plants?"

"That one is anemone." Persephone found herself blushing. "Hades wore one in his suit the night I met him."

Persephone gathered her tools, and Hecate showed her where to store the items—in a small alcove near the palace.

After, Hecate took Persephone on a tour of the grounds. As they passed Hades's obsidian home, she noted a few new things she hadn't before—a stone courtyard attached to the palace and stables.

They continued, following a slate path among tall shoots of grass.

"Asphodel! I love these!" Persephone exclaimed, recognizing the flowers mixed among the grass with their long stems and spikes of white flowers. The farther they walked, the more abundant they became.

"Yes, we're close to Asphodel." Hecate held out her hand to stop Persephone from moving too far forward. When she looked down, she stood at the edge of a steep canyon; the asphodel grew right up to the edge of the incline, making the chasm almost impossible to see as they approached.

Persephone wasn't sure what she expected from Asphodel, but she guessed she'd always thought of death as a sort of aimless existence—a time when souls occupied space but had no purpose. At the bottom of this canyon, however, there was life.

A field of green stretched for miles, flanked by sloping hills in the distance. Several small homes were scattered over the emerald plane, all slightly different—some crafted of wood and others of obsidian brick. Smoke rose from some chimneys, flowers bloomed in a few window boxes, and warm light illuminated windows. A wide path cut right through the center of the field, crowded with souls and colorful tents.

"Are they…celebrating something?" Persephone asked.

Hecate smiled. "It is market day. Would you like to explore?"

"Very much," Persephone said.

Hecate took the young goddess's hand and teleported, landing on the ground inside the valley. When Persephone looked up, she could see Hades's palace rising tall toward his muted sky. She realized it was similar to the way Nevernight towered over the mortals in the world above. It was both beautiful and ominous, and Persephone wondered what feelings the sight of their king's tower inspired in these people.

The path they followed through Asphodel was lined with lanterns. Souls wandered about, looking as solid as living humans. Now that Persephone was on ground level, she saw that the colorful tents were filled with a variety of goods—apples and oranges, figs and pomegranates. Others held beautifully embroidered scarves and woven blankets.

"You look puzzled," Hecate commented.

"I just... Where does all this stuff come from?" Persephone asked.

"It is made by the souls."

"Why?" Persephone asked. "Do the dead need this stuff?"

"I think you misunderstand what it means to be dead," Hecate said. "Souls still have feeling and perception. It pleases them to live a familiar existence."

"Lady Hecate!" someone called in greeting.

Once one of the souls spotted the goddess, others did too and approached, bowing and grasping her hands. Hecate smiled and touched every one, introducing Persephone as the Goddess of Spring.

At that, the souls seemed confused.

"We do not know the Goddess of Spring."

Of course they didn't—no one did.

Until now.

"She is the daughter of the Goddess of Harvest," Hecate explained. "She will be spending time with us here in the Underworld."

Persephone blushed. She felt compelled to offer an explanation, but what was she supposed to say? *I entered into a game with your lord and he held me to a contract I must fulfill?* She decided staying silent was best.

She and Hecate walked for a long while, exploring the market. Souls offered them everything—fine silk and jewels, fresh breads and chocolate. Then a young girl ran up to Persephone with a small, white flower and held it out in her pale hand, bright-eyed, looking as alive as ever. It was a strange sight, and it made Persephone's heart feel heavy.

Her gaze fell to the flower, and she hesitated, knowing if she touched the petal, it would shrivel. Instead, she bent and allowed the girl to thread the flower into her hair. After, several more souls of all ages approached to offer flowers.

By the time she and Hecate left Asphodel, a crown of flowers decorated Persephone's head, and her face hurt from smiling so much.

"The crown suits you," Hecate said.

"They're just flowers," Persephone replied.

"Accepting them from the souls means a lot."

They continued toward the palace, and as they crested a hill, Persephone stopped short, spotting Hades in the clearing. He was shirtless, sun-kissed and chiseled, sweat glistening over his defined back and biceps. His arm was back as he prepared to throw the red ball his three hounds had brought her earlier.

For a moment, she felt panicked, like she was intruding or seeing something she wasn't meant to see—this moment of abandon when he was engaged in something so...*mortal*. It ignited something low in her stomach, a fluttering that spread to her chest.

Hades threw the ball, his strength and power evident in how impossibly far it went. The hounds bolted after it and Hades laughed, deep and loud; the sound was warm like his skin and echoed in Persephone's chest.

Then the god turned, and his eyes found hers immediately, as if he was drawn to her. Her eyes widened as she took him in, trailing from his broad shoulders to the deep vee of his abs. He was beautiful—a work of art, carefully sculpted. When she managed to look at his face again, she found him smirking, and she quickly averted her eyes.

Hecate marched forward, like she wasn't even fazed by Hades's physique. "You know they never behave for me after you spoil them."

Hades grinned. "They grow lazy under your care, Hecate." His eyes slid to Persephone. "I see you have met the Goddess of Spring."

"Yes, and she is quite lucky I did. How dare you not warn her to stay away from the Lethe!"

Hades's eyes widened, and Persephone tried not to smile at Hecate's tone. "It seems I owe you an apology, Lady Persephone."

Persephone wanted to tell him he owed her far more—but she couldn't make her mouth work. The way Hades looked at her took her breath away. She swallowed hard and was relieved when a horn sounded in the distance.

Hecate and Hades turned in its direction.

"I am being summoned," she said.

"Summoned?" Persephone echoed.

Hecate smiled. "The judges are in need of my advice."

Persephone didn't understand, and Hecate didn't explain.

"My dear, call the next time you are in the Underworld," she said in parting. "We'll return to Asphodel."

"I would love that," Persephone said.

Hecate vanished, leaving her alone with Hades.

"Why would the judges need Hecate's advice?" Persephone demanded.

Hades cocked his head to the side, as if he were trying to decide whether he should tell her the truth. "Hecate is the Lady of Tartarus. And particularly good at deciding punishments for the wicked."

Persephone shivered. "Where is Tartarus?"

"I would tell you if I thought you would use the knowledge to avoid it."

"You think I want to visit your torture chamber?"

He leveled his dark gaze upon her. "I think you are curious," he said. "And eager to prove I am as the world assumes—a deity to be feared."

"You're afraid I'll write about what I see."

He chuckled. "Fear is not the word, darling."

She rolled her eyes. "Of course, you fear nothing."

Hades responded by reaching to pluck a flower from her hair. "Did you enjoy Asphodel?"

"I did." She couldn't help smiling. Everyone had been so kind. "Your souls... They seem so happy."

"You are surprised?"

"Well, you aren't exactly known for your kindness," Persephone said and immediately regretted the harshness of her words.

Hades's jaw tightened. "I'm not known for my kindness to mortals. There is a difference."

"Is that why you play games with their lives?"

His eyes narrowed, and she could feel the tension rise between them like the restless waters of the Styx. "I seem to recall advising that I would answer no more of your questions."

Persephone's mouth fell open. "You can't be serious."

"As the dead," he said.

"But...how will I get to know you?"

That stupid smirk on his face returned. "You want to get to know me?"

She averted her gaze, scowling. "I'm being forced to spend time here, right? Shouldn't I get to know my jailer better?"

"So dramatic," he said, but he was quiet for a moment, considering.

"Oh no," Persephone said.

Hades raised a brow. "What?"

"I know that look."

He raised a curious brow. "What look?"

"You get this...look. When you know what you want." She felt ridiculous saying that out loud.

His eyes darkened and his voice lowered. "Do I?" He paused. "Can you guess what I want?"

"I'm not a mind reader!"

"Pity," he said. "If you would like to ask questions, then I propose a game."

"No. I'm not falling for that again."

"No contract," he said. "No favors owed, just questions answered—like you want."

She lifted her chin and narrowed her eyes. "Fine. But I get to pick the game."

He clearly hadn't expected that, and the surprise showed on his face. Then he grinned. "Very well, Goddess."

CHAPTER IX
Rock Paper Scissors

"This game sounds horrible," Hades complained, standing in the middle of his study—a beautiful room with floor to ceiling windows and a large obsidian fireplace. He'd found a shirt since they returned to the palace, and Persephone was only glad because his nakedness would have proved a distraction during their game.

"You're just mad because you haven't played."

"It sounds simple enough. Rock beats scissors, scissors beats paper, and paper beats rock. How exactly does paper beat rock?"

"Paper covers rock," Persephone said. Hades frowned at her reasoning, and the goddess shrugged. "Why is an ace a wild card?"

"Because it's the rules."

"Well, it's a rule that paper covers rock," she said. "Ready?"

They lifted their hands, and Persephone couldn't help giggling. Witnessing the God of the Dead playing rock paper scissors should be on every mortal's bucket list.

"Rock, paper, scissors, shoot!" they said in unison.

"Yes!" Persephone squealed. "Rock beats scissors!"

She mimicked smashing Hades's scissors with her fist—the god blinked. "Damn. I thought you'd choose paper."

"Why?"

"Because you just sang paper's praises."

"Only because you asked why paper covers rock. This isn't poker, Hades. It's not about deception."

He met her gaze, eyes burning. "Isn't it?"

She looked away, drawing in a breath before she asked, "You said you had successes before with your contracts. Tell me about them."

Hades moved to a bar cabinet across the room, poured his drink of choice—whiskey—and took a seat on his black leather sofa. "What is there to tell? I have offered many mortals the same contract over the years. In exchange for money, fame, love, they must give up their vice. Some mortals are stronger than others and conquer their habit."

"Conquering a disease is not about strength, Hades."

"No one said anything about disease."

"Addiction is a disease. It cannot be cured. It must be managed."

"It is managed," he argued.

"How? With more contracts?"

"That is another question."

She lifted her hands, and they played another round. When she threw rock and he scissors, she didn't celebrate but demanded, "How, Hades?"

"I do not ask them to give everything up at once. It is a slow process."

They played again, and this time, Hades won. "What would you do?"

She blinked. "What?"

"What would you change? To help them?"

Her mouth fell open a little at his question. "First, I wouldn't allow a mortal to gamble their soul away. Second, if you're going to request a bargain, challenge them to go to rehab if they're an addict, and do one better—pay for it. If I had all the money you have, I'd spend it helping people."

He studied her a moment. "And if they relapsed?"

"Then what?" she asked. "Life is hard out there, Hades, and sometimes living it is penance enough. Mortals need hope, not threats of punishment."

Silence stretched between them, and then Hades lifted his hands—another game. This time, when Hades won, he took her wrist and pulled her to him. He laid her palm flat, his fingers brushing the bandage Hecate had helped her tie. "What happened?"

She offered a breathy laugh. "It's nothing compared to bruised ribs."

Hades's face hardened, and he was quiet. After a moment, he pressed a kiss to her palm, and she felt the healing warmth of his lips seal her skin. It happened so quickly, she had no time to pull away.

"Why does it bother you so much?" She wasn't sure why she was whispering. She guessed it was because this all felt so intimate—the way they sat, facing each other on the couch, leaning so close she could kiss him.

Instead of answering, he placed a hand on the side of

her face, and Persephone swallowed thickly. If he kissed her now, she wouldn't be responsible for what happened next.

Then the door to Hades's study opened, and Minthe entered the room. She wore an electric-blue dress that hugged her curves in ways that left little to the imagination, and Persephone was surprised by the shock of jealousy that ricocheted through her. She had a thought that if she were mistress of the Underworld, Minthe would always wear turtlenecks and knock before she entered any room.

The flaming-haired nymph stopped short when she saw Persephone sitting beside Hades, her anger obvious. A smile curled Persephone's lips at the thought that Minthe might be jealous too.

The god withdrew his hand from her face and asked in an irritated voice, "Yes, Minthe?"

"My lord, Charon has requested your presence in the throne room."

"Has he said why?"

"He has caught an intruder."

Persephone looked at Hades. "An intruder? How? Would they not drown in the Styx?"

"If Charon caught an intruder, it's likely he attempted to sneak onto his ferry." Hades stood and held out his hand. "Come. You will join me."

Persephone took his hand—a move that Minthe watched with fire in her eyes before she twisted on her heels and left the study ahead of them. They followed her down the hall and to Hades's cavernous, high-ceilinged throne room. Rounded glass windows let in muted light. Black flags bearing images of gold narcissus flanked either side of the room all the way to the precipice of Hades's throne. Like him, it was sculpted and looked as if it were composed of thousands of pieces of shattered, sharp obsidian.

A man with umber skin stood there near the precipice, draped in white and crowned with gold. Two long braids hung over his shoulders, clamped with gold. His dark eyes first fell upon Hades, then on her.

Persephone tested Hades's grip on her hand, but the god only held her tighter, guiding her past the ferryman and up the steps to his throne. Hades waved his hand, and a smaller throne materialized beside his; Persephone hesitated.

"You are a goddess. You will sit in a throne." He guided her to be seated and only then released her hand. When he took his place upon his throne, Persephone thought for a moment that he might drop his glamour, but he didn't. "Charon, to what do I owe the interruption?"

"You're Charon?" Persephone asked the man in white. He looked nothing like the drawings in her Ancient Greek textbook that always depicted him as either an old man, a skeleton, or a figure cloaked in black. This version almost resembled a god—beautiful and charming.

Charon grinned, and Hades's jaw tightened. "I am indeed, my lady."

"Please call me Persephone," she said.

"My lady will do," Hades said sharply. "I am growing impatient, Charon."

The ferryman bowed his head. Persephone got the sense Charon was amused by Hades's mood. "My lord, a man named Orpheus was caught sneaking onto my ferry. He wishes for an audience with you."

"Show him in. I am eager to return to my conversation with Lady Persephone."

Charon snapped his fingers, and a man appeared before them on his knees, hands tied behind his back. Persephone inhaled, surprised by the manner in which he'd been restrained. The man's curly hair was plastered to his forehead, still dripping with river water from the Styx. He looked defeated.

"Is he dangerous?" Persephone asked.

Charon looked at Hades, so Persephone did too.

"You can see to his soul. Is he dangerous?" she asked again.

She could tell by the way the veins in Hades's neck rose that he was gritting his teeth. Finally, he said, "No."

"Then release him from those bindings."

Hades's eyes bored into hers. Finally, he turned to the man and waved his hand. When the bonds disappeared, he fell forward, hitting the floor. As he climbed to his feet, he looked at Persephone. "Thank you, my lady."

"Why have you come to the Underworld?" Hades asked.

Persephone was impressed; the mortal kept Hades's gaze and showed no sign of fear. "I have come for my wife." Hades did not respond, and the man continued. "I wish to propose a contract—my soul in exchange for hers."

"I do not trade in souls, mortal," the god answered.

"My lord, please—"

Hades held up his hand, and the man turned his gaze to Persephone, pleading.

"Do not look upon her for aid, mortal. She cannot help you."

Persephone took that as a challenge. "Tell me of your wife." She ignored Hades's gaze and focused on Orpheus. "What was her name?"

"Eurydice. She died a day after we were married."

"I am sorry. How did she die?"

"She just went to sleep and never woke up." His voice broke.

"You lost her so suddenly." Persephone's chest ached and her throat felt tight. She felt such sympathy for the man who stood broken before them.

"The Fates cut her life thread," Hades said. "I cannot return her to the living, and I will not bargain to return souls."

Persephone's fists curled. She wanted to argue with the god in that moment—before Minthe and Charon and this mortal. Was that not what he had done during the Great War? Bargained with the gods to bring back their heroes?

"Lord Hades, please—" Orpheus choked. "I love her."

Something hard and cold settled in her stomach when Hades laughed—a single harsh bark. "You may have loved her, mortal, but you did not come here for her. You came for yourself." Hades reclined in his throne. "I will not grant your request. Charon."

The daimon's name was a command, and with a snap of his wrist, both he and Orpheus were gone.

Persephone seethed, refusing to look at Hades. She was surprised when Hades broke the silence.

"You wish to tell me to make an exception."

"You wish to tell me why it's not possible," she countered.

His lips twitched. "I cannot make an exception for one person, Persephone. Do you know how often I am petitioned to return souls from the Underworld?"

She imagined often, but still. "You barely offered him a voice. They were only married for a day, Hades."

"Tragic," he said.

She glared at him. "Are you so heartless?"

"They are not the first to have a sad love story, Persephone, nor will they be the last, I imagine."

"You've brought mortals back for less," she said.

Hades looked at her. "Love is a selfish reason to bring the dead back."

"And war isn't?"

Hades's eyes darkened. "You speak of what you do not know, Goddess."

"Tell me how you picked sides, Hades," she said.

"I didn't."

"Just like you didn't offer Orpheus another option. Would it have been relinquishing your control to offer him even a glimpse of his wife, safe and happy in the Underworld?"

"How dare you speak to Lord Hades—" Minthe began, but she stumbled when Persephone glared at her. She wished she had the power to turn Minthe into a plant.

"Enough." Hades stood, and Persephone followed. "We are done here."

"Shall I show Persephone out?" Minthe asked.

"You may call her Lady Persephone," Hades said. "And no. *We* are not finished."

Minthe did not take her dismissal well, but she left, her heels clicking against the marble as she went. Persephone watched her leave until she felt Hades's fingers under her chin. He lifted her eyes to his.

"It seems you have a lot of opinions on how I manage my realm."

"You showed him no compassion," she said. He stared at her for a moment but said nothing, and she wondered what he was thinking. "Worse, you mocked the love he had for his wife."

"I questioned his love. I did not mock it."

"Who are you to question love?"

"A god, Persephone."

She glared at him. "All of your power and you do nothing with it but hurt." He flinched at that, and she continued, "How can you be so passionate and not believe in love?"

Hades offered a humorless laugh. "Because passion doesn't need love, darling."

Persephone knew just as well as he did that lust fueled the passion they shared, and yet she was surprised and angered by his response. Why? He had not treated her with compassion, and she was a goddess. Perhaps she hoped to see him as moved by Orpheus's plea as she had been. Maybe she had hoped to see a different god in the moment—one who would prove all her assumptions wrong.

And yet it had only confirmed them.

"You are a ruthless god," she said and snapped her fingers, leaving Hades alone in his throne room.

CHAPTER X
Tension

Persephone arrived at the Acropolis early on Monday. She wanted to start her article, and Hades had given her more than enough to work with during her visit to the Underworld. She was still angry with him for how he had treated Orpheus, could still hear his bitter laugh at the poor man's expression of love for his deceased wife, and it made her shiver.

At least he had shown his true nature—and at the precise instant she had begun to think he possessed a conscience.

The Fates must be on my side, she thought.

When she stepped off the elevator on her floor, she found Adonis standing at the front with Valerie, leaning over her desk and chatting. They immediately stopped talking when she arrived, and Persephone felt like she was intruding on a private moment.

"Persephone, you're here early." Adonis cleared his throat and straightened.

"Just hoping to get a head start. I have a lot to do," she said and passed them, heading straight for her desk.

Adonis followed. "How'd Nevernight go?"

She froze for a moment. "What do you mean?"

"Hades invited you to Nevernight before we left the interview. How did it go?"

Oh, right. You're too paranoid, Persephone, she thought.

"It was fine." She stowed her purse and opened her laptop.

"I thought he might convince you not to write about him."

Persephone took a seat and frowned. She hadn't considered that Hades's intention in inviting her on a tour of the Underworld might be a tactic to keep her from writing about him. "At this point, nothing could convince me not to write about him. Even Hades himself."

Especially Hades. Every time he opened his mouth, she found another reason to dislike him, even if that mouth inflamed her.

Adonis smiled, oblivious to her treacherous thoughts. "You're going to make a great journalist, Persephone." He took a step back and pointed at her. "Don't forget to send me the article. You know, when you're finished."

"Right," she said.

When she was alone, she attempted to sort out her thoughts on the God of the Dead. So far, she felt like she'd seen two sides to him. One was a manipulative, powerful god who'd been exiled from the world so long, he didn't seem to understand people. That same god had bound her to a contract with the very hands he'd used to heal her. He'd been so careful and gentle until it came to kissing, and then his passion was barely restrained.

It was like he starved for her.

But that couldn't be true—because he was a god and he had lived for centuries, which meant centuries of experience, and she was only obsessing over this because she had none.

She hung her head in her hands, frustrated with herself. She needed to reignite the anger she felt when Hades so arrogantly admitted to abusing his power under the pretense that he was helping mortals.

Her eyes fell to the notes she'd taken after interviewing him. She'd written so fast, the words were hardly legible, but after a few careful readings, she was able to piece it together.

If it is help Hades truly wants to offer, he should challenge the addict to rehab. Why not go a step further and pay for it?

She sat up a little straighter and typed that out, feeling the anger spark in her bloodstream again. It was like flame to an accelerant, and soon her fingers flew across the keys, adding word after angry word.

I see the soul. What burdens it, what corrupts it, what destroys it—and challenge it.

Those words pierced all the wrong parts of her. What was it like to be the God of the Underworld? To only see the struggle, the pain, and the vices of others?

It sounded miserable.

He must be miserable, she decided. Tired of being the God of the Dead, he inserted himself in the fate of mortal lives for entertainment. What did he have to lose?

Nothing.

She stopped typing and sat back, taking a deep breath.

She had never felt so many emotions about a single person before. She was angry with him, and curious, caught between surprise and disgust at the things he had created and the things he said. At war with both of those was the extreme attraction she felt when she was with him.

How could she want him? He represented the opposite of everything she'd dreamed of in her whole life. He was her jailer when all she'd wanted was freedom.

Except that he had freed something inside her. Something long-repressed and never explored.

Passion and lust and desire—probably all the things Hades looked for in a burdened soul.

She flexed her fingers over the keyboard and imagined what it would be like to kiss him with all this anger in her veins.

Stop! she commanded herself, biting down hard on her lip. *This is ridiculous. Hades is the enemy. He is your enemy.*

He only kissed her to bestow favor so she wouldn't cause any chaos for him. More than likely, her near-death experience in the Underworld had taken him away from important things.

Like Minthe.

She rolled her eyes and focused on her screen again, reading the last line she'd typed.

If this is the god we are presented with in our life, what god will we meet upon our death? What hopes can we have of a happy afterlife?

Those words stung, and she knew she was probably being a little unfair. After touring part of the Underworld, it was clear Hades cared about his realm and those who occupied it. Why else would he go through the trouble of maintaining such a grand illusion?

Because it likely benefits him, she reminded herself. *It's*

143

obvious he likes pretty things, Persephone. Why wouldn't he cultivate a pretty realm?

Her desk phone rang suddenly, scaring her so badly, she jumped and fumbled to pick up the receiver, silencing the sound.

"Persephone speaking." Her heart was still racing, and she took a deep breath to calm herself.

"Persephone, it's Valerie. I think your mother is here?"

Her racing heart fell into her stomach. What was Demeter doing here?

She worried her lip for a moment—had Demeter found out about her visit to the Underworld over the weekend? She recalled her words in the Garden of the Gods—"*Need I remind you a condition of your time here was that you stay away from the gods? Especially Hades.*" She still hadn't figured out how her mother knew she was at Nevernight, but she assumed the Goddess of Harvest probably had a spy among those at Hades's club.

"I'll be right up." Persephone managed to keep her voice even.

It was easy to spot Demeter. She looked as close to her Divine form as possible, maintaining her sun-kissed glow and bright eyes. She wore a light pink sundress and white heels that stood out against the muted wall.

"My flower!" Demeter approached her with open arms, pulling Persephone into a hug.

"Mother." Persephone pushed away. "What are you doing here?"

Demeter cocked her head to the side. "It's Monday."

It took a moment for Persephone to remember what that meant.

Oh no.

The color drained from her face.

How could she have forgotten? Every Monday, she and her mother had lunch, but with everything that had happened in the last few days, it completely slipped her mind.

"There is a lovely café down the street," Demeter continued, but Persephone sensed the tightness in her voice. She knew Persephone had forgotten, and she didn't like it. "I thought we might try it today. What do you think?"

Persephone thought that she didn't want to be alone with her mother. Not to mention she had just gained the momentum needed to write this article about Hades; if she stopped now, she might not finish.

"Mother, I'm…so sorry." Those words felt like glass coming out of her mouth. They were a lie, of course—she wasn't sorry for what she was about to say. "I'm really busy today. Can we reschedule."

Demeter blinked. "Reschedule?"

She said the word like she had never heard it before. Her mother hated when things didn't go her way, and Persephone had never asked her to rearrange her schedule. She'd always remembered lunch like she always remembered her mother's rules—two things she'd ignored in the last week.

She knew her mother was making a list of offenses she had committed against her and it was just a matter of time before Demeter made her pay.

"I'm so sorry, Mother," Persephone said again.

Demeter finally met her gaze. The Goddess of Harvest tightened her jaw and managed in a perfectly flat tone, "Another time, then."

Demeter turned on her heels without saying goodbye and stormed out of the office.

Persephone released the breath she'd been holding. She'd spent all this time preparing to fight with her mother, and now that the adrenaline was gone, she felt exhausted.

"Wow, your mother is beautiful." Valerie's comment drew Persephone's gaze. The girl had a dreamy look on her face. "It's too bad you couldn't go to lunch with her."

"Yeah," Persephone said.

She made her way back to her desk slowly, weighed down by a cloud of guilt—until she noticed Adonis standing behind her chair, looking at her laptop screen.

"Adonis." She slammed her laptop closed as she reached the desk. "What are you doing?"

"Oh, hey, Persephone," he said and smiled. "Just reading your article."

"It's not finished." She tried to remain calm, but it was hard when he'd just invaded her privacy.

"I think it's good," he said. "You've really got something."

"Thanks, but I'd really appreciate it if you didn't look at my computer, Adonis."

He sort of laughed. "I'm not going to steal your work, if that's what you're worried about."

"I told you I'd send the article when I was finished!"

He put his hands up and stepped away from her desk. "Hey, calm down."

"Don't tell me to calm down," she said between her teeth. She hated when people told her to calm down; the disparaging remark only made her angrier.

"I didn't mean anything by it."

"I don't really care what you meant," she snapped.

Adonis was finally silent. She guessed he realized he wasn't going to be able to charm his way out of this one.

"Everything okay out here?" Demetri appeared at his door, and Persephone glared at Adonis.

"Yeah, everything's fine," Adonis said.

"Persephone?" Demetri looked at her expectantly.

She should have told him no, that in fact everything was not fine—that she was balancing an impossible contract with the God of the Underworld and hiding the fact from her mother, who would ensure she never saw the gleaming skyscrapers of New Athens again if she found out. On top of that, this mortal seemed to think it was perfectly acceptable to read her personal thoughts— because that was what this was, a draft of an article she was planning.

And maybe that was why she was so angry, because the words she'd written were raw, furious, and impassioned. They made her vulnerable, and if she opened her mouth to contradict Adonis, she wasn't sure what would come out.

She took a deep breath before forcing the words out. "Yeah, everything's fine."

And when she saw the smug expression on Adonis's face, she got the sense she'd regret lying.

———

A few days later, Persephone was late getting to Nevernight. Her study group had run over, and though she was tired, she knew she needed to check on her garden. The dirt in the Underworld held moisture like the desert, which meant she had to water her garden every day if she wanted it to have a chance in hell of surviving.

She stepped off the bus to the scrutiny of the line waiting to enter Hades's club, all staring at her like she'd grown talons and wings. She was sharply aware of her appearance, dressed in yoga pants and a tank, long hair still pulled into a messy bun from the start of her study session. She hadn't bothered to even look in the mirror today, and she hadn't wanted to waste time running home to change just to water a garden. The thought of squeezing into a dress and heels at this point in the day made her cringe anyway. Hades and these club-goers would just have to deal with it.

You aren't here to impress anyone, she reminded herself. *Just get in there and get to the Underworld as soon as possible.* She adjusted the straps of her heavy backpack, wincing at the soreness in her shoulders, and marched toward the door.

Mekonnen emerged from the dark. He wore a scowl until he recognized her, and then a charming, yellow smile spread across his face as he reached for the door. "My lady—I mean, Persephone."

"Good evening, Mekonnen." She grinned at the ogre as she passed into the club.

Persephone paused in the dark foyer. She preferred not to enter the club proper this time and decided to teleport. She snapped her fingers and expected to feel the familiar shift in the air around her.

But nothing happened.

She tried again.

Still nothing.

She would just have to go to Hades's office and enter the Underworld there.

She kept her head down as she cut through the

packed floor of the club. She knew people were staring, and she could feel her face growing flush with their judgment.

A hand clamped down on her shoulder. She turned, expecting to find an ogre or another one of Hades's employees stopping her because of the way she was dressed. An argument was poised on the tip of her tongue, but when she turned, she looked into a familiar pair of gold eyes.

"Hermes," she said, relieved. Even glamoured up, he was ridiculously handsome in his white shirt and gray pants, drink already in hand. His golden hair was perfectly styled—shorn on the sides, long curls on top, catching the light.

"Sephy!" he exclaimed. "What are you wearing?"

She looked down at herself, though she didn't need to. She knew perfectly well what she was wearing. "I just came from class."

"College chic." He raised his golden brows. "Hot."

She rolled her eyes and twisted away from him, making her way toward the steps. The God of Trickery followed.

"What are you doing here?" Persephone asked.

"Well, I am the Messenger of the Gods," he said.

"No, what are you doing here? On the floor of Nevernight?"

"Gods gamble too, Sephy," he answered.

"Don't call me that," she said. "And why would gods gamble with Hades?"

"For the thrill." Hermes smiled mischievously.

Persephone topped the stairs with Hermes in tow.

"Where are we going, Sephy?"

She thought it was funny that he included himself in that statement. "*I'm* going to Hades's office."

"He won't be in there," Hermes said, and it occurred to her that perhaps he didn't know about her and Hades's bargain.

She looked at the god, and though she wasn't here to see Hades, she still wondered aloud, "Then where is he?"

Hermes grinned. "He is reviewing propositions for contracts across the way."

Persephone's jaw tightened. *Of course he is.*

"I'm not here for Hades," she said and hurried ahead to his office. Once inside, she dropped her backpack on the couch and rolled her shoulders, rubbing at the pain.

She looked up to find Hermes at the bar, picking up various bottles and reading the labels. Whatever he had in his hands must have been appealing, because he unscrewed it and poured it into an empty glass.

"Should you be doing that?" she asked.

The god shrugged. "Hades owes me, right? I saved your life."

Persephone looked away. "*I* owe you. Not Hades."

"Careful, Goddess. One bargain with a god is enough, don't you think?"

She startled. "You know?"

Hermes smiled. "Sephy, I wasn't born yesterday."

"You must think I'm incredibly stupid," she said.

"No. I think you were lured by Hades's charms."

"So you agree Hades has wronged me?"

"No," he said. "I'm saying you're attracted to him."

Persephone rolled her eyes and turned from the god. She crossed Hades's office and tried the invisible door behind his desk, but her hands didn't sink into the surface like last time.

Her way into the Underworld was barred. Had he revoked her favor because she'd brought Adonis to Nevernight? Or was he angry because of how she'd left him in his throne room a few days before? Hadn't he bestowed favor so she wouldn't have to bother him?

The doors to Hades's office rattled suddenly, and Hermes grabbed Persephone and dragged her toward the mirror over the mantle. She resisted, but Hermes pressed his lips close to her ear and murmured, "Trust me. You'll want to see this."

He snapped his fingers, and Persephone felt her skin tighten across her bones. It was the strangest feeling, and it didn't go away even when they were inside the mirror. The sensation was like being behind a waterfall and looking out at the hazy world.

She started to ask if they could be seen, but Hermes pressed a finger to his lips. "Shh."

Hades came into view on the other side of the mirror, and Persephone's breath caught. No matter how often she saw him, she didn't think she'd ever get used to his beauty. Today he looked tense and severe. She wondered what had happened.

She soon received her answer; Minthe followed close behind and Persephone felt a rush of hot jealousy at the sight of her.

They were arguing.

"You are wasting your time!" Minthe said.

"It's not like I'm running out," Hades snapped, clearly not wanting to listen to the nymph lecture him.

Minthe's face hardened. "This is a *club*. Mortals

bargain for their desires. They do not make *requests* of the God of the Underworld."

"This club is what I say it is."

Minthe glared at him. "You think this will sway the goddess to think better of you?"

The goddess? Was Minthe referring to her?

Hades's eyes darkened at the comment. "I do not care what others think of me, and that includes you, Minthe." Her face fell, and Hades continued, "I will hear her offer."

The nymph said nothing and turned on her heels, walking out of sight. After a moment, a woman entered Hades's office. She wore a beige trench coat, a large sweater, and jeans, her hair pulled back into a ponytail. Despite being fairly young, she looked exhausted, and Persephone didn't need Hades's powers to know that whatever burden she carried at this point in her life was heavy.

When the woman saw the god, she froze.

"You have nothing to fear," Hades said in his warm, soothing baritone, and the mortal was able to move again.

She offered a small, nervous laugh, and when she spoke, her voice was rough. "I told myself I wouldn't hesitate. I wouldn't let fear get the best of me."

Hades tilted his head to the side. Persephone knew that look—he was curious. "But you have been afraid. For a very long time."

The woman nodded, and tears spilled down her face. She brushed at them fiercely, hands shaking, and offered that nervous laugh again. "I told myself I wouldn't cry either."

"Why?"

Persephone was glad Hades asked, because she was just as curious. When the woman met the god's gaze, she was serious, her face still glistening with tears. "The Divine are not moved by my pain."

Persephone flinched. Hades did not.

"I suppose I cannot blame you," the woman continued. "I am one in a million pleading for myself."

Again, Hades tilted his head. "But you are not pleading for yourself, are you?"

The woman's mouth quivered, and she answered in a whisper, "No."

"Tell me," he coaxed. It was like a spell, and the woman obeyed.

"My daughter." The words were a sob. "She's sick. Pineoblastoma. It's an aggressive cancer. I wager my life for hers."

"No!" Persephone said out loud, and Hermes quickly hushed her, but all she could think was, *He can't! He won't!*

Hades studied the woman for a long moment. "My wagers are not for souls like you."

Persephone started forward. She would come out of this mirror and fight for that woman, but Hermes held on to her shoulder tight. "*Wait.*"

Persephone held her breath.

"Please," the woman whispered. "I will give you anything—whatever you want."

Hades dared to laugh. "You could not give me what I want."

The woman stared, and Persephone's heart wrenched at the look in her eyes. She was defeated. The woman hung her head, and her shoulders shook as she sobbed into her hands. "You were my last hope. My last hope."

Hades approached her, placed his fingers under her chin, and lifted her head. After he brushed her tears away, he said, "I will not enter into a contract with you because I do not wish to take from you. That does not mean I will not help you."

The woman gaped. Persephone eyes widened, and Hermes chuckled under his breath.

"Your daughter has my favor. She will be well and just as brave as her mother, I think."

"Oh, thank you! Thank you!" The woman threw her arms around Hades, and the god stiffened, clearly unsure of what to do. Finally, he conceded and embraced her.

After a moment, he pulled her away and said, "Go. See to your daughter."

The woman took a few steps back. "You are the most generous god."

Hades offered a dark chuckle. "I will amend my previous statement. In exchange for my favor, you will tell no one I have aided you."

The woman looked surprised. "But—"

Hades put up his hand—he would hear no argument. Finally, the woman nodded. "Thank you." She turned to leave, practically racing out of the office. "Thank you!"

Hades watched the door for a moment before locking it with a snap of his fingers. Before Persephone knew what was happening, she and Hermes fell out of the mirror.

Persephone wasn't prepared and hit the floor with a loud thud. Hermes landed on his feet.

"Rude," the God of Trickery said.

"I could say the same," the God of the Dead replied, his eyes falling unfavorably to Persephone as she got to her feet. "Hear everything you wanted?"

"I *wanted* to go to the Underworld, but *someone* revoked my favor."

It was like she hadn't even spoken. Hades's gaze turned to Hermes. "I have a job for you, messenger."

Hades snapped his fingers, and without warning, Persephone was dumped in her desolate garden on her backside. A growl of frustration erupted from her mouth, and as she got to her feet, brushing dirt off her clothes, she yelled to the sky.

"Ass!"

CHAPTER XI
A Touch of Desire

Persephone watered her garden, cursing Hades while she worked. She hoped he could hear every word. She hoped it cut him deep. She hoped he felt it every time he moved.

He'd ignored her.

He'd dumped her in the Underworld like she was nothing.

She had questions. She had demands. She wanted to know why he'd helped the woman, why he'd demanded her silence. What was the difference between this woman's request and Orpheus's wish to bring Eurydice back from the dead?

When she finished watering her garden, she tried to teleport back to Hades's office, but when snapping her fingers didn't work, she realized she was stuck.

Then she tried cursing Hades's name, and when that didn't work, she kicked the garden wall.

Why did he send her here? Did he have plans to find

her after he was finished with Hermes? Would he restore her favor, or would she have to find him every time she wanted to enter the Underworld?

That would be annoying.

She must have made him very angry.

She decided she would explore his palace in his absence. She had only seen a few rooms—Hades's office, bedchamber, and the throne room. She was curious about the rest, and it was well within her rights to explore. If Hades got mad, she could argue that, judging by the state of her garden, it would be her home in six months anyway.

While she investigated, she noted Hades's attention to detail. There were gold accents and various textures—fur rugs and velvet chairs. It was a luxurious palace, and she admired the beauty of it, just as she admired the beauty of Hades. She tried to argue with herself—it was in her nature to admire beauty. It didn't mean anything to think the God of the Dead and his palace were extraordinary. He was a god, after all.

Her exploration of the palace ended when she found the library.

It was magnificent. She had never seen anything like it—shelves and shelves of books with gorgeous, thick spines and gold embossing. The room itself was well-furnished. A large hearth took up the far wall, flanked by dark shelves. These weren't full of books but ancient clay vases inked with images of Hades and the Underworld. She could imagine settling into one of the cozy chairs, curling her toes into the soft rug, and reading for hours.

This would be one of her favorite places, Persephone decided, if she lived here.

But she should not be thinking about living in the Underworld at all. Maybe, after all this was over, Hades would extend his favor to the use of his library.

She wondered idly if there was a kiss for that.

She wandered down the stacks, brushing her fingers along the spines. She managed to pull a few history books and searched for a table where she could look through them. She thought she finally located one when she found what looked like a round table, but when she went to place the books on it, she discovered it was actually a basin full of dark water, similar to the Styx.

She set the books on the floor to get a better look at the basin. As she stared, a map appeared before her; she could see the river Styx and the Lethe, Hades's palace and gardens. Though the map appeared to sit in the black water, glorious color as vibrant as Hades's gardens soon bled across the landscape. She found it funny that the God of the Dead, who wore so much black, took such pleasure in color.

"Hmm." Persephone was sure this map was missing vital parts of the Underworld—like Elysium and Tartarus. "Strange." She reached into the basin.

"Curiosity is a dangerous quality, my lady."

She gasped and turned to find Hades behind her, framed by a set of shelves. Her heart throbbed hard in her chest.

"I'm more than aware," she snapped. The mark on her wrist had taught her that. "And don't call me *my lady*." Hades simply watched her, saying nothing, so Persephone added, "This map of your world is not complete."

Hades glanced at the water. "What do you see?"

"Your palace, Asphodel, the river Styx, and the Lethe... That's it." All places she'd been before. "Where is Elysium? Tartarus?"

The corners of Hades mouth quirked. "The map will reveal them when you've earned the right to know."

"What do you mean *earned*?"

"Only those I trust most may view this map in its entirety."

She straightened. "Who can see the whole map?" He just smirked, so she demanded, "Can Minthe see it?"

His eyes narrowed. "Would that bother you, Lady Persephone?"

"No," she lied.

His eyes hardened and his lips thinned; he turned and disappeared into the stacks. She hurried to pick up the books she pulled from the shelf and followed after him.

"Why did you revoke my favor?" she demanded.

"To teach you a lesson," he replied.

"To not bring mortals into your realm?"

"To not leave when you are angry with me," he said.

"Excuse me?" She halted and set the books on a nearby shelf. She hadn't expected that reply.

Hades stopped too and faced her. They were standing in the narrow stacks, and the smell of dust floated in the air around them. "You strike me as someone who has a lot of emotions and has never quite been taught how to deal with it all, but I can assure you, running away is not the solution."

"I had nothing more to say to you."

"It's not about words," he said. "I'd rather help you understand my motivations than have you spy on me."

"It was not my intention to spy," she said. "Hermes—"

"I know it was Hermes who pulled you into that mirror," he said. "I do not wish for you to leave and be angry with me."

She should have taken his comment as endearing, but she couldn't stop herself from sounding disgusted when she asked, "Why?"

It really wasn't disgust; it was confusion. Hades was a god. Why did he care what she thought of him?

"Because," he said and then thought for a moment. "It is important to me. I would rather explore your anger. I would hear your advice. I wish to understand your perspective." She started to open her mouth and ask why again when he added, "Because you have lived among mortals. You understand them better than I. Because you are compassionate."

She swallowed. "Why did you help the mother tonight?"

"Because I wished to."

"And Orpheus?"

Hades sighed, rubbing his eyes with his forefinger and thumb. "It isn't so simple. Yes, I have the ability to resurrect the dead, but it does not work with everyone, especially where the Fates are involved. Eurydice's life was cut short by the Fates for a reason. I cannot touch her."

"But the girl?"

"She wasn't dead, just in limbo. I can bargain with the Fates for lives in limbo."

"What do you mean *bargain with the Fates*?"

"It is a fragile thing," he said. "If I ask the Fates to spare one soul, I do not get a say in the life of another."

"But...you are the God of the Underworld!"

"And the Fates are Divine," he said. "I must respect their existence as they respect mine."

"That doesn't seem fair."

Hades raised a brow. "Doesn't it? Or is it that it doesn't sound fair to mortals?"

It was exactly that. "So mortals have to suffer for the sake of your game?"

Hades's jaw tightened. "It is not a game, Persephone. Least of all *mine*."

His stern voice gave her pause, and she glared at him. "So you've offered an explanation for part of your behavior, but what of the other bargains?"

Hades's eyes darkened, and he took a step toward her in the already-restricted space. "Are you asking for yourself or the mortals you claim to defend?"

"*Claim*?" She would show him—her arguments against his tricks were not for show.

"You only became interested in my business ventures after you entered into a contract with me."

"Business ventures? Is that what you call willfully misleading me?"

His brows rose. "So this *is* about you."

"What you have done is unjust—not just to me but to all the mortals—"

"I do not want to talk about mortals. I would like to talk about *you*." Hades moved toward her, and she took a step away, the bookcase pressing into her back. "Why did you invite me to your table?"

Persephone looked away. "You said you'd teach me."

"Teach you what, Goddess?" He stared at her a moment, eyes seductive and dark. Then his head dropped into the crook of her neck and his lips brushed lightly over her skin. "What did you truly desire to learn then?"

"Cards," she whispered, but she could barely breathe, and she knew she was lying. She'd wanted to learn him—the feel of him, the smell of him, the power of him.

He whispered words against her skin. "What else?"

She dared to turn her head then, and his lips brushed hers.

Her breath caught hard in her throat. She couldn't answer—wouldn't. His mouth remained close to hers, but he didn't kiss her. He waited.

"Tell me."

His voice was hypnotic, and his warmth had her under a wicked spell. He was the adventure she craved. He was temptation she wanted to indulge. He was a sin she wanted to commit.

Her eyes fluttered closed and her lips parted. She thought he might claim her then, but when he didn't, she took a deep breath, her chest rising against his, and said, "Just cards."

He drew back, and Persephone opened her eyes. She thought she caught his surprise just before it melted into an unreadable mask.

"You must wish to return home," he said and started walking down the stacks. If she wasn't talking to the God of the Dead, she would have thought he was embarrassed. "You may borrow those books if you wish."

She gathered them into her arms and quickly followed after him. "How? You withdrew my favor."

He turned to her, his gaze emotionless. "Trust me, Lady Persephone. If I stripped you of my favor, you would know."

"So I'm Lady Persephone again?"

"You have always been Lady Persephone, whether you choose to embrace your blood or not."

"What is there to embrace?" she asked. "I'm an unknown god at best—and a minor one at that."

She hated the look of disappointment that shadowed his face. "If that is how you think of yourself, you will never know power."

Her lips parted in surprise, and she noted how his eyes tightened right before his hand twitched. He was about to send her away without warning again.

"Don't," she commanded, and Hades paused. "You asked that I not leave when I'm angry, and I'm asking you not to send me away when *you're* angry."

He dropped his hand. "I am not angry."

"Then why did you drop me in the Underworld earlier?" she asked. "Why send me away at all?"

"I needed to speak with Hermes," he said.

"And you couldn't say that?"

He hesitated.

"Don't request things of me you cannot deliver yourself, Hades."

He stared at her. She wasn't sure what she expected of him—that her demands would make him angry? That he would argue that this was different? That he was a powerful god and he could do what he willed?

Instead, he nodded. "I will grant you that courtesy."

She took a breath, relieved. "Thank you."

He extended his hand. "Come. We can return to Nevernight together. I have...unfinished business there."

She took him up on the offer, and they teleported

163

back to his office, appearing right in front of the mirror she and Hermes had hidden inside.

Persephone tilted her head back so she could meet his eyes. "How did you know we were in there? Hermes said we couldn't be seen."

"I knew you were here because I could feel you."

His words made her shiver, and she withdrew from his warmth, picked up her backpack where she'd left it on the couch, and heaved it on her shoulders. On the way out the door, she paused. "You said the map is only visible to those you trust. What does it take to gain the trust of the God of the Dead?"

He responded simply, "Time."

CHAPTER XII
God of the Game

"Persephone!"

Someone was calling her name. She rolled over and covered her head with her blanket to muffle the sound; she left the Underworld late last night and, too keyed up to sleep, stayed awake to work on her article.

She had a hard time choosing how she should proceed after watching Hades help that mother. In the end, she decided she had to focus on the bargains Hades made with mortals—the ones where he chose to offer impossible terms. While she worked on the article, she found she was still frustrated, though she couldn't tell if it was over her bargain with Hades or their time in the stacks—the way he'd asked her what she wanted and refused to kiss her.

Her skin had prickled with anticipation at the memory, though she wasn't anywhere near him.

She'd pressed Save on her article at four in the morning and decided to rest a few hours before rereading it. But as she started to drift off, Lexa burst through her bedroom door. "Persephone! Wake up!"

She groaned. "Go away!"

"Oh no, you're going to want to see this. Guess what's in the news today!"

Suddenly, she was wide awake. Persephone shoved off her blankets and sat up, her imagination already taking hold—had someone snapped a picture of her in her goddess form outside Nevernight? Had someone caught her inside the club with Hades? Lexa shoved her tablet into Persephone's face, and her eyes focused on something much worse.

"It's all over social media today," Lexa explained.

"No, no, no," Persephone gripped the tablet with both hands. The title across the top of the page was black and bold and familiar:

Hades, God of the Game by Persephone Rosi.

She read the first line aloud. "Nevernight, an elite gambling club owned by Hades, God of the Dead, can be seen from anywhere in New Athens. The sleek pinnacle expertly mimics the imposing nature of the god himself and is a reminder to mortals that life is short—even shorter if you agree to gamble with the Lord of the Underworld."

This was her draft. Her real article remained safely on her computer.

"How did this get published?" she hissed.

Lexa looked confused. "What do you mean? Didn't you submit it?"

"No." She scrolled through the article, her stomach in knots. She noticed some additions, like a description of Hades she never would have written. Hades's eyes were described as colorless chasms, his face callous, his manner cold and boorish.

Boorish?

She wouldn't dream of describing Hades in such a manner. His eyes were inky but expressive, and every time she met his gaze, she felt like she could see the threads of his lifetimes there. In truth, his face could be callous at times, but when he looked at her, she saw something different—a softness to his jaw, an amusement alight in his face, a curiosity that burned. And his manner was anything but cold and boorish—he was passionate and charming and refined.

There was only one person who had gone with her and seen Hades in the flesh, and that was Adonis. He'd also invaded her workspace and read her article without permission.

Guess he was doing more than just reading it. Persephone's anxiety was now as strong as her fury. She tossed the tablet aside and jumped out of bed, angry and vengeful words racing through her head. They sounded more like her mother's than her own.

He will be punished, she thought. *Because I will be punished.*

She took a few deep breaths to cool her anger and consciously worked to uncurl her fingers. If she wasn't careful, her glamour would melt away. It always seemed to react to her emotions—maybe because her magic was borrowed.

In reality, Persephone didn't want Adonis punished, at least not by Hades. The God of the Dead had made his dislike of this mortal abundantly clear, and bringing him to Nevernight had been a mistake for several reasons—that was clear now. Perhaps this was part of the reason Hades had wanted her to stay away from him.

A third emotion rose inside her—fear—and she tamped it down. She wouldn't allow Hades to get the best of her. Besides, she'd planned on writing about the god despite his threat.

"Where are you going?" Lexa asked.

"Work." Persephone disappeared into her closet, trading her nightshirt for a simple green dress. It was one of her favorite outfits, and if she was going to get through this day, she figured she needed every weapon in her arsenal to feel as powerful as possible. Maybe she could get the article taken out of publication before Hades saw it.

"But…you don't work today," Lexa pointed out from her perch on Persephone's bed.

"I have to see if I can get ahead of this." Persephone reappeared, hobbling on one foot to buckle her sandals.

"Ahead of what?"

"The article. Hades can't see it."

Lexa laughed and then covered her mouth quickly, speaking between her fingers. "Persephone, I hate to break it to you, but Hades has already seen the article. He has people who look for this kind of stuff." Persephone met Lexa's gaze, and her friend winced. "Whoa."

"What?" Hysteria rose in Persephone's voice.

"Your eyes, they're…freaky."

Avoiding Lexa's gaze while her emotions ricocheted all over her body, Persephone reached for her purse. "Don't worry about it. I'll be back later."

She left her room and slammed the door to her apartment closed as Lexa called her name.

The bus wouldn't run for another fifteen minutes, so she decided to go on foot. She dug her compact out of her purse and applied more magic as she walked.

No wonder Lexa had been freaked out. Her eyes had lost all their glamour and glowed bottle-green. Her hair was brighter, her face sharper. She looked more Divine than she ever had in public.

By the time Persephone arrived at the Acropolis, her mortal appearance was restored. When she walked off the elevator, Valerie rose from behind her desk.

"Persephone," she said nervously. "I didn't think you were in today."

"Hey, Valerie." She tried to keep her voice cheerful and act like nothing was out of the ordinary—like Adonis hadn't stolen her article and Lexa hadn't woken her up to shove said angry article in her face. "Just coming in to take care of a few things."

"Oh, well, you have several messages. I, uh, transferred them to your voicemail."

"Thanks."

But Persephone wasn't interested in her voicemails; she was here for Adonis. She dropped her purse at her desk and stalked across the workroom to his. Adonis sat with his earbuds in, focused intently on his computer. At first, she thought he was working—probably editing something he stole, she thought angrily—but as she came up behind him, she discovered he was watching some sort of television show—*Titans After Dark*.

She rolled her eyes. It was a popular soap opera about how the Olympians defeated the Titans. Though she'd only watched parts of it, she'd started to imagine most of the gods as they were portrayed on the show. Now she knew Hades was all wrong—a pale, lithe creature with a hollow face. If he were going to seek revenge for anything, it should be how they depicted him on that show.

She tapped Adonis's shoulder and he jumped, taking out an earbud. "Persephone! Congr—"

"You stole my article," she cut him off.

"Stealing is a harsh term for what I did." He pushed away from his desk. "I gave you all the credit."

"You think that matters?" she seethed. "It was *my* article, Adonis. Not only did you take it from me, you added to it. Why? I told you I would send it to you once I finished!"

In all honesty, she wasn't sure what she expected him to say, but it wasn't the answer he gave. "I thought you would change your mind."

She stared at him a moment. "I told you I wanted to write about Hades."

"Not about that. I thought he might convince you he was justified in his contracts with mortals."

"Let me get this straight. You decided that I couldn't think for myself, so you stole my work, altered it, and published it?"

"It's not like that. Hades is a god, Persephone—"

And I'm a goddess, she wanted to yell. Instead, she ground out, "You're right. Hades is a god, and for that very reason, *you* didn't want to write about him. You feared him, Adonis. Not me."

He cringed. "I didn't mean—"

"What you meant doesn't matter," she snapped.

"Persephone?" Demetri called, and she and Adonis looked in the direction of their supervisor's office. "A moment?"

Her gaze slid back to Adonis, and she pinned him with a final glare before heading into Demetri's office.

"Yes, Demetri?" she said from the doorway.

He was sitting behind his desk, a fresh edition of the paper in hand. "Take a seat."

She did—on the edge, because she wasn't sure what Demetri would think of the article; she had a hard time calling it hers. Would his next words be "you're fired"? It was one thing to say you wanted the truth, another to actually publish it.

She considered what she would do when she lost her internship. She now had less than six months until graduation. It was unlikely another paper would hire the girl who dared call the God of the Underworld the worst god. She knew many people shared Adonis's fear of Tartarus.

Just as Demetri started to speak, Persephone said, "I can explain."

"What is there to explain?" he asked. "It's clear by your article what you were trying to do here."

"I was angry."

"You wanted to expose an injustice," he said.

"Yes, but there's more. It's not the whole story," she said. She'd really only shown Hades in one light—and that was really in no light at all, just darkness.

"I hope it's not," Demetri said.

"What?" Persephone straightened.

"I'm asking you to write more."

The Goddess of Spring was quiet, and Demetri

continued. "I want more. How soon can you have another article out?"

"About Hades?"

"Oh yes. You have only scratched the surface of this god."

"But I thought… Aren't you…afraid of him?"

Demetri laid the paper down and leveled his gaze with hers. "Persephone, I told you from the beginning. We seek truth here at *New Athens News*, and no one knows the truth of the King of the Underworld. You can help the world understand him."

Demetri made it all sound so innocent, but Persephone knew she would only bring hatred upon Hades from the article published today.

"Those who fear Hades are also curious. They will want more, and you're going to deliver."

Persephone straightened at his direct order. Demetri stood and walked to the wall of windows, his hands behind his back. "How about a biweekly feature?"

"That's a lot, Demetri. I'm still in school," she reminded him.

"Monthly, then. What do you say to…five, six articles?"

"Do I have a choice?" she muttered, but Demetri still heard.

The corner of his mouth quirked. "Don't underestimate yourself, Persephone. Just think—if this is as successful as I think it will be, there will be a line of people waiting to hire you when you graduate."

Except it wouldn't matter, because she'd be a prisoner—not just of the Underworld but of Tartarus. She wondered how Hades would choose to torture her.

He'll probably refuse to kiss you, she thought and rolled her eyes at herself.

"Your next article is due on the first," he said. "Let's have some variety. Don't just talk about his bargains. What else does he do? What are his hobbies? What does the Underworld really look like?"

Persephone felt uncomfortable at Demetri's questions, and she wondered if they were for him rather than the public.

With that, he dismissed her. Persephone walked out of Demetri's office and sat down at her desk. Her head felt foggy and she couldn't concentrate.

A monthly feature following the God of the Dead? What have you gotten yourself into, Persephone? She groaned out loud. Hades was never going to agree to this.

Then again, he didn't have to.

Perhaps this would give her a chance to bargain with him. Could she leverage the threat of more articles to convince him to let her out of the contract?

And would his promise of punishment turn out to be true?

―――――

Persephone went straight to class after leaving the Acropolis, and it seemed like everyone had a copy of *New Athens News* today. That bold, black headline glared back at her on the bus, on her walk across campus, even in class.

Someone tapped her on the shoulder, and she twisted to find two girls huddled together in the row behind her. She wasn't sure of their names, but they'd sat behind her since the beginning of the semester and said nothing until today. The girl on the right held a copy of the paper.

"You're Persephone, right?" one of them asked. "Is everything you wrote true?"

That question made her cringe. Her instinct was to say no, because she hadn't written the story, not in its entirety—but she couldn't. She settled on "The story is evolving."

What she didn't anticipate was the excitement in the girls' eyes. "So there will be more?"

Persephone cleared her throat. "Yeah...yes."

The girl on the left leaned farther over the table. "So you've met Hades?"

"That's a stupid question," the other girl chided. "What she wants to know is what's Hades like? Do you have pictures?"

A strange feeling erupted in Persephone's stomach—a metallic twist that made her feel both jealous and protective of Hades. Ironic, since she had promised to write more about him. Still, now that she was posed with these questions, she wasn't sure she wanted to share her intimate knowledge of the god. Did she want to talk about how she'd caught him playing fetch with his dogs in a grove in the Underworld? Or how he'd amused her by playing rock paper scissors?

These were...human aspects of the god, and all of a sudden, she felt possessive of them. They were hers.

She offered a small, unamused smile. "I guess you'll have to wait and see."

Demetri had been right—the world was just as curious about the god as they were afraid of him.

The girls in her class weren't the only people who

stopped her to ask about her article. On her way across campus, several other strangers called out to her. She guessed they were testing her name, and once they discovered she was Persephone, they ran up to her to ask the same questions—"*Did you really meet Hades? What does he look like? Do you have a picture?*"

She made excuses to get away quickly. If there was one thing she hadn't anticipated, it was this—the attention she would receive. She couldn't decide if she liked it or not.

She was just passing through the Garden of the Gods when her phone rang. Grateful for the excuse to ignore more strangers, she answered it. "Hello?"

"Adonis told me the good news! A series on Hades! Congrats! When do you interview him next and can I come?" Lexa laughed.

"Th-thanks, Lex," Persephone managed. After stealing her article, it didn't surprise her that Adonis had also taken the opportunity to text her friend about her new work assignment before she even got a chance to tell her.

"We should celebrate! La Rose this weekend?" Lexa asked.

Persephone groaned. La Rose was an upscale nightclub owned by Aphrodite. She had never been inside, but she'd seen pictures. Everything was cream and pink, and like Hades's Nevernight, there was an impossible waiting list. "How are we supposed to get into La Rose?"

"I have my ways," Lexa replied mischievously. Persephone wondered if those ways included Adonis, and she was about to ask as much when she caught a flash in the corner of her eye. Whatever Lexa was saying on the other line was lost as her attention moved to her mother, appearing through the garden's foliage a few feet in front of her.

"Hey, Lex. I'll call you back." Persephone hung up and acknowledged Demeter with a curt, "Mother. What are you doing here?"

"I had to ensure you were safe after that ridiculous article you wrote. What were you thinking?"

Persephone felt the shock run deep, like an electrical current splicing through her chest. "I thought—I thought you'd be proud. You hate Hades."

"Proud? You thought I'd be proud?" Demeter scoffed. "You wrote a critical article on a god—but not just any god, Hades! You deliberately broke my rule—not once but multiple times." Persephone's surprise must have shown on her face because her mother added, "Oh yes. I know you have returned to Nevernight on multiple occasions."

Persephone glared at Demeter. "How?"

Demeter's eyes fell to the phone in Persephone's hand. "I tracked you."

"Through my phone?" Persephone knew her mother wasn't above violating her privacy to keep tabs on her; she'd proven that by having her nymphs spy on her. Still, Demeter hadn't bought her phone, nor did she pay the bill. She had no right to use it as a GPS. "Are you serious?"

"I had to do something. You weren't talking to me."

"Since when?" Persephone demanded. "I saw you Monday!"

"And you canceled our lunch," the goddess sniffed. "We hardly spend time together anymore."

"And you think stalking me will encourage me to spend more time with you?" Persephone demanded.

Demeter laughed. "Oh, my flower, I cannot stalk you. I am your mother."

Persephone glared. "I don't have time for this." She tried to sidestep her and leave, but she found she couldn't move—her feet felt as though they were welded to the ground. Hysteria erupted in her stomach and lodged in her throat. Persephone met her mother's dark gaze, and for the first time in years, she saw Demeter as the vengeful goddess she was—the one who lashed nymphs and killed kings.

"I have not dismissed you," her mother said. "Remember, Persephone, you are only here by the grace of my magic."

Persephone wanted to scream at her mother, *Keep reminding me I'm powerless.* But she knew challenging her was the wrong move. It was what Demeter wanted so she could dole out her punishment, so instead, Persephone inhaled a shaky breath and whispered, "I'm sorry, Mother."

For a tense moment, Persephone waited to see if Demeter would release her or abduct her. Then she felt her mother's hold loosen around her shaking legs. "If you return to Nevernight again, see Hades ever again, I will take you from this world."

Persephone wasn't sure where she gathered her courage, but she managed to look her mother in the eyes and say, "Don't think for a second that I will ever forgive you if you send me back to that prison."

Demeter gave a sharp laugh. "My flower, I don't require forgiveness."

Then she vanished.

Persephone knew Demeter meant her warning. The

problem was, there was no way to get around going back to Nevernight; she had a contract to fulfill and articles to write.

Persephone's phone vibrated in her hand and she looked down to see a message from Lexa: *Yes to La Rose??*

She texted back: *Sounds great.*

She was going to need a lot of alcohol to forget this day.

CHAPTER XIII
La Rose

Persephone and Lexa took a taxi to La Rose. It wasn't her preferred method of travel—she felt like they were a game of chance. She never knew what she was going to get—a smelly cab, a talkative driver, or a creepy one.

Tonight, they'd gotten a creepy one. He kept taking long looks at them in the rearview mirror and had become so distracted he had to swerve hard to miss oncoming traffic.

She glared at Lexa, who had insisted they couldn't arrive at La Rose on a bus.

Better that than dead, she thought now.

"Five articles about the God of the Dead," Lexa said dreamily. "What do you think you'll write about next?"

She honestly didn't know, and right now, she didn't care to think about Hades, but Lexa wasn't going to let it go.

Before Persephone could muster a response, Lexa gasped—the sound she always made when she had an idea or something terrible was happening. Persephone was sure that whatever was about to come out of her mouth was probably both.

"You should write about his love life."

"What?" Persephone sputtered. "No. Absolutely not."

Lexa pouted. "Why not?"

"Uh, what makes you think Hades would share that information with me?"

"Persephone, you're a journalist. Investigate!"

"I'm not really interested in Hades's past lovers." Persephone stared out the window.

"Past lovers? That makes it sound like he has a current lover…like you're the current lover."

"Uh, no," Persephone said. "I'm pretty sure the Lord of the Underworld is sleeping with his assistant."

"So write about that!" Lexa encouraged.

"I'd rather not, Lexa. I work for *New Athens News*, not the *Delphi Divine*. I'm interested in truth." Besides, she'd rather not learn whether that was true. Just thinking about it made her sick.

"You're pretty sure Hades is banging his assistant. Just get it confirmed, and it's truth!"

Persephone sighed, frustrated. "I don't want to write about trivial things. I want to write about something that will change the world."

"And bashing Hades's godly antics will change the world?"

"It might," Persephone argued, and Lexa shook her head. "What?"

Her friend sighed. "It's just…all you did in publishing that article was confirm everyone's thoughts and fears about the God of the Dead. I'm guessing there are other truths about Hades that weren't in that article."

"What's your point?"

"If you want your writing to change the world, write about the side of Hades that makes you blush."

Persephone's face heated. "You're such a romantic, Lexa."

"There you go again," Lexa said. "Why can't you just admit you find Hades attractive—"

"I *have* admitted—"

"And that you're attracted to him?"

Persephone's mouth snapped shut, and she crossed her arms over her chest, withdrawing her gaze from Lexa back to the window.

"I don't want to talk about this."

"What are you afraid of, Persephone?"

Persephone closed her eyes against that question. Lexa wouldn't understand. It didn't matter if she liked Hades or not, if she found him attractive or not, if she wanted him or not. He was not for her. He was forbidden. Maybe the contract was a blessing—it was a way to think of Hades as a temporary thing in her life.

"Persephone?"

"I told you I don't want to talk about it, Lexa," she said tightly, hating the direction this conversation had gone.

They didn't speak again even after they arrived at La Rose. When Persephone left the cab, the distinct smell of rain hit her nose, and when she looked up, lightning illuminated the sky. She shivered, wishing she had chosen a different outfit. Her slippery, shimmery teal dress only reached midthigh, hugging the curves of her breasts and hips, and the deep V-neck left little to the imagination—and protection from the elements.

She had chosen it to spite Hades. It was silly. She'd wanted to look like power, like temptation, like sin—all for him. She wanted to dangle herself in front of him and then draw back at the last moment when he was close enough to taste her.

She wanted him to want her.

It was all pointless, of course. La Rose was another god's territory. It was unlikely Hades would see her tonight. This dress was a stupid idea.

La Rose was a beautiful building that looked like several crystals jutting from the earth. They were made of mirrored glass so that at night, they reflected the light of the city. Like Nevernight, there was a huge line to get inside.

A sudden chill of unease spread over Persephone and she glanced around, unsure of where it was coming from—until her eyes landed on Adonis.

He was grinning ear to ear, striding toward her and Lexa dressed in a black shirt and jeans. He looked comfortable, confident, and smug. She was about to ask what he was doing here when Lexa called out to him. "Adonis!"

She hugged him around the middle the moment he reached them, and he returned the embrace. "Hey, babe."

"Babe?" Persephone echoed flatly. "Lexa, what is he doing here?"

Her best friend pulled away from Adonis. "Adonis wanted to celebrate you, so he reached out to me. We thought it would be fun to surprise you!"

"Oh, I am surprised." Persephone glared at Adonis.

"Come on. I have a suite." Adonis took Lexa's hand and looped it through his arm, but when he offered the same to Persephone, she declined.

Adonis's smile faltered for a moment, but he quickly recovered, grinning down at Lexa as if nothing were amiss.

Persephone considered leaving, but she had come with Lexa, and she really didn't feel comfortable leaving her with Adonis. At some point tonight, she was going to have to tell her best friend about what her crush had done.

Adonis led them past the line and inside the club; music vibrated through Persephone's body as they entered under the misty, pink hue of the laser lights. The ground floor had room for dancing and places to sit that were curtained in crystals. Suites dominated the upper tiers of the club, overlooking a stage and the dance floor.

Adonis led them up a set of stairs to a suite on the second floor and through a crystal curtain that created a barrier from the outside world. The interior was luxurious, with soft pink couches on either side of a fire pit, which offered warmth and an ambiance Persephone found annoying.

"This is my personal suite," Adonis said.

"This is amazing." Lexa went straight to the balcony overlooking the dance floor.

"You like?" Adonis asked, hovering near the entrance.

"Of course! You'd have to be crazy not to."

"What about you, Persephone?" Adonis looked at her expectantly. Why was he seeking praise from her?

"You must be very lucky," she said curtly. "You're on the VIP list at two clubs owned by gods."

Adonis's eyes dulled, but he didn't miss a beat. "You should know I'm lucky, Persephone. I set your career in motion."

She glared at him and he smirked, then crossed the room to stand beside Lexa, who seemed oblivious to their exchange over the pounding music. She leaned into him and Adonis placed his hand on the small of her back.

Persephone stared at them for a moment, conflict splitting her chest, caught between her anger with Adonis and love for her friend. Lexa was clearly infatuated with the man. Did Adonis make Lexa's heart feel like it wanted to leave her chest? Did her whole body turn electric when he touched her? Did her thoughts scatter when he entered the room?

A waitress came to take their order, interrupting Persephone's thoughts. She was mortal, having no aura of magic around her, and dressed in a tight, iridescent dress; its shimmering surface reminded Persephone of the inside of a shell.

Once she took Lexa's and Adonis's orders, the waitress turned to Persephone.

"A cab, please," Persephone said, glancing at her friend. "Make it two."

Shortly after she returned with their drinks, Sybil, Aro, and Xerxes arrived—Sybil in a short, black leather skirt and a lacy top and the twins matching in their dark jeans, black shirts, and leather jackets. They took a seat opposite Persephone and placed their orders with the waitress. After she left, Sybil looked around the suite.

"My, my, my, Adonis. Looks like favor has its perks."

The air in the room grew heavy, like there was some

kind of history behind Sybil's comment. Persephone sought Lexa's gaze, but she wasn't looking at her—or anyone; she had turned her attention back to the dance floor.

This was what Persephone had feared; if Adonis did have a god's favor, it meant that any mortal he set his sights on was possibly in danger. Lexa knew that, and she wasn't going to risk the wrath of a god—was she?

"Don't believe everything you hear, Sybil," Adonis said.

"You expect us to believe you get all these passes because you work for *New Athens News*?" asked Xerxes.

Adonis sighed, rolling his eyes.

"Persephone," Aro said. "You work for the *News*. Do you get passes to popular clubs?"

She hesitated. "No—"

"Persephone here was invited to Nevernight by Hades himself."

She glared at Adonis; she knew what he was doing, trying to take the attention off himself. Luckily, no one took the bait.

"Keep denying it. I know a charmed one when I see one," said Sybil.

"And we all know you're fucking Apollo, but we don't say anything," said Adonis.

"Whoa, that was out of line, man," said Aro, but Sybil raised her hand to silence her friend's defense.

"At least I'm honest about my favor," she said.

The longer this went on, the more Persephone knew she had to get her friend out of this suite. Lexa was going to need air and some time to get over the disappointment of getting her hopes up about Adonis.

Persephone stood and crossed the room. "Lexa, let's dance." She took her hand and led her out of the suite. Once they were downstairs, she turned to Lexa.

"I'm okay, Persephone," Lexa said quickly.

"I'm sorry, Lex."

She was quiet a moment, nibbling on her lip. "Do you think Sybil is right?"

The girl was an oracle, which meant she was probably more in tune with the truth than anyone in the party, but still, all Persephone could say was, "Maybe?"

"Who do you think it is?"

It could be anyone, but there were a few goddesses and gods who were notorious for taking mortal lovers—Aphrodite, Hera, and Apollo, just to name a few. "Don't think about it. We came here to have fun, remember?"

A waitress approached them and handed them two drinks.

"Oh, we didn't order—" Persephone started to say, but the waitress interrupted.

"On the house," she said and smiled.

Persephone and Lexa each took a glass. The liquid inside was pink and sweet, and they drank fast—Lexa to drown her sadness and Persephone for courage to dance. Once they finished, she grabbed Lexa's hand and dragged her into the throng.

They danced together and with strangers, the tempo of the music, the flash of the laser lights, and the alcohol in their systems leaving them feeling happily disconnected from the events of the day. There was just the here and now.

The crowd moved around them, rocking them back and forth. Persephone panted, her mouth dry and sweat trickling off her forehead. She felt flushed and dizzy. She came to a stop on the dance floor, the crowd pulsing around her, but the world still spun, sending her stomach turning.

It was then she noticed she'd become separated from Lexa. The faces blurred around her as she pushed through the crowd, growing dizzier with each jolt to her body. She thought she caught sight of her friend's electric-blue dress and followed its shimmer, but when she came to the edge of the dance floor, Lexa wasn't there.

Maybe she'd gone back up to the suite.

Persephone started back up the steps. Each move made her head feel like it was full of water. At one point, the dizziness was too much, and she paused to close her eyes.

"Persephone?"

She peeled her eyes open to find Sybil standing in front of her.

"Are you okay?"

"Have you seen Lexa?" Persephone asked. Her tongue felt thick and swollen.

"No. Have you—"

"I have to find Lexa." She turned away from Sybil, heading back downstairs. At this point, she knew something was wrong with her. She needed to find her friend and go home.

"Whoa, whoa—wait." Sybil stepped in front of her. "Persephone, how much have you had to drink?"

"One glass," she said.

The girl shook her head, brows pinched together. "There's no way you've just had one glass."

Persephone pushed past her. She wasn't going to

argue about how much alcohol she had tonight. Maybe Lexa was in the bathroom.

She tried to keep to the wall as she searched for her friend but found herself pulled into the sea of moving bodies. Just when she felt the crowd would swallow her completely, someone grabbed her wrist and drew her toward them. She put her hands out, and they landed on a hard chest. She looked up into Adonis's face.

"Whoa, where you going, babe?"

"Let me go, Adonis." She tried to pull away, but he held her fast.

"Shh, it's alright. I'm your friend."

"If you were my friend—"

"You're going to have to get over that little article thing, babe."

"Don't call me babe, and don't tell me what to do."

"Has anyone ever told you you're a handful?" he asked, and then his hold on her tightened, forcing their hips together.

She thought she just might vomit.

"I just want to talk," he said.

"No."

Adonis's face changed in that moment. His playful smirk turned down, and his bright eyes darkened. "Fine. We don't have to talk."

His hand snaked behind her head, fisting in her hair, and he pressed his lips hard against hers. She clamped her mouth shut and wrenched against him, but he held tight, tongue prying at her closed mouth, and tears sprang to her eyes.

Rough hands clamped down on Adonis's arms, and a pair of ogres yanked him off and dragged him away from

Persephone. She wiped her hands across her mouth to remove the feel of Adonis's lips on hers when she saw the God of the Dead moving toward her.

"Hades," she breathed.

She closed the distance between them, wrapping her arms around his waist, welding herself to him. One of Hades's hands pressed into her back, the other one twisting into her hair. He held her close for a moment before drawing her away. He reached for her chin and tilted her head up so their eyes met.

"Are you well?" he asked.

She shook her head, swallowing thickly. There were so many things wrong with this day and night. "Let's go."

He guided her toward him, wrapping a protective arm around her shoulder, and led her through the crowd. It parted for him easily, and she was vaguely aware that Hades's presence in the club had caused a type of silent chaos. The music still blared in the background, but no one was dancing. They'd all stopped to watch as he steered her off the dance floor.

"Hades—" she started to warn him, but he seemed to know what she was thinking and answered before she could form the words.

"They will not remember this."

That satisfied her enough to follow him toward the exit, until she remembered that she needed to find her best friend.

"Lexa!" She turned back too fast, and her vision swam. When she swayed, Hades caught her, scooping her into his arms.

"I will ensure she gets home safe," Hades said.

Any other time, she would have protested or argued,

but the world was still spinning, even with her eyes closed.

"Persephone?" Hades's voice was low, and his breath brushed her lips.

"Hmm?" she asked, her brows knitted together, and she squeezed her eyes shut tight.

"What's wrong?"

"Dizzy," she whispered.

He didn't speak again. She could tell when they'd stepped outside because the cool air touched every inch of her exposed skin, and the rain pattered on the awning over La Rose's entrance. She shivered, snuggling nearer to Hades's warmth, and inhaled his now-familiar scent of ash and spice.

"You smell good." She fisted his jacket, pressing as close to him as possible. His body was like a rock. He'd had centuries to chisel this physique.

Hades chuckled, and she opened her eyes to find him looking at her. Before she could ask what he was laughing at, he shifted, holding her tight as he folded into the back seat of a black limo. She caught a glimpse of Antoni as he shut their car door.

The cabin was cozy and private, and Hades slid her off his lap and into the leather seat beside him. She watched his lithe fingers adjust the controls so that the vents were pointed at her and the heater was on full blast.

As they pulled out on the road, she asked, "What are you doing here?"

"You don't listen to orders."

She laughed. "I don't take orders from you, Hades."

He raised a brow. "Trust me, darling. I'm aware."

"I'm not yours and I'm not your darling."

"We've been through this, haven't we? You *are* mine. I think you know that just as well as I do."

She folded her arms over her chest. "Have you ever thought that maybe you're mine instead?"

His lips twitched and his eyes fell to her wrist. "It is *my* mark upon *your* skin."

Maybe the alcohol made her brave. She shifted, sliding her leg across Hades's lap so that she straddled him. Her dress rose, and she could feel him against her, hard and aroused. She smiled and his gaze returned to hers instantly; this time, it was like fire scorching her skin.

"Should *I* leave a mark?" she asked.

"Careful, Goddess." His words were a growl.

She rolled her eyes. "Another order."

"A warning," Hades said through gritted teeth, and then his hands clasped her bare thighs and she inhaled sharply at the feel of his skin against hers. "But we both know you don't listen, even when it's good for you."

"You think you know what's good for me?" she asked, dangerously close to his lips. "You think you know what I need?"

His hands moved up, pushing her dress higher, and she gasped as his fingers neared the apex of her thighs. Hades laughed. "I don't think, Goddess. I know. I could make you worship me."

Persephone bit her lip, and his eyes fell there and remained. So she closed the distance between them, sealing her lips to his.

He opened to her immediately, and she tasted him deep, taking what was hers to claim. Her fingers tangled into his hair, tilting his head back to kiss him deeper. In this position, she felt powerful.

When she finally pulled away, it was to nibble at his ear. "You will worship *me*," she said and rolled her hips against him. His hands dug into her skin, and she moved in, her cheek brushing his as she whispered. "And I won't even have to order you."

She didn't think his hands could grasp her any tighter, and then he lifted her up effortlessly and maneuvered her so that she was cradled tight against him. He fixed her dress, then covered her with his own jacket. "Don't make promises you can't keep, Goddess."

She blinked, confused by the sudden change in him. He had rejected her. "You're just afraid."

Hades didn't speak, but when she glanced at him, he was glaring out the window, jaw locked tight, hands fisted, and she got the sense she might be right.

It wasn't long after that she fell asleep in his embrace.

CHAPTER XIV
A Touch of Jealousy

When Persephone woke, she was aware of two things: one, she was in a stranger's bed, and two, she was naked. She bolted up, holding black silk sheets to her chest. She was in Hades's room—she recognized it from the day she'd fallen into the Styx and he'd healed her—and she found Hades sitting before his blazing fireplace. It was probably the most godlike she'd ever seen him. He looked perfectly untouched—not a hair out of place, not a wrinkle in his jacket, not a button undone. He held his whiskey in one hand, and the fingers of his other hand rested against his lips. The halo of fire roaring behind him was also fitting, raging like his eyes.

It was how she knew that though he appeared to be reclining, he was wound tight.

He kept her gaze, not speaking, and took a sip of his drink.

"Why am I naked?" Persephone asked.

"Because you insisted on it," he answered in a voice

void of the barely restrained desire he'd exhibited in the limo. She didn't have many memories from last night, but she was sure she'd never forget the press of Hades's fingers into her thighs or the delicious friction that sent shock waves through her body. "You were very determined to seduce me."

Persephone blushed fiercely and averted her gaze. "Did we—"

Hades laughed darkly, and Persephone clenched her teeth so hard, her jaw hurt. Why was he laughing? "No, Lady Persephone. Trust me, when we fuck, you'll remember."

When? "Your arrogance is alarming."

His eyes flashed. "Is that a challenge?"

"Just tell me what happened, Hades!" she demanded.

"You were drugged at La Rose. You're lucky you are immortal. Your body burned through the poison fast."

Not fast enough to prevent embarrassment, apparently.

She remembered a waitress approaching once they'd hit the dance floor, how she'd brought them drinks and said they were on the house. Soon after she'd consumed hers and started dancing, the music had sounded far away, the lights were blinding, and every move she made sent her head spinning.

She also remembered hands on her body and cold lips closing over hers.

"Adonis," Persephone said. Hades's jaw tightened at hearing the mortal's name. "What did you do to him?"

Hades looked at his glass, swirling the whiskey before downing the last bit. Once he finished, he set the glass aside, not looking at her. "He is alive, but that is only because he was in his goddess's territory."

"You knew!" Persephone pushed off the bed and stood, Hades's silk sheets rustling around her. His penetrating gaze drifted from her face down, tracing every line of her body. She felt as if she were standing bare before him. "Is that why you warned me to stay away from him?"

"I assure you, there are more reasons to stay away from that mortal than the favor Aphrodite has bestowed upon him."

"Like what? You can't expect me to understand if you don't explain anything." She'd taken a step toward him, even though some part of her knew it was dangerous. Whatever Hades had gone through in the night was clearly still racing through his mind.

"I expect that you will trust me," he said, standing. The blunt admission shocked her. "And if not me, then my power."

She hadn't even considered his powers—the ability to see the soul for what it was, raw and burdened. What did he see when he looked at Adonis?

A thief, she thought. *A manipulator.*

Hades put distance between them, refilling his glass at the small bar in his room.

"I thought you were jealous!"

Hades was about to take a drink, but he paused to laugh. She was both angry and hurt at his dismissal.

"Don't pretend you don't get jealous, Hades. Adonis kissed me last night."

Hades slammed the glass down. "Keep reminding me, Goddess, and I'll reduce him to ash."

"So you are jealous!" she accused.

"Jealous?" He stalked toward her. "That...leech...

touched you after you told him not to. I have sent souls to Tartarus for less."

She recalled Hades's anger at Duncan, the ogre who had laid his hands on her, and she realized that was why he was on edge. He probably did want to find Adonis and incinerate him.

"I'm…sorry." She wasn't sure what to say, but his distress seemed so great, she thought she might ease it with an apology.

She only made it worse.

"Don't you dare apologize." He cupped her face. "Not for him. Never for him." He studied her and whispered, "Why are you so desperate to hate me?"

Her brows came together, and she covered his hands with hers. "I don't hate you," she said quietly, and Hades stiffened, tearing away from her. The violence with which he moved surprised her, and the anger and tension returned.

"No? Shall I remind you? *Hades, Lord of the Underworld, Rich One, and arguably the most hated god among mortals, exhibits a clear disregard for mortal life.*"

He quoted her article word for word, and Persephone cringed. How many times had he read it? How he must have seethed.

Hades's jaw worked. "This is what you think of me?"

She opened her mouth and closed it before deciding to explain. "I was angry—"

"Oh, that is more than obvious." Hades's voice was sharp.

"I didn't know they would publish it!"

"A scathing letter illustrating all of my faults? You didn't think the media would publish it?"

She glared at him. "I warned you."

It was the wrong thing to say.

"You warned me?" He set his gaze upon her, dark and angry. "You warned me about what, Goddess?"

"I warned you that you would regret our contract."

"And I warned you not to write about me." He stepped closer to her, and she didn't back down, tilting her head to keep his gaze.

"Perhaps in my next article, I'll write about how bossy you are," she said.

"Next article?"

"You didn't know? I've been asked to write a series on you."

"No," he said.

"You can't say no. You're not in control here."

"And you think you are?"

"I'll write the articles, Hades, and the only way I'll stop is if you let me out of this Gods-damned contract!"

Hades went rigid, then hissed, "You think to bargain with me, Goddess?" The heat coming off him was almost unbearable. He inched forward, though it wasn't like he had much space—he was already so close to her. She stuck out one hand, clutching the sheet to her body with the other. "You've forgotten one important thing, *Lady Persephone*. To bargain, you need to have something I want."

"You asked me if I believed what I wrote!" she argued. "You care!"

"It's called a bluff, darling."

"Bastard," she hissed.

Hades reached out. Burying his hand in her hair, he hauled her against him and pulled her head back so that her throat felt taut. It was savage and possessive. Her breath caught in her throat, and the space between her thighs felt damp. She craved him. "Let me be clear—you bargained, and you lost. There is no way out of our contract unless you fulfill its terms. Otherwise, you remain here. With me."

"If you make me your prisoner, I will spend the rest of my life hating you."

"You already do."

She flinched again. She didn't like that he thought that and kept saying it. "Do you really believe that?"

He didn't answer, just offered a mocking laugh, and then pressed a hot kiss to her mouth before tearing away viciously. "I will erase the memory of him from your skin."

She was surprised by his ferocity, but it thrilled her. He tore away the silk sheet, leaving her naked before him, and when he lifted her off the ground, she wrapped her legs around his waist without a second thought. He gripped her bottom tight and his mouth crashed into her. The friction of his clothes against her bare skin drove her to the edge, and liquid heat pooled at her core. Persephone raked her hands into Hades's hair, grazing his scalp as she freed the long strands, gripping them hard in her hands. She pulled his head back and kissed him hard and deep. A guttural sound escaped Hades's mouth at that, and he moved, backing her into the bedpost, grinding into her hard. His teeth grazed her skin, biting and sucking in a way that kept her from breathing, eliciting gasps from deep in her throat.

Together they were mindless, and when she found herself sprawled out on the bed, she knew she would give Hades anything. He wouldn't even have to ask.

But the God of the Dead stood over her, breathing hard. His hair spilled over his shoulders; his eyes were dark, angry, aroused—and instead of closing the distance he had created between them, he smirked.

It was unsettling, and Persephone knew she wasn't going to like what came next.

"Well, you would probably enjoy fucking me, but you definitely don't like me."

Then he was gone.

———

Persephone found her dress neatly folded on one of the two chairs in front of Hades's fireplace with a black cloak beside it. As she pulled on the dress and the cloak, she thought of how Hades had looked at her when she awoke. How long had he sat watching her sleep? How long had he simmered in his rage? Who was this god who appeared out of nowhere to rescue her from unwanted advances, claimed it wasn't jealousy, and folded her clothes? Who accused her of hating him but kissed her like he had never partaken of something so sweet?

Her body flushed as she thought about how he'd lifted her and moved her to the bed. She couldn't recall what she'd been thinking, but she knew it wasn't telling him to stop. Still, he'd left her.

That heady flush turned to anger.

He'd laughed and left her.

Because this is a game to him, she reminded herself. She couldn't let her strange and electric attraction to him overpower that reality. She had a contract to fulfill.

Persephone left Hades's room via the balcony to check on her garden. Despite her resentment of the greenhouse, she still loved flowers, and the God of the Underworld had managed to create one of the most beautiful gardens she'd ever seen. She marveled at the colors and the scents—the sweet smell of wisteria, the heady and sultry scent of gardenias and roses, the calming aroma of lavender.

And it was all magic.

Hades had lifetimes to learn his powers, to craft illusions that deceived the senses. Persephone had never known the feel of power in her blood. Did it burn hot like the need Hades ignited within her? Did it feel like last night when she'd boldly straddled him and whispered challenges in his ear as she tasted his skin?

That had been power.

For a moment, she'd controlled him.

She'd seen lust cloud his gaze, heard his growl of passion, felt his hard arousal. But she'd not been powerful enough to keep him under her spell.

She was beginning to think she would never be powerful enough.

Which was why a mortal life suited her so well—why she could not let Hades win.

Except she wasn't sure how she was supposed to win when her garden still looked like a scorched piece of earth. As she came to the end of the path, the lush gardens gave way to a bald patch where the soil was more like sand and black as ash. It had been a few weeks since she'd planted the seeds in the ground. They should be sprouting by now. Even without magic, mortal gardens at least produced that much life. If it had been her mother's garden, it would already be fully grown. Persephone had harbored a secret hope that through this process, she would discover some dormant power that didn't involve stealing life—but standing before this barren patch of earth made her realize how ridiculous that hope was.

She couldn't just wait around for power to manifest or for mortal seeds to sprout in the Underworld's impossible soil. She had to do something more.

She straightened and went in search of Hecate.

Persephone found the Goddess in a grove near her home. Hecate wore purple robes today, and her long hair was braided and snaked over her shoulder. She sat cross-legged in the soft grass, petting a furry weasel. Persephone squealed when she saw it.

"What is that?" she demanded.

Hecate smiled softly and scratched the creature behind its small ear. "This is Gale. She is a polecat."

"That is not a cat."

"Polecat." Hecate laughed quietly. "She was once a human witch, but she was an idiot, so I turned her into a polecat."

Persephone stared at the goddess, but Hecate didn't seem to notice her stunned silence.

"I like her better this way," Hecate added, then looked up at Persephone. "But enough about Gale. What can I help you with, my dear?"

That question was all it took. Persephone erupted, breaking into a seething tangent about Hades, the contract, and her impossible wager, avoiding details about this morning's disaster. She even admitted her greatest secret—that she could not grow a single thing. When she finished, Hecate pursed her lips, looking thoughtful but not surprised.

"If you cannot give life, what can you do?" she asked.

"Destroy it."

Hecate's pretty brows furrowed over her dark eyes. "You have never grown anything at all?"

Persephone shook her head.

"Show me."

"Hecate...I don't think that's—"

"I'd like to see."

Persephone sighed and turned her hands over. She stared at her palms for a long moment before bending and pressing them to the grass. Where it was green before, it yellowed and withered beneath her touch. When she looked at Hecate, the goddess was staring at her hands. "I think that is why Hades challenged me to create life— because he knew it was impossible."

Hecate did not look so certain. "Hades does not challenge people with the impossible. He challenges them to embrace their potential."

"And what is my potential?"

"To be the Goddess of Spring." The polecat hopped off Hecate's lap as she got to her feet, brushing off her skirts. Persephone expected the goddess to continue asking questions about her magic, but instead she said, "Gardening is not the only way to create life."

Persephone stared at her. "How else should I create life?"

She could tell by the amused look on her face that she wasn't going to like what Hecate had to say. "You could have a baby."

"*What?*"

"Of course, to fulfill the contract, Hades would have to be the father," she continued as if she hadn't heard Persephone. "He would be furious if it were anyone else."

She decided she was going to ignore that comment. "I'm not having Hades's child, Hecate."

"You asked for suggestions. I was merely trying to be a good friend."

"And you are—but I am not ready for children and Hades is not a god I would want as a father to them anyway." Though she did feel a bit guilty for saying that last part out loud. "What am I going to do? Ugh, this is impossible!"

"It is not as impossible as it seems, my dear. You are in the Underworld, after all."

"You do realize the Underworld is the realm of the dead, don't you, Hecate?"

"It is also a place for new beginnings," she said. "Sometimes, the existence a soul leads here is the best life they've ever had. I'm sure you, of all the gods, understand that best."

The realization settled heavy on Persephone's shoulders. She did understand that.

"Living here is no different than living up there," Hecate added. "You challenged Hades to help mortals lead a better existence. He has merely charged you with the same here in the Underworld."

CHAPTER XV
Offer

Another busy week passed, full of reading articles, writing papers, and taking tests. Persephone had thought that by now, the hype over her article would die down, but it hadn't. She still got stopped on her way to the Acropolis and the university; strangers asked her when the next article about Hades was coming out and what she planned to write about.

She was a little tired of the questions and even more tired of repeating herself—*the article is out in a few weeks, and you'll have to buy the paper.* She started putting her headphones in on her walks just so she could claim she couldn't hear people when they called her name.

"Persephone?"

Too bad she couldn't do that at work right about now.

Demetri poked his head out of his office. Somehow, he looked younger and older at the same time in his denim shirt and polka-dot bow tie, maybe because the blue brought out the gray in his hair, and the bow tie was fun.

"Yes?" she asked.

"Have a moment?"

"Sure." She saved what she was working on and closed her laptop, following Demetri into his office where she took a seat.

Her boss leaned against his desk. "How's that article coming along?"

"Fine. It's...fine." If he was looking for a summary of what she planned to write, she didn't have one. She had thought about writing about the mother who came to Hades to ask for her daughter's life, but though she didn't understand why Hades wished to keep that a secret, she wanted to honor the request he made of the woman.

Since the morning after La Rose, when Hades had confused her with his passion and anger, she'd just focused on avoiding him. She knew that wasn't best, especially if she was going to get this article submitted in a few weeks, but she still had the weekend, and with her and Hades's track record, he was bound to do something to piss her off, which meant ideal writing material.

"'God of the Game' was our most popular story to date. Millions of views, thousands of comments and papers sold."

"You were right," she said. "People are curious about Hades."

"Which is why I called you in," he said.

Persephone straightened, her thoughts shooting in all sorts of directions. She'd been waiting for Demetri to request more from her. So far, he'd let her have creative control over how she covered Hades, and she didn't want to lose that.

"I've got an assignment for you."

"An assignment?" she echoed.

"I've been holding on to these." He reached for an envelope on his desk and handed it to her. "I hadn't decided who to send, but I had no doubt after the success of your article."

"What is it?" She was too nervous to open the envelope, but her boss just smiled.

"Why don't you open it?"

Persephone did and found two tickets inside to Saturday's Olympian Gala at the Museum of Ancient Arts. They were beautiful invitations—black with gold leaf lettering—and looked just as expensive as the gala itself.

Persephone's eyes went wide. The Olympian Gala was the biggest event of the year. It was a huge fashion show, party, and charity event. Every year, a theme was chosen, inspired by a god or goddess, and that god or goddess got to choose what charity project was funded with the money raised at the gala. Tickets were coveted and cost hundreds of dollars.

"But...why me?" she demanded. "You should be going to this. You're the editor in chief."

"I have another obligation that night."

"Bigger than the Olympian Gala?"

Demetri smirked. "I have been many times, Persephone."

"I don't understand. Hades doesn't even go to the gala." She'd watched live coverage of the event with Lexa and had never seen him enter with the other gods, and no one had ever snapped a photo of him.

"Lord Hades doesn't allow himself to be photo-graphed, but he always attends."

"I can't go," she said after a long silence.

Her boss leveled his gaze with hers. "Persephone, what are you so afraid of?"

"I'm not...afraid." Though she kind of was. The last time she'd seen her mother, she'd threatened to send her back to the greenhouse if she went to Nevernight or saw Hades again. It didn't matter where. Plus, she wasn't even supposed to be around the gods, and it wasn't like she could hide the fact that she was there from her mother—Demeter would be there too.

But that was all too complicated to say to Demetri.

"Consider it an opportunity for research and obser-vation," he said. "We always write about the Olympian Gala. You'll just put the spotlight on Hades."

"You don't understand—" she started.

"Take the tickets, Persephone. Think it over—but don't take too much time. You don't have long to decide."

She didn't feel comfortable taking the tickets because she was certain she wasn't going to the gala. Still, Demetri sent her back to her desk with them, and she sat down in a daze, staring at the envelope. After a moment, she pulled the tickets out to read them:

Join us for an Evening in the Underworld

She'd had no idea this year's theme was the Underworld. Her curiosity heightened—how would the organizers of this event interpret Hades's realm? She bet they'd never guess there was so much life below. She also wondered what charity Hades would choose to donate to.

Gods, she really wanted to go.

But there were so many cons—her mother, for one.

It was also a few days away and she didn't have a gown just lying around.

Her gaze dropped to the tickets again where the dress code was printed further down the page and indicated the gala was a masquerade.

It wasn't likely she could hide from her mother in a mask, but now she wondered if Hecate had any spells up her sleeve that would help. She made a mental note to ask when she visited the Underworld this evening.

Her desk phone rang, and she picked up. "This is Persephone."

"Hades's...assistant is here to see you?" Valerie said.

It took Persephone a moment to respond. "Minthe?" What could Minthe possibly have to say to her?

"Oh, Adonis is bringing her back," Valerie added.

Persephone looked up to see the nymph heading for her across the room. She was dressed in black, and her hair and green eyes shone like fire. Adonis walked beside her like an escort, expression utterly smitten, and suddenly Persephone's dislike for him deepened.

"Hey, Persephone," Adonis said, oblivious to her frustration. "You remember Minthe?"

"How could I forget?" Persephone replied matter-of-factly.

The nymph smiled. "I came to speak with you regarding the article you published about my employer."

"I'm afraid I don't have time to meet with you today. Maybe some other time."

"I'm afraid I must demand an audience."

"If you have complaints about the article, you should speak with my supervisor."

"I'd rather voice my concerns with you." Minthe's

eyes flashed, and Persephone knew it would take a force of nature—likely Hades—to remove this lady from the building.

They stared at one another for a long moment, and Adonis cleared his throat. "Well, I'll let you two work this out."

Neither woman acknowledged Adonis as he slithered away, leaving them alone. After a moment, Persephone asked, "Does Hades know you're here?"

"It is my job to advise Hades on matters that might harm his reputation and, when he will not listen to reason, act."

"Hades doesn't care about his reputation."

"But I do. And you are threatening it."

"Because of my article?"

"Because you exist," she said.

Persephone leveled her gaze. "Hades's reputation preceded his knowledge of my existence. Don't you think it's a little absurd to blame me?"

"I'm not talking about his bargains with mortals. I'm talking about his bargain with you." Minthe spoke louder, and though Persephone knew what she was doing, the tactic worked; she wanted to shut her up. "Now, if you will so kindly give me the time I have requested."

"Right this way," Persephone said through gritted teeth.

She led the nymph into an interview room, shutting the door louder than necessary. She turned to Minthe and waited, crossing her arms over her chest. Neither sat down, an indication this wouldn't last long.

"You seem to think you have Hades all figured out," Minthe said, her eyes narrowed.

Persephone stiffened. "And you disagree?"

She smiled. "Well, I have known him for centuries."

"I don't think I need to know him for centuries to understand he has no grasp of the human condition. Nor does he understand how to help the world." Although what he'd done for that mother was more than generous. She was starting to understand there were rules at work that prevented even Hades, a powerful and long-existing god, from doing whatever he wanted.

"Hades will not kneel to your every whim," Minthe said.

"I don't expect him to kneel," Persephone said. "Though it would be a nice touch."

Minthe took a step forward and spat, "Arrogant girl!"

Persephone stiffened and lowered her arms. "I am not a girl."

"Do you know what? I don't know what such a powerful god sees in you. You are entitled and magicless and yet he continues to let you into our realm—"

"Trust me, nymph. It's not a choice."

"Isn't it? Isn't it a choice every time you let him put his hands on you? Every time he kisses you? I know Lord Hades, and if you asked him to stop, he would—but you don't. You never do."

Persephone's blush was fierce, but she managed, "I don't want to discuss this with you."

"No? Then I will get to the point. You are making a mistake. Hades isn't interested in love, nor is he made for it. Keep walking this path and you will get hurt."

"Are you threatening me?"

"No, it's the promise of falling in love with a god."

"I'm not falling for Hades," Persephone argued.

The nymph offered a cruel smile. "Denial," she said. "It's the first stage of reluctant love. Don't make this mistake, Persephone."

She hated her name on the nymph's tongue and couldn't repress a shudder. Swallowing, Persephone felt her glamour ripple. "Is this why you came to my work? To warn me against Hades?"

"Yes," Minthe said. "And now I have an offer to extend."

"I want nothing from you." Persephone's voice shook.

"If you truly wish to be free of your contract, you will take my offer."

Persephone glared, still mistrusting, but she couldn't deny she wanted to hear what the nymph had to say.

Minthe chuckled. "Hades has asked you to create life in the Underworld. There is a spring in the mountains where you will find the Well of Reincarnation. It will give life to anything—even your desolate garden."

Persephone had never heard of such a place in any of her readings of the Underworld, though that wasn't saying much. Those books also described the Underworld as dead and desolate. "And why should I trust you?"

"It has nothing to do with trust. You want to be free from your contract with Hades, and I want Hades to be free from you."

She stared at Minthe for a moment. She wasn't sure what compelled her to ask the question, but she found the words rolling off her tongue. "Do you love him?"

"You think this has to do with love?" Minthe demanded. "How sweet. I'm protecting him. Hades loves nothing but a good bargain, and you, my young goddess, are the worst wager he's ever made."

Then Minthe was gone.

CHAPTER XVI
A Touch of Darkness

"You are the worst wager he's ever made."

Minthe's words rolled around in Persephone's head. Now and then, they hit a chord so sensitive she felt a fresh flush of rage as she made her way to Nevernight.

Despite realizing that her garden might not succeed in fulfilling the contract between her and Hades, she felt like it would be giving up to ignore it completely, so she returned, watered her garden, and then sought out her new friends in Asphodel.

Persephone made a point to stop by Asphodel every time she visited the Underworld now. There, in the green valley, she found the dead lived—they planted gardens and harvested fruit. They made jams, butter, and bread. They sewed and knitted and weaved, making clothing and scarves and rugs. It was the reason they had an extensive market that twisted throughout the alleyways between the strange, volcanic-glass homes.

More than usual, the dead were out in droves and

the market was bustling with an energy she had yet to experience in the Underworld: excitement. A few of the souls strung lanterns between their homes, decorating the alleyway they shared. Persephone watched them for several moments until she heard a familiar voice.

"Good evening, my lady!" Persephone turned to find Yuri, a pretty young woman with thick curls, approaching her on the road. She wore pink robes and carried a large basket of pomegranates.

"Yuri." Persephone smiled and hugged the girl. The two had gotten to know each other one day when Yuri offered her one of her signature tea blends. Persephone had loved it so much she tried to purchase a tin, but Yuri refused her money and offered it for free.

"What would I do with money in the Underworld?" she'd asked.

The next time Persephone visited, she brought Yuri a jeweled clip so she could pin back her thick hair. The girl had been so grateful, she threw her arms around Persephone and then quickly backed away, apologizing for being so forward. Persephone had only laughed and said, "I like hugs."

The two had been friends ever since.

"Is...something happening today?" Persephone asked.

Yuri smiled. "We are celebrating Lord Hades."

"Why?" She didn't mean to sound so surprised, but she wasn't feeling generous toward the God of the Dead these days. "Is it his birthday?"

Yuri laughed at that question, and Persephone realized how dumb it was to ask—Hades likely didn't celebrate a birthday or even remember when he was born. "Because he is our king and we wish to honor him." There were several festivals celebrating gods above ground, but none of them celebrated the God of the Underworld. "We've been hopeful that he will soon have a queen."

Persephone paled. Her first thought was who? And then why? What had given them the impression that they might have a queen? "A...what?"

Yuri smiled. "Come now, Persephone. You aren't so blind."

"I think I am."

"Lord Hades has never given a god so much freedom over his realm."

Oh, Yuri was referring to her.

"What about Hecate? Hermes?" she argued. They each had access to the Underworld and came and went as they pleased.

"Hecate is a creature of this world and Hermes is merely a messenger. You...you're something more."

Persephone shook her head. "I'm no more than a game, Yuri."

She could tell by the tilt of her head that the soul was confused by her statement, but Persephone wasn't going to argue. The souls of the Underworld might see Hades's treatment as special, but she knew it for what it was.

Yuri reached into her basket and offered Persephone a pomegranate. "Even so, will you not stay? This celebration, it's just as much for you as it is for Hades."

The shock of Yuri's words went deep. "But I'm not... You can't worship me."

"Why not? You are a goddess, you care for us, and you care for our King."

"I—" She wanted to argue that she didn't care for Lord Hades, but the words wouldn't come.

Before she could think of a good response, her attention was drawn away by a chorus of voices.

"Lady Persephone! Lady Persephone!"

Something small but powerful rammed into her legs, and she almost fell into Yuri and her basket.

"Isaac! Apologize to your—" Yuri paused, and she got the sense the souls in Asphodel had already started calling her by a title she didn't own. "Apologize to Lady Persephone."

The child in question withdrew his embrace from Persephone's legs. He'd been followed by an army of children ranging in age, all of whom Persephone had met before and played several games with. Joining them were Hades's dogs, Cerberus, Typhon, and Orthrus. Cerberus clasped their large, red ball in his jowls.

"Sorry, Lady Persephone. Will you play with us?" Isaac begged.

"Lady Persephone is not dressed to play, Isaac," Yuri said, and the boy frowned. It was true that Persephone hadn't been prepared to play in the meadow. She still wore her work attire—a form-fitting white dress.

"It's perfectly alright, Yuri," she said and reached to lift Isaac into her arms. He was the youngest of the group, she guessed only about four. It pained her to think of why this child was here in Asphodel. What had befallen him in the Upperworld? How long had he been here? Were any of these souls his family?

She shut down those thoughts as quickly as they came. She could spend hours thinking about all the reasons any of these people were here, and it did no good. The dead were the dead, and she was learning their existence here really wasn't so bad.

"Of course I'll play," she said.

A chorus of cheers erupted as she walked with the children to a clear part of the meadow, out of the way of the souls preparing for Hades's celebration.

Persephone played catch with the dogs, along with tag and a million other games the children made up. She spent more time sliding in the wet grass to avoid being tagged than she did on her feet. By the time she walked away from the field, she was covered in mud but happily exhausted.

It had grown dark in the Underworld, and musicians stepped into the thoroughfare, playing sweet notes. Souls filled the streets to chat and laugh, and the smell of meat cooking and sweets baking thickened the air. It wasn't long before Persephone found Hecate in the crowd, and the goddess smiled at her appearance.

"My dear, you are a mess."

The Goddess of Spring smiled. "It was an intense game of tag."

"I hope you won."

"I was a complete failure," she said. "The children are far more adept."

The two laughed, and another soul approached them—Ian, a blacksmith who always kept his forge hot, working metal into beautiful blades and shields. She'd asked him once why he seemed to be preparing for battle, and the man replied, "Habit."

Persephone didn't think too long on that just as she tried not to think too long on Isaac.

"My lady," Ian said. "Asphodel has a gift for you."

Persephone waited, curious, as the soul dropped to his knee and drew a beautiful gold crown from behind his back. This wasn't just any crown; it was a series of carefully crafted flowers made into a circlet. Among the bouquet, she spied roses and lilies and narcissus. Tiny gems of various colors sparkled at the center of each flower.

"Will you wear our crown, Lady Persephone?"

The soul wasn't looking at her, and she wondered if he feared her rejection. She glanced up, eyes going wide as she realized that the whole place had gone quiet. The souls waited, expectant.

She remembered Yuri's comments earlier. These people had come to think of her as a queen, and accepting this crown would only encourage that, but not accepting would hurt them.

Against her better judgment, she placed a hand on Ian's shoulder and knelt to him. She looked into his eyes and answered, "I will gladly wear your crown, Ian."

She allowed the soul to place the crown on her head, and everyone broke into cheers. Grinning, Ian offered his hand, leading her into a dance at the center of the dirt walkway beneath the lights strung overhead. Persephone felt ridiculous in her stained dress and gold crown, but the dead didn't seem to notice or care. She danced until she could scarcely breathe, and her feet hurt. When she moved toward Hecate for respite, the Goddess of Witchcraft said, "I think you could use some rest. And a bath."

Persephone laughed. "I think you're right."

"They will celebrate all night long," she added. "But you have made their night. Hades has never visited to celebrate with them."

Persephone's heart fell. "Why not?"

Hecate shrugged. "I cannot speak for him, but it is a question you may ask."

The two returned to the palace. On their way to the baths, Persephone explained that she had received two tickets to the Olympian Gala and asked if Hecate had any spells that might help her go unseen by her mother. The goddess considered her question, then asked, "Do you have a mask?"

Persephone frowned. "I planned to pick one up tomorrow."

"Leave it to me."

The baths were located at the back of the fortress and accessed through an archway. When Persephone stepped inside, she was greeted by the smell of fresh linen and lavender, and a warm mist coated her skin and sank into her bones. She flushed with the heat of the air, and it was welcomed after her evening spent in the muddy meadow.

Hecate led her down a network of steps, past several smaller pools and showers.

"This is a public bath?" Persephone asked. In antiquity, public bath houses were very common, but they'd fallen out of popularity in modern times. She wondered how many in the palace used this house—among them, Minthe and Hades.

Hecate laughed. "Yes, though Lord Hades has his own private pool. That is where you will bathe."

Persephone didn't protest. She wasn't keen on bathing in public. Hecate paused to gather supplies for her—soap and towels and a lavender peplos. Persephone hadn't worn the ancient garment in nearly four years—since she left Olympia and the greenhouse for New Athens. Wearing one now felt strange after four years in mortal clothes.

They descended a final set of steps and came to Hades's pool. It was a large oval surrounded by columns. Overhead, the ceiling was exposed to the sky.

"Call for me if you need anything," Hecate said and left Persephone to undress in private. "When you are finished, join us in the dining room."

Naked, Persephone took a tentative step toward the water, dipping her foot in to test the temperature—it was hot but not scalding. She entered the pool and groaned with pleasure. Steam rose around her and drew perspiration from her skin—the water was cleansing, and she felt like it washed away the day. Thankfully, the celebration in Asphodel had relieved a lot of the stress from Minthe's earlier visit, and now that she was back in his realm and thinking of where he and Minthe might bathe, all those thoughts came rushing back to the surface.

How was she the one threatening Hades's reputation? The God of the Dead did enough damage on his own. Despite the fact that Persephone wanted a way out of her contract, she wasn't sure she trusted Minthe enough to listen.

Persephone scrubbed her skin until it was raw and pink. She wasn't sure how long she soaked in the water after that, because she'd gotten lost in the details of the bath, noticing a line of white tiles with red narcissus peering over the edge of the water around the pool. The columns she had thought were white were actually brushed with gold. The sky overhead deepened, and tiny stars glimmered.

She was amazed by Hades's magic—how he blended scents and textures. He was a master with his brush, smoothing and stippling, creating a realm that rivaled the beauty of the most sought-after destinations in the Upperworld.

She was so lost in thought, she almost didn't hear the sound of boots treading on the steps into the bath until Hades appeared at the edge of the pool, and their eyes met. She was glad the water had already flushed her skin and he couldn't see how hot she'd grown at his presence.

He didn't say anything for a long moment, just stared at her in his bath. Then his eyes fell to the clothes she'd stripped off at his feet. Among them, the gold crown.

Hades bent and picked it up. "This is beautiful."

She cleared her throat. "It is. Ian made it for me." She didn't bother asking him if he knew Ian. Hades had told her before that he knew all the souls in the Underworld.

"He is a talented craftsman. It is what led to his death."

Persephone frowned. "What do you mean?"

"He was favored by Artemis, and she blessed him with the ability to create weapons that ensured their bearer could not be defeated in battle. He was killed for it."

Persephone swallowed—it was just another way a god's favor could result in pain and suffering.

Hades spent a moment longer inspecting the crown before setting it down again. When he rose to his feet, Persephone was still staring at him and hadn't moved an inch. "Why didn't you go? To the celebration in Asphodel. It was for you."

"And you," he said.

It took her a moment to figure out what he meant.

"They celebrated you," he said. "As they should."

"I am not their queen."

"And I am not worthy of their celebration."

She stared. How could this confident and powerful god feel unworthy of his people's celebration? "If they feel you're worthy of celebration, don't you think that's enough?"

He did not respond. Instead, his eyes grew darker and a strange feeling pervaded the air—heavy, heated, and spiced. It made her chest feel tight, restricting her breath.

"May I join you?" His voice was deep and sultry.

Persephone's brain short-circuited.

He meant in the pool. Naked. Where only water would provide cover.

She found herself nodding, and she wondered briefly if she had gone insane having been in the water too long, but there was a part of her that burned so hot for this god she would do anything to sate the flame, even if it meant testing it.

He didn't smile and he didn't take his eyes from her as he stripped off his clothes. Her eyes made a slow descent from his face to his arms and chest, his torso, and held at his arousal. She wasn't the only one who felt this electric attraction, and she feared when they entered the water together, they might incinerate.

He stepped into the pool, saying nothing. He stopped a few inches from her. "I believe I owe you an apology."

"For what, specifically?" she asked. There were several things he might be apologizing for in her mind—Minthe's unannounced visit (if he knew about it), the way he'd treated her the morning after La Rose, the contract.

Hades smirked, but the humor didn't touch his gaze. No, his gaze burned.

The King of the Underworld reached out and touched her face, drawing a finger across her cheek. "Last time we saw each other, I was unfair to you."

He had stripped her bare and teased her in the most vicious way, and when he had left her, she felt embarrassed and angry and abandoned. She didn't want him to see any of that in her eyes, so she looked away. "We were unfair to each other."

When she managed to look at him again, he was studying her. "You like your life in the mortal realm?"

"Yes." At his question, she put distance between them, swimming backward, but Hades followed, slow and calculated. "I like my life. I have an apartment and friends and an internship. I'm going to graduate from university soon." And she would get to stay if she kept Hades and the contract a secret.

"But you are Divine."

"I have never lived that way and you know it."

Again, he studied her, quiet for a moment. Then, "You have no desire to understand what it is to be a goddess?"

"No," she lied. The claws of that long-ago dream still had a hold on her, and the more she visited the Underworld, the more her heart ached for it. She'd spent her childhood feeling inadequate, surrounded by her mother's magic. When she'd come to New Athens, she'd finally found something she was good at—school and writing and research—but once again, she found herself in the same situation as before; different god, different realm.

"I think you're lying," he said.

"You don't know me." She stopped moving and glared at him, angry that he saw right through her.

Hades was now toe to toe with her, looking down, eyes like coals. "I know you." He trailed his fingers over her collarbone and moved so that he was behind her. "I know the way your breath hitches when I touch you. I know how your skin flushes when you're thinking about me. I know there is something beneath this pretty facade."

Hades's fingers continued their featherlight caress over Persephone's skin. His words weren't far behind, whispering along the path of heat he left. He kissed her shoulder.

"There is rage. There is passion. There is darkness."

He paused a moment and let his tongue swirl against her neck. Her breath caught in her throat so hard, she thought she might choke.

"And I want to taste it."

His arm came around her waist and her back met his chest. The arch of her body fit against him perfectly. His arousal pressed into her, and she wondered what it would feel like to have that flesh inside her.

"Hades," she breathed.

"Let me show you what it is to hold power in your hands," he said. "Let me coax the darkness from you—I will help you shape it."

Yes, she thought. *Yes.*

Hades's head rested in the crook of her neck as his hand brushed along her stomach and lower. When he cupped her sex, she gasped, arching against him.

"Hades, I've never—"

"Let me be your first," he said—begged—and his voice rumbled in her chest.

She couldn't speak, but she took a few breaths and then nodded.

He answered by brushing his fingers through her curls, then grazing his thumb against that sensitive bud at the apex of her core. She inhaled sharply and then held her breath as he toyed with her there, stroking and circling.

"Breathe," he said.

And she did—as much as she could anyway, until his fingers sank into her flesh. Persephone threw her head back, crying out as Hades groaned, his teeth grazing her shoulder.

"You're so wet." His mouth was warm against her skin.

He moved slowly in and out, and Persephone held on to his arm, nails digging into his skin. Then she felt Hades's other hand guide hers down.

"Touch yourself. Here," he said. He helped her circle the sensitive flesh he'd toyed with for so long before entering her. Pleasure curled through her stomach. She rocked against him, arching her back. Hades kissed her skin ruthlessly and cupped her breast, kneading her nipples until they were hard and taut. She thought she would explode.

Hades moved faster and Persephone rubbed harder and then suddenly, he withdrew. The absence of him was so shocking, she cried out.

She twisted toward him in anger, and he grabbed her wrists, pulling her toward him, his mouth descending on hers. His kiss was consuming. Their tongues collided, desperate and searching. She thought he might be trying to taste her soul.

He pulled away, resting his forehead against hers. "Do you trust me?"

"Yes," she breathed—and she felt the truth of her words deep in her soul. It was a knowledge so primal and so pure, she thought she might weep. In this, she trusted him. In this, she would always trust him.

He kissed her again and lifted her onto the edge of the bath.

"Tell me you have never been naked with a man," he said. "Tell me I am the only one."

She cupped his face, searching his eyes, and answered, "You are."

He kissed her before moving his arms under her knees, shifting her so that she barely rested on the edge of the pool. She couldn't breathe as he kissed along the inside of her thigh, pausing when he reached the bruises on her flesh. She hadn't noticed them, but looking at them now, she knew exactly where they had come from: the night in the limo when Hades had gripped her tight. It was a sign of his need and of his restraint.

He looked up at her. "Was this me?"

"It's okay," she whispered and ran her fingers through his hair.

But Hades frowned and kissed each bruise—eight in total. Persephone counted.

Slowly, he moved from the outside in, closer to her core. And then his mouth was on her and a cry escaped her. She felt molten where he touched her, and it spread all over her body. His tongue circled her clit and parted her damp flesh, drinking her until she came apart.

He rose to his full height and kissed her hard on the lips. She melted into him, wrapping her legs around his waist. She could feel his cock pressing into her entrance, and she wanted desperately to feel him inside her. To know what it was to be filled up and whole.

Hades pulled away from the kiss, wordlessly asking for permission, and she would have granted it had she not heard a soft, feminine voice call out, "Lord Hades?"

Hades twisted her so that the woman who approached could only see her back. They were chest to chest, and Persephone's legs were still wrapped around Hades's waist. She let her hand slip between them and wrapped her fingers around his hard flesh. Hades's eyes bore into hers as she touched him.

"Ha—"

Persephone recognized the voice now—it was Minthe. She couldn't see the beautiful nymph but knew by her voice that she was shocked to find them together. She had probably expected Persephone to heed her earlier warning and stay away.

"Yes, Minthe?" Hades's voice was tight. Persephone wasn't sure if it was because he was angry at being interrupted or the fact that she had just stroked him from root to tip. He was thick and hard and soft.

"We...missed you at dinner," Minthe said. "But I see that you are busy."

Another stroke.

"Very," he gritted out.

"I will let the cook know you have been thoroughly sated."

Another.

"Quite," he gritted out.

The soft click of Minthe's heels echoed and disappeared. When she was out of earshot, Persephone pushed away from Hades.

She couldn't believe she'd let this happen. She was insane—enticed by pretty words and a stunningly attractive god. She should have stayed away—not because of Minthe's warning but because of Minthe herself.

"Where are you going?" he demanded, following after her.

"How often does Minthe come to you in the bath?" she asked as she stepped out of the pool.

"Persephone."

She didn't look at him as she grabbed a towel to cover herself. She reached for the peplos and the crown Ian had made for her.

"Look at me, Persephone."

She did.

He hadn't quite exited the pool but stood on the steps, his feet and calves submerged. He was huge—his body and his erection.

"Minthe is my assistant."

"Then she can assist you with your need," she said, looking right at his cock. She started to move away, but Hades reached for her and pulled her to him.

"I don't want Minthe," he growled.

"I don't want you."

Hades tilted his head to the side, and his eyes flashed. "You don't…want me?"

"No," she said, but it was as if she was trying to convince herself, especially since Hades's eyes had dropped to her lips.

"Do you know all of my powers, Persephone?" he asked, finally leveling his gaze with hers.

It was really hard to think when he was so close,

and she looked at him warily, wondering what he was getting at. "Some of them."

"Enlighten me."

She recalled the passage she'd read about the Lord of the Dead's magic. "Illusion."

As she spoke, he leaned in, lightly kissing the column of her neck. "Yes."

"Invisibility?"

A press of his tongue in the hollow of her throat. "Very valuable."

"Charm?" she breathed.

"Hmm." The hum of his words vibrated against her skin, lower this time, closer to her breast. "But it doesn't work on you, does it?"

"No." She swallowed hard.

"You seem to not have heard of one of my most valuable talents." He pulled the towel down, exposing her breasts, and took one tight bud between his teeth, sucking until a guttural sound escaped her mouth. He pulled back and leveled his gaze with hers. "I can taste lies, Persephone. And yours are as sweet as your skin."

She pushed at him, and he took a step back. "This was a mistake." That part, she believed. She had come here to meet the terms of her contract. How had she ended up naked in a pool with the God of the Dead? Persephone grabbed her clothes from the floor and moved up the steps.

"You might believe this was a mistake," he said, and she paused but didn't turn to look at him. "But you want me. I was inside you. I tasted you. That is a truth you will never escape."

She shivered and ran.

CHAPTER XVII
The Olympian Gala

Persephone couldn't sleep.

Unspent energy coursed through her veins, making her body feel flushed beneath the blankets. She pushed them off but found little relief. Her thin cotton night gown was like a weight against her skin, and when she moved, the fabric brushed against her sensitive breasts. She curled her fingers into fists and clamped her thighs together to stop the pressure building in her core.

And she could think of no one else but Hades—the press of his body against hers, the heat of his kiss, the feel of his tongue tasting more than the skin of her collarbone.

She sighed, frustrated, and shifted in bed, but the pulsing didn't stop.

"This is ridiculous," she said aloud and got to her feet. She paced her room. She should be focusing on fulfilling the terms of the contract with Hades, not kissing the King of the Dead.

Stupid favor, she thought.

Each time Hades kissed her, things went further and further. Now she'd been brought to the edge of something she didn't understand—something she hadn't explored and couldn't shake.

She looked at her bed—the rumpled comforter made it appear like she'd shared it with someone. She clenched and unclenched her fists. She had to make this feeling go away or she wasn't going to sleep, and she had too much to do. She and Lexa had to go shopping and get ready for the Olympian Gala.

She made a split-second decision and stepped out of her panties. The cool air eased the tension in her core— just barely. It also made her hyperaware of the dampness between her thighs. Lying down again, she moved her legs apart and drew her fingers along her thigh until they trailed her sex. She was wet and hot, and her fingers sank into a part of her she had never touched. She gasped, arching her back as she pleasured herself. Her thumb found that sensitive place at the apex of her thighs, and she worked it the way Hades had taught her, until her body felt electric and waves of pleasure made her dizzy and unaware.

She rolled onto her knees, working herself hard, imagining it was Hades's hand in place of hers, imagining that she could feel his hard length inside her. She knew that if Minthe hadn't interrupted, she would have let Hades take her in the pool. That thought spurred her on. Her breath came harder and she moved faster.

"Tell me you're thinking about me." His voice came from the shadows—a chill breeze against a bright flame.

Persephone froze and rolled, finding Hades standing at the end of her bed. She couldn't tell what he was wearing in the dark, but she could see his eyes, and they glittered like coals in the night.

When she said nothing, he prompted, "Well?"

Her thoughts scattered. A small shaft of light fell across a cheekbone and his full lips. She wanted those lips in all the places she felt fire. She rose onto her knees and kept his gaze as she removed her nightshirt completely. Hades growled low in his throat and braced himself against the footboard of the bed.

"Yes," she breathed. "I was thinking about you."

The tension in the air thickened. Hades spoke in a growl that made Persephone's skin prick. "Don't stop on my account."

Persephone began where she left off. Hades inhaled between gritted teeth as he watched her pleasure herself. At first, she maintained eye contact, reveling in the feel of his eyes roving every inch of her skin, reveling in this sin. Soon the pleasure was too much, and her head rolled back, her hair spilling down her back, exposing her breasts for Hades's viewing.

"Come for me," he urged and then commanded again. "Come, my darling."

And she did with a strangled cry. Sweet release pulsed through her and she collapsed onto the bed. Her body shook, coming off the high. She breathed deep, inhaling the smell of pine and ash, and as she regained her scattered thoughts, the reality of her boldness descended like her mother's wrath.

Hades.

Hades was in her bedroom.

She sat up with a start, scrambling for her nightshirt to cover her bare skin. It was a little ridiculous, given what had happened between them. She started to lecture Hades on his abuse of power and breach of privacy when she discovered she was alone.

She craned her neck around the room.

"Hades?" She whispered his name, feeling both ridiculous and nervous at the same time. She pulled on her nightshirt and slipped off the bed, checking every corner of her room, but he was nowhere to be found.

Had her desire been so strong she hallucinated?

Feeling uncertain, she climbed into bed, eyes heavy, and fell asleep to the rhythmic reminder that hallucinations don't smell like pine and ash.

———

"You look like a goddess," Lexa said.

Persephone studied her red silk gown in the mirror. It was simple but fit her like a glove, accentuating the curve of her hips where the fabric gathered and then split midthigh to expose one creamy leg. A pretty black floral appliqué spilled from her right shoulder down the right side of the open back. Lexa had styled her hair for her, pulling it into a high, curled ponytail, and done her makeup, choosing a dark smoky eye. Persephone accessorized with simple gold earrings and the gold cuff she wore to cover Hades's mark. Right now, she felt the burn of it on her skin.

Persephone blushed. "Thank you."

But Lexa wasn't finished. She added, "Like…the Goddess of the Underworld."

Persephone remembered Yuri's words and the soul's hope that Hades would soon have a queen. "There is no Goddess of the Underworld."

"The spot's just vacant," Lexa said.

Persephone didn't want to talk about Hades. She would see him soon enough, and she had never felt so confused about anything in her life. She knew her attraction to him would only get her in trouble; despite hating Minthe's words, she believed them. Hades wasn't the type of god who wanted a relationship, and she already knew he didn't believe in love.

Persephone wanted love. Desperately. She'd been denied so much all her life. She wouldn't be denied love too.

Persephone shook her head, clearing those thoughts away. "How's Jaison?"

Lexa had met Jaison at La Rose. They'd exchanged numbers and had been talking ever since. He was a year older than them and a computer engineer. When Lexa talked about him, it sounded like they were complete opposites, but somehow it was working.

Lexa blushed. "I really like him."

Persephone grinned. "You deserve it, Lex."

"Thank you."

Lexa popped back into her room to finish getting ready and Persephone had just started to look for her clutch when the doorbell rang.

"I'll get it!" she called to Lexa.

When she answered, she found no one there, but a package rested on their doorstep—a white box with a red ribbon tied in a bow. She picked it up and brought it inside, looking to see if it was addressed to anyone.

She found a tag that read *Persephone*.

Inside, resting on black velvet, was a mask and a note: *Wear this with your crown.*

Persephone set it aside and pulled out a beautiful filigree gold mask. Despite its detail, it was simple and didn't cover much of her face.

"Is that from Hades?" Lexa asked, stepping into the kitchen. Persephone's mouth fell open when she saw her best friend. Lexa had chosen a strapless royal-blue taffeta gown for tonight's affair; her white mask, embellished with silver, had a poof of feathers coming out of the top right side.

"Well?" she prompted when Persephone didn't answer.

"Oh." She looked down at the mask. "No, it's not from Hades."

Persephone took the box to her room. She felt a little silly putting the crown Ian had given her on her head, but once her mask was on, she understood Hecate's instruction. The combination was striking, and she really did look like a queen.

Persephone and Lexa took a cab to the Museum of Ancient Arts. Their tickets indicated an arrival time of five thirty—an hour and a half earlier than the gods. No one wanted pictures of mortals unless they draped the arm of one of the Divine.

They waited in the back of the stuffy cab at the end of a long line of vehicles before they were finally let out at the edge of a grand set of steps covered in red carpet. Persephone was grateful for the fresh air—except that she was immediately accosted by the flash of camera lights. She felt crowded and claustrophobic, her chest tightening once again.

Attendants ushered them up the steps into the ominous museum, the facade of which was modern—made of concrete pillars and glass. Once inside, they were led down a hall lined with glittering crystals that hung on strands like lights. It was beautiful and an element Persephone did not expect.

Anticipation rose as they neared the end of the hallway and passed through a curtain of the same crystals into a richly decorated room. There were several round tables covered in black cloth and crowded with fine china, organized around a ballroom's edge—leaving space in the center for dancing. The real masterpieces decorated the center—marble statues that paid homage to the gods of Ancient Greece.

"Persephone, look." Lexa elbowed her, and she tilted her head back to study the beautiful chandelier at the center of the room. Strands of shimmering crystals draped the ceiling and gleamed like the stars in the Underworld's sky.

They found their table, snagged glasses of wine, and spent time mingling. Persephone admired Lexa's ability to make friends with anyone; she started chatting with a couple at their table and their group grew to include several more by the time a chime sounded in the room. Everyone exchanged looks, and Lexa gasped.

"Persephone, the gods are coming! Come on!" Lexa took Persephone's hand, dragging her across the floor and to a set of stairs that led to the second floor.

"Lexa, where are we going?" Persephone asked as they headed to the stairs.

"To watch the gods arrive!" Lexa said, as if that were obvious.

"But…won't we see them inside?"

"Not the point! I've watched this part on television for years. I want to see it in person tonight."

There were several exhibits on the second floor, but Lexa made a beeline for a spot on the outdoor terrace, which overlooked the entrance to the museum. There were already several people crowded around the balcony's edge to get a look at the Divine as they arrived, but Persephone and Lexa managed to squeeze into a small space. A mass of screaming fans and journalists crowded the sidewalks and the other side of the street, and camera lights flashed like lightning all around.

"Look! There's Ares!" Lexa squealed, but Persephone's stomach turned.

She did not like Ares. He was a god who thirsted for blood and violence. He was one of the loudest voices before the Great Descent, persuading Zeus to descend to the Earth and make war upon the mortals, and Zeus had listened—ignoring the advice and wisdom of Ares's counterpart, Athena.

The God of War made his way up the steps in a gold chiton with a red cape covering one shoulder. Part of his chest was uncovered, revealing statuesque muscles and golden skin, and instead of a mask, he bore a golden helm with a red plume of feathers falling down his back. His scimitar-like horns were long, lithe, and lethal, bowing back with his feathers, completing a regal, beautiful, and frightening image.

After Ares came Poseidon. He was huge, his shoulders, chest, and arms bulging beneath the fabric of his aquamarine suit jacket. He had pretty blond hair that reminded Persephone of restless waves, and he wore a minimal mask that shimmered like the inside of a shell. She had the thought that Poseidon wanted no mystery to his presence.

Following Poseidon was Hermes, handsome in a flashy gold suit. He had dropped the glamour from his wings, and the feathers created a cloak about his body. It was the first time Persephone had seen the God of Trickery without his glamour. Upon his head, he wore a crown of gold leaves. Persephone could tell he liked walking the red carpet; he rejoiced in the attention, smiling broadly and posing. She thought about calling to him, but she didn't need to—he found her quickly, winking at her before disappearing from view.

Apollo arrived in a gold chariot pulled by white horses, recognizable at once with his dark curls and violet eyes. His skin was a burnished brown and made his white chiton glow like a flame. Instead of showing off his horns, he wore a gold crown that resembled the sun's rays. And he was accompanied by a woman Persephone recognized.

"Sybil!" she and Lexa called happily, but the beautiful blond couldn't hear them over the cries of the crowd. Journalists screamed questions at Sybil, asking for her name, demanding to know who she was, where she was from, and how long she'd been with Apollo.

Persephone admired the way Sybil handled it all. She seemed to enjoy the attention, smiling and waving, and she actually answered the questions. Her beautiful red gown shimmered as she walked beside Apollo into the museum.

Persephone recognized Demeter's vehicle—a long, white limo. Her mother went for a more modern look, choosing a lavender ball gown that dripped with pink petals. It literally looked like a garden was growing up her skirts. Tonight her hair was up, her antlers on display, and her expression grim.

Lexa leaned in and whispered to Persephone, "Something must be wrong. Demeter always works the red carpet."

Lexa was right. Her mother usually put on a fashionable and flamboyant show, smiling and waving at the crowd. Tonight, she frowned, barely glancing at the journalists when they called to her. All Persephone could think was that, whatever her mother was going through, it was all her fault.

She shook her head.

Stop, she told herself. She wasn't going to let Demeter ruin her fun. Not tonight.

The crowd grew louder as the next limo arrived, and Aphrodite stepped out wearing a surprisingly tasteful evening gown, the bodice decorated in white and pink flowers, the middle see-through with flowers trailing down into folds of tulle. She wore a headpiece of pink peonies and pearls, and her graceful gazelle horns sprouted from her head behind it. She was stunning, but the thing about Aphrodite—all the goddesses, really—was that they were warriors too. And the Goddess of Love, for whatever reason, was particularly vicious.

She waited outside her limo, and both Persephone and Lexa groaned when they saw none other than Adonis clamber from the back seat. Lexa leaned in and whispered, "Rumor has it Hephaestus didn't want her."

Persephone snorted. "You can't believe everything you hear, Lexa."

Hephaestus was not an Olympian, but he was the God of Fire. Persephone didn't know much about him except that he was quiet and a brilliant inventor. She'd heard a lot of rumors about his marriage to Aphrodite, and none of them were good—something about how Hephaestus was forced to marry Aphrodite.

The last to arrive were Zeus and Hera.

Zeus, like his brothers, was huge and wore a chiton that exposed part of his well-muscled chest. His brown hair fell in waves to his shoulders, threaded through with hints of silver-white, matching his full and well-manicured beard. He wore a golden crown that fit between a pair of ram horns that curled down around his face, fierce and terrifying.

Beside him, Hera walked with an air of grace and nobility, her long brown hair pulled over her shoulder. Her dress was beautiful but simple—black, the bodice embroidered with colorful peacock feathers. A gold circlet rested on her head, fitting perfectly around a pair of stag horns.

Though Demetri had told her Hades never arrived alongside the other gods, Persephone thought he might make an exception this time, with the evening being themed after his realm; but when the crowds began to disperse at Zeus and Hera's arrival, she realized he wasn't coming—at least not via this entrance.

"Weren't they all magnificent?" Lexa asked as she and Persephone headed inside.

They were—each and every one of them. And yet for all their style and glamour, Persephone still yearned to see one face among the crowd.

She started down the stairs and halted abruptly.

He's here. The feeling tore through her, straightening her spine. She could feel him, taste his magic. Then her eyes found what they sought, and the room was suddenly too hot.

"Persephone?" Lexa asked when she didn't move. Then she followed Persephone's stare, and it wasn't long before the whole room grew quiet.

Hades stood at the entrance, the crystal backdrop creating a beautiful and sharp contrast to his tailored black suit. The jacket was velvet with a simple red flower in the breast pocket. His hair was slick and tied in a bun at the back of his head, his beard trimmed close and sharp, and he wore a plain black mask that only covered his eyes and the bridge of his nose.

Her eyes trailed from his shiny black shoes up his tall, powerful frame and over his broad shoulders to his glittering coal eyes. He had found her too. The heat of his gaze tracked her, roving every inch of her body, and she felt like a flame exposed to a chill wind.

She might have spent all night staring at him if it wasn't for the red-haired nymph who appeared beside him. Minthe was gorgeous, dressed in an emerald gown with a sweetheart neckline. It hugged her hips and flared out, leaving a train of fabric behind her. Her neck and ears were laden with fine jewels that gleamed as the light hit them. Persephone wondered if Hades had supplied them as Minthe looped her arm through his.

Her anger burned hot, and she knew her glamour was melting. Her gaze shifted to Hades, and she glared at him. If he thought he could have her and Minthe too, he was wrong.

She downed the remainder of her wine and then looked at Lexa. "Let's find another drink."

Persephone and Lexa cut through the crowd, flagging down a server to exchange their empty glasses for full ones.

"Can you hold this?" Lexa asked. "I need the restroom."

Persephone took Lexa's glass and started to drink from her own when she heard a familiar voice behind her.

"Well, well, well, what do we have here?" She turned to find Hermes approaching through the crowd. "A Goddess of Tartarus."

Persephone raised a brow in question.

"Get it? Torture?" She gave him a blank stare, and he frowned. "Because you're torturing Hades?"

It was Persephone's turn to roll her eyes.

"Oh, come on! Why else would you wear that dress?"

"For myself," she answered a little defensively. She hadn't chosen her dress with Hades in mind; she had wanted to look beautiful and sexy and feel powerful.

This dress did all those things.

The God of Trickery lifted a brow, smirked, and conceded, "Fair. Still, the whole room noticed you were eye-fucking Hades."

"I was not—" She clamped her mouth shut, her cheeks reddening..

"Don't worry. Everyone noticed him eye-fucking you too."

Persephone rolled her eyes. "Did they also notice Minthe on his arm?"

Hermes's smile became wicked. "Someone's jealous."

She started to deny it but decided it was silly to even try. She *was* jealous, so she admitted, "I am."

"Hades isn't interested in Minthe."

"It sure doesn't look that way," she muttered.

"Trust me. Hades cares for her, but if he was interested, he would have made her his queen a long time ago."

"What's that supposed to mean?"

Hermes shrugged. "That if he loved her, he would have married her."

Persephone scoffed. "That doesn't sound like Hades. He doesn't believe in love."

"Well, who am I to say? I have only known Hades for centuries, and you—a few months."

Persephone frowned.

It had been hard for her to see Hades in any other light than the one her mother cast upon him—and it was ugly and unflattering. She had to admit, the more time she spent in the Underworld and with him, the more she was starting to question just how much truth there was to what her mother had said and the rumors spread by mortals.

Hermes nudged her with his shoulder. "Don't worry, love. When you're jealous, just make a point to remind Hades of what he's missing."

She looked at him and he kissed her cheek. The move surprised her, and Hermes laughed, calling back as he flounced away, his white wings dragging the ground like a regal cape, "Save a dance for me!"

Lexa returned just then, looking bewildered. "Um, did Hermes just kiss you on the cheek?"

Persephone cleared her throat. "Yeah."

"Do you know him?"

"I met him at Nevernight."

"And you didn't tell me?"

Persephone frowned. "I'm sorry. I just didn't think about it."

Lexa's eyes softened. "It's okay. I know things have been insane recently."

There was a reason Lexa was her best friend, and it was moments like this when Persephone felt the most thankful for her.

They cut through the crowd and returned to their table for dinner. They were served a combination of ancient and modern foods—an appetizer of olives, grapes, figs, wheat bread, and cheese, an entrée of fish, vegetables, and rice, and rich chocolate cake for dessert.

Despite the beautiful spread, Persephone found she wasn't all that hungry.

Conversation around the table wasn't lacking. The group talked about various topics including the Pentathlon and *Titans After Dark*, their conversation interrupted only when clapping began and Minthe strolled across stage to take the podium.

"Lord Hades is honored to reveal this year's charity—the Halcyon Project," she announced.

The lights in the room dimmed, and a screen lowered to play a short video about Halcyon, a new rehabilitation center specializing in free care for mortals. The video detailed statistics about the large number of accidental deaths due to overdoses, suicide rates, and other challenges mortals faced in the post-Great War era and how the Olympians had a duty to help.

They were words Persephone had spoken, repackaged for his audience.

What is this? Persephone wondered. Was this Hades's way of making fun of her? Her hands curled into fists in her lap.

Then the video ended, and the lights came up. Persephone was surprised to see Hades standing on the stage. His presence elicited cheers from the audience.

"Days ago, an article was published in *New Athens News*. It was a scathing critique of my performance as a god, but among those angry words were suggestions on how I could be better. I don't imagine the woman who wrote it expected me to take those ideas to heart, but in spending time with her, I started to see things her way." He paused to chuckle under his breath, as if recalling something they'd shared, and Persephone shivered. "I've never met anyone who was so passionate about how I was wrong, so I took her advice and initiated the Halcyon Project. As you move through the exhibit, it is my hope that Halcyon will serve as a flame in the dark for the lost."

The crowd erupted in applause, standing to honor the god. Even a few of the Divine followed, including Hermes.

It took Persephone a moment to rise to her feet. She was shocked by Hades's charity but also wary. Was he only doing this to reverse the damage she'd done to his reputation? Was he trying to prove her wrong?

Lexa shot Persephone a quizzical look.

"I know what you're thinking," Persephone said.

Lexa arched a brow. "And what am I thinking?"

"He didn't do this for me. He did this for his reputation."

"Keep telling yourself that." Lexa grinned. "I think he's besotted."

"Besotted? You've been reading too many romance novels."

Lexa walked toward the exhibit with the others at their table, but Persephone hung back, afraid to see more of the creation inspired by her. She couldn't explain her hesitation. Maybe it was because she knew she was in danger of falling for this god who her mother hated and who'd lured her into a contract she couldn't win. Maybe it was because he listened to her. Maybe it was because she had never felt more attracted to another person in her short, sheltered life.

She wandered into the exhibit slowly. The space was dimmed so the spotlight showed on the exhibits, which illustrated the plans and mission for the Halcyon Project. Persephone took her time and stopped at the center of the room to observe a small, white model of the building. The card beside it stated it was Hades's design. It was not a modern building like she had expected; it looked like a country mansion, nestled on ten acres of lush land.

She spent a long time roaming through the exhibit, reading every presentation, learning about the technology that would be incorporated into the facility. It was truly state-of-the-art.

By the time she left, people had already begun dancing. She caught sight of Lexa with Hermes and Aphrodite with Adonis. She was glad her coworker hadn't tried talking to her and had been keeping his distance from her at work.

It took her a moment, but she realized she was searching for Hades. He was not among the dancers or those in attendance at the tables. She frowned and turned to find Sybil approaching.

"Persephone." She smiled, and they hugged. "You look beautiful."

"So do you."

"What do you think of the exhibit? Marvelous, isn't it?"

"It is." She couldn't deny, it was everything she'd imagined and more.

"I knew great things would come of your union," Sybil said.

"Our…union?" Persephone echoed slowly.

"You and Hades."

"Oh, we're not together—"

"Perhaps not yet. But your colors, they're all tangled up. They have been since the night I met you."

"Colors?"

"Your paths," Sybil said. "You and Hades—it was destiny, woven by the Fates."

Persephone was speechless. Sybil was an oracle, so the words that came from her mouth were truth, but could it really be that she was fated to wed the God of the Dead? The man her mother hated?

Sybil frowned. "Are you okay?"

Persephone wasn't sure what to say.

"I'm sorry. I…should not have told you. I thought you would be happy."

"I'm not…unhappy," Persephone assured her. "I just…"

She couldn't finish her sentence. Tonight and the last few days were weighing on her, the emotions varying and intense. If she were destined to be with Hades, it explained her insatiable attraction to the god—and yet it complicated so many other things in her life.

"Will you excuse me?" She headed for the bathroom.

Once inside, safely alone, she took a few deep breaths, braced her hands on either side of the sink, and looked at herself in the mirror. She turned on the faucet, running cold water over her hands, and splashed her heated cheeks lightly, trying not to disturb her makeup. She patted her face dry and prepared to return to the floor when she heard an unfamiliar voice.

"So you are Hades's little muse?" The tone was rich, seductive—a voice that lured men and bewitched mortals. Aphrodite came into view behind her, and Persephone wasn't sure where the goddess had come from, but once she met her gaze, she found it hard to move.

Aphrodite was beautiful, and Persephone got the feeling she had met this goddess before, though she knew that was impossible. Her eyes were the color of sea foam and framed by thick lashes, her skin like cream and her cheeks lightly flushed. Her lips were of a perfect fullness and pout. Yet despite her beauty, there was something behind her expression—something that made Persephone think she was lonely and sad.

Maybe what Lexa said was true, and Hephaestus didn't want her.

"I don't know what you're talking about," Persephone said.

"Oh, don't play coy. I saw the way you looked at him. He has always been handsome. I used to tell him all he would have to do is show his face and his realm would fill with the willing and faithful."

That made Persephone feel a little sick. She didn't wish to discuss this with anyone, much less Aphrodite. "Excuse me." She tried to step around Aphrodite, but the goddess stopped her.

"But I am not finished speaking."

"You misunderstand. I don't want to speak to you."

The Goddess of Spring pushed past Aphrodite and left the bathroom, snatching a glass of champagne from a server and finding a spot to watch the dancers. She considered leaving; Jaison had already agreed to pick Lexa up, as she was planning to spend the night at his house.

Just when she had decided to call the cab, she felt Hades's approach. She straightened, preparing for his closeness, but did not turn to face him.

"Anything to critique, Lady Persephone?" His voice rumbled low in his throat like a heady spell.

"No," she whispered and looked to her right. She still couldn't see him, even in her peripheral. "How long have you been planning the Halcyon Project?"

"Not long."

"It will be beautiful."

She felt him lean closer. She was surprised when his fingers brushed along her shoulder, tracing the edge of the black appliqué. Now and then, he touched skin to skin, and she shivered.

"A touch of darkness." His fingers tracked down her arm and threaded through hers. "Dance with me."

She didn't pull away and instead turned to face him. He never failed to take her breath away, but there was a gentleness to his face that made her heart hammer in her chest. "All right."

Eyes tracked them, curious and surprised, as Hades led her onto the floor. Persephone did her best to ignore the stares and instead focused on the god beside her. He was so much taller, so much bigger, and when he turned to face her, she was reminded of how he'd touched her in his pool.

His fingers remained twined with hers as the other hand landed on her hip. She didn't take her eyes from his as he drew her close, growling low under his breath as they moved together. He guided her, and each brush of their bodies inflamed her. For a while, neither of them spoke, and Persephone wondered if Hades found it hard to speak for the same reasons she did.

That was probably why she chose to fill the silence with her next comment. "You should be dancing with Minthe."

Hades's lips thinned. "Would you prefer that I dance with her?"

"She's your date."

"She is not my date. She is my assistant, as I have told you."

"Your assistant doesn't arrive on your arm to a gala."

His hold on her tightened, and she wondered if he was frustrated. "You are jealous."

"I'm not jealous," she said—and she wasn't anymore. She was angry. He smirked at her denial, and she wanted to hit him. "I will not be used, Hades."

That wiped the smirk off his face. "When have I used you?"

She didn't respond.

"Answer, Goddess."

"Have you slept with her?"

It was the only question that mattered.

He stopped dancing, and those who shared the floor with them did too, watching with obvious interest. "It sounds like you are requesting a game, Goddess."

"You want to play a game?" she scoffed, stepping away from him. "Now?"

He did not answer and simply held out his hand for her to take. A few weeks ago, she would have hesitated, but tonight she'd had a few glasses of wine, her skin was hot, and this dress was uncomfortable.

Besides, she wanted answers to her questions.

She clasped his hand, and as his fingers closed over hers, he smiled wickedly before teleporting to the Underworld.

CHAPTER XVIII
A Touch of Passion

Hades appeared in his office where they'd played their game of rock paper scissors. A fire crackled in the hearth, but the heat wasn't necessary; Persephone was already an inferno from their dance, and that smile he'd offered just before they teleported hadn't helped. It had promised something sinful.

Gods. Would it ever be possible to control her body's reaction to him? She was terrible at resisting him, and maybe it was because the darkness in her responded to the darkness in him.

Hades offered her wine, and she accepted a glass while he chose his usual—whiskey.

He lifted his gaze from his drink and asked, "Hungry? You barely ate at the gala."

Persephone narrowed her eyes. "You were watching me?"

"Darling, don't pretend you weren't watching *me*. I know your gaze upon me like I know the weight of my horns."

Her cheeks colored. "No, I'm not hungry."

Not for food, anyway—but she didn't say that out loud.

He accepted this and walked to a table in front of the fireplace. It was like the one in Nevernight, and instead of sitting side by side, Hades and Persephone took up opposite ends.

A single deck of cards waited. She never imagined that a few pieces of plastic would hold so much power. These cards could take or bestow riches. They could grant freedom or become the jailer. They could answer questions and strip away dignity.

Hades took a sip from his glass and then set it down with an audible click, reaching for the cards.

"The game?" Persephone asked.

"Poker," Hades replied.

He took the cards from the box and started to shuffle them, and the sound drew Persephone's attention, as did his graceful fingers. The air in the room grew thick and heavy, and she took a breath before asking, "The stakes?"

Hades smiled. "My favorite part—tell me what you want."

A thousand things came to her at once, and all of them had to do with returning to the baths and finishing what they started. Finally, she said, "If I win, you answer my questions."

"Deal." When he finished shuffling the cards, he added, "If I win, I want your clothes."

"You want to undress me?" she asked.

He chuckled. "Darling, that's only the start of what I want to do to you."

She cleared her throat. "Is one win equal to a piece of clothing?"

"Yes." He eyed her dress, and it really wasn't fair, because it was all she had on except for her jewels. She touched her necklace where it dipped between her breasts and Hades's eyes followed. He seemed to assess her jewels.

"And...what about jewelry?" Persephone asked. "Do you consider that undressing?"

He took a sip from his drink before answering. "That depends."

"On?"

"I might decide I want to fuck you with that crown on."

She smirked. "No one said anything about fucking, Lord Hades."

"No? Pity."

She leaned over the table, and though she felt shaky inside, she managed in as steady a voice as possible, "I'll accept your bargain."

His brows rose, eyes alight. "Confident in your ability to win?"

"I'm not afraid of you, Hades."

Except that she was—afraid that she wouldn't have the strength to resist him when he came for her. She was very aware of the fluttering low in her belly, reminding her that Hades's lithe fingers had been inside her. That he had drank her passion and need from her body and he hadn't finished.

She needed him to finish.

Persephone shivered.

"Cold?" he asked as he dealt the first hand.

"Hot." She cleared her throat.

Heat pooled at her core and suddenly she couldn't get comfortable. She shifted, crossing her legs harder, smiling at Hades, hoping he couldn't tell how terribly nervous she was.

Hades laid his cards down—a pair of kings. She clamped her lips together, glaring, before she laid down her cards, already knowing she had lost. A smile tugged at the corners of his lips, and his eyes brightened with lust. He sat back, assessing. After a moment, he said, "I suppose I will take the necklace."

She reached to unclasp it, but he stopped her. "No, let me."

She hesitated but slowly dropped her hands into her lap. Hades stood and walked to her side, the click of his shoes making her heart race. He gathered her hair into his hands and drew it over her shoulder. When his fingers touched her skin, she inhaled and held her breath until he unclasped the necklace. He let one side drop, and the cool metal fell between her breasts. As he pulled it away, the chain slid along her collarbone, and his lips replaced it.

"Still hot?" he asked against her skin.

"An inferno," she breathed.

"I could free you from this hell." His lips trailed up the column of her neck and she swallowed hard.

"We're just getting started," she answered.

His breathy laugh was warm against her skin, and she felt cold when he pulled away and returned to his seat to deal another hand.

Persephone smiled when their cards were on the table and said, "I win."

Hades kept his gaze narrowed upon her. "Ask your question, Goddess. I am eager to play another hand."

She bet he was. "Have you slept with her?"

Hades's jaw tightened, and after what seemed like an eternity, he answered. "Once."

The word was like a stone, dropped right in the pit of her stomach. "How long ago?"

"A very long time ago, Persephone."

She had other questions, but the way he said her name—soft and gentle, like he really regretted having been with Minthe at all—kept her from saying anything else. It wasn't really an option anyway. He'd already given her two answers—she'd only won the right to one.

She swallowed and looked away, surprised when he added, "Are you...angry?"

She met his gaze. "Yes," she admitted. "But...I don't know why exactly."

She thought it might have something to do with the fact that she was not his first, but that was silly and irrational. Hades had existed in this world far longer than she, and to expect him to abstain from pleasure was ridiculous.

He stared at her for a moment before dealing another hand. Each snick of the cards made her more and more tense. The air in the room was thick with the deal they'd made. When he won the third round, he requested her earrings. That was slow torture, as he took them out and nibbled her earlobe. She gasped at the scrape of his teeth, clenching the edge of the table to keep from threading her hands through his hair and forcing his lips on hers.

When he sat down in front of her again, she was still trying to catch her breath. If Hades won the next round, he'd ask for the only thing she had left—her dress. She'd be naked before him, and she wasn't so sure she could withstand him undressing her.

She was spared from finding out when she won. She had another burning question.

"Your power of invisibility," she said. "Have you ever used it…to spy on me?"

Hades seemed both amused and suspicious of her question, but she was asking for a very important reason. She needed to know if he had been in her bedroom that night, or had her desire for him simply caused her to fantasize?

"No," he answered.

She was relieved. She'd been completely consumed by her own pleasure and hadn't thought twice about the appearance of Hades at the end of her bed…until after.

"And will you promise to never use invisibility to spy on me?"

Hades studied her, as if he was trying to figure out why she was asking this of him. Finally, he answered.

"I promise."

As he started to deal another hand, she asked another question. "Why do you let people think such horrible things about you?"

He shuffled the cards, and for a moment, she thought he might not answer, but then he said, "I do not control what people think of me."

"But you do nothing to contradict what they say about you," she argued.

He raised a brow. "You think words have meaning?"

She stared at him, confused, and he dealt another hand.

"They are just that—words. Words are used to spin stories and craft lies, and occasionally they are strung together to tell the truth."

"If words hold no weight for you, what does?"

Their eyes locked, and something changed in the air between them—something charged and powerful. He approached her, cards in hand, and placed them on the table—a royal flush.

Persephone stared at the cards. She had yet to reach for hers, but she didn't need to. There was no doubt in her mind that he had won this round.

"Action, Lady Persephone. Action holds weight for me."

She rose to meet him, and their lips collided. Hades's tongue twined with hers, and his hands gripped her hips. He twisted, sitting down and dragging her into his lap, drawing the straps of her dress down, cupping her breasts, squeezing her nipples until they were taut between his fingers.

Persephone gasped and bit down hard on his lip, eliciting a growl that made her shudder. His lips left hers and descended upon her breasts, licking and sucking, grazing each nipple with his teeth. Persephone clung to him, fingers twining in his hair, freeing it from its binding, pulling the strands harder the longer he worked.

Then he yanked up her dress, and he hauled her onto the table.

"I have thought of you every night since you left me in the bath," he said, spreading her legs wide, pressing in against her. "You left me desperate, swollen with need only for you," he gritted out. For a moment, she thought he might leave her desperate in return, but then he said, "But I will be a generous lover."

He lowered and kissed the inner part of her thigh, following with his swirling tongue until he reached her center. Then his hands spread her further and she felt him there—a testing tongue, then a deeper exploration, and she arched off the table, crying out. She reached for him, wishing to tangle her fingers in his dark hair, but he grabbed her wrists and held them against her sides and spoke against her. "I said I would be a generous lover, not a kind one."

She writhed against him as he worked, pressing her hips into him just to feel him deeper, and he delivered, releasing her to sink his fingers into her damp center. She couldn't stop the moans from escaping her mouth. He drove her to the edge, and she resisted, wanting to prolong this ecstasy as long as possible, but he grew fierce and wicked, and she called his name over and over again—a chant that matched his strokes until she came apart.

She had no time to collect herself. Hades reached for her, dragging her to his mouth. She tasted herself on his lips and reached for the buttons of his shirt, but Hades caught her wrists, stopping her. She was even more confused when he pulled the straps of her dress into place.

"What are you doing?" she demanded.

He dared to laugh. "Patience, darling,"

She was anything but patient—the heat between her legs had only been stoked, and she was desperate to be filled.

He gathered her into his arms and strolled out of his study into the palace halls.

"Where are we going?" she asked, hands fisted into his shirt. She was ready to rip it from his body—to see him naked before her, to know him as intimately as he knew her.

"To my chambers," he said.

"And you can't teleport?"

"I'd prefer the whole palace know we aren't meant to be disturbed."

Persephone blushed. She only shared half of that wish—and it was to not be disturbed.

He held her close as he walked, and the reality of why they were going to his bedroom descended. There was no returning from this—she'd known that from the beginning. The evening they shared in the pool had been one of the most exhilarating experiences of her life, but this night would be one of the most devastating.

Their darkness would come together. After tonight, this god would always be a part of her.

After they were inside Hades's chambers, he seemed to sense the change in her thoughts. He lowered her to the ground, keeping her close. She fit against his body perfectly, and she had the fleeting thought that they were always meant to come together like this

"We don't have to do this," he said.

She reached for the lapels of his jacket and helped him out of it. "I want you. Be my first. Be my everything."

It was all the encouragement he needed. Hades's lips met hers—softly at first, and then they came together more urgently. He tore away and turned her around, unzipping her dress. The red silk fell away, puddling on the floor at her feet. She still wore the heels but stood naked before him.

Hades groaned and walked around to face her. His shoulders were bunched, his hands fisted, and his jaw clenched, and she knew he was doing everything in his power to maintain control. "You are beautiful, my darling."

He kissed her again, and Persephone fumbled with his shirt until Hades took over, making quick work of the buttons, then he reached for her, but she took a step back. For a moment, Hades's eyes darkened, and then Persephone said, "Drop your glamour."

He looked at her curiously.

She shrugged a shoulder. "You want to fuck me with this crown. I want to fuck a god."

His smirk was devilish, and he answered, "As you wish."

Hades's glamour evaporated like smoke curling into the air. The black of his eyes melted to an electrifying blue, and two black gazelle horns spiraled out of his head. He seemed bigger than ever, filling the whole space with his dark presence.

She had no time to enjoy the look of him, because as soon as his glamour fell, he reached for her and lifted her off the floor, lowering her on the bed. He kissed her lips again, then her neck, trailing his tongue over one nipple and the other. He stayed there for a while, working each into a tight bud. Persephone tried to reach for the button of his pants, but he pulled away, laughing.

"Eager for me, Goddess?" He kissed down her stomach and then her thighs. He sat back on his knees, and Persephone thought he was going to press his mouth to her core once more, but instead he stood, removing each of her shoes and then the rest of his clothing.

She would never tire of seeing him naked. He was sin and sex, and his smell was all around her, clinging to her hair and to her skin. Her eyes fell to his arousal, thick and swollen. She reached for it, unafraid, unthinking, and as her hands surrounded his hot shaft, he hissed.

She liked the sound. She worked him—up and down, from root to tip, and with each groan that escaped his mouth, Persephone grew more confident. She leaned forward and pressed a kiss to the tip of his cock.

"Fuck."

And then she took him into her mouth and Hades braced himself against her shoulders. She didn't know what to do—she had never done this before, but she liked the taste of salt on his skin. Her teeth grazed the top of his head as she moved him in and out, and soon his hips moved too—harder and faster until he pulled her away.

Confused, she asked, "Did I do something wrong?"

His laugh was dark, his voice husky, his eyes predatory. "No."

His hand gripped the back of her neck and he kissed her, his tongue reaching deep before he tore away and said, "Tell me you want me."

"I want you." She was breathless and desperate.

He pushed her back and climbed over her, covering her body with his, stretching out so she felt the press of his erection against her stomach.

"Tell me you lied," he said.

"I thought words meant nothing."

He gave her a bruising kiss, and his touch lifted heat from her skin, searing a path everywhere he went.

"Your words matter," he said. "Only yours."

She wrapped her legs around his waist and drew him against her heat.

"Do you want me to fuck you?" he asked.

She nodded.

"Tell me," he said. "You used words to tell me you didn't want me. Now use words to say you do."

"I want you to fuck me," she said.

He groaned and kissed her hard before teasing her by moving his cock up and down her damp entrance. She pulled him toward her, urging him inside, and Hades laughed. She growled, frustrated.

"Patience, darling. I had to wait for you."

"I'm sorry," she said, her voice quiet, sincere—and then he filled her completely.

She cried out, head falling back into her pillow. She covered her mouth to keep quiet, but Hades removed her hand, holding her wrists above her.

"No, let me hear this," he growled.

He impaled her over and over again. There was nothing slow or gentle about his movements, and with each thrust, he spoke, and she cried in ecstasy.

"You left me desperate," he said, pulling out until he was barely inside her. Then he thrust into her hard.

"I have thought about you every night since."

Thrust.

"And each time you said you didn't want me, I tasted your lies."

Thrust.

"You are mine."

Thrust.

"Mine."

He moved deeper and faster, pumping into her. She

lost herself in him, and pressure built in her stomach and exploded. Hades came soon after. She felt him pulse inside her, and then he withdrew, a gush of warmth spreading over her thigh. He collapsed against her, sweat-soaked and breathless.

After a moment, he drew back, pressing kisses to her face—her eyes, her cheeks, her lips. "You are a test, Goddess. A trial offered to me by the Fates."

She couldn't think straight enough to respond. Her legs felt shaky, and she was gloriously exhausted.

When Hades moved, she reached for him, "No. Don't leave."

He chuckled, kissing her once more. "I will come back, my darling."

He was gone a moment and returned with a damp cloth. He cleaned her, then moved her, fitting her back against his chest and pulling her close. Wrapped in his warmth, she fell asleep.

Sometime later, Persephone woke to Hades grinding into her from behind, his arousal hard and thick against her bottom. As he gripped her hips, he trailed kisses up her neck. Her need for him overpowered her exhaustion, and she turned her head, meeting his soft lips, desperate to taste him again.

Hades guided her onto her back and climbed on top of her, kissing her until she was breathless. She tried reaching for him, wishing to twine her fingers into his soft hair, but he restrained her, pinning her wrists over her head. He used the position to his advantage, nibbling her earlobes, kissing down her neck and grazing her nipples with his teeth. Each sensation drew a breathy moan from Persephone's throat, and the sounds seemed to fuel Hades's lust. He made his way to her thighs and wasted no time parting her legs and lapping at her wet heat. His fingers joined, thrusting into her hard and fast, working her until her moans came in quick succession, until she could hardly take in breath, and when she came, it was with his name on her lips—the only word she'd spoken since this began.

Hades said nothing, lost in a haze of want, and rose to cover her once more, positioning himself at her entrance. He sank deep, his thrusts rough and wild.

At some point, he lifted her as if she weighed nothing. Sitting back on his heels and gripping her hips, he moved her up and down his shaft. The feel of him inside her was perfection, and she grew hungry to feel him deeper and faster. She wrapped her arms around his neck and moved against him. Their mouths came together, teeth scraping, tongues searching. Together, they rode wave after wave of mindless sensation and came together, collapsing in a heap of limbs and sweat and hard breaths.

Before she fell asleep again, she had the fleeting thought that, if this was her fate, she would gladly claim it.

CHAPTER XIX
A Touch of Power

Persephone woke to find Hades asleep beside her. He lay on his back, black sheets covering the lower half of his body, leaving the contours of his stomach exposed. His hair spilled over his pillow, his jaw covered in stubble, and she longed to reach out and trace his perfect brows, nose, and lips. But she didn't want to wake him, and the move seemed too intimate.

She realized that sounded ridiculous considering what had taken place between them last night. Still, touching him without invitation or initiation seemed like something a lover might do, and Persephone did not feel like Hades's lover.

She wasn't even sure she wanted to be a lover. She'd always imagined falling in love as something heady, almost shy—but things with the Lord of the Dead had been anything but shy. Their attraction was carnal and greedy and burning. It stole her breath, crowded her mind, invaded her body.

Heat started to build in the pit of her stomach, igniting the desire she'd felt so strongly yesterday. *Breathe*, she told herself, willing the warmth to dissipate.

After a moment, she slipped out of bed, found the black robe Hades had let her borrow when she'd first come to the Underworld, and tugged it on. Wandering onto the balcony, she let herself take a deep breath, and in the quiet of the day, the full weight of what she had done with Hades crashed down on her. She had never been so confused or afraid.

Confused because her feelings for the god were all tangled up. She was angry with him, mostly because of the contract, but otherwise intrigued; and the way he'd made her feel last night—well, nothing compared. He had worshipped her. He had laid himself bare, admitting his desire for her. Together, they had been vulnerable and senseless and savage. She didn't need to look in the mirror to know that her skin was discolored in all the places Hades had bit and sucked and gripped. He had explored parts of her no one else had.

And that was where the fear came in.

She was losing herself in this god, in this world beneath her own. Before, when all they'd shared was a moment of weakness in the baths, she might have sworn to stay away and meant it; but if she said it now, it would just be a lie.

Whatever was between them, it was powerful. She had felt it the moment she laid eyes on the god. Knew it deep in her soul. Every interaction since then had been a desperate attempt to ignore their truth—that they were meant to come together—and Sybil had confirmed that last night.

It was destiny, woven by the Fates.

But Persephone knew there were many such alliances, and being meant for each other didn't mean perfection or even happiness. Sometimes it was chaos and strife—and given how tumultuous her life had been since she met Hades, nothing good would come from their love.

Why was she thinking about love?

She pushed those thoughts away. This wasn't about love. It was about satisfying the electric attraction that had been building between them since that first night in Nevernight. Now it was done. She wouldn't let herself regret it; instead, she would embrace it. Hades had made her feel powerful. He had made her feel like the goddess she was supposed to be—and she had enjoyed every bit of it.

She took another breath as heat rose from the bottom of her stomach. As she inhaled the crisp Underworld air, she felt something...different.

It was warm. It was a pulse. It was *life*.

It felt distant, like a memory she knew existed but couldn't quite recall, and when it started to fade, she chased it.

Descending the steps into the garden, she halted on the black stone, her heart racing. She tried to calm herself again, holding her breath until her chest grew tight.

Just when she thought she'd lost it, she felt the featherlight pulse at the edges of her senses.

Magic.

It was magic. *Her* magic!

She stepped off the path and wandered into the gardens. Surrounded by roses and peonies, she closed her eyes and breathed deep. The calmer she became, the more life she felt around her. It warmed her skin and soaked deep into her veins, as heady as the lust she felt for Hades.

"Are you well?"

Persephone's eyes flew open, and she turned to face the God of the Dead a few paces behind her. She'd stood beside him often enough, but this morning, in the garden surrounded by flowers and wearing only a wrap around his waist and still in his Divine form, he seemed to swallow her vision. Her eyes fell from his face to his chest and down, tracing all the planes of his body she'd touched and tasted last night.

"Persephone?" His voice took on a lustful tone, and when she met his gaze again, she knew he was restraining himself. She managed a smile.

"I'm well," she said.

Hades took a breath and approached her, clasping her chin between his fingers. She thought he would kiss her, but instead he asked, "You are not regretting our night together?"

"No!" Her eyes lowered, and she repeated herself quietly. "No."

Hades's thumb passed over her bottom lip. "I don't think I could handle your regret."

He kissed her, his fingers threaded through her hair, and cupped the back of her head, holding her to him. It wasn't long before her robe parted, leaving her most sensitive skin exposed to the morning. Hades's hands trailed down her body, gripping her thighs, and he lifted and thrusted into her. She gasped and held him tightly, moving against him harder and faster, feeling wave after wave of pleasure rush through her body while life fluttered around her.

It was intoxicating.

Persephone buried her face in the crook of Hades's neck, biting down hard as she shattered in his arms. A growl tore through his throat, and he pumped into her harder until she felt him pulse inside her. He held her a moment while they breathed hard against each other before he withdrew and helped her to the ground. She held on to him, legs shaky, fearing she might fall. Hades seemed to notice and picked her up, cradling her against him.

Persephone closed her eyes. She didn't want him to see what was in them. It was true she didn't regret last night or this morning, but she had questions—not only for him but for herself. What were they doing? What did this night mean for them? Their future? Her contract? What would she do the next time things started to go too far?

They returned to Hades's room and showered, but when Persephone went to pick up her discarded dress, she frowned. It was far too dressy to wear around the Underworld, and she planned to stay a while. "Do you... have something I can wear?"

Hades gave her an appraising look. "What you have on will be just fine."

She gave him a pointed look. "You'd rather I wander your palace naked? In front of Hermes and Charon—"

Hades's jaw tightened. "On second thought—" He disappeared and returned in an instant, carrying a length of fabric in a beautiful shade of green. "Will you allow me to dress you?"

She swallowed hard. She was getting used to these kinds of words coming out of his mouth, but still, it was odd. He was ancient and powerful and gorgeous. He was known for his ruthless assessment of souls and impossible bargains, and yet he was asking to dress her after a night of passionate sex.

Would wonders never cease?

She nodded, and Hades set to work wrapping the fabric around her body. He took his time, using the task as an excuse to touch and kiss and tease, and by the time he finished, her body was flush. It took everything in her power to let him pull away. She wanted to demand that he finish what he started, but then they would never leave this room.

He kissed her before they left his chambers for a beautiful dining room. It was almost a little ridiculous; several chandeliers cut through the middle of the ceiling, and a gold coat of arms hung on the wall over an ornate throne-like chair at the end of an ebony banquet table crowded with chairs. It was a banquet hall for more than just her and Hades.

"You actually eat in here?" Persephone asked.

Hades's lips quirked. "Yes, but not often. I usually take my breakfast to go."

Hades pulled out a chair and helped Persephone sit. Once he took his seat, a couple of nymphs entered the dining hall with trays of fruit, meat, cheese, and bread. Minthe followed them, and as the nymphs placed the food on the table, she came to stand between Persephone and Hades.

"My lord," Minthe said. "You have a full schedule today."

"Clear the morning," he said without looking at her.

"It's already eleven, my lord," Minthe said tightly.

Hades filled his plate and, when he finished, looked at Persephone. "Are you not hungry, darling?"

Though he had been calling her *darling* since they met, he'd never said it in front of anyone. A glance at Minthe told her the nymph didn't like it.

"No," she said. "I…usually only drink coffee for breakfast."

He stared at her for a moment, and then, with a flick of his wrist, a steaming cup of coffee appeared before her. "Cream? Sugar?"

"Cream." She smiled, and when it was given, she cupped her hands around the mug. "Thank you."

"What are your plans today?" Hades asked.

It took Persephone a moment to realize he was talking to her. "Oh, I need to write—"

She stopped abruptly.

"Your article?" Hades finished. She could not tell what he was thinking, but she felt it wasn't good.

"I will be along shortly, Minthe," Hades said at length, and Persephone's heart fell. "Leave us."

"As you wish, my lord." There was a note of amusement to Minthe's voice that Persephone hated.

When they were alone, Hades asked, "So you will continue to write about my faults?"

"I don't know what I'm going to write this time," she said. "I…"

"You what?"

"I hoped I might be able to interview a few of your souls."

"The ones on your list?"

271

"I don't want to write about the Olympian Gala or the Halcyon Project," she explained. "All the other newspapers will jump on those stories."

Hades stared at her for a long moment, then wiped his mouth with his napkin, pushed away from the table, and stood, striding toward the exit. Persephone followed. "I thought we agreed we wouldn't leave each other when we're angry? Didn't you request that we work through it?"

Hades twisted toward her. "It's just that I'm not particularly excited that my lover is continuing to write about my life."

She blushed at hearing him call her lover. She thought about correcting him but decided against it. "It's my assignment. I can't just stop."

"It wouldn't have been your assignment if you had heeded my request."

Persephone crossed her arms over her chest. "You never request anything, Hades. Everything is an order. You ordered me not to write about you. You said there would be consequences."

His face changed then, and the look he gave her was more endearing than angry. It made her heart flutter. "And yet you went through with it anyway."

She opened her mouth to deny it, because the reality was that she hadn't—Adonis had, and despite the fact that she really disliked the creep of a mortal, she didn't want Hades to know he was responsible. In truth, she'd rather deal with Adonis herself.

"I should have expected it," he said, drawing his finger along her jaw, tipping her head back. "You are defiant and angry with me."

"I'm not…" she started to say, but then Hades's hands cupped her face.

"Shall I remind you that I can taste lies, darling?" He brushed her bottom lip with his thumb. "I could spend all day kissing you."

"No one's stopping you," she said, surprised by the words that came out of her mouth. Where was this boldness coming from?

But Hades only chuckled and pressed his lips to hers.

CHAPTER XX
Elysium

It was an hour or so later when Hades walked Persephone outside. He held her hand, fingers laced, and called a name into the air. "Thanatos!"

Persephone was surprised when a god dressed in black appeared before them. He was young and his hair was white, which made the rest of his features stand out in vivid color—sapphire eyes and bloodred lips. Two short black gayal horns, slightly curved and coming to sharp points, stuck out on the sides of his head. Large black wings, heavy and ominous, sprouted from his back.

"My lord, my lady." Thanatos bowed to them.

"Thanatos, Lady Persephone has a list of souls she'd like to meet. Would you mind escorting her?"

"I would be honored, my lord."

Hades looked at her then. "I will leave you in Thanatos's care."

"Will I see you later?" she asked.

"If you wish." He lifted her hand to his lips. She

blushed when Hades kissed her knuckles, which seemed so silly considering all the places those lips had been.

Hades must have thought the same thing, because he laughed quietly and vanished.

Persephone turned to face Thanatos, meeting those striking blue eyes. "So you're Thanatos."

The god smiled. "The very one."

She was struck by how kind and soothing his voice sounded. She instantly felt comfortable with him, and there was a part of her brain that realized it must be one of his gifts—to comfort the mortals whose souls he was about to harvest.

"I confess, I have been eager to meet you," Thanatos added. "The souls speak well of you."

She smiled. "I enjoy being with them. Until I visited Asphodel, I didn't have a very peaceful view of the Underworld."

His smile was sympathetic, as if he understood. "I imagine so. The Upperworld has made death evil, and I suppose I cannot blame them."

"You're very understanding," she observed.

"Well, I do spend a lot of time in the company of mortals, and always in their worst or hardest moments."

She frowned. It seemed sad that this was Thanatos's existence, but the God of Death quickly soothed, "Do not mourn for me, my lady. The shadow of death is often a comfort to the dying."

She decided she really liked Thanatos.

"Shall we find these souls you wish to speak to?" he asked, quickly changing the subject.

"Yes, please." She handed him the list she'd made

her first day at *New Athens News* when she'd begun her research into Hades. "Can you take me to any of these?"

Thanatos's brows came together as he read the list, and he grimaced. She did not think that was a good sign. "If I may, why these souls?"

"I believe they all had something in common before they died: a contract with Hades."

"They did." It surprised Persephone that he knew so much. "And you wish to…interview them? For your paper?"

"Yes." Persephone found herself answering hesitantly, suddenly unsure. Did Thanatos share Minthe's view of her?

The God of Death folded the piece of paper and said, "I will take you to them. Though I think you will be disappointed."

She didn't have time to ask why, as Thanatos stretched his wings, folded them around her, and teleported.

When he released her from his feathery hold, they were at the center of a field. The first thing Persephone noticed was the silence; it was different here, a tangible thing that had weight and pressed against her ears. The grass beneath her feet was golden and the trees tall and lush, heavy with fruit, completing the image of beauty and peace. "Where are we?"

"These are the Elysium Fields. The list of names you offered, those souls reside here."

"I…don't understand. Elysium is paradise."

The Elysium Fields were known as the Isle of the Blessed, reserved for heroes and those who lived a pure and righteous life dedicated to the gods. That was far from the truth of the souls on the list she'd given Thanatos.

These were people who had struggled in life, who had made bad decisions—one of those being a bargain with Hades—that ended their lives.

Thanatos offered her a small smile, as if he understood her confusion. "It is a paradise. It is a sanctuary. It is where the pained come to heal in peace and solitude. It is where Hades sent the souls on the list you gave once they died."

She looked out at the plain where several souls lingered. They were beautiful phantoms, dressed in white and glowing—but more than that, she knew this place was healing them. Her heart felt lighter, unburdened by the frustration and anger she felt over the last couple of months. "Why? Did he feel guilty?"

Thanatos shot her a confused look.

"He is the reason they died," she explained. "He made a bargain with them, and when they couldn't fulfill it, he took their souls."

"Ah," Thanatos said. "You misunderstand. Hades does not decide when souls come to the Underworld. The Fates do."

"But he is the Lord of the Underworld. He makes the contracts!"

"Hades is the Lord of the Underworld, but he is not death, nor is he destiny. You may see a bargain with a mortal, but Hades is really bargaining with the Fates. He can see the thread of each human's life, knows when their soul is burdened, and wishes to change the trajectory. Sometimes the Fates weave a new future. Sometimes they cut the thread."

"Surely he has influence?"

Thanatos shrugged. "It is a balance. We all understand

that. Hades cannot save every soul, and not every soul wants to be saved."

She was quiet for a long moment, realizing now that she hadn't really been listening to Hades at all. He had told her before that the Fates were involved in his decision-making and that it was a balance—a give and take. Yet she hadn't thought twice about his words.

She hadn't thought about a lot of things.

But that didn't change the fact that he could offer mortals a better path to overcome their struggles. What it did mean was that Hades's intentions were far nobler than anything Persephone had given him credit for.

"Why didn't he tell me?" she snapped.

Why did he let her think those horrible things about him? Did he want her to hate him?

Thanatos kept smiling. "Lord Hades is not in the habit of trying to convince the world he is a good god."

"*You are the worst sort of god,*" she'd told him.

Her chest tightened at the memory, and she could not reconcile her feelings. While she was relieved Hades was not as monstrous or uncaring as she first believed, why had he drawn her into a contract? What did he see when he looked at her?

Thanatos offered his arm to Persephone, and she accepted. They strolled through the field unnoticed; unlike Asphodel, the souls here were quiet and content to be alone. It didn't even seem like they realized two gods walked among them.

"Do they speak?" she asked.

"Yes, but souls who reside in Elysium must drink from the Lethe. They cannot have memories from their time in the Upperworld if they are to reincarnate."

"How can they heal if they don't possess memory?"

"No soul has ever healed by dwelling on the past," Thanatos answered.

"When do they reincarnate?"

"When they heal."

"And how long does it take for them to heal?"

"It varies…months, years, decades, but there is no rush," Thanatos answered. "All we have is time."

She supposed that was true of all souls—living or dead.

"There are a few souls who will incarnate within the week," Thanatos said. "I believe the souls in Asphodel are planning a celebration. You should join them."

"What about you?" Persephone asked.

He offered a small laugh. "I do not think the souls wish to have their reaper join them for a celebration."

"How do you know?"

Thanatos opened his mouth, hesitated, then admitted, "I suppose I don't."

"I think you should go. We all should, even Hades."

Thanatos's brows rose and a smile broke out across his face. "You can count on my presence, my lady, though I cannot speak for Lord Hades."

They walked a little while in silence, and then Persephone said, "Hades does so much for his souls… except live alongside them."

Thanatos did not answer immediately, and Persephone paused, facing the God of Death.

"When Asphodel celebrated him, he told me he didn't go because he wasn't worthy of their celebration," she added. "Why?"

"Lord Hades carries many burdens, as we all do. The heaviest of them is regret."

"Regret for what?"

"That he was not always so generous."

Persephone let that comment sink in. So Hades regretted his past and therefore refused to celebrate his present? That was ridiculous and damaging. Maybe the reason he never tried to change what others thought of him was because he believed all the things people said.

He probably believed *her*, which was why her words were so important to him.

"Come, my lady," Thanatos said. "I will show you back to the palace."

As the two walked, she asked, "How long has it been since he hosted a party at the palace?"

Thanatos's brows rose. "I don't know that he ever has."

That was about to change—and so was Hades's opinion of himself.

Before Persephone left the Underworld, she stopped to let Hecate know her plans and also of her newfound ability to sense life.

Hecate's eyes widened. "You're sure?"

Persephone nodded. "Can you help me, Hecate?"

She was glad to sense magic, but she had no idea how to harness it. If she could learn how to use it and fast, she could fulfill the terms of her contract with Hades.

"My dear," Hecate said. "Of course I'll help you."

CHAPTER XXI
A Touch of Insanity

When Persephone returned home on Sunday, she stayed up late and worked on her article, finishing around five o'clock in the morning. She decided to write about the gala and the Halcyon Project and started the article with an apology, writing, *I was wrong about the God of the Underworld. I accused him of carelessly engaging mortals in bargains that led to their deaths. What I have learned is that these contracts are far more complicated and the motives far more pure.*

She stood by her original statement that Hades should offer help in a different manner but acknowledged that that Halcyon Project was, in fact, a direct result of a conversation they'd had, adding, *When other gods might retaliate for my candid review of their character, Lord Hades asked questions, listened, and changed. What more could we want from our gods than that?*

Persephone laughed to herself. Never in her lifetime would she have thought she'd suggest that Hades was the standard by which all other gods should be measured, but the more she learned about him, the more she felt that might be the case. Not that Hades was perfect—in fact, it was his imperfection and willingness to acknowledge it that made him a god unlike any other.

You're still in a contract with him, she reminded herself before she put the Lord of the Underworld on too high a pedestal.

After her visit to Elysium and her conversation with Thanatos, she'd wanted to ask Hades so many questions yesterday—*Why me? What did you see when you looked at me? What weakness did you want to challenge in me? What part of me were you hoping to save? What destiny did the Fates forge for me that you wanted to challenge?*

But she hadn't gotten the chance. When Hades had returned to the Underworld, he'd gathered her into his arms and taken her to bed, shattering all rational thoughts.

Coming home had been exactly what she needed—it had given her the distance to remind herself that if she wanted...whatever was between her and Hades to work, the contract had to end.

After a couple hours of sleep, Persephone got ready for the day; she had to put in a few hours at her internship and then head to class. While she was in the kitchen making coffee, she heard the front door bang open.

"I'm back!" Lexa called.

Persephone smiled and poured her a cup, sliding it across the counter as she came into view. "How was your weekend?"

Lexa beamed. "Magical."

Persephone snorted, but she could relate—she wondered if she and her best friend had similar experiences.

"I'm happy for you, Lex." She'd said it before, and she'd say it many times after.

"Thanks for the coffee." Lexa started toward her room but paused. "Oh, I meant to ask. How was the Underworld?"

Persephone froze. "What do you mean?"

"Persephone. I know you left with Hades Saturday night. It's all anyone could talk about—the girl in red, stolen to the Underworld."

She paled. "Did anyone—no one knew it was me, right?"

Lexa looked a little sympathetic. "I mean, Hades had just announced the Halcyon Project, which was inspired by you, so people came to their own conclusions."

Persephone groaned. That was all she needed, more press on her supposed relationship with Hades.

A very dark and very loud part of her mind suddenly wondered if Hades's behavior at the gala had been intentional. Was he looking for a way to divert attention from his antics by shining a spotlight on a relationship? And if that were the case, was she just a pawn?

"I know you'd rather not acknowledge whatever's going on between you and Hades," Lexa added, "but I'm your best friend. You can tell me anything. You know that, right?"

"I know, I know. I really didn't intend to leave with him. I was going to call a cab and then..." Her voice trailed away.

"He swept you off your feet?" Lexa waggled her brows, and Persephone couldn't help but laugh. "Just tell me one thing. Did he kiss you?"

Persephone blushed and admitted, "Yes."

Lexa squealed. "Oh my gods, Persephone! You have to tell me everything!"

Persephone looked at the clock. "I have to go—lunch with Sybil?"

"I wouldn't miss it for the world."

Despite leaving her apartment late, Persephone took her time walking to work, reveling in the feel of life around her. She was still in disbelief. Her magic had surfaced, and it had awakened in the Underworld. She still had no idea what to do with it—she didn't know how to harness what she felt or use it to create illusions, but she planned to meet Hecate this evening for lessons.

When she arrived at the Acropolis, Demetri asked to see her. He offered a few edits to her article, and before she sat down to work on them, she went into the break room to get some coffee.

"Hey, Persephone," Adonis said as he joined her. He put on his most charming smile, as if it could erase the past and build a whole new future.

She glanced at him. "I don't really feel like talking to you."

She didn't need to look at him to know he had stopped grinning. He was probably shocked his smile hadn't worked its usual magic. "You're really just gonna stop talking to me? You know that's impossible. We work together."

"I'll still be professional," she said.

"You aren't being very professional right now."

"Actually, I don't have to make small talk with you to be professional. I just have to get my job done."

"Or you could forgive me," Adonis said. "I was drunk, and I barely touched you."

Barely touched? He had pulled her hair and attempted to force her mouth open. Besides that, his touch—no matter how light or aggressive—was completely unwanted.

Persephone ignored him, leaving the break room. He followed.

"Is this about Hades?" he demanded. "Are you sleeping with him?"

"That is not an appropriate question, Adonis, and it's also none of your business."

"He told you to stay away from me, didn't he?"

Persephone turned to face him. She'd never met anyone who was so oblivious to their own wrongdoing. "I am capable of making my own decisions. I thought you would remember that after you stole my article," she snapped. "But just so we're clear, I don't want to talk to you because you are a manipulator, you never take responsibility for your mistakes, and you kissed me when I specifically told you not to, which makes you a predator."

There was a heavy pause as Persephone's words hit home. It took Adonis a moment, but he finally seemed to understand what she was saying. His nostrils flared, and he clenched his fists, knuckles turning white.

"You bitch!"

"Adonis." Demetri's voice cut through their conversation like a whip. Stunned, Persephone turned to see her boss standing outside his office. She had never thought him capable of the anger she saw on his face. "A moment."

Adonis looked stricken, and he glared at Persephone as if she were to blame.

When the mortal disappeared into Demetri's office, her boss gave her an apologetic look before following him in and closing the door. Ten minutes later, a security officer arrived on the floor and walked into Demetri's office. After a moment, the officer, Demetri, and Adonis emerged. Adonis was flanked by the two and as he passed Persephone's desk, he was rigid, his hands fisted. He muttered under his breath, "This is ridiculous. She's a snitch."

"You told on yourself," Demetri said.

They disappeared in the direction of his desk and reappeared leading Adonis to the elevator with a box in his hands.

When Demetri returned, he approached Persephone's desk. "You have a moment?"

"Yeah," she said quietly and followed him into his office.

Once inside, she took a seat, and Demetri did the same. "Want to tell me what happened?"

She explained—only the part where Adonis stole her article and submitted it without her knowledge, because that was the only part that really counted at work.

"Why didn't you tell me?"

Persephone shrugged. "I wanted to submit it anyway. It just happened faster than I anticipated."

Demetri grimaced. "In the future, I want you to come to me when you feel wronged, Persephone. Your satisfaction in this job is important to me."

"I...appreciate that."

"And I will understand if you want to cease writing articles about Hades."

She stared at him. "You would? But why?"

"I won't pretend that I'm not aware of the frustration and stress it has caused you," he said, and she had to admit, she was a little surprised he'd noticed. "You became famous overnight and you're not even finished with college yet."

She let her eyes fall to her hands, twisting her fingers nervously. "But what about the readership?"

Demetri shrugged. "That's the thing about news. There's always something new."

Persephone managed a small laugh and considered things. If she stopped writing now, she didn't feel she would have done Hades's story justice. She'd started out with such a harsh critique of him, and, maybe selfishly, she wanted to explore other facets of his character. She realized she didn't have to write an article to do that, but a part of her wanted to show Hades in the light. She wanted others to see him as she had come to—as kind and caring.

"No," she said. "It's okay. I want to continue with the series...for now."

Demetri smiled. "Alright, but if you wish to end it, I want you to let me know."

She agreed and went back to her desk, unable to focus on her tasks. She still felt a little shaky from her encounter with Adonis. In truth, she'd hoped it wouldn't come to this, but after today, she knew it was the right decision. She didn't think she would forget the look on his face—she'd seen and felt his rage.

After work, she headed to campus. During class, she found it harder to concentrate. Her sleepless night was catching up to her, and though she took notes, at the end of class, when she tried to read what she had written, it was just scribbles.

She really needed some rest.

A tap on the shoulder made her jump. She turned and looked into the face of a girl with small, fairylike features and a dust of pretty freckles. Her eyes were large and round.

"You're Persephone Rosi, right?"

She was getting used to that question and learning to dread it.

"I am," she said hesitantly. "Can I...help you?"

The girl picked up a magazine that rested on top of the books she cradled against her chest. It was the *Delphi Divine,* its cover a picture of Hades this time. Persephone was shocked—Hades had actually allowed himself to be photographed. The headline read:

God of the Underworld Credits Journalist for the Halcyon Project

Persephone took it, flipped to the full spread, and started reading, rolling her eyes.

Probably the worst part—aside from the article suggesting that the reason for the project was because Hades had fallen for the "beautiful, blond mortal"— was that they'd sourced a picture of her. It was the headshot they'd taken for her internship at *New Athens News.*

"Is it true?" the girl asked. "Are you really dating Lord Hades?"

Persephone looked at her and stood, shouldering her backpack. She didn't think there was a word to describe what was happening between her and the God of the Dead. Hades had called her his lover, but Persephone would still describe herself as a prisoner—and that would be the case until the contract was removed.

Instead of answering the girl, she asked, "You do know the *Divine* is a gossip magazine?"

"Yes, but...he created the Halcyon Project just for you."

"It isn't for me." Persephone pushed past the girl. "It's for mortals in need."

"Still, don't you think that's romantic?"

Persephone paused and turned to face the girl. "He listened. There's nothing romantic about that."

The girl blinked, confused.

Persephone explained, "I'm not interested in romanticizing Hades for doing something all men should be doing."

"So you don't think he likes you?" the girl asked.

"I'd much rather he respect me," Persephone answered. Respect could build an empire. Trust could make it unbreakable. Love could make it last forever. And she would know Hades respected her when he removed this stupid mark on her skin.

"Excuse me," she said and left. It was close to lunch and she had that date with Lexa and Sybil.

Persephone left Hestia Hall and crossed campus, cutting through the Garden of the Gods, following the familiar stone path, passing Apollo's marble statue, when the scent of Hades's magic hit her. It was the only warning she had before she was teleported. She appeared in a different part of the garden where narcissus bloomed, standing face-to-face with Hades.

He reached forward, gripped the back of her neck, and brought his lips to hers. She kissed him eagerly, but she was distracted by the article and her thoughts around the contract.

When he pulled away, he stared at her a moment, then asked, "Are you well?"

Her stomach flipped. She wasn't used to that question or the way he asked it—in a voice echoing with sincerity and concern.

"Yes," she answered breathlessly. *Tell him—ask him about the contract*, she commanded herself. *Demand he free you if he wants to be with you.* Instead, she asked, "What are you doing here?"

The corners of his mouth turned up, and he brushed his thumb over the bottom of her lip. "I came to say goodbye."

"What?" The question came out more demanding than she wanted. What did he mean he was saying goodbye?

He chuckled under his breath. "I must go to Olympia for Council."

Council for the gods occurred quarterly unless there was a war. If Hades was going, that meant Demeter would be going too. "Oh." She lowered her head, disappointed. "How long?"

He shrugged. "If I have anything to say about it, a day and no more."

"Why wouldn't you have a say?"

"It depends on how much Zeus and Poseidon argue."

She wanted to laugh, but after seeing them at the gala, she got the feeling their arguing wasn't cute but brutal. Even worse than Zeus or Poseidon, Persephone wondered how her mother would treat the God of the Dead.

She shivered and tried to meet Hades's gaze, but his

eyes had fallen to the magazine. He plucked it from the top of her things and frowned—then frowned deeper after she asked, "Is this why you announced the Halcyon Project at the gala? So people would focus on something other than my assessment of your character?"

"You think I created the Halcyon Project for my reputation?"

She shrugged. "You didn't want me to continue writing about you. You said so yesterday."

He stared at her for a moment, clearly frustrated. "I didn't start the Halcyon Project in hopes that the world would admire me. I started it because of you."

"Why?"

"Because I saw truth in what you said. Is that really so hard to believe?"

She couldn't really answer, and Hades's brows drew together tightly.

"My absence will not affect your ability to enter the Underworld. You may come and go as you please."

She didn't like how distant he suddenly felt, and he wasn't even gone yet. She stepped closer to him and tilted her head back so she could look into his eyes. "Before you go, I was thinking," she said and reached for the lapels of his jacket. "I'd like to throw a party in the Underworld...for the souls."

Hades's hands closed over her wrists. His eyes were searching, and she wasn't sure if he would push her away or pull her closer. "What kind of party?"

"Thanatos tells me souls will reincarnate at the end of the week and that Asphodel is already planning a celebration. I think we should move it to the palace."

"We?"

Persephone bit her lip and blushed. "I'm asking you if I can plan a party in the Underworld." He just stared at her, so she went on, "Hecate has already agreed to help."

His brows rose. "Has she?"

"Yes." Her eyes fell to where her palms now rested, flat on his chest. "She's thinking we should have a ball."

He was quiet so long, she thought he must be angry, so she looked up to meet his gaze.

"Are you trying to seduce me so I'll agree to your ball?" he asked.

"Is it working?"

He chuckled and drew her closer. His arousal was hard against her stomach and she gasped. It was the only answer she required, and still he said against her ear, "It's working." He kissed her thoroughly and released her. "Plan your ball, Lady Persephone."

"Come home soon, Lord Hades."

He smiled wickedly before vanishing.

She realized in that moment she was afraid to say anything about the contract because that might mean disappointment. It might mean the realization that this would never work.

And that would break her.

———

Persephone met Lexa and Sybil for lunch at the Golden Apple. Luckily, with Sybil present, Lexa didn't ask any questions about the kiss, though it was possible Sybil already knew the details. The girls talked about finals, graduation, the gala, and Apollo.

It all started because Lexa asked Sybil, "So are you and Apollo…?"

"Dating? No," Sybil said. "But I think he hopes I will agree to be his lover."

Persephone and Lexa exchanged a look.

"Wait," Lexa said. "He asked? Like…for permission?"

Sybil smirked, and Persephone admired how the oracle could talk about this so easily. "He did, and I told him no."

"You told Apollo, the God of the Sun, perfection incarnate, no?" Lexa looked slightly appalled. "Why?"

"Lexa, you can't ask that!" Persephone chided.

Sybil just smiled and said, "Apollo will not love one person, and I do not wish to share."

Persephone understood why Sybil wouldn't want to get involved with the god. Apollo had a long list of lovers that spanned divine, semidivine, and mortal—and as the God of Light's list had proven, he never stayed with one person too long.

Conversation lapsed into making plans for the weekend, and once they had decided where they would meet for drinks and dancing, Persephone left for the Underworld.

She watered her garden and went to find Hecate in her cottage. It was a small home, nestled in a dark meadow, and while it was charming, there was something…foreboding about it. Perhaps it was because of the coloring—the siding was dark gray, the door a dark purple, and ivy crawled up the house, covering the windows and roof.

Inside, it was like she had stepped into a garden filled with night-blooming flowers—thick, purple wisteria hung overhead like clusters of stars in a blackout night while a carpet of white nicotiana covered the ground.

A table, chairs, and bed were crafted of soft black wood that looked as if it had grown into the formation of each piece. Orbs rose into the air and it took Persephone a moment to recognize what they really were—lampades, small and beautiful fairylike creatures with hair like night, laced with white flowers and silvery skin.

Hecate wasn't sitting on the bed or at the table but on the grassy floor. Her legs were folded under her, and her eyes were closed. A lit black candle flickered in front of her.

"Hecate?" Persephone asked, knocking on the doorframe, but the goddess didn't stir. She stepped farther into the room. "Hecate?"

Still no response. It was like she was asleep.

Persephone bent and blew out the candle, and Hecate's eyes snapped open. For a moment, she looked positively wicked, her eyes an endless black, and Persephone suddenly understood the kind of goddess Hecate could become if she was pushed—the kind of goddess that turned Gale the witch into Gale the polecat.

When she recognized Persephone, she smiled. "Welcome back, my lady."

"Persephone," she corrected, and Hecate's smile widened.

"I'm only trying it out," she said. "You know, for when you become mistress of the Underworld."

Persephone blushed fiercely. "You're getting ahead of yourself, Hecate."

The goddess raised a brow, and Persephone rolled her eyes.

"What were you doing?" Persephone asked.

"Oh, just cursing a mortal," Hecate replied almost

cheerfully, grabbing the candle and getting to her feet. She put it away and turned to face Persephone. "Watered your garden already, dear?"

"Yes."

"Shall we begin?"

She was quick to get down to business, directing Persephone to sit on the floor. Persephone hesitated, but after encouragement from Hecate to see if her touch still took life, she knelt to the ground. When she pressed her hands to the grass, nothing happened.

"Amazing," Persephone whispered.

Hecate spent the next half hour leading her through a meditation that was supposed to help her visualize and use her power.

"You must practice calling to your magic," Hecate said.

"How do I do that?"

"Magic is malleable. As you call for it, imagine it as clay—mold it into what you desire and then...give it life."

Persephone shook her head. "You make it sound so easy."

"It is easy," Hecate said. "All it takes is belief."

Persephone wasn't sure about that, but she tried to do as Hecate instructed. She imagined the life she felt in the wisteria above her as something she could shape and willed the plants to grow larger and more vibrant, but when she opened her eyes, nothing had changed.

Hecate must have noticed her disappointment, because she placed a hand on Persephone's shoulder. "It will take time, but you will master this."

Persephone smiled at the goddess but wilted on the inside. She had no choice but to master this if she was going to fulfill her contract with Hades, because as much as she liked the King of the Underworld, she had no desire to be a prisoner of his realm.

"Persephone?"

"Huh?"

She blinked, looking at Hecate, who grinned.

"Thinking of our king?"

Persephone looked away. "Everyone knows, don't they?"

"Well, he did carry you through the palace to his bedroom."

She stared at the grass. She hadn't intended to have this conversation, and though it pained her to speak the words, she said, "I'm not sure it should have happened."

"Why ever not?"

"For so many reasons, Hecate."

The goddess waited.

"The contract, for one," Persephone explained. "And my mother will never let me out of her sight again if she finds out." She paused. "What if she can see it when she looks at me? What if she knows I'm not the virginal goddess she's always wanted?"

Hecate chuckled. "No god has the power to determine if you are a virgin."

"Not a god but a mother."

Hecate frowned. "Do you regret sleeping with Hades? Forget your mother and the contract—do you regret it?"

"No. I could never regret him."

"My dear, you are at war with yourself. It has created darkness within you."

"Darkness?"

"Anger, fear, resentment," Hecate said. "If you do not free yourself first, no one else can."

Persephone knew darkness had always existed within her, and it had deepened over the last few months, rising to the surface when she felt challenged or angry. She thought of how she'd threatened that nymph at the Coffee House, how she'd snapped at her mother, how jealous she'd been of Minthe.

Her mother might claim that the mortal world had done this to her—grew the darkness into something tangible—but Persephone knew otherwise. It had always been there, a dark seed, fueling her dreams and her passions, and Hades had roused it, charmed it, fed it.

Let me coax the darkness from you—I will help you shape it.

And she had let him.

"When did you feel life for the first time?" Hecate asked, curious.

"After Hades and I..." She didn't need to finish her sentence.

"Hmm." The Goddess of Magic tapped her chin. "I think, perhaps, the God of the Dead has created life within *you*."

CHAPTER XXII
The Ascension Ball

By Friday, Hades had not returned from Olympia, and Persephone was surprised by how anxious that made her. She knew he planned to be at the Ascension Ball this evening, because when she arrived in the Underworld to help decorate, Hecate ushered her into another part of the palace to get ready and greeted her with, "Lord Hades has sent your gown. It's beautiful."

Persephone had no idea Hades planned on sending her a gown at all. "May I see it?"

"Later, dear," Hecate said, opening a set of gilded doors to a suite unlike the rest of the palace. Instead of dark floors and walls, they were marble white and inlaid with gold. The bed was luxurious and covered in fluffy blankets, the floors in soft furs. Overhead, a large chandelier dropped from a dome ceiling.

"These rooms, who are they for?" Persephone asked as she entered, trailing her fingers along the edge of a white vanity.

"The mistress of the Underworld," Hecate replied.

Persephone let that sink in a little. She knew Hades had created everything in his realm, so adding a suite for a wife must have meant he'd considered having one. She remembered what Hermes had alluded to about the subject at the gala. Did these rooms prove the god had hopes of marrying?

"But...Hades has never had a wife," Persephone hedged.

"He has not."

"So...these rooms have never been occupied?"

"Not that we are aware. Come. Let's get you ready."

Hecate called for her lampades and they set to work. Persephone bathed, and while she reclined in the tub, Hecate's nymphs polished her toes and nails. Once she was dry, they rubbed oils into her skin. They smelled of lavender and vanilla—her favorite scents. When she said as much, Hecate smiled.

"Ah, Lord Hades said you loved them."

"I don't recall telling Hades my favorite scents."

"I don't suppose you had to," Hecate said absently. "He can smell them."

She directed Persephone to the vanity with a mirror so large, she could see the whole wall on the opposite side of the room. The nymphs took time arranging her hair, piling it atop her head. When they finished, pretty ringlets framed her face, and gold clips glistened in her blond hair.

"It's beautiful," Persephone told the lampades. "I love it."

"Just wait until you see your gown," Hecate said.

The Goddess of Witchcraft disappeared into the

closet and returned with a strip of shimmering gold fabric. Persephone couldn't tell what it looked like until she slipped it on. The fabric was cool against her skin, and when she looked in the mirror, she hardly recognized herself. The gown Hades had chosen for her hung on her body like liquid gold. With a plunging neckline, backless design, and thigh-high split, it was beautiful, daring, and delicate.

"You are a vision," Hecate said.

Persephone smiled. "Thank you, Hecate."

The Goddess of Witchcraft left to get ready for tonight's festivities, leaving Persephone alone.

"This is the closest I have ever looked to a goddess," she said aloud, smoothing her hands over her dress.

The sudden feel of Hades's magic, warm and safe and familiar, gave her pause. She braced to teleport, since the last time she had felt it, that was exactly what had happened. This time, however, Hades appeared behind her. She met his dark eyes in the mirror and started to turn, but Hades's voice rang out, "Don't move. Let me look at you."

His instructions were more of a request than a command, and she swallowed, barely able to handle the heat his presence ignited inside her. He radiated power and darkness, and her body responded—craved the power, hungered for the heat, yearned for the darkness. She burned to touch him but held his gaze for a breath before he started a slow circle around her.

When he finished, he wrapped an arm around her waist, pulling her back against his chest, welding their bodies together. "Drop your glamour."

She hesitated. In truth, her human glamour was her

security, and Hades's command made her want to hold on to it tighter. "Why?"

"Because I wish to see you," he said.

Her grip tightened on the glamour, but Hades coaxed in a voice that made her melt, "Let me see you."

She closed her eyes and released her hold. Her glamour slipped away like water dripping down her skin, and she knew when it was completely gone because she felt both unburdened and raw.

"Open your eyes," Hades encouraged, and when she did, she was in her goddess form.

Everything about her presence had intensified, and she glowed against Hades's darkness.

"Darling, you are a goddess," Hades said and pressed his lips to her shoulder. Persephone wrapped her hand around his neck, pulling him to her; their lips crashed together, and when Hades growled, Persephone turned in his arms.

"I have missed you." He cupped her face, eyes searching. She wondered what he was looking for.

"I missed you too."

The admission made her blush, and Hades smirked, pulling her in for another kiss. His lips brushed hers— once, twice—teasing, before Persephone sealed their lips together. She was ravenous and he tasted rich and smoky, like the whiskey he drank. Her hands slipped down his chest; she wanted to touch him, feel his skin against her own, but Hades stopped her with his hands on her wrists, breaking their kiss.

"I am just as eager, my darling," he said. "But if we do not leave now, I think we shall miss your party."

She wanted to pout, but she also knew he was right.

"Shall we?" he asked, holding out his hand.

When she took it, Hades dropped his glamour. She could watch it all day—the way his magic moved like shadow, peeling off him like smoke, revealing his striking form. His hair fell over his shoulders, and a silver crown made of jagged edges decorated the base of his massive horns. The suit he had been wearing moments ago was replaced by black robes, the edges embroidered in silver.

"Careful, Goddess," Hades warned in a low growl. "Or we won't leave this room."

She shivered and quickly looked away.

Fingers laced, he led her out of the suite and into the hallway to a set of gilded doors. Beyond them, she could hear the low rumble of a large crowd. Her anxiety spiked, probably because she had no glamour to protect her. She realized that was silly—she knew these people and they knew her.

Still, she felt like an impostor—an impostor goddess, an impostor queen, an impostor lover.

Each of those thoughts hurt worse than the other so she shoved them down deep and entered the ballroom beside Hades.

Everything went silent.

They stood at the top of a staircase that led to the packed ballroom floor. The room was crowded from wall to wall, and she recognized many of those in attendance— gods and souls and creatures alike. She spotted Euryale, Ilias, and Mekonnen. She smiled at them, her anxiety forgotten, and when they bowed, Hades led her down the stairs.

As they made their way through the crowd, Persephone smiled and nodded, and when her eyes fell on Hecate, she broke from Hades to take her hands. "Hecate! You look beautiful!"

The Goddess of Witchcraft was luminous—she wore a silver, glittering gown that fit her frame and flared out. Her thick, dark hair spilled over her shoulders and sparkling stars glittered in her long locks.

"You flatter me, my dear," she said as they embraced.

Suddenly, Persephone found herself surrounded by souls. They hugged her and thanked her, told her how amazing the palace looked and how beautiful she was. She didn't know how long she stood there, accepting embraces and talking to the people of the Underworld, but it was music that broke up the crowd.

Persephone's first dance was with a few children from the Underworld. They moved in circles and begged to be lifted and twirled. Persephone obliged, marveling at their joy as they moved about the ballroom.

When that dance finished, Charon approached. He was dressed all in white, his usual color, except the edges of his robes were embroidered with azure thread. He bowed, one hand covering his heart. "My lady, may I have the next dance?"

She smiled and took his hand. "Of course!"

Persephone joined a line dance, weaving through the souls. The tempo was quick, and she was soon out of breath and flushed. She clapped and laughed and grinned until her face hurt. Two dances later, she turned to find Hermes bowing behind her.

"My lady," he said.

"It's Persephone, Hermes," she said, taking his hand.

303

The music was different now, coasting into a charming, slow melody.

"You look almost as amazing as me," he said smugly as they moved about the room.

"What a thoughtful compliment," she teased.

The god grinned and then leaned in. "I can't tell if it's the dress or all the sex you've been having with the god of this realm."

Persephone blushed. "Not funny, Hermes!"

He lifted a brow. "Isn't it?"

"How do you even know?"

"Well, it's rumored he carried you through the palace to his bed."

She blushed fiercely. She would never forgive Hades for that.

"I see it's true."

Persephone rolled her eyes but didn't deny it.

"So tell me—how was it?"

"I'm not going to talk to you about it, Hermes."

"I bet he's rough," Hermes mused.

Persephone looked away both to hide her blush and her laugh. "You're impossible."

Hermes chuckled. "But truly—love looks good on you."

"Love?" she almost choked.

"Oh dear. You haven't realized it yet, have you?"

"Realized what?"

"That you're in love with Hades."

"I'm not!"

"Are too," he said. "And he loves you."

"I almost preferred your questions about my sex life," she muttered.

Hermes laughed. "You walked into this room like you were his queen. You think he would let just anyone do that?"

She honestly didn't know.

"I think the Lord of the Underworld has found his bride."

She wanted to argue that Hades hadn't found her—he'd captured her—but instead of saying that, she raised her brow at the God of Trickery. "Hermes, are you drunk?"

"A little," he admitted sheepishly.

Persephone laughed, but his words worked into her mind. Did she love Hades? She had only let herself think of it briefly after their first night together and then crushed those thoughts altogether.

As Hermes spun her, she glanced around, searching the crowd for Hades. She hadn't seen him since they had come down the stairs together and she'd immediately been surrounded by souls. She spotted him sitting on a dark throne. He was reclined, a hand raised to his lips, staring at her. Thanatos stood on one side, dressed in black, his wings folded neatly like a cape. Minthe loomed on the other looking radiant in shimmery black. They were like an angel and a devil on the shoulders of the God of the Dead.

Persephone looked away quickly, but Hermes seemed to notice she was distracted and stopped dancing.

"It's alright, Sephy." He released her. "Go to him."

Persephone hesitated. "It's okay—"

"Claim him, Persephone."

She smiled at Hermes, and the crowd parted as she made her way to Hades. He watched her, and she

305

couldn't quite place the look on his face, but something inside her was drawn to him. As she neared, his hand fell, resting on the arm of his throne. She bowed low, then rose.

"My lord, will you dance?"

Hades's eyes were alight, and his lips twitched. He stood, a towering and commanding figure, and took her hand, leading her to the floor. The souls made room, packing in against the walls to give them space and to watch. Hades drew her against him, his hand firm on her back, the other laced between her fingers.

She had been closer to him than this, but there was something about the way he held her now before all his subjects that made her skin burn. The air grew thick and charged between them. They didn't speak for a long moment, just looked at one another.

"Are you displeased?" she asked after some time.

"Am I displeased that you have danced with Charon and Hermes?" he asked.

Was that what she was asking? She stared at him and he leaned forward, pressing his lips against her ear. "I am displeased that I am not inside you."

She tried not to smile. "My lord, why didn't you say so?"

His eyes darkened. "Careful, Goddess. I have no qualms taking you before my whole realm."

"You wouldn't."

His look challenged: *Dare me.*

She didn't.

They glided across the floor in silence for a little while longer before Hades pulled her off the floor and up the stairs. Behind them, the crowd clapped and whistled.

"Where are we going?" she asked.

"To remedy my displeasure," he replied.

Once they left the ballroom, he led her outside onto a balcony at the end of the hall. It was a large space, and Persephone became distracted by the view it offered, an Underworld cloaked in darkness, ignited by glimmering starlight. She marveled at the craftsmanship, the attention to detail.

This was Hades's magic.

But when she started to walk ahead of Hades, he pulled her back to him. His eyes were dark, communicating his need.

"Why did you ask me to drop my glamour?" she asked.

Hades brushed a stray piece of hair behind her ear. "I told you—you will not hide here. You needed to understand what it is to be a god."

"I'm not like you," she said.

His hands trailed up her arms and he smiled. "No, we have only two things in common."

She raised a brow. "And those are?"

"We are both Divine," he said, inching closer. "And the space we share."

He lifted her into his arms, and her back met the wall. Hades's hands were almost desperate, drawing up her dress and parting his robes. He sank deep inside her without warning and they both groaned. His forehead rested against hers, and she inhaled a shaky breath. "Is this what it's like to be a god?"

Hades pulled back to meet her gaze. "This is what it is like to have my favor," he answered and moved, sliding in and out, invading her in the most delicious way. Their gazes held and their breaths became heavier, faster.

Persephone's head fell back. The stone bit into her scalp and back, but she didn't care. Each thrust touched something deep inside her, building sensation after sensation.

"You are perfect," he said, fingers twisting into her hair. He cupped the back of her head, his thrusts taunting as he slowed, moving at a pace that ensured she could feel every part of him.

"You are beautiful. I have never wanted like I want with you."

His admission came with a kiss, and then Hades pumped in and out of her harder than ever and her body devoured him. They came together, their cries smothered by their clasped lips.

Hades withdrew carefully, holding her against him until her legs stopped shaking. Then the sky ignited behind them, and Hades drew her to the edge of the balcony.

"Watch," he said.

On the dark horizon, fire shot into the sky, disappearing into a trail of glimmering sparks.

"The souls are returning to the mortal world," Hades said. "This is reincarnation."

Persephone watched in awe as more and more souls rose into the sky, leaving trails of fire in their wake.

"It's beautiful," she said.

It was magic.

Below, the residents of the Underworld had gathered in the stone courtyard, and when the final souls rose into the air, they broke into applause, music began again, and the merriment continued. Persephone found herself smiling, and when she looked at Hades, he was staring at her.

"What?" she asked.

"Let me worship you," he said.

She remembered the words she had whispered to him in the back of the limo after La Rose. *"You will worship me, and I won't even have to order you."* His request felt sinful and devious, and she reveled in it.

She answered, "Yes."

CHAPTER XXIII
A Touch of Normal

Persephone was looking forward to a date with Hades.

It had been a few weeks since the Ascension Ball, and she had spent a lot of time with him. He'd started seeking her out while she was in the Underworld, asking her to go for walks or play a game of her choosing. She'd begun making requests of him too; he'd played with the children in the Underworld, added a new play area for them, and hosted a few dinners for the souls and his staff.

It was during these moments that her connection to him grew, and she found she felt far more passion for him than she ever had before. It manifested when they came together late at night, making love as if they'd never see one another again. Everything felt so desperate, and Persephone realized it was because neither of them were using words to communicate how they felt.

And she felt like she was falling.

One evening, after a particularly intense game of strip poker, they lay in bed, Persephone's head on Hades's chest while he brushed his fingers absently through her hair. "Allow me to take you to dinner."

Her gaze snapped to his. "Dinner? Like...out in public?"

Her stomach clenched at the thought, worried about the media attention. Since Hades had announced the Halcyon Project, more articles about her were appearing in magazines across New Greece—the *Corinth Chronicle,* the *Ithaca Inquirer.* The ones that made her the most anxious were those that tried to research her background. Right now, they'd found enough to satisfy them, writing things like she'd been homeschooled until eighteen, at which point she came to New Athens University from Olympia. Majoring in journalism, she found an internship with *New Athens News* and began her relationship with Hades after an interview.

It was just a matter of time before they wanted more. She should know; she was a journalist.

"Not in public exactly," he said. "But I do want to take you to a public restaurant."

She hesitated, and Hades gave her a meaningful look. "I would keep you safe."

She knew that was true, and this god had managed to avoid the media for a very long time—though she knew that was due in part to his power of invisibility and the fear he struck in mortals.

"Okay," she said and smiled. Despite her reservations, it *was* terribly romantic that Hades wanted to do something so...simple. Like take her to dinner.

Since that night, everything had been hectic. School was busy, work was stressful, and she had been accosted by strangers in person and via email. People stopped and questioned her about her relationship with Hades on the bus, during walks, and while writing at the Coffee House. Some journalists emailed to ask if they could interview her for their newspapers; others offered jobs. She had gotten into a habit of checking her inbox once a day and mass deleting the majority of the emails she received without reading them, but this time when she logged in, she noticed a disturbing subject line: *I know you're fucking him.*

Journalists were a little more professional than that.

Dread pooled in her stomach as she clicked on the email and found a string of photos. They were images of her with Hades, all taken in the Underworld while they were on the balcony during the Ascension Ball. The email concluded with: *I want my job back or I'll release these to the media.*

The email was from Adonis. She pulled out her phone to call him—she hadn't deleted his number yet, and she figured this was the best way to reach him.

She could tell he picked up the phone, but he didn't offer a greeting, just waited for her to speak.

"What the hell, Adonis?" she demanded. "Where did you get the photos?"

"I'm sure you'd like to know."

"Hades will crush you."

"He can try, but then he probably doesn't want to face Aphrodite's wrath."

"You're a bastard."

"You have three weeks," he said.

"How am I supposed to get your job back for you?" she snapped.

"You'll think of something. You did get me fired."

"You got yourself fired, Adonis," she hissed. "You shouldn't have stolen my article."

"I made you famous," he argued.

"You didn't make me anything but a victim, and I'm not interested in continuing that trend."

There was a long pause on the other side before Adonis spoke again. "Time is running out, Persephone."

He hung up, and she put the phone down, thoughts racing. The easiest thing to do was to ask Demetri if he'd consider hiring Adonis back, so she rose from her seat and knocked on his door. "Do you have a moment?"

Her boss looked up from his computer, glasses reflecting his blue shirt and yellow tie, making eye contact almost impossible. "Yes, come in."

Persephone only took a few steps into the room. "What are the chances Adonis could...come back?"

"He was dishonest, Persephone. I have no interest in employing him again." When she nodded, he asked, "Why?"

"Just feeling...a little bad for him is all," she managed, though the words tasted like blood in her mouth.

Demetri took his glasses off. She could now see his eyes, full of concern and a little suspicious. "Is everything alright?"

She nodded. "Yes. Yeah. Excuse me."

She exited Demetri's office, packed her things, and left. The images in her email were damning, and if released to the public, they would prove everything in the gossip magazines true.

Well, not everything.

Persephone really couldn't say that she and Hades were dating. As before, she was hesitant to assign any

313

label to their current status given their contract. Not to mention the fact that if those photos were released, her mother would see them, and that would mean the end of her time in New Athens. She wouldn't even have to worry about the media storm that would ensue as a result, because she wouldn't be here for it. Demeter would lock her back up forever.

Even while Persephone got ready for her date—something that should've been enjoyable—her mind was on Adonis's threat. She considered how she should handle the situation; she could tell Hades, and everything would be over as quickly as it began, but she didn't want the God of the Dead fighting her battles for her. She wanted to solve this problem herself.

She decided Hades would be the last resort, a card she would pull if she couldn't find a solution.

She must have looked troubled when Hades arrived to pick her up, because the God of the Underworld asked as she approached his limo, "Is everything okay?"

"Yes," she managed in her cheeriest voice possible. He had been asking that a lot, and she wondered if he was paranoid. "It was just a busy day."

He smiled. "Then let's get you off your feet."

He helped her into the limo and followed close behind. Antoni was in the driver's seat.

"My lady." He bowed his head.

"It is good to see you, Antoni."

The cyclops smiled. "Just press the com if you need anything." Then he rolled up a tinted window that kept his cabin separate from theirs.

She and Hades sat side by side, close enough that their arms and legs touched. The friction ignited a fever beneath her skin. Suddenly, she couldn't get comfortable, and she shifted, crossing and uncrossing her legs. It drew Hades's attention, and after a moment, he placed a hand on her thigh.

She wasn't sure what possessed her to say it. Maybe it was the stress of the day or the tension in the cabin, but right now, all she wanted was to lose herself in him. "I want to worship you."

The words were quiet and casual. As if she had just asked him how his day went or commented on the weather. She felt his eyes on her and slowly peeked up at him. His gaze had darkened.

"And how would you worship me, Goddess?" His voice was deep and controlled.

She tried to repress a smile and kneeled to the floor board in front of him, wedging herself between his legs. "Shall I show you?"

His throat worked, and he managed in a husky tone, "A demonstration would be appreciated."

Her hands moved to the button of his trousers where she freed his sex and clasped it in her hand. It was soft but hard, and she met Hades's gaze as she stroked him once. His hands became fists on his thighs, and when she tasted him, he groaned and rolled his head back.

Then the car came to a stop.

"Fuck," he said and reached for the intercom button. Persephone continued to take him deep into the back of her throat, licking and sucking him. When Hades spoke, he was breathless. "Antoni. Drive until I say otherwise."

"Yes, sir."

He hissed, inhaling breath between his teeth. His fingers dug into her scalp, loosening her braid as she worked him with her hand and moved her tongue and teeth over the head of his cock. He tasted like salt and darkness, and he grew harder and heavier in her mouth.

She knew when she had driven him into mindlessness because he ground out her name and started thrusting into her mouth. She braced herself against the seat of the limo, unable to breathe, only able to take. He hit the back of her throat over and over until he came with her name on his lips.

Persephone took all of him, licking him clean. When she finished, Hades reached for her, dragging her up for a hard kiss before tearing away to growl, "I want you."

She tilted her head, questioning. "How do you want me?"

He answered without so much as a second thought. "To start, I'll take you from behind on your hands and knees."

"And then?"

"I'll pull you on top and teach you how to ride me until you come apart."

"Hmm, I like that one."

She lifted herself, and Hades helped her sit on his shaft. She groaned as he filled her, and Hades's hands spanned her waist, helping her establish a rhythm until she moved of her own accord, using him for her pleasure. Her arms went around his neck, and she held him close. She bit his ear, and when he groaned, she whispered, "Tell me how I feel."

"Like life," he answered.

His hands moved between them, and he worked her, building the tension, until she could no longer stand it. Her labored breathing gave way to a cry of ecstasy, and she collapsed against him, her face burrowed into the crook of his neck.

She didn't know how long he held her like that, but at some point, Persephone slid from his lap, and Hades restored his appearance before letting Antoni know they were ready to arrive at their destination. Antoni entered a garage and parked near an elevator where Hades helped Persephone out of the limo. Once inside, he took out a key card and scanned it, punching the button for floor fourteen.

"Where are we?" she asked.

"The Grove," Hades replied. "My restaurant."

"You own the Grove?" It was a favorite among the mortals of New Athens because of its unique decor and cozy, garden-inspired dining. "How does no one know?"

"I let Ilias run it," he said. "And prefer that people think he owns it."

The elevator opened to the roof, and Persephone gasped at what she saw. The rooftop of the Grove looked like a forest in the Underworld; a stone path wound through beds of flowers and trees strung with lights. Hades led her down the path, which opened onto an open space with a table and two plush chairs. The lights in the trees crisscrossed overhead.

"This is beautiful, Hades."

He smiled and led her to the table where a collection of breads and a bottle of wine waited. Hades poured them each a glass and toasted their evening.

She found herself laughing more than she ever remembered, the burden of her day long forgotten as Hades told her stories of Ancient Greece. When they finished eating, they walked through the forest on the roof and Persephone asked, "What do you do for fun?"

It seemed like a silly question, but she was curious. Over the months, she gathered that Hades liked cards, walks, and playing with his animals, but she wondered what else.

"What do you mean?"

She laughed. "The fact that you just asked that says everything. What are your hobbies?"

"Cards. Riding." He swirled his hand in the air, thinking. "Drinking."

"What about things not related to being the God of the Dead?"

"Drinking is not related to being God of the Dead."

"It also isn't a hobby. Unless you're an alcoholic."

Hades raised a brow. "Then what are *your* hobbies?"

Persephone smiled, and though she knew he was avoiding talking about himself, she answered, "Baking."

"Baking? I feel like I should have known about this sooner."

"Well, you never asked."

Silence fell between them, and they walked a little further before Hades came to a stop. Persephone turned to look at him when he said, "Teach me."

She stared at him for a moment, stunned. "What?"

"Teach me," he said. "To bake something."

She couldn't help but laugh, and he raised a brow, clearly not amused. "I'm sorry. I'm just imagining you in my kitchen."

"And that's difficult?"

"Well…yeah. You're the God of the Underworld."

"And you're the Goddess of Spring," he said. "You stand in your kitchen and make cookies. Why can't I?"

She couldn't take her eyes off him. It wasn't until now that she realized something had changed between them. It had been happening gradually, but today, it hit her hard.

She was in love with him.

She hadn't realized she was frowning until he touched her face, brushing her cheek with his finger. "Are you well?"

She smiled. "Very well." She stood on the tips of her toes and pressed a kiss to his mouth, pulling away. "I'll teach you."

Hades smiled too. "Well then. Let's get started."

"Wait. You want to learn *now*?"

"Now is as good a time as any," he said.

She opened her mouth to argue that she didn't have the right supplies to do this in the Underworld when Hades said, "I thought maybe...we could spend time at your apartment." She stared at him, and he shrugged. "You're always in the Underworld."

"You...want to spend time in the Upperworld? In my apartment?"

He just stared at her. He'd already told her exactly what he wanted to do.

"I...have to prepare Lexa for your arrival."

He nodded. "Fair enough. I'll have Antoni drop you off." He looked down at his suit. "I need to change."

———

Persephone had no difficulty convincing Lexa to have Hades over for an evening of food, baking, and movies.

In fact, she screamed when Persephone brought it up, which summoned Jaison from her room armed with a lamp, his blue-gray eyes wide and his dark brown curls wild. He looked ready for a fight, and when the girls saw him, they laughed.

Jaison lowered the lamp. "I heard someone scream."

"And you were going to save me with a lamp?" Lexa asked.

"It was the heaviest thing I could find," he said defensively.

They laughed again, and Persephone explained why Lexa was screaming.

Jaison rubbed the back of his neck. "Wow, Hades, huh?"

"Yes, Hades!" Lexa reached for Jaison's hand. "Come on! We have to clean the living room. He's going to think we're peasants."

Persephone smiled as the two disappeared into the adjoining room, Jaison still in possession of the lamp.

They cleaned, and just as she finished putting on her pajamas, the doorbell rang. Despite all the time she'd spent with Hades, her heart still hammered in her chest as she went to answer the door.

Hades stood on their porch in a black shirt that fit his muscles like a dream and loose sweatpants. Persephone was shocked by his appearance; the manicured god could dress down and he was still magnificent.

"Did you own those before today?" she asked, pointing to the pants.

Hades looked down at them, grinning. "No."

She let him in, feeling slightly embarrassed. This apartment was way too small for him—he was nearly as wide as the doorway, and he had to duck to enter. Persephone frowned.

"What?" he asked.

"Nothing," she said quickly and moved around him. She brought him into the living room where Lexa and Jaison had finished cleaning and now lounged on the couch. "Um, Hades, this is Lexa, my best friend, and Jaison, her boyfriend."

Jaison waved from the couch, but Lexa got to her feet and hugged Hades around the middle.

Persephone's brows rose. She was impressed with Lexa's fearlessness and by Hades's reaction; he didn't seem surprised at all and returned Lexa's hug.

"It's nice to meet you," she said.

"Very few have ever spoken those words," he told her.

Lexa pulled away and grinned. "So long as you treat my best friend right, I'll continue to be happy to see you."

Hades's lips curled. "Noted, Lexa Sideris," he said and gave a little bow "May I say, it is a pleasure to meet you."

Lexa blushed.

Damn, the Lord of the Underworld was charming.

Persephone took Hades into her kitchen. It was small for her and Lexa, even tinier with him. His head practically touched the ceiling, but his height came in handy, as much of what Persephone needed was on the top shelf in her cabinets.

"Why do you put everything up so high?" he asked as he helped retrieve her supplies.

"It's the only place it will fit. In case you haven't noticed, I don't live in a palace."

He gave her a look as if to say, *I could change that.*

When everything was on the counter, Hades turned to look at her. "What would you do without me?"

"Get it myself," she said simply.

Hades snorted. She turned to face him and found he was leaning against the counter, arms crossed over his chest. He was absolutely breathtaking, and she wanted to laugh because he was standing in her ugly kitchen making cookies. "Well, get over here. You can't learn from there."

Hades raised a brow, smirking, and approached. She hadn't expected him to stand so close, but he came up behind her, cradling her body with his, hands braced on either side of her.

His mouth touched her ear, warm and honeyed. "Please, instruct."

She took a breath and cleared her throat. "The most important thing to remember when baking is that the ingredients have to be measured and mixed right or it could mean disaster."

His lips brushed along her neck and then her shoulder. Her breath caught, and she added, "Scratch that. The most important thing to remember is to pay attention."

She glared at him over her shoulder while he tried to look innocent, and she handed him the measuring cup.

"First, flour," she said.

Hades took the cup and measured out the required amount of flour. He kept his arms around her, working almost as if she weren't there—except she knew he was aware of her because she could feel his body hardening against hers.

"Next?"

Concentrate, she commanded herself. "Baking soda."

He continued like that until all the ingredients were in the bowl and mixed. Persephone took that opportunity to duck under his arm, reaching for a cookie sheet and a spoon. She instructed Hades to form the dough into balls no more than an inch in diameter and place them on the sheet.

Once the cookies were in the oven, Hades turned to her expectantly, but she was already prepared for him.

"We make icing." She rubbed her hands together. This was the best part. Hades raised a brow, clearly amused.

Persephone began to instruct again, handing Hades a whisk.

"What am I supposed to do with this?"

"You'll beat the ingredients together," she said, pouring powdered sugar, vanilla, and corn syrup into a bowl. She pushed it toward him. "Beat."

He smirked. "Happily."

When the icing was made, they divided it into separate bowls and mixed food coloring into them. Persephone was not the cleanest baker, and by the time they finished incorporating all the colors, her fingers were covered in icing.

Hades reached for her hand. "How does it taste?" he asked and drew her fingers deep into his mouth, sucking them clean. He groaned. "Delicious."

She flushed and drew her hand away.

There was a long pause, and Hades asked, "Now what?"

Their eyes met.

Hades took two steps, planted his hands on her

waist, and lifted her onto the counter. She yelped and then laughed, drawing him close as she wrapped her legs around his waist. He kissed her hungrily, tilting her head back so he could reach deep into her mouth—but it was short-lived, because Lexa came into the kitchen and cleared her throat.

Persephone broke the kiss while Hades's head fell into the crook of her neck.

"Lexa." Persephone blushed. "What's up?"

"I was wondering if you guys wanted to watch a movie?"

"Say no," Hades whispered against her ear.

Persephone laughed and asked, "What movie?"

"*Clash of the Titans*?"

Hades snorted and drew away from her, looking at Lexa. "Old or new?"

"Old."

He considered, tilting his head. "Fine," he said, and then he kissed Persephone on the cheek. "Going to need a minute."

He left the kitchen, and Persephone stayed seated on the counter, kicking her legs back and forth. When Hades was out of sight, Lexa started. "Okay, first. Not in the kitchen! Second, he's completely in love with you."

Persephone's cheeks heated. "Stop, Lexa."

"Girl, he worships you."

Persephone ignored Lexa and started cleaning up.

Once the cookies were done, she left them to cool and the four settled in to watch the movie. Persephone cuddled next to Hades, and it was there, nestled against him, that she realized how weird her life had become since she met the God of the Underworld, and yet she had some of her happiest times with him. This was one. He was willing to try mortal things with her. He had wanted to do the things that made her happy and learn them.

She giggled at the thought of him in the kitchen, mittens on, trying to retrieve the hot pan of cookies from the oven.

Hades's arms tightened around her, and he whispered against her ear. "I know what you're thinking."

"You can't possibly know."

"After what I put myself through this evening, I'm sure there are several things you are laughing at."

It wasn't long before she fell asleep. At some point, Hades lifted her and carried her to her bedroom. "Don't leave," she said sleepily when he lowered her onto the bed.

"I'm not." He kissed her forehead. "Sleep."

She woke to Hades's hot mouth on her skin and she groaned, reaching for him. He kissed her urgently, like he hadn't tasted her in weeks, before trailing his lips along her jaw, her throat, her chest. Then his fingers found the hem of her shirt. She arched her back and helped him pull it over her head. Tossing it aside, he descended, caressing her breasts with his hands and his tongue. It wasn't long before she wiggled out of her pants and he parted her center, tasting her with his mouth. His thumb worked that sensitive bundle of nerves, sending her into delirious bliss.

When he finished, he climbed up her body and kissed her before divesting himself of his clothes and fitting himself between her thighs. She spread her legs wide to accommodate him as his cock pressed against her entrance. He sank into her easily, and she arched with the pleasure of him filling her so full. She had never felt more complete.

He leaned down to press his forehead against hers, breathing hard.

"You are beautiful," he said.

"You feel good," she said, hissing as she took in breath between her teeth, fighting the pressure building behind her eyes. The longer she experienced this euphoria, the less control she had. "You feel...like power."

He moved slowly at first and she savored every bit of him, but this god was starved, and his thoughtfulness soon gave way to something far more mindless and carnal.

A fierce growl came from deep in his throat, and he leaned into her, kissing and biting her lips, her neck, pumping harder and harder, moving her entire body.

Persephone clung to him, her heels dug into him, her nails raked his skin, and her fingers twined into his hair. She reached for anything that would ground her to him, to this moment.

Hades braced his hands against the top of her head to keep her from hitting the headboard as he drove into her. The whole bed shook, and the only sounds were their ragged breathing, their soft moans, their desperate attempts to feel more of each other. Her body was electric, fueled by his intoxicating heat, and he pushed her further and further until she could hold on no longer. Her final cry of ecstasy gave way to his, and she reveled in the sensation of him pulsing inside her. She would take all of him, drain him.

In the aftermath, they were quiet. Hades's slick body

rested against hers, and he slowly came off his high, as if his consciousness was returning to his body. It was then he seemed to realize he had lost his mind, that he had pumped into her so hard they were crammed against the headboard.

He studied her, and under his scrutiny, she realized she was crying.

"Persephone." A note of panic colored his voice. "Did I hurt you?"

"No," she whispered, covering her eyes. He hadn't hurt her, and she didn't know why she was crying. She took in a shaky breath. "No, you didn't hurt me."

After a moment, Hades pried her hand away from her eyes. She met his gaze as he brushed tears from her face, and she was relieved when he didn't ask any more questions.

He moved to his side and tucked her against him, covering them both with the blankets. He kissed her hair and whispered, "You are too perfect for me."

She felt like she had just fallen asleep when Hades sat up suddenly beside her. She felt cold immediately and rolled over, half asleep, to reach for him.

"Come back to bed," she said.

"Get away from my daughter." Demeter's voice thundered throughout the room.

That roused her immediately. She sat up, clutching her blanket to her chest. "Mother! Get out!"

Demeter's chilling gaze fell on Persephone and she saw the promise of pain—of destruction—in her eyes. She could see the headline now: *Olympian Gods Battle, Destroy New Athens.*

"How dare you." Demeter's voice shook, and

Persephone wasn't sure if she was talking to her or Hades—maybe both.

Persephone threw off the blankets and pulled on her nightshirt. Hades remained sitting in the bed.

"How long?" Demeter asked.

"It's really none of your business, Mother," Persephone snapped.

Her mother's eyes darkened. "You forget your place, Daughter."

"And you forget my age. I am not a child!"

"You are my child, and you have betrayed my trust."

Persephone knew what was about to happen. She could feel her mother's magic building in the air.

"No, Mother!" Persephone looked frantically to Hades, and he looked back, tense but calm. It did nothing to ease her fear.

"You will no longer live this disgraceful, mortal life!"

Persephone closed her eyes, cringing as Demeter snapped her fingers, but instead of teleporting to the glass prison like she expected, nothing happened.

Slowly, she opened her eyes and straightened, looking at her mother, whose eyes went wide, then narrowed on Persephone's gold cuff.

The goddess struck, snatching her forearm. Gripping too hard, she pulled the bracelet from Persephone's wrist and revealed the darkness marking her creamy skin.

"What did you do?" This time, Demeter looked at Hades.

"Don't touch me!" Persephone tried to wrench away, but Demeter's hold tightened, and Persephone cried out.

"Release her, Demeter." Hades's voice was calm, but

there was something deadly in his eyes. Persephone had seen that look before—rage was building inside him.

"Don't you dare tell me what to do with my daughter!"

Hades snapped his fingers and suddenly he was dressed in the same clothes from last night. He rose to his full height, and as he approached, Demeter released Persephone. She put distance between herself and her mother at once.

"Your daughter and I have a contract," Hades explained. "She will stay until she fulfills it."

"No." Demeter's gaze focused on Persephone's wrist, and she got the sense her mother would do just about anything to take her from this place, including cutting her hand off. "You will remove your mark. Remove it, Hades!"

The god clearly wasn't fazed by Demeter's growing anger. "The contract must be fulfilled, Demeter. The Fates command it."

The Goddess of Harvest paled when she looked at Persephone. "How could you?"

"How could I?" Persephone echoed sharply. "It's not like I wanted this to happen, Mother!"

From the corner of her eye, she saw Hades flinch.

"Didn't you? I warned you about him!" Demeter pointed to Hades. "I warned you to stay away from the gods!"

"And in doing so, you left me to this fate."

Demeter lifted her chin. "So you blame me? When all I did was try to protect you? Well, you will see the truth very soon, Daughter."

The goddess extended her hand and stripped Persephone of the magic she had given.

It felt like a thousand tiny needles were pricking her skin at once as the glamour she had crafted to hide her Divine appearance was stripped away. The pain knocked the breath out of her, and she fell to the floor, gasping.

"When the contract is fulfilled, you will come home with me," Demeter said, and Persephone glared up at her. "You will never return to this mortal life and you will never see Hades again."

Then Demeter was gone.

Hades scooped Persephone up from the floor and held her close when she burst into tears. All she could manage to say was, "I don't regret you. I didn't mean that I regretted you."

"I know." Hades kissed her tears away.

There was a knock on the door and they both looked up to find Lexa standing just inside the room, eyes wide. "What the fuck?"

Persephone pulled away from Hades.

"Lexa," she said. "I have something to tell you."

CHAPTER XXIV
A Touch of Trickery

Lexa took the news that she'd been living with a goddess the last four years in stride. Her emotions ranged from feelings of betrayal to disbelief, which Persephone understood. Lexa valued truth, and she had just discovered that the person she called her best friend had been lying about a huge chunk of her identity.

"Why did you keep it from me?" Lexa asked.

"It was an agreement I made with my mom," Persephone said. "Plus, I wanted to know what it was like to live a normal life."

"I get that," Lexa said. "Man, your mother is a bitch," she said and then hunkered down as if she expected lightning to strike her. "Will she kill me for saying that?"

"She's too angry with me and full of hatred for Hades to even think about you," Persephone replied.

Lexa shook her head and just stared at her best friend. They sat in the living room together. It would have felt like any other day had she not been stripped of her mother's magic and exposed as a goddess. Luckily, Hades helped her call up a human glamour. "I can't believe you're the Goddess of Spring. What can you do?"

Persephone flushed. "Well, that's the thing. I'm just now learning my powers. Up until recently, I couldn't even feel my magic. I used to want to be like the other gods," she said. "But when my powers never developed, I just wanted to be somewhere where I was good at something."

Lexa placed her hand on Persephone's. "You are good at so many things, Persephone. Especially at being a goddess."

Persephone scoffed. "How would you know? You just found out what I was."

"I know because you are kind and compassionate and you fight for your beliefs, but mostly, you fight for people. That's what gods are supposed to do, and someone should remind them, because a lot of them have forgotten." Lexa paused. "Maybe that's why you were born."

Persephone wiped tears from her eyes.

"I love you, Lex."

"I love you too, Persephone."

———

Persephone had a hard time sleeping in the weeks following Demeter's threats. Her anxiety skyrocketed, and she felt even more trapped than before. If she didn't fulfill the terms of her contract with Hades, she would be stuck in the Underworld forever. If she managed to create life, then she would become a prisoner in her mother's greenhouse.

It was true she loved Hades, but she preferred to come and go from the Underworld as she pleased. She wanted to continue living her mortal life, graduate, and start her career in journalism. When she'd said as much to Lexa, her best friend had responded, "Just talk to him. He's the God of the Dead. Can't he help?"

But Persephone knew talking would do no good. Hades had said over and over that the terms of the contract were not negotiable, even when facing Demeter. The choice was to fulfill the contract or not—freedom or not.

And that reality was breaking her apart.

Worse, she was using Hades's magic, and while there were a few advantages, it was like having him around all the time. He was a constant presence, a reminder of her predicament, of how she'd spiraled out of control and found herself in love with him.

It was two weeks from graduation—and from the end of her contract with Hades.

When Persephone arrived at the Acropolis for work, she noticed something was off. Valerie was already standing behind her desk when Persephone stepped off the elevator, and she stopped her to whisper before she headed to her desk. "Persephone, there's a woman here to see you. She says she has a story on Hades."

She almost groaned out loud. "Did you vet her?" Persephone had given Valarie a list of questions to ask anyone who called claiming they had a story about Hades. Some of the people who'd made calls or came in person to interview had only been curious mortals or undercover journalists trying to get a story.

"She seems legitimate, although I think she's lying about her name."

Persephone tilted her head. "Why?"

She shrugged. "I don't know. It was the way she said it. Like it was an afterthought."

That didn't make Persephone feel too confident. "What name?"

"Carol."

Weird.

Then Valerie offered, "If you want someone to go with you into the interview, I can."

"No," Persephone said. "That's okay. Thanks, though."

She put her things away, grabbed coffee, and scrolled quickly through her emails on her phone as she entered the room.

"So you have a story for me?" she said, looking up.

"A story? Oh, no, Lady Persephone—I have a bargain."

Persephone froze. She knew that bright blond hair anywhere.

"Aphrodite." Persephone's breath left her. Why was the Goddess of Love here to see her? "What are you doing here?"

"I thought I would pay you a visit, seeing as you are close to the end of your contract with Hades."

Persephone covered her wrist unconsciously, though the mark was hidden by a bracelet. "How do you know about that?"

Aphrodite smiled, but there was pity in her gaze. "I fear Hades has placed you in the middle of our bet."

Persephone felt a painful twist in her stomach, and she swallowed something thick in her throat.

"Bet?" she echoed.

Aphrodite pursed her lips. "I see he has not told you."

"You can drop the false concern, Aphrodite, and get to the point."

The goddess's face changed, and she became more severe and more beautiful than before. When she'd seen Aphrodite at the gala, Persephone had sensed her loneliness and sadness, but now it was clear across her face. It shocked her that Aphrodite, the Goddess of Love—the goddess who had affairs with gods and mortals alike—was lonely.

"My, my," Aphrodite said. "You are awfully demanding. Perhaps that is why Hades likes you so much."

Persephone's fists clenched, and the goddess offered a small smile.

"I challenged Hades to a game of cards. It was all for fun, but he lost. My wager was that he had to make someone fall in love with him within six months," she said.

It took a moment for what she said to sink in. Hades had a contract with Aphrodite—*make someone fall in love with him*.

Persephone swallowed hard.

"I must admit, I was impressed with how quickly he zeroed in on you. Not an hour after I set my terms, he lured you into a contract, and I have been observing his progress ever since."

Persephone wanted to accuse the goddess of lying, but she knew every word Aphrodite had spoken was true.

All this time, she'd been used. The weight of the truth settled on her, broke her, ruined her.

She should have never suspected Hades was capable

of change. The game was life for him. It meant everything, and he would do anything to win.

Even if it broke her heart.

"I am sorry to hurt you," Aphrodite said. "But I see now that I have truly lost."

Persephone glared at the Goddess of Love through watery eyes.

"You do love him."

"Why would you be sorry?" Persephone asked through her teeth. "This is what you wanted."

The goddess shook her head. "Because...until today, I didn't believe in love."

―――――

Persephone had never wanted to choose between Demeter's or Hades's prisons. She'd wanted to find a way to be free, but given the realization she'd been used, she made a choice.

After Aphrodite vanished from the interview room, she made a split decision—she would end the bargain with Hades once and for all and deal with the consequences later. She gathered her things, let Demetri know she needed to leave immediately, and took the bus to Nevernight.

She appeared in the Underworld, making her way across a field, heading toward a dark wall of mountains, intent on finding the Well of Reincarnation.

She should have listened to Minthe.

Gods, she never thought she'd be thinking that.

She was so angry, she couldn't think straight, and she was happy to feel this way now, because she knew when she calmed down, all she would feel was crushing sadness.

She had given everything to Hades—her body, her heart, her dreams.

She'd been so stupid.

Charm, she rationalized. He must have charmed her.

Her thoughts quickly spiraled out of control as she recalled memories from the last six months, each one bringing more pain than the last. She couldn't understand why Hades had gone through so much trouble to orchestrate this plan. He'd fooled her. He'd fooled so many people.

What about Sybil?

The oracle had told her their colors were intertwined. That she and Hades were meant to be together.

Perhaps she's just a really bad oracle.

Now close to tears, she almost didn't hear the rustling of grass beside her. Persephone turned to see movement a short distance from her. Her heart stuttered out of control, and she stumbled back, tripping on something hidden in the grass. When she fell, whatever was in the grass charged toward her.

Persephone closed her eyes and covered her face only to feel a cold, wet nose press against her hand; she opened her eyes to find one of Hades's three dogs staring at her.

She laughed and sat up, petting Cerberus on the head, his tongue rolling out of his mouth. With a glance, she found that what she'd tripped over had been his red ball.

"Where are your brothers?" she asked, scratching behind his ear, and he responded by licking her face. Persephone pushed him away and got to her feet, scooping up the ball. "You want this?"

Cerberus sat back on his haunches but could barely stay still.

"Fetch!" Persephone threw the ball. The hound took off, and she watched him for a few moments before continuing toward the base of the mountain.

The closer she got, the more the ground beneath her feet became uneven, rocky, and bare. A short time later, Cerberus joined her again, ball in his mouth. He didn't drop it at her feet but looked ahead at the mountains.

"Can you lead me to the Well of Reincarnation?" Persephone asked.

The dog looked at her and then took off.

She followed—up a steep incline and into the heart of the mountains. It was one thing to see these landforms from a distance, another to walk among them and beneath the halo of black, swirling clouds. Lightning flashed and thunder shook the earth. She continued to follow Cerberus, fearful of losing sight of the dog—or worse, that he would be hurt.

"Cerberus!" Persephone called as he disappeared around another turn in the maze. She wiped the back of her hand over her forehead, slick with sweat; it was warm in the mountains and growing hotter.

Rounding the corner, she hesitated, noticing a small stream at her feet—but this stream was fire. Unease trickled down her spine. She heard Cerberus barking ahead and jumped over the rivulet only to find the dog at the edge of a cliff where a river of raging flame roiled below. Its heat was almost unbearable, and Persephone suddenly realized where she'd wandered.

Tartarus.

This was the river Phlegethon.

"Cerberus, find a way out!" she commanded.

The dog barked as if accepting her direction and raced toward a set of stairs carved into the mountains. They were sleek and steep and disappeared into the folds above.

But they would take her higher into the mountains.

"Cerberus!"

The dog continued on, so she chased after him.

The steps led to an open cavern above. Lanterns lined the passage but barely illuminated her feet. The tunnel provided an escape from the heat of the Phlegethon. Perhaps Cerberus was leading her to the Well of Reincarnation as she had requested.

Just as she had that thought, she came to the end of the cavern, which led to a beautiful grotto full of lush vegetation and trees heavy with golden fruit. The pool at her feet held water that glittered like stars in an inky sky.

This must be the Well of Reincarnation, she thought.

At the pool's center, there was a stone pillar with a gold goblet at the top. Persephone wasted no time as she waded through the water to reach the cup, but with the movement of water, there came a voice.

"Help," it rasped. "Water."

She froze and looked around but saw nothing.

"H-hello?" she called to the dark.

"The pillar," the voice said.

Persephone's heart raced as she came around the post to find a man chained to the other side of it. He was thin—literally skin stretched over bones—and his hair and beard were long, white, and matted. The manacles around his wrists were just short enough to prevent him from reaching the cup at the top of the pillar or the low-hanging fruit just out of reach.

She inhaled sharply at the sight of him, and when the man looked at her, his pupils appeared to be swimming in blood.

"Help," he said again. "Water."

"Oh my gods."

Persephone climbed the pillar for the goblet, filled it with water from the pool, and helped the man drink.

"Careful," she warned the faster he gulped. "You'll be sick."

She pulled the goblet away, and the man took a few breaths, chest heaving.

"Thank you," he said.

"Who are you?" she asked, studying his face.

"My name"—he took a breath—"is Tantalus."

"And how long have you been here?"

"I do not remember." Every word he spoke was slow and seemed to take all his energy. "I was cursed to be eternally deprived of nourishment."

She wondered what he had done to be assigned such a punishment.

"I have begged daily for an audience with the lord of this realm so that I might find peace in Asphodel, but he will not hear my pleas. I have learned from my time here. I am not the same man I was all those long years ago. I swear it."

She considered this, and despite what she'd learned about Hades today, she believed in the god's powers. Hades knew the soul. If he felt this man had changed, he would grant him his wish to reside in Asphodel.

Persephone took a step away from Tantalus, and his eyes seemed to ignite, his teeth clenched. *There it is*, she realized, *the darkness that Hades saw.*

"You do not believe me," he said, suddenly able to speak without pause.

"I'm afraid I don't know enough either way," Persephone said, trying to remain as neutral as possible. She had the unsettling feeling that this man's rage was to be feared.

At her words, the strange, angry glint that had clouded his eyes disappeared, and he nodded. "You are wise."

"I think I should go," Persephone said.

"Wait," he called as she started to move. "A bite from the fruit—please."

Persephone swallowed. Something told her not to do it, but she found herself plucking a plump, golden fruit from the tree. She approached the man, stretching her arms in an effort to keep a good distance from him. Tantalus strained his neck to reach the fleshy fruit.

That was when something hard plowed into Persephone's legs from under the water.

She lost her footing and was submerged. Before she could break the surface, she felt the man's foot on her chest. Despite his suffering, he was strong and held her under the water while she writhed against him until she grew too weak to fight. The hold she had on her glamour slipped away, and she returned to her Divine form.

When she stopped struggling, Tantalus removed his foot.

That was when Persephone moved.

She pushed her way through the water, which felt more like swimming in tar. She fell, spraying water everywhere.

"A goddess!" She heard Tantalus croon. "Come back, little goddess. I've been starved so long. I require a taste!"

The grotto's bank was slick, and she struggled to climb it, scraping her knees on the jagged rock. She didn't notice the pain, desperate to get out of this place. When she made it to the dark exit, she slammed into a body, and hands clamped down on her shoulders.

"No! Please—"

"Persephone," Hades said, pushing her back only a step.

She froze, meeting his gaze, and at the sight of him, she couldn't contain her relief.

"Hades!" She threw her arms around him and sobbed. He was steady and strong and warm; one of his hands curled against her head and the other on her back.

"Shh." His lips pressed into her hair. "What are you doing here?"

Then the man's horrible voice cut through the air.

"Where are you, little bitch?"

Hades went rigid and pulled her behind him, approaching the grotto's opening. When he snapped his fingers, the column turned so Tantalus faced them now. He didn't appear to be afraid of Hades's arrival.

The god flung out his hand and Tantalus's knees gave out, his arms pulled tight in his chains.

"My goddess was kind to you." Hades's voice was cold and resonant. "And this is how you repay her?"

Tantalus started to heave, and the water Persephone had given him spilled from his mouth. Hades took deliberate steps toward the prisoner, parting the water, creating a dry path straight to the man. Tantalus struggled to

342

find his footing to relieve the pain in his arms, taking deep, shaky breaths that rattled in his chest.

"You deserve to feel as I have felt—desperate and starved and alone!" Tantalus gritted out.

Hades watched Tantalus for a moment; then in a flash, he lifted the man, holding him by the neck. Tantalus's legs kicked back and forth, and Hades laughed at his struggle.

"How do you know I haven't felt like that for centuries, mortal?" he asked, and as he spoke, his glamour melted away. Hades stood clothed in darkness. "You are an ignorant mortal. Before, I was merely your jailer, but now I shall be your punisher, and I think my judges were too merciful. I'll curse you with an unquenchable hunger and thirst. I'll even put you within reach of food and water—but everything you partake of will be fire in your throat."

With that, Hades dropped Tantalus. The chains yanked on his limbs, and he hit the stone hard. When he was able, he lifted his gaze to Hades and growled like an animal. Just as he started to lunge for the god, Hades snapped his fingers and Tantalus was gone.

In the quiet, he turned to Persephone, and she couldn't control her reaction. She took a step back, slipping on the slimy stone. Hades lunged forward and caught her, cradling her in his arms.

"Persephone." His voice was warm and low—a plea. "Please don't fear me. Not you."

She stared up at him, unable to look away. He was beautiful and fierce and powerful—and he had deceived her.

Persephone couldn't hold in her tears. She broke,

and when Hades's hold on her tightened, she buried her face in the crook of his neck. She wasn't aware of when they teleported, and she didn't look up to see where he'd taken her; she only knew that a fire was near. The heat did little to banish the cold raking her body, and when she didn't stop shivering, Hades took her to the baths.

She let him undress her and cradle her against him as they entered the water, but she wouldn't look at him. He allowed the silence to go on for a while, until, she imagined, he couldn't handle it any longer.

"You are unwell," he said. "Did he…hurt you?"

She was quiet and kept her eyes closed, hoping that would keep her from crying.

"Tell me," he begged. "Please."

It was at the word *please* that she opened her watery eyes. "I know about Aphrodite, Hades." His face changed at her words. She'd never seen him look so shocked or stricken. "I'm no more than a game to you."

He scowled. "I have never considered you a game, Persephone."

"The contract—"

"This has nothing to do with the contract," he all but snarled, releasing her.

Persephone struggled to gain her footing in the water and shot back at him. "This has everything to do with the contract! Gods, I was so stupid! I let myself think you were good even with the possibility of being your prisoner."

"Prisoner? You would think yourself a prisoner here? Have I treated you so poorly?"

"A kind jailer is still a jailer," Persephone snapped.

Hades's face darkened. "If you considered me your warden, why did you fuck me?"

"It was you who foretold this." Her voice shook. "And you were right—I did enjoy it, and now that it's done, we can move on."

"Move on?" His voice took on a deadly edge. "Is that what you want?"

"We both know it's for the best."

"I'm beginning to think you don't know anything," he said. "I'm beginning to understand that you don't even think for yourself."

Those words pierced her like a blade to her sternum. "How dare you—"

"How dare I what, Persephone? Call out your bullshit? You act so powerless, but you've never made a damn decision for yourself. Will you let your mother determine who you fuck now?"

"Shut up!"

"Tell me what you want." He cornered her, pinning her against the edge of the pool.

She looked away and ground her teeth so hard, her jaw hurt.

"Tell me!"

"Fuck you!" She snarled and jumped, twining her legs around his waist. She kissed him hard, their lips and teeth crashing together painfully, but neither of them stopped. Her fingers tangled into his hair, and she pulled hard, tipping his head back, kissing down his neck. In seconds, they found themselves outside the pool, on the marble walkway, and Persephone pushed Hades onto his back and impaled herself on his shaft, taking him deep.

The brutal movement of their bodies and breathing

filled the baths. It was the most erotic thing she'd ever done, and as she moved, she felt a rush inside her—something separate from the heady pull of Hades's body. She couldn't place it, but it was awake in her veins and vibrating.

Hades reached between them, squeezing her breasts and gripping her thighs, then rose into a sitting position, taking her nipples into his mouth. The sensation drew a guttural sound from Persephone, and she squeezed Hades to her, moving harder and faster.

"Yes," Hades said between his teeth and then commanded, "Use me. Harder. Faster."

It was the only command she ever wanted to obey.

They came together, and in the aftermath, Persephone rose from Hades, grabbed her clothes, and left the baths. Hades followed after her, naked.

"Persephone," he called. She kept walking, pulling on her clothes as she went. Hades cursed and finally caught up with her, pulling her into a nearby room—his throne room.

She turned on him, pushing him away angrily. He didn't move an inch and instead caged her with his arms.

"I want to know why." Persephone could feel something burning in her veins. It ignited deep in her belly and rushed through her like venom when he didn't speak. "Was I an easy target? Did you look at my soul and see someone who was desperate for love, for worship? Did you choose me because you knew I couldn't fulfill the terms of your bargain?"

"It wasn't like that."

He was too calm.

"Then tell me what it was!" she seethed.

"Yes, Aphrodite and I have a contract, but the bargain I struck with you had nothing to do with it." She crossed her arms, prepared to reject that statement, when he added, "I offered you terms based on what I saw in your soul—a woman caged by her own mind."

Persephone glared at him.

"You are the one who called the contract impossible," he said. "But you are powerful, Persephone."

"Do *not* mock me." Her voice shook.

"I would never."

The sincerity in his voice made her sick. "Liar."

His eyes darkened. "I am many things, but a liar I am not."

"Not a liar then, but a self-admitted deceiver."

"I have only ever given you answers," he said. "I have helped you reclaim your power, and yet you haven't used it. I have given you a way to walk out from underneath your mother, and yet you will not claim it."

"How?" she demanded. "What did you do to help me?"

"I worshipped you!" he yelled. "I gave you what your mother withheld—worshippers."

Persephone stood for a moment in stunned silence. "You mean to tell me you forced me into a contract when you could have just told me I needed worshippers to gain my powers?"

"It's not about powers, Persephone! It's never been about magic or illusion or glamour. It's about confidence. It's about believing in yourself!"

"That's twisted, Hades—"

"Is it?" he snapped. "Tell me, if you'd known, what would you have done? Announced your divinity to the whole world so that you might gain a following and consequently your power?" She knew the answer, and so did he. "No, you've never been able to decide what you want because you value your mother's happiness over your own!"

"I had freedom until you, Hades."

"You thought you were free before me?" he asked. "You just traded glass walls for another kind of prison when you came to New Athens."

"Why don't you keep telling me how pathetic I am," she spat.

"That's not what I—"

"Isn't it?" she cut him off. "Let me tell you what else makes me pathetic: I fell for you." Tears stung her eyes. Hades moved to touch her, but she held out her hand. "Don't!"

He halted, looking far more pained than she could have ever imagined. She took a moment, waiting to speak until she was sure her voice was even. "What would Aphrodite have gotten if you had failed?"

Hades swallowed and answered in a low, rough voice, "She asked that one of her heroes be returned to the living."

Persephone pressed her lips together and nodded. She should have known. "Well, you won. I love you. Was it worth it?"

"It wasn't like that, Persephone!" She turned from him, and he called out, "You would believe Aphrodite's words over my actions?"

She paused at that and turned to face him. She was so angry her body vibrated. If he was trying to tell her he loved her, he needed to say it. She needed to hear the words.

Instead, he shook his head and said, "You are your own prisoner."

Something within her snapped. It was painful and moved through her veins like fire. Beneath their feet, the marble rattled. Their eyes met just as great black vines erupted from the floor, twisting around the God of the Dead until his wrists and ankles were restrained.

For a moment, they were both frozen, stunned.

She had created life—though what rose from the floor looked far from alive. It was withered and black, not bright and beautiful. Persephone breathed heavily; unlike before, the magic she now felt was strong. It made her body throb with a dull pain.

Hades regarded his bound wrists, testing the restraints. When he looked at Persephone, he offered a humorless chuckle, his eyes a dull, lifeless black.

"Well, Lady Persephone. It looks like *you* won."

CHAPTER XXV
A Touch of Life

Persephone didn't remove the gold cuff until she was in her own shower. She stood under a hot stream of water until it ran ice cold, then slid to the floor of the tub. When she pulled off the bracelet, the mark was gone.

She'd always envisioned this moment differently. In truth, she'd imagined gaining her powers *and* Hades. She'd imagined having the best of both worlds.

Instead, she had neither.

She knew it was just a matter of time before her mother came to collect her. A sob caught in her throat, but she held it back and dragged herself out of the bathroom.

She was her own prisoner.

Hades was right, and the weight of his words crashed down on her in the night, eliciting a renewed stream of tears. At some point—she didn't know when—Lexa climbed into bed with her, drew her into her arms, and held her. That was how Persephone fell asleep.

When she woke the next morning, Lexa was awake and watching her. Her best friend brushed her hair out of her face and asked, "Are you okay?"

"Yes," she said quietly.

"Is it…over?"

Persephone nodded and forced the tears away. She was tired of crying. Her eyes were swollen, and she couldn't breathe out of her nose.

"I'm sorry, Persephone," Lexa said and bent down to hug her close.

Persephone shrugged. She was afraid to say anything—afraid she would cry again.

Despite this, she felt different. She had a renewed determination to take control of her life.

As if on cue, her phone vibrated, and when she looked down, she found a message from Adonis: *Tick tock.*

She'd forgotten his deadline. She was supposed to have his job reinstated by tomorrow. Knowing that was impossible, Persephone had no other options.

If only she could get those photos, he'd have nothing to blackmail her with.

"Lexa," Persephone said. "Isn't Jaison a programmer?"

"Yeah…why?"

"I have a job for him."

———

Persephone waited in the Garden of the Gods on campus. She'd chosen Hades's garden, mostly because it offered more privacy from prying eyes and eavesdroppers.

She'd spent the morning telling Lexa everything that had happened with Adonis and asked Jaison if he could hack into the mortal's computer and delete the photos he was using for blackmail. The amount of joy he'd gotten from the request was comical; during the hack, he'd uncovered a wealth of information, including Adonis's informant.

Persephone's phone buzzed, and as she checked it, she saw Adonis had texted.

Here.

When she looked up, she spotted Minthe and Adonis approaching from opposite directions—Minthe glaring, Adonis wide-eyed.

They came to a stop a few feet from her.

"What is he doing here?" Minthe snapped.

"What's *she* doing here?" Adonis asked.

"It's so I won't have to repeat myself," Persephone said. "I know Minthe took the photos you're blackmailing me with." Her phone buzzed and she checked it before adding, "Or rather, I should say, were blackmailing me with. As of this second, your devices have been hacked and the photos removed."

Adonis paled, and Minthe's glare deepened.

"You can't do that. It's—it's illegal!" Adonis argued.

"Illegal like blackmail?"

That shut him up. Persephone turned her attention to Minthe.

"I suppose you'll run and tell on me?" the nymph asked.

"Why would I do that?" Persephone's question was genuine, but Minthe just seemed irritated, pressing her lips together and snarling.

"Let's not play act, Goddess. Revenge, of course. I'm surprised you didn't tell Hades I was the one who sent you into Tartarus."

"Did she just call you Goddess?" Adonis jumped in, but glares from Minthe and Persephone had him silent again.

"I prefer to fight my own battles," Persephone said.

"With what? Your words?" Minthe offered a sarcastic laugh.

"I understand that you're jealous of me," Persephone said. "But your anger is misplaced." If anything, she should be angry with Hades, or maybe angry with herself for wasting time pining after a man who didn't love her.

"You understand nothing!" Minthe seethed. "All these years, I stood beside him, only to wither in your shadow as he flaunted you to his whole kingdom like you were already his queen!"

Minthe was right—Persephone didn't understand. She couldn't imagine what it would feel like to dedicate your life—your love—to a person who never returned it.

Then Minthe added in a shaky voice, "You were supposed to fall in love with him, not the other way around."

Persephone flinched. So Minthe had been aware of the terms of the bargain. She wondered if Hades had told her or if she'd been present when Aphrodite had set her terms. It made her embarrassed to think that Minthe had watched her fall in love with Hades, knowing his deception.

"Hades doesn't love me," Persephone said.

"Stupid girl." Minthe shook her head. "If you cannot see it, then maybe you aren't worthy of him."

Anger ignited in her veins, and her fingers curled into fists.

"Hades betrayed me." Persephone's voice shook.

Minthe snorted.

"How? Because he chose not to tell you about his contract with Aphrodite? Given that you wrote a derisive article about him within a few days of meeting him, I'm not at all surprised he didn't confide in you. He was probably afraid that if you found out, you would act like the child you are."

Minthe was treading on thin ice.

"You should have been more thankful for your time in our world," she added. "It's the most powerful you will ever be."

It was at that moment Persephone knew how it felt to be truly wicked. A smile curled her lips, and Minthe suddenly sobered as if she sensed something had changed.

"No," Persephone said, and with a flick of her wrist, a vine shot out from the ground and curled around Minthe's feet. As the nymph started to scream, another vine closed over her mouth, silencing her. "*This* is the most powerful I will ever be."

She snapped her fingers, and Minthe shrunk and morphed until she was nothing more than a lush mint plant.

Adonis's eyes went wide with disbelief. "Oh my gods! You—you—"

Persephone approached the plant and plucked it from the ground, then she turned and kneed Adonis in the groin. The mortal collapsed, writhing on the ground, clutching himself and moaning. Persephone watched him a moment, content to see him suffer.

"If you ever threaten me again, I will curse you," she said, a deadly calm overtaking her voice.

He spoke between breaths. "You…can't…have… Aphrodite's…favor!"

Persephone smirked and tilted her head to the side. It wasn't until a slender vine reached around to caress his face that Adonis started to scream.

Persephone had turned his arms into literal limbs, and they were quickly growing foliage.

His pain forgotten, he shrieked. "Turn me back! Turn me back!"

When he saw she was not moved by his demands, he turned to pleading.

"Please." Tears spilled from his eyes. "Please. I'll do anything. Anything."

"Anything?" Persephone echoed.

"Yes! Just turn me back!"

"A favor," Persephone bargained. "To be collected at a future time."

"Whatever you want! Do it! Do it now!"

But Persephone didn't, and when Adonis realized she was making no move to reinstate his arms, he grew quiet.

"Do you know what a corpse lily is, Adonis?"

He glared at her and didn't speak.

"Don't make me repeat myself, mortal." She dropped her glamour and took a threatening step forward. "Yes or no?"

Adonis's eyes widened, and he wiggled away, whimpering, "No."

"Pity. It is a parasitic flower that smells like decaying flesh. I'm sure you're wondering what this has to do with you. Well, it's a wager. If you touch any woman without consent, I will turn you into one."

Adonis went pale but managed to glare at her. "A wager usually implies I get something in return."

She shook her head at his stupidity. "You do." She leaned close. "Your life." For emphasis, she held Minthe—the newly transformed mint plant—aloft, examining its green leaves. "She'll make a fine addition to my garden."

She snapped her fingers, and Adonis's arms were restored. He floundered for a moment during the transition, but once he was on his feet again, she turned on her heels and walked away.

"Who the fuck are you?" he called after her. Persephone paused, then turned to look at Adonis over her shoulder.

"I am Persephone, Goddess of Spring," she answered and disappeared.

———

Her mother's greenhouse was just as she remembered: an ornate metal structure covered in glass, nestled in the rich woods of Olympia. It was two stories, the ceiling was rounded, and at this moment, the sun shone in a way that made the whole thing look like gold.

It was a shame she hated being here, because it was breathtaking.

Inside, it smelled like her mother—sweet and bitter, like a bouquet of wildflowers. The scent made her heart ache. There was a part of her that missed her mother and mourned how their relationship had changed. She had never wanted to be a disappointment, but more than that, she didn't want to be a prisoner.

Persephone spent time walking the paths, passing colorful beds of lilies and violets, roses and orchids, and a variety of trees with plump fruit. The flutter of life was all around her. The feeling was growing stronger and more familiar.

She stopped along the path, recalling all the dreams she'd had when trapped behind these walls. Dreams of sparkling cities and exciting adventures and passionate love. She'd found all of that, and it had been beautiful and wicked and heartbreaking.

And she'd do it all again just to taste, to feel, to live again.

"Kore."

Persephone cringed, as she always did when her mother used her childhood name. She turned and found Demeter standing a few feet away, her face cold and unreadable.

"Mother." Persephone nodded.

"I have been looking for you," said Demeter, and her eyes fell to Persephone's wrist. "But I see you have come to your senses and returned to me of your own volition."

"Actually, Mother, I came to say that I know what you did."

Her mother's expression remained distant. "I don't know what you mean."

"I know you kept me hidden here to prevent my powers from manifesting," she said.

Demeter lifted her head a fraction. "It was for your own good. I only ever did what I thought was best."

"What you thought was best," Persephone repeated. "Didn't you ever consider how I might feel?"

"If you had just listened to me, none of this would have happened! You didn't know any different until you left. That's when you changed." Demeter said it like it was a horrible thing—like she resented who Persephone had become. And maybe that was true.

"You're wrong," Persephone argued. "I wanted adventure. I wanted to live outside these walls. You knew that. I begged you."

Demeter looked away.

"You never gave me a choice—"

"I couldn't!" she snapped and then took a deep breath. "I suppose it didn't matter in the end. It all happened as the Fates predicted."

"What?"

Demeter glared. "When you were born, I went to the Fates and asked of your future. A goddess had not been born in ages, and I worried for you. They told me you were destined to be a Queen of Darkness, the Bride of Death. Hades's wife. I could not let that happen. I did the only thing I could do—kept you hidden and safe."

"No, not safe," Persephone said. "You did it so I would always need you, so you would never have to be alone."

The two stared at each other for a moment before Persephone added, "I know you do not believe in love, Mother, but you had no right to keep me from mine."

Demeter blinked in shock. "Love? You can't...*love* Hades."

Persephone wished she didn't; then she wouldn't feel this aching in her chest. "See, that's the problem with you trying to control my life. You're wrong. You've always been wrong. I know I'm not the daughter you wanted, but I am the daughter you have, and if you want to be in my life, you will let me live it."

Demeter glared. "So this is it? You have come to tell me you've chosen Hades over me?"

"No, I came to tell you that I forgive you…for everything."

Demeter's expression was one of contempt. "You forgive me? It is you who should be begging for my forgiveness. I did everything for you!"

"I don't need your forgiveness to live an unburdened life, and I most certainly will not beg for it."

Persephone waited. She wasn't sure what she expected her mother to say—maybe that she loved her? That she wanted a relationship with her, and they would figure out this new normal?

But she said nothing, and Persephone's shoulder fell.

She was emotionally exhausted. What she wanted now more than anything was to be surrounded by people who loved her for who she was.

She was tired of fighting.

"Whenever you're ready to reconcile, let me know."

Persephone snapped her fingers, intent on teleporting from the greenhouse, except that she remained where she was—trapped.

Demeter's face darkened with a devious smile.

"I am sorry, my flower, but I cannot allow you to leave. Not when I have just managed to reclaim you once again."

"I asked you to let me live." Persephone's voice shook.

"And you will. Here. Where you belong."

"No." Persephone's fists curled.

"In time, you will understand. This moment will be forgotten in the vastness of your lifetime."

Lifetime. The word made Persephone breathless. She couldn't imagine a lifetime locked in this place—a lifetime without adventure, without love, without passion.

She wouldn't.

"Things will be as they were before," Demeter added.

But things could never be as they were before, and Persephone knew it. She had a taste—a touch of darkness—and she would crave it the rest of her life.

When Persephone began to shake, so did the ground, and Demeter frowned. "What is the meaning of this, Kore?"

It was time for Persephone to smile.

"Oh, Mother. You don't understand, but everything has changed."

And out of the ground shot thick, black stalks, rising until they shattered the glass of the greenhouse above, effectively breaking the spell Demeter had placed upon the prison. From the stalks, silver vines twisted, filling the space, breaking the structure, flattening flowers and destroying trees.

"What are you doing?" Demeter screamed over the sounds of bending metal and breaking glass.

"Freeing myself," Persephone replied—and vanished.

CHAPTER XXVI
A Touch of Home

Graduation came and went in a flurry of black robes, blue and white tassels, and parties. It was a bittersweet end, and Persephone had never felt prouder as she walked across that stage…or more alone.

Lexa had been spending more time with Jaison. Persephone hadn't heard from her mother since she destroyed the greenhouse, and she hadn't returned to Nevernight or the Underworld since she'd left Hades tangled in her vines.

Her only distraction was work. Persephone had started full-time at *New Athens News* as an investigative journalist the week after graduation. She arrived early and stayed late, and when she had nothing left to do, she'd spend the evening deep in the Garden of the Gods practicing her magic.

She was getting better, and while the instinct to reach for her power was stronger, she hadn't managed to reclaim the abilities she'd had when she'd transformed

Minthe into a plant and Adonis's limbs into vines and destroyed her mother's home. The things she grew now had returned to resembling dead vines. She found herself wishing she could train with Hecate.

She missed Hecate, the souls, the Underworld.

She missed Hades.

Now and then, she considered returning to the Underworld to visit. She knew Hades hadn't revoked her favor, but she was too afraid, too embarrassed, and too ashamed to go. How was she supposed to explain her absence, and would they forgive her?

As more days passed, the less Persephone felt she could return, and so she continued her daily routine: work, lunch with Lexa and Sybil, and an evening walk through the park.

Today, that routine was disrupted.

She checked her watch as she sat her usual table at the Coffee House. She was waiting for a text from Lexa. It was her birthday weekend, and they were going out tonight to celebrate with Jaison, Sybil, Aro, and Xerxes, and while Persephone was excited for the distraction, she needed to finish her final article on the God of the Dead.

Writing the article had been more painful than she expected. She'd written through tears and clenched teeth. As a result, the publication was delayed. She hadn't expected to be so emotional, but she guessed she'd gone through a lot in the last six months. The worry and stress over fulfilling the terms of her contract with Hades had taken a toll in so many ways. Against her better judgment, she had fallen for the god, and she had slowly been trying to figure out how to put the pieces of her heart back together.

The problem was it didn't fit together the same way. She was changed.

And it was both beautiful and terrible. She had taken control of her life, severing relationships as she went. The people she trusted six months ago were not the people she trusted now.

The most painful part of it all was her mother's betrayal and subsequent silence. After she'd destroyed the greenhouse, Demeter had kept her distance. Persephone wasn't even sure where her mother had gone, though she suspected she was in Olympia.

Still, she had expected something from her—even an angry text.

Nothing was a stab in the heart.

Her phone beeped with a message from Lexa: *Ready for tonight?*

She texted back, *You know it! Have you made a decision?*

She hadn't decided where to celebrate yet. They'd both agreed Nevernight and La Rose were out of the question.

I'm thinking Bakkheia or the Raven. Bakkheia was a bar owned by Dionysus and the Raven was owned by Apollo. *What do you think?*

Hmm. Definitely the Raven.

But you hate Apollo's music.

It was true. Persephone dreaded every album the God of Light released. She wasn't sure why—something about the way he pronounced his words irritated her, and it was the only music that played at his club.

But it's your birthday. Persephone reminded her. *And the Raven is more your style.*

It's settled. The Raven it is! Thanks, Persephone!

Despite seeing less of Lexa, Persephone was happy for her. Lexa was thriving with Jaison, and Persephone would forever be indebted to the two mortals for their service to her—especially Lexa, who had stayed with her for a whole week while she reeled from her breakup with Hades and managed to keep Minthe the mint plant alive after she had promptly forgotten her existence in the kitchen window.

She'd had plans to return the nymph to the Underworld and offer her to Hades, but she didn't have the courage to face him.

She texted Lexa that she was heading out and started to pack her things when a shadow fell over her. She looked up into a familiar pair of dark, gentle eyes.

"Hecate!" Persephone stood and threw her arms around the goddess's neck. "I missed you."

Hecate returned her embrace and inhaled sharply with relief. "I missed you too, my dear." She pulled away and studied Persephone's face, her brows knitted together over her caring eyes. "We all do."

Guilt slammed into Persephone, and she swallowed. She'd essentially been avoiding everyone. "Sit with me?"

"Of course." The Goddess of Witchcraft took a seat beside Persephone.

She couldn't stop staring at Hecate. The goddess looked different in human glamour, with her hair in a braid and wearing a long, black maxi dress instead of regal robes.

"I hope I'm not interrupting," Hecate added.

"No, just…working," Persephone said.

The goddess nodded. They were quiet for a

moment, and Persephone hated the awkwardness between them.

"How is everyone?" she hedged.

"Sad," Hecate said, and Persephone felt a pang in her chest.

"You're really not one to beat around the bush, are you, Hecate?"

"Come back," she said.

Persephone couldn't look at Hecate. Her eyes burned. "You know I can't."

"What does it matter that you found each other through this contract?" Hecate asked.

Persephone's eyes widened, and she looked at the Goddess of Witchcraft. "Did he tell you?"

"I asked."

"Then you know he deceived me."

"Did he? As I recall, he told you your contract had nothing to do with Aphrodite's wager."

"You cannot tell me that he didn't consider I might help him fulfill his contract with her."

"I am sure he considered it, but only because he was already in love with you. Was it so wrong for him to hope?"

Persephone sat, stewing in her silence. Was Hecate only here to attempt to convince her to return to Hades?

She knew the answer—but it was more complicated than a yes.

Hecate was here to convince her to return to the Underworld, to a kingdom of people who had treated her like a queen—to her friends.

She knew Hecate was right. Did it really matter that they had found love for each other because of a contract? People found love in all sorts of ways.

The hardest thing, though, was that when she'd told Hades she loved him, he hadn't said it in return. He hadn't said anything at all.

She felt Hecate watching her, and the goddess asked, "How do you think you fulfilled the terms of your contract?"

Persephone looked at her, confused. "I…grew something."

It wasn't beautiful. She wasn't even sure it could be called a plant, but it was alive and that was what mattered.

The goddess shook her head. "No. You fulfilled the contract because you created life within Hades. Because you brought life to the Underworld."

Persephone looked away, closing her eyes against the words. She couldn't hear this.

Then Hecate whispered, "It is bleak without you." She took Persephone's hand. "Do you love him?"

The question brought tears to her eyes, and she wiped at them furiously before uttering a breathless, "Yes." She sniffed. "Yes. I think I've loved him since the beginning. That's why it hurts."

Hades had challenged her to look at the whole picture, to not be blinded by her passion—except when it came to her passion for him.

"So go to him. Tell him why you hurt. Tell him how to fix it. Isn't that what you're good at?"

Persephone couldn't help laughing at that and then groaned, rubbing her eyes. "Oh, Hecate. He doesn't want to see me."

"How do you know?" she asked.

"Don't you think if he wanted me, he would have come for me?"

"Perhaps he was just giving you time," she said.

Hecate looked away, down the pedestrian street, and Persephone followed her gaze. Her breath caught, and her heart pounded in her chest.

Hades stood a few feet away. Dressed from head to toe in black, he had never looked more handsome. His gaze, dark and piercing, settled on her, and it was the most vulnerable she'd ever seen him—hopeful but afraid.

Persephone rose from her chair, but it took her a moment to get her legs moving. She stumbled forward, and then broke into a run. He caught her as she jumped into his arms, legs twining around his waist. He held her close, burying his face into the crook of her neck.

"I missed you," he whispered.

"I missed you too," she said and then pulled back. She studied his face, brushing the curve of his cheek and the bow of his lips. "I'm sorry."

"As am I," he said, and she realized he was examining her just as intently, like he was trying to memorize every part of her. "I love you. I should have told you sooner. I should have told you that night in the bath. I knew then."

She smiled, her fingers coiling into his hair. "I love you too."

Their lips crashed together, and it was like the whole world melted away—though they were surrounded by a legion of people taking photos and filming. Hades broke the kiss first, and Persephone looked up at him, both frustrated and slightly dazed.

"I wish to claim my favor, Goddess," he said, his eyes darkening.

Persephone's heart hammered in her chest.

"Come to the Underworld with me."

She started to protest, but he silenced her with a kiss.

"Live between worlds," he said. "But do not leave us forever—my people, your people…me."

She blinked back tears—he understood. She would have the best of both worlds. She would have him.

Her smile turned mischievous, and she smoothed his shirt. "I'm eager for a game of cards."

The corners of his mouth twitched and his eyes darkened. "Poker?" he asked.

"Yes."

"The stakes?"

"Your clothes," she answered.

Then they vanished.

Minthe the Mint Plant

Hades's dark eyes held Persephone's gaze as he reclined in the chair behind his obsidian desk, lithe fingers covering his full lips. When Persephone had entered his office, she'd been surprised to find him there. Since meeting the God of the Dead six months ago, she'd never seen him use the desk.

"Oh, so the desk isn't just for show." A smile curled her lips, and for a moment, she was unburdened by the reason she'd come here.

Hades raised a brow and looked her up and down, eyes glittering. She'd chosen her outfit strategically: a red dress that hugged her curves. The straps were thin and the neckline a deep V, accentuating the rise and fall of her chest. It was probably unfair, but she thought it might lessen the blow she'd come to deliver.

"I can be very productive when I wish," he said.

"Oh?"

"Yes, as you are aware, darling, I am exceptional

at multitasking," he said, and the air thickened with an electric pulse she felt in her gut.

"Hmm. I seem to have forgotten you possessed *that* particular skill. Perhaps you can enlighten me?"

Hades's fingers fisted but he did not move, eyes falling to the plant she cradled in her arms. "Have you brought me something?"

The moment was ruined, which wasn't all that surprising. Minthe had ruined many things when she'd been a nymph; now she ruined things as a plant too.

Persephone placed the mint plant on the edge of Hades's desk. "Actually, I'm returning what was already yours."

Hades's brows knitted together over his coal-black eyes. "I think I would remember leaving a mint plant at your home, Persephone."

"Well, you see, this…*plant* wasn't always a plant."

Hades waited.

"She was a nymph. Minthe."

Persephone couldn't tell what he was thinking, but her heart was racing, and anxiety pulled at her chest. She'd practiced delivering her news in the mirror before she'd teleported to Nevernight, marched up the stairs, and barged into Hades's office. She'd had to walk fast, or she would have turned around and gone back home.

But it was time he knew the truth.

Now that the words were out of her mouth, he sat silent and still. She had expected more of a reaction from him.

After a moment, he spoke.

"You're saying that"—Hades pointed to the mint plant—"is my assistant?"

"Yes."

He didn't look at the plant but at her. "And why is my assistant a plant, Persephone?"

"Because"—She averted her eyes and admitted—"She upset me."

Hades waited, his silence questioning, and when she said nothing more, he asked, "What did Minthe do to upset you?"

There was a long list—her closeness to Hades, her opinion that Persephone was all wrong for him, the fact that the nymph had tricked her into entering Tartarus—but what had really pissed her off was when Minthe had called her powerless.

But she wasn't here to snitch, so she answered, "That doesn't matter anymore. I took care of it." Hades raised a brow, and before he could say anything else, she continued. "I thought I would give you the option of returning her to her true form."

The corners of his mouth lifted, and his eyes glittered. He was clearly amused, and her anxiety lessened. "You wish for me to make that decision?"

She blinked and said, "She's *your* assistant."

Hades tilted his head to the side, studying her. He was deciding how to proceed, and that made her nervous. When he rose to his feet and came around the desk, Persephone turned toward him, and Hades captured her chin between his fingers, tilting her head back until her throat was taut.

"How shall I convince you to tell me the truth?" His voice was low, husky. It promised passion.

"Are you asking to play?"

He watched her a moment. She still couldn't figure

out exactly what he thought about this whole situation. Then he pressed his lips to the hollow of her throat, tracing the column of her neck and the edge of her jaw with his mouth. Persephone clung to him, her hands fisted into his jacket, and when she gasped, Hades moved. Gripping her hips, he guided her to the edge of his pristine, obsidian desk.

"I'm multitasking," he said as his hands slid up her thighs and under her dress. His mouth closed over hers. Teeth and tongue and breaths twined together, and as he consumed her, he slipped her panties off and spread her legs wide, straining her dress at the seams and exposing her heat to the cool air.

Anticipation coiled low in her stomach as Hades's wicked gaze fell upon her. His fingers parted her hot flesh, and as he entered her, her head fell back.

Did Hades intend to pleasure her into answering his questions?

His fingers thrust, working hard and deep. He drew back to watch her, and as her breath quickened, she moaned his name.

"Do you like that?" he asked, moving in and out, the friction of his fingers driving her to the edge of a cliff she would kill to fall off.

"Yes," she breathed.

"Tell me what you want."

"More. Harder," she said, breathless. "Faster."

And that was when he withdrew.

His sudden absence was shocking, and a guttural sound came from her throat. She glared at him and reached for him, but Hades took a step back, chest rising and falling. For a moment, she thought someone might be approaching the office, but when Hades made no move to help cover her, she knew something else was amiss. "Why did you stop?"

"Tell me why you snapped," he said. "What did she say to upset you?"

Persephone glared at him. "This is your game?"

"You think this is a game?"

Her anger was so fierce and so acute, she thought she might turn him into a plant too, recognizing the feel of her magic awakening in her veins. It was strongest when she was angry.

She started to push off the desk, but Hades trapped her, bringing his lips to hers again. Fingers twisting into her hair, he pulled her head back so he could explore her mouth deeper. For a moment, she stiffened in his arms, hands pressed firmly against his chest. It was like she had thought to push him away but couldn't, wouldn't resist him.

But she'd make him pay.

He was wrong if he thought he could do this—even more wrong if he thought he could resist *her*.

Persephone unbuttoned his shirt; her hands sought the planes of his chest, rock-hard abs, and the waistband of his slacks. His arousal strained against the fabric, and when she freed him, he groaned against her mouth.

Her fingers closed over his shaft and she pushed into him, slipping off the desk and directing him backward until his back hit the wall.

Then she snapped her fingers, and they found themselves in the Underworld—in the garden Hades had granted her at the start of their contract. Hades's back was pressed against the stone wall. She still held his cock in her hand, and she smiled. She loved having Hades's favor.

"Persephone—"

She snapped her fingers again, and this time vines wound their way around Hades's wrists and ankles. His eyes darkened, his jaw tightened, and her name came out as a warning. "*Persephone.*"

"Yes, my lord?" she asked innocently.

"What are you doing?"

She stroked him, and his chest heaved.

"What does it look like?" she asked.

She worked him up and down and used her thumb to stroke the head of his member. She rose on the tips of her toes to kiss his lips and down his neck. Hades strained against the bindings she had put in place, desperate to reciprocate.

"Tell me what you want," she whispered as she nibbled his ear.

Hades growled, "You, Goddess."

She pulled away, smiling deviously, and then kneeled to take him into her mouth. He tasted like salt, and she took him deeper, the head of his cock hitting the back of her throat. Hades groaned over her. She held on to his legs, feeling his muscles cord beneath her hands. She worked him until he exploded in her mouth, and when she was finished, she rose to her feet, keeping his dark gaze, and stepped away.

"Is it torturous?" she asked. It was a challenge.

He didn't answer but his eyes burned, and the vines around his wrists were taut.

"To take pleasure from me and not give it in return?"

She lifted her dress over her head and tossed it aside. Standing naked before him, she asked, "What do you want, Hades?"

She underestimated his strength and will to possess her. The vines she'd called forth to hold him snapped, and he pounced, dragging her up his body and entering her without hesitation. Persephone's moan shattered the air as he stretched her and took her deep. His hands gripped her thighs so hard, it felt like he was holding her bones. The god shifted, resting her against the stone wall, thrusting into her hard. The jagged rock scraped her back, but she didn't even feel it. She was too busy clawing at Hades, reaching for his hair, lost in his body as he filled her to bursting.

Hades had awakened a darkness within her, an ache that constantly needed attention. She would always crave him.

Her climax was violent, as was his.

He knelt in the dirt then, holding Persephone close. She clung to him for a long time, legs shaking, unable to move or stand.

Once their breathing returned, Persephone pulled away and met Hades's gaze. "You will not use sex to get what you want, do you understand?"

"Yes, my queen."

Persephone's eyes widened.

"But I will tell you what I want," he said quickly. "An answer when I ask for it."

Persephone reddened. "Why? Don't you trust me?"

"I could ask the same of you."

Persephone looked away. "It's not so easy to answer you."

"Why?" She was quiet, and Hades touched her chin, drawing her eyes back to his. "Are you ashamed?"

It took her a moment, and then she said, "I was angry and rash in my decision, but she questioned my power and I thought I'd teach her just how powerful I was."

Hades was quiet for a moment before he kissed her.

"If you had not punished her, I would have for leading you to Tartarus."

Persephone looked at him, surprised. "You knew?"

"I suspected," he said. "You confirmed."

She glared at him, swatting at his arm. "That's deceptive."

Hades chuckled but grew more serious. "Still, why protect her when she put you in danger?"

"I wasn't protecting her. I was handling her on my own. I don't want you to fight my battles, Hades."

The look he gave her was one of admiration and astonishment. "My lady, it is very clear to me that you do not need my helping fighting your battles." Hades helped Persephone dress, and once their appearances were restored, he snapped his fingers, and Minthe the mint plant appeared in his hand. "Now, what shall we do with her?"

"I haven't completely forgiven her," Persephone admitted. "But I should like to provide her with at least one comfort, and that's to be returned to the Underworld."

Hades observed a few wilted leaves on the mint plant. "Is that because you have neglected her in the Upperworld?"

"No!" Persephone snapped defensively, and Hades

laughed. "If you *must* know, I spend more time here anyway. I'd rather she not die under my watch."

Hades, still smiling, kissed the top of her head. "As you wish, darling."

Hades helped Persephone plant Minthe in the coarse, black soil. Once she was settled, the two set off on a stroll through the fields of the Underworld.

The day was bright, full of the Underworld's strange, unnatural light. Around them were tall shoots of grass and flowers the color of blood oranges. Black mountains and dark forests encroached. This world was beautiful, surreal, magical; it was a haven to the dead, a prison to some, and in the last few months, it had become one of her favorite places.

She looked forward to her visits to the Underworld, not just to see Hades or the lands but to visit Hecate and the souls in Asphodel. They had come to expect her, celebrate her. They called her queen.

It was that thought that gave her pause, and the fact that Hades had too. She had tried to put a stop to their use of the title, but why would they listen if their king used it too?

"Hades… I want to ask that you not call me my—"

"Lady?"

"Queen," she said.

The god came to a stop, his expression unreadable.

She hurried to continue. "I recognize you spoke in a moment of passion—"

"I meant it," he said. "You are my queen. Only you hold sway over me."

"Hades—"

"Why do you fear it? The title?"

"It's not fear; it's…" She couldn't find words. "Your people already call me their queen. Don't you think it's a little…too early?"

"So it is fear," he said. "Fear that you and I will not work."

Persephone didn't need to say anything. It *was* fear.

"My people will always see you as their mistress because of how you have treated them, whether you choose to love me or not." His words made her heart hurt. She wanted to tell him that she did love him, but he continued. "As for me, well—you will always be the ruler of my heart."

"You cannot know that," she said. No matter how much she wanted it to be true.

"I have waited lifetimes for you," he said as if it was an oath he was swearing upon every star in the sky, every drop of water in the ocean, every soul in the entire universe. "I know it."

He walked on, and she followed, feeling a weight settle on her shoulders. Perhaps she shouldn't have doubted their love, but she had fears—fears that still loomed like clouds over their future.

Her mother was just one. The other was far more complicated.

Persephone was a goddess, but she still hoped to keep that part of her life a secret from the rest of the world. The biggest problem? The whole world wanted to know everything about her since she'd been revealed as Hades's lover.

They came to a stop on the edge of a sliver of cliff. Beyond, silver trees glistened like a foaming sea, and the muted sky above was growing dusty with night.

Persephone had never seen this part of the Underworld before, and that was one thing she loved about being here. Every day was an adventure.

"This is beautiful," she said.

She felt Hades's gaze on her, but she kept her eyes on the grove below, partly because she was in awe of the sight and partly because she was ashamed to face him.

"I am glad you think so," he said. "Because it is yours. Welcome to the Grove of Persephone."

She had to look at him now, shock evident upon her face. "But—"

"I thought you might like to have a place to yourself—somewhere to practice your magic. A place that doesn't...remind you of our beginning."

He was referring to her garden in the Underworld—and their bargain.

She reached for him, placing her palm against his cheek. "Hades, I love our beginning." He smiled faintly, but she could tell he didn't believe her, and that was painful too. So she explained, "It's true I haven't always loved it, but I could never hate anything that brought me to you."

He took her hand and pressed his lips to her palm, then drew her against him, their bodies aligned hip to hip, chest to chest. He kissed her, holding her tight, as if he feared she might vanish. When he pulled away, she was breathless, her fingers twisted into his jacket.

He stared at her, eyes burning into hers, and swore fiercely, "You will be my queen. I do not need the Fates to tell me that."

Keep reading for
a sneak peek of
A Game of Fate

CHAPTER I
A Game of Balance

Hades manifested near the Coast of the Gods.

In the sunlight, the shoreline boasted turquoise water and pristine, white beaches, all set before the backdrop of cliffs, grottoes, and a monastery made of white and green marble that could be accessed after ascending three hundred steps. Mortals flocked here to swim, sail, and snorkel. It was an oasis, up until the sun made its fiery descent in the sky.

After twilight, evil moved in the darkened night, beneath a sky of stars and an ocean of moonlight. It came on ships and moved across New Greece, and Hades was here to neutralize it.

He turned, the gravel crunching beneath his feet, and walked in the direction of the Corinth Company, a fishery that took up an extensive amount of real estate on the coast. The plaster facade of the warehouse blended flawlessly with the ancient architecture adorning the shoreline, appearing worn, bleached, and charming. A simple, black lamp highlighted a sign bearing the company's name, written in a font that boasted prestige and power—admirable characteristics when they belonged to the best of society.

Dangerous when they belonged to the worst.

A mortal moved in the shadow. He had been there since Hades arrived and no doubt thought he was well hidden, which perhaps he was to other mortals, but Hades was a god and he owned the shadows.

As he passed, the man moved and Hades twisted, his hand biting down on the mortal's. A gun was clutched in his fingers. Hades looked at the weapon and then at the man, a wicked smile crossing his lips.

In the next second, sharp spires extended from the tips of Hades's fingers, sinking into the man's flesh. His weapon clattered to the ground and he dropped to his knees with a guttural cry.

"Please spare me, my lord," the man begged. "I did not know."

Hades always found the seconds before a mortal's death intriguing. Especially when he encountered one like this—one who had killed without thought and yet feared his own demise.

Hades tightened his hold, and as the man trembled, the god laughed.

"Your death is not imminent," Hades said, and the mortal looked up. "But I will have words with your employer."

"My employer?"

Hades almost groaned. So the mortal would play dumb.

"Sisyphus de Ephyra."

"H-he's not here."

Lie.

The knowledge coated his tongue like ash, drying his throat.

Hades lifted the man by his arm, spikes still embedded in his skin, until their gazes were level. It was from this angle that Hades noticed a tattoo on the man's wrist. It was a triangle, now spliced by the spears extending from his fingers.

"I do not need your aid to enter that warehouse," Hades said. "What I need from you is an example."

"A-An example?"

Hades decided to use actions to explain, carving two deep fissures in the man's face. As blood coated his skin, neck, and clothes, the god dragged him to the entrance of the warehouse, kicked open the doors, and strolled inside.

What had looked like a building from the shore now appeared to be a wall, because instead of walking into an enclosed space, Hades found himself in a yard open to the inky sky above. The earth was bare, and there were large above-ground pools holding fish. The air smelled like ocean and rot and salt. Hades hated the stench.

Workers dressed in black jumpsuits turned to watch as the god pushed the bleeding mortal forward. The man floundered but caught himself before he hit the ground. Opposite Hades, another man approached, flanked by two large bodyguards. He was dressed in a white suit, and his fingers were fat and suffocated with gold rings. His hair was short and black, his beard manicured and threaded with silver.

"Sis, i-i-it wasn't my fault," the man said as he stumbled forward. "I—"

Sisyphus withdrew a gun and shot the man. He fell, hitting the ground with a loud thud. Hades looked at the still body and then at Sisyphus.

"He was not wrong," Hades said.

"I did not kill him because he let you enter my property. I killed him because he has disrespected a god."

A display like that usually came from a loyal subject. Of those, Hades had few, and he knew Sisyphus was not one.

"Is this your version of a sacrifice?"

"Depends," the man replied, cracking his neck and handing his gun to the bodyguard on the right. "Do you accept?"

"No."

"Then it was business."

Sisyphus straightened the lapels of his jacket and adjusted his cuff links, and Hades noted the same triangle tattoo on his wrist.

"Shall we?" The mortal gestured for Hades to walk in front, toward an office on the opposite side of the yard. "Divine first."

"I insist," Hades declined.

Despite his power, he was never eager to have his back turned.

Sisyphus's eyes narrowed slightly. The mortal probably saw Hades's refusal to lead as a form of disrespect, mostly because it showed that Hades did not trust him. Ironic, considering Sisyphus had broken one of the most ancient rules of hospitality—the law of Xenia—by killing his competition after inviting them into his territory.

It was just one of Sisyphus's transgressions Hades was here to address.

"Very well, my lord." The mortal offered a cold smile before starting toward his office, the two bodyguards in tow. Their presence was amusing, as if the two mortal men could protect Sisyphus from him.

Hades found himself considering how he would take them out. He had a number of options—he could call forth the shadows and let them consume the two, or he could subdue them by himself. He supposed the only real consideration was whether he wanted blood on his suit.

The two bodyguards took their places on either side of the door as Sisyphus entered his office. Hades did not look at them as he passed.

Sisyphus's office was small. His desk was solid wood, stained dark, and stacked with paperwork. An old-fashioned telephone sat to one side, and a crystal decanter and two glasses on the other. Behind him, a set of windows overlooked the yard, obstructed by blinds.

It was behind the desk where Sisyphus chose to stand, a strategic move, Hades imagined. It put something physical between them. It was also probably where he kept a store of weapons. Not that they would do any good against him, but Hades had existed for centuries and knew desperate mortals would try anything.

"Bourbon?" Sisyphus asked as he uncorked the decanter.

"No."

The mortal stared at Hades for a moment before pouring himself a glass. He took a sip and asked, "To what do I owe the pleasure?"

Hades looked toward the door. From here, he could see the pools, and he nodded toward them now.

"I know you are hiding drugs in your pools," Hades said. "I also know that you use this company as a front to move them across New Greece and that you kill anyone who gets in the way."

Sisyphus stared at Hades for a moment, and then took a slow sip from his glass before asking, "Have you come to take my life?"

"No."

It was not a lie. Hades did not reap souls—Thanatos did, but the God of the Underworld could see Sisyphus was due for a visit and soon. The vision had come, unbidden, like a memory from long ago. Sisyphus, dressed smartly, would collapse as he left a high-ending dining room.

He would never regain consciousness.

And before that happened, Hades would have balance.

"Then should I assume you want a cut?"

Hades tilted his head to the side. "Of sorts."

Sisyphus chuckled. "Who would have thought, the God of the Dead came to bargain."

Hades gritted his teeth. He did not like the implication of Sisyphus's words, as if the mortal thought he had the upper hand.

"As penance for your crimes, you will donate half your income to the homeless. You are, after all, responsible for many of them."

The drugs Sisyphus trafficked had destroyed lives, eating mortals up from the inside out with addiction and igniting violence in communities, and while he wasn't the only one responsible, it was his ships that brought it into the mainland, his trucks that transported it across New Greece.

"Is penance not served in the afterlife?" Sisyphus asked.

"Consider it a favor. I am allowing you an early start."

Sisyphus used his tongue to pick between his teeth, then he snickered quietly.

"You know they never describe you as a righteous god."

"I am not righteous."

"Forcing crooks like myself to donate to charities is righteous."

"It is balance. A price you pay for the evil you spread."

Hades did not believe in eradicating the world of evil, because he did not believe it was possible. What was evil to one was a fight for freedom to another—the Great War was an example. One side fought for their gods, their religion, the other fought for freedom from their perceived oppressor. The best he could do was offer a touch of redemption so that their sentence in the Underworld might eventually lead to Asphodel.

"But you are not the God of Balance. You are the God of the Dead."

It would do no good to explain the workings of the Fates, the balance they strove to create in the world, and so he remained silent. Sisyphus pulled a metal case from the inside pocket of his jacket and withdrew a cigarette.

"I'll tell you what." He put the cigarette to his lips and lit it. The smell of nicotine filled the small shop—ashy, stale, and chemical. "I'll donate one million, and I won't violate the law of Xenia anymore."

Hades paused a moment and used the silence to quell the rush of anger the mortal's words ignited, his fingers curling into fists. Not so long ago, he would have let the fury overtake him, sending the mortal to Tartarus without a second thought. Instead, he let the darkness do the work for him. Outside Sisyphus's office, Hades called to the shadows and they slithered across the exterior of the building, darkening the windows as they went.

Hades watched as Sisyphus turned, eyes following the shadows until they approached the two bodyguards at the front of the office. In the next second, they slipped into every orifice of their bodies and they collapsed, dead.

Sisyphus's eyes returned to Hades's and he grinned.

"On second thought, you have a deal, Lord Hades," Sisyphus said. "Two hundred and fifty million it is."

"Three," Hades replied.

Defiance flashed in the mortal's eyes. "That is more than half my income."

"A punishment for wasting my time," Hades said. He started to turn and leave the office before pausing. He looked over his shoulder at the mortal. "And I would not worry about breaking the law of Xenia, mortal. You don't have much time left."

Sisyphus was silent after Hades's words. Ribbons of smoke danced from the cigarette poised between his fingers. After a moment, he put it out in his drink.

"Tell me something," he said. "Why do it? Bargain and balance? Have you hope for humanity?"

"Have you none?" Hades countered.

"I live among mortals, Lord Hades. Trust me, when given the choice to tip the scale one way or the other, they'll choose darkness. It's the fastest path with the quickest benefit."

"And the most to lose," Hades said. "Do not educate

me on the nature of mortals, Sisyphus. I have judged your kind for a millennium."

Hades paused outside the door, looking down at the two men who lay at his feet. He did not revel in the idea of restoring them to life to spread violence and death themselves, but he knew the Fates would demand a sacrifice—a soul for a soul—and it was likely they would choose souls that were good and pure and innocent.

Balance, Hades thought, and he suddenly hated the word.

"Wake," he commanded.

And as they inhaled sharp breaths, Hades vanished.

Author's Note

I never thought I would write romance, but sometime in the last year, I became brave enough to do just that, and it is fitting that I started with a retelling of Hades and Persephone.

I have always loved Greek mythology. It's creepy and violent and vicious, and when it came to the tale of Hades and Persephone, I was always intrigued by Persephone, who was the Goddess of Spring but also the Queen of the Underworld. She, like so many, straddled the light and the dark.

When I started writing about Hades and Persephone, I wrote short snippets—pieces of dialogue between the two that kept popping into my head, so I started posting pieces on Tumblr. This was my first:

> *The garden is my solace.*
> *It's the only life in this horrid place—this dark desert.*
> *The roses smell sweet. The wild flowers smell bitter.*
> *The stars shine bright.*

In the back of my mind, I marvel at how he crafts such
    an illusion. How he can blend scents and texture—a
    master with his brush, stippling and smoothing.
As quick as awe descends, I scoff.
Of course he can stir the air and prick holes in the dark
    above so light shines through—he is a god.
And my jailer.
I could do better, I think bitterly. I could turn this
    death-scape into an oasis—the air would smell of
    spring, and this black canvas would be painted in
    vibrant, vivacious color.
But that would be a gift.
And I'm not in a giving mood.
The air changes. He is near. I have learned the feel of
    him. The ruler of the dead is not cold. He blazes,
    like a hearth in the dead of winter. I shiver as he
    casts me in his shadow and scent. He smells of
    pine—of home.
I curl my fingers into my gown.
He is everything I hate and everything I want.

The tone of this is very different from what I ended
up writing, but the dynamics are still the same—an
ancient god who takes pleasure in crafting his world and
an envious goddess who both marvels and despises his
work.

From this first scene, I started to ask questions and
formulate my world and characters. I ended up with a
Persephone who wants adventure and passion more than
anything in the world. She wants desperately to be good
at something and is very quick to judge Hades, who
she believes is abusing his power as a god by agreeing to

bargain with mortals. I ended up with a Hades who was just as desperate for passion and was very tired of being alone. When Persephone comes along to challenge him, he does the opposite of what she expects and listens.

A Touch of Darkness is Hades and Persephone's first book, but I plan to explore their story more. Persephone must embrace her power, both as the Goddess of Spring and eventually as the Queen of the Underworld, and Hades has secrets that will challenge the new life he wishes to lead with Persephone.

I'm so happy to finally share my version of the Hades and Persephone story with you. I hope you enjoy it as much as I enjoyed writing it.

About the Author

Scarlett St. Clair lives in Oklahoma with her excellent dog. She has a master's degree in library science and information studies. She is obsessed with Greek mythology, murder mysteries, love, and the afterlife. For information on books, tour dates, and content, please visit scarlettstclair.com.